EDWARD D. HOCH
(Photograph by Michael Culligan)

Funeral
in the
Fog

Books by Edward D. Hoch
Published by Crippen & Landru

The Cases of Dr. Sam Hawthorne

Diagnosis Impossible: The Problems of Dr. Sam Hawthorne. Available as a print book and as Kindle e-book

More Things Impossible: The Second Casebook of Dr. Sam Hawthorne. Available as a print book and as a Kindle e-book

Nothing Is Impossible: Further Problems of Dr. Sam Hawthorne. Available as a print book and as a Kindle e-book

All But Impossible: The Impossible Files of Dr. Sam Hawthorne. Available as a print book and as a Kindle e-book

Challenge the Impossible: The Final Problems of Dr. Sam Hawthorne. Available as a print book and as a Kindle e-book

Other Sleuths

The Ripper of Storyville and Other Ben Snow Tales. Available as a Kindle e-book

The Velvet Touch: Nick Velvet Stories. Available as a Kindle e-book

The Old Spies Club and Other Intrigues of Rand. Available as a Kindle e-book

The Iron Angel and Other Tales of the Gypsy Sleuth. Available as a Kindle e-book

Hoch's Ladies. Available as a print book and as a Kindle e-book

Funeral in the Fog: The Strange Mysteries of Simon Ark. Available as a print book and (forthcoming) as a Kindle e-book

Funeral
in the
Fog

Edward D. Hoch

Introduction by Gigi Pandian

Crippen & Landru Publishers
Cincinnati, Ohio
USA
2020

FIRST EDITION

Printed in the United States of America
on recycled acid-free paper

Jeffrey A. Marks, Publisher
Douglas G. Greene, Senior editor

Crippen & Landru Publishers
5436 Douglas Fir Court
Cincinnati, OH 45247
USA

Email: info@crippenlandru.com
Web: www.crippenlandru.com

CONTENTS

INTRODUCTION

A man who claims the Devil is trying to kill him after he witnessed a woman killed by an invisible hand. Lightning bolts that strike from a clear sky, at locations across the globe, to kill a series of former astronauts. A group of friends who sold their soul to the Devil as a joke when they were students find their time is up and Devil has come to collect. A knife that vanished as it was being thrown during a Revolutionary War battle reappears from thin air two centuries later in the same spot. A cursed trumpet that immediately causes anyone who plays it to age decades within seconds and die of old age.

These are but a handful of the sixteen baffling mysteries solved by occult detective Simon Ark in this collection. And no, it's not a spoiler to tell you that each of the seemingly impossible crimes has a rational explanation. But *how?*

Ed Hoch (1930-2008) wrote more than 950 short stories over the course of his career. Many of them appeared in *Ellery Queen Mystery Magazine*, and Hoch has the distinction of appearing in every issue published for 35 years, beginning in 1973. He was so prolific that he needed to invent more than a dozen main characters. It might be the biggest mystery of all how Ed Hoch created characters that are so distinct. Capers featuring thief Nick Velvet, who only steals items with no monetary value; code and cipher puzzles solved by Jeffery Rand; historical Westerns with sleuth Ben Snow and real life historical figures; police procedurals starring Captain Leopold; and many more, including two I'll mention in more detail below. *Crippen & Landru* has collected many of Hoch's stories together.

As an avid reader of impossible crime stories, I first learned of Ed Hoch from *Crippen & Landru's* collections of the tales of Dr. Sam Hawthorne, a small town doctor who solved dozens of locked room and other seemingly impossible mysteries. I discovered the Sam Hawthorne stories at the same time I was devouring short stories featuring other locked room mystery sleuths including John Dickson Carr's Dr. Gideon Fell, Clayton Rawson's The Great Merlini, and Jacques Futrelle's The Thinking Machine.

Hoch's character Simon Ark is less well known than Sam Hawthorne, but I would argue is an even more intriguing character. Much like John Dickson Carr's impossible crime novels and stories with an atmospheric backdrop of a Gothic, supernatural ghost story, Hoch's Simon Ark is drawn to mysteries that appear to be the work of the Devil.

In a Simon Ark tale, you get the best of so many types of stories rolled into one: the challenge of a puzzle plot, the pleasure of curling up with fascinating characters including an old friend, and the chills of a good ghost story.

Simon Ark claims to be 2,000 years old. He travels the world searching out evil and the work of the Devil, which is why he's drawn to mysteries that seem to have a supernatural explanation. With his unnamed Watson-like narrator in tow, he travels the world seeking out evil, to eradicate it. In each of their adventures, Simon Ark proves the seemingly supernatural evil is indeed the work of a diabolical human.

I'm disappointed I never had a chance to meet Ed Hoch, but I'm glad to have gotten to know him through his ingenious stories.

Gigi Pandian
June 2020

Gigi Pandian is the Agatha Award winning author of ten mystery novels and more than a dozen locked room mystery short stories.

DAY OF THE WIZARD

Yesterday it was like this.

The big four-engined bomber coming in low over the Red Sea, catching now and then the glint of sunlight on the water and the sand below. The crew singing and joking, because they were nearly home, near to the home-away-from-home where the bombers now no longer waited, and the world no longer stood still for the falling bombs and the screaming men and the cities glowing brightly in the flame of war.

For the war was over. Here against the quiet of the desert and everywhere the world around, there was no war any longer. The legions of Hitler had long since surrendered, and Tokyo had announced acceptance of the surrender terms only a few days earlier. So the men sang, and occasionally one of them would go back to check on the very special cargo that was bringing this plane almost halfway around the world.

The sky was empty that day, dotted only with occasional puffs of cloud so rare against the desert sun. No longer were there the dangerous tiny specks on the the horizon, specks that grew into Nazi fighter-planes on the prowl. But there was another danger here, even in the empty sky. The pilot had time for nothing but the half-formed thought of a silent prayer; and then in an instant the great silver bird was screeching, flaming, screaming its swansong to the silent skies, plunging, billowing in under waiting blankets of sand and stone; digging its own grave in a world untouched by any civilized man till now.

Somewhere nearby, a desert scorpion tensed at the sound of the dying, curling itself into a tiny defenseless ball. But then no sound followed the first, only the simple gradual settling of the silent dust cloud of sand, and soon the scorpion uncurled to continue its journey across the changeless, ever-changing sands ...

That was how it must have been, back on that August day in 1945. At least that was the picture which formed itself in my own mind as I listened to the man across the table from me. He was a youngish sort, perhaps in his mid-thirties, and I had the distinct feeling of superiority that four or five years of prior existence can give one—superiority that went far towards outweighting the official-looking cards he carried in his wallet.

"You want me to go?" I asked, not quite believing the words he'd just spoken.

"We need Simon Ark," the man from Washington answered simply and truthfully. "You're probably the only person on Earth who can find him for us. You know him, you know where he is."

I snorted a bit at that. "Does anyone really know him? Certainly I don't. Besides, that plane of yours went down nearly seventeen years ago, in one of the remotest areas on Earth. For all you know, the plane might even be at the bottom of the Red Sea."

But the man from Washington only shook his head with a tired smile. He dipped into his briefcase and came out holding a dull, rusty piece of metal. "Our man in Cairo found this three weeks ago in a little curio shop."

"What is it?"

"At one time it was a cigarette case. The man in the shop apparently figured he could sell it to some stupid tourist. Open it and look at the engraving."

The thing I hold in my hand might truly have been a hundred or more years old. Only the familiar trademark of the American manufacturer told me it must be of more recent vintage. "*Carey W. Lindhurst*," I read with difficulty. "*U. S. Army Air Force.*"

The man across the table nodded. "Lindhurst was the pilot, a major. It was a million-to-one chance finding that thing in Cairo after all these years."

"So the plane is out there somewhere in the desert. So what?" I lit another cigarette and thought about all the business piling up on my desk during this long lunch hour.

"There was ... something on it," he said. "Something that would be out there still."

"What?"

But he only spread his hands flat on the soiled tablecloth and frowned slightly. "I'm not at liberty to say."

"You want me to fly halfway around the world, find Simon Ark, get him to tramp through the desert for a couple of months, and dig out an old airplane—and you won't even tell me what's in it?" I sipped my drink to cool off a bit. "What am I supposed to do, close my eyes when we find it?"

"Naturally, if and when the plane is found you will be made aware of its contents. Till then, I have my orders."

They always had their orders. "Is it an atomic bomb?"

"No," he said simply. "Nothing like that."

"How do you know the people who found the cigarette case didn't make off with your treasure too?"

"It isn't the sort of thing anybody would want to take," he answered mysteriously. "It must still be there."

"Look," I said, on the last legs of my argument, "I'm forty years old. Tramping through the desert is for younger guys."

"We're certainly not asking you to attempt the journey alone. All we really want is a contact with Simon Ark. He knows the region and he knows the people. If that plane is out there anyplace, he can find it for us."

"Simon Ark can be a tough man to locate."

The man nodded. "We know. That's why we came to you. He's in the Middle East, probably in Cairo, and if anybody can contact him, you can. We'll arrange for you to fly to Egypt, where you'll be met by one of our men. As soon as you place him in contact with Simon Ark, your job is done."

It had been many months since I'd last seen Simon, and then only briefly for dinner one night in New York. Egypt, I suppose, was his home if he had a home, and I wasn't surprised to hear that he'd returned there. I knew I could find him, or let him find me, among the shadowed streets of Cairo or Alexandria. "All right," I agreed suddenly, for no real reason except a desire to see Simon once more. "I'll go, but only for a week. If I haven't contacted him in seven days I'll have to get back to work."

"Fair enough," the man from Washington said. And that was the beginning of it ...

Cairo in summer is hot and horrible, with a peculiar odor all its own. The streets for the most part are filled with white-robed figures, blending with and overpowering what European manner or influence had penetrated this far East. Truly the British were gone, departed with the ebb of empire, and what remained in their place seemed only a shadow of existence, a modern city struggling against the past but not really winning the struggle.

I made it somehow into the city from the airport, and found the promised room awaiting me at the new Shepherd's Hotel. The first thing I wanted was a cold shower, but my preparations for it were interrupted by the arrival of my contact. He was a tall, handsome chap in his early thirties, with rippling muscles. When he spoke, it was with a quick alertness which extended to his eyes. "Blake's the name," he said, offering his hand. "Harry Blake, assigned to the American Embassy."

"Oh," I said, probably showing my surprise. "I hadn't really expected a State Department man."

"It gives me an excuse for being around," he explained with a smile. "I can be other things on occasion."

"Glad to hear it."

"I understand you're a friend of this Ark fellow."

"I've known him for many years. I suppose if he has any friends I'm one of them."

"Odd sort of guy, isn't he? Claims to be a couple thousand years old?"

I offered him a cigarette and took one myself. "It's actually closer to fifteen hundred years. And whether you believe him or not, he's certainly a man of vast knowledge."

"He was once a Coptic priest, here in Egypt?"

"Something like that. If anybody knows this part of the world, it's Simon Ark."

Blake smiled, a friendly sort of smile that made you like him. "I don't go along with this supernatural stuff, but if Ark can find that plane, he's the man we need."

"I must warn you that Simon is far more interested in Satanism and evil than in the quirks of modern warfare. Even if I find him, there's no assurance that hell do the job for you. He may very well be working on something he considers more important. After all, if we don't even know what's on this plane that makes it so valuable after seventeen years ..."

But I could see I wasn't going to get any more out of Blake than I had from the man back in New York. He simply shrugged. "Let's just say it's a lot of money, gold bricks or something."

"It isn't, though. They wouldn't still be there if someone had found the plane already."

Another shrug. "Who knows? But let's get down to business. Where do we find Simon Ark?"

I sighed and ground out my cigarette. Now that I was in Cairo, thousands of miles from home, how *was* I going to find Simon? It had all seemed so easy, flying over and registering at a hotel and finding him. Now somehow it wasn't so easy at all. The streets and alleys of the city teemed with white-robed Egyptians and mysterious-looking Europeans. Since the Suez trouble it was a far different city from the one I remembered during a brief war stay in the early Forties. "I'll do the looking," I said finally. "You just keep in touch."

"We're anxious to get started on the journey."

"Journey?"

"To the crash site." Just like that.

"Well, I'll do the best I can. I have to be back in New York next week."

He nodded, shook hands, and promised to call that evening. I waited till he was gone and then slipped off my sticky clothes and stepped into the long-awaited shower. The coolness of the water helped relax me, and I had a few moments to think about Simon and the whole crazy business. But when I finished bathing and started to dress I still had no real plan for finding him.

I went out into the heat of the city, deciding to at least prowl the more likely places. Across the street from the hotel, a small band of noisy students scuffled with police, intent on starting some sort of demonstration. "Go home, American," one of them yelled in my direction, but I pretended I hadn't heard it.

The alleys of Cairo were strange to me after all these years, though here and there a half-remembered landmark still remained. Presently I found myself on a street hung with multicolored banners, where tattered signs proclaimed in a half-dozen languages the merits of past and present stage and screen attractions to be found at nearby theaters. It was here that one sign caught my eye, a blazing red thing with an unmistakable figure of Satan rising from the ashes of a smouldering fire like some great phoenix. Printed below the picture, in large Arabic characters with the English translation helpfully supplied, was the legend: *The Wizard – World's Greatest Magician.*

The Wizard. A simple name for a magician, though it looked somehow more imposing in the Arabic. If Simon Ark were to be found anywhere in Cairo, I had the feeling it would be here. I located the bannered entrance to the theater in question and entered, past a sleepy ticket-seller who hardly noticed me. The afternoon show was just beginning, playing to a depressingly empty house hot with the sweat of un-air-conditioned bodies.

The Wizard, when he appeared in a puff of pale smoke, proved to be amazingly good, even by American standards. He vanished a long series of beautiful Egyptian girls with all the ease of an old pro, and then settled down to some original versions of famous continental tricks. During the next hour he somehow managed to walk through a wall, eat fire and swallow swords, catch bullets in his teeth, and saw a girl quite convincingly in half. But even all this only moved the audience to mild applause, and I decided they must consider the Wizard only an American or some other despised foreigner.

After the show I made my way backstage, because the Wizard still seemed the best path I had to Simon Ark. I knocked on the dressing-room door and entered at his request, finding a man somewhat older than I'd expected. The pointed black beard he'd worn on stage was indeed phoney, but the face beneath his Satanic makeup was older than my own. I guessed him to be about forty-five. "Ah," he greeted me. "An American!"

The accent was unmistakably German, though the tone was friendly enough. I introduced myself as a New York publisher and got right to the point. "I'm looking for a friend, Mr. Wizard. I thought you might help."

"Mr. Wizard! Ha! I sound like someone on your American television, no?"

I smiled and kept going. "My friend is named Simon Ark. He has an interest in magic and I thought you might know him."

"Simon? Simon Ark? a familiar name."

"You do know him?"

"I have heard of him. He is well known in the East."

"I think he might be in Cairo."

The Wizard shrugged and continued removing his make-up. "It is possible, though I have never met the man."

My heart sank a little at his words, but I still had a plan. "It's important that I find him before the week is out. I was wondering ... You're not drawing much of a crowd here."

"No. It is the heat! But night shows are a little better."

"You could use some publicity in the local papers."

"The local papers are too full of threats of war, and hate-the-English, and Communist activities. There is no room for a poor but honest magician."

"There's room if you've got one good trick. If you make a direct challenge to Simon Ark, it would be good for some space. You said yourself his name is well known here."

"I have a good trick," the Wizard said simply. "Tell me a little more."

"We call in the reporters and announce that you are challenging the great mystic, Simon Ark, to solve your riddle. How's that? You get the publicity and I find Simon."

"You are a smart American. Smart, smart! I do it."

I sighed and pulled up a chair. That had been easy, and with Simon not too far off this would surely bring him to me. "Start working on your trick, then," I told him. "I'll have the newsmen here tonight."

"On your way," he said with a mysterious smile, "bring me a lock, a simple padlock of some sort. Buy one in a store."

"A padlock?" I made a note of it. "You need it for your trick?"

He nodded. "This is not a trick quite right for the stage, but I believe it will certainly baffle your friend Simon Ark."

"I don't know about that. But at least it should bring him into the open. See you tonight." I left him there, puttering about the dressing-room with the quaint mannerisms of an aging German professor, humming low to himself some half-remembered melody from Gilbert and Sullivan.

It was an easy job to round up some representatives of the Egyptian press, easier in fact than I'd expected. They seemed to think that anything concerning an American was news, and especially if the half-legendary Simon Ark was involved. I gathered he was always good copy in the Cairo newspapers. They promised happily to appear at the theater at the appointed hour, and I went off in search of a padlock for the Wizard. I found one without much trouble, a standard model that seemed sturdy enough for most purposes. It came complete with two keys, and a small yellow tag which announced it had been *Made in Brooklyn, U.S.A.* I figured that should be good enough for any Wizard.

The crowd was a bit better at the evening show that night, sprinkled with a cross-section of foreign faces apparently taking in the sights of the city by night. A few were British, businessmen no doubt, trying hard to hold their ties with the slipping Middle Eastern markets. Others were French, German, American and even Russian. A group of girls perhaps just out of college giggled in a back row, obviously American, incongruously clashing with the surroundings. I stood quietly near the back of the darkened house, watching the Wizard run through his familial ad on the nearly barren stage. The same raven-haired Egyptian girl was sawed once more in half, and now even the fire from the Wizard's fingertips seemed familiar and less frightening than before. When finally the curtain ran down, I found three of the reporters outside and led them backstage.

"Ah, good evening!" the Wizard greeted us. "I am waiting for you." The English was still a bit broken and the face was still aging as he patted his beard. "You brought the lock?"

I nodded and produced it from my pocket. He took it carefully from my fingers, turned it over once or twice as if studying it, and said finally, "Very good. We proceed."

One of the leathery-skinned newsmen, his stub of pencil poised in the best Manhattan tradition, asked. "Do we understand that you are challenging Simon Ark to solve this trick?"

"You call it a trick?" The Wizard scowled in the best stage tradition. "It is a miracle, a true miracle. Observe, gentlemen, this door to my closet."

We observed seeing only a thick wooden door that swung open at his touch, revealing a barren closet that he'd apparently emptied only recently. "Step into it, examine it, assure yourselves there is no secret panel or trickery. No trickery, only a miracle."

The little closet was certainly solid enough, with room for only one or two people. The walls, ceiling and floors resisted every effort at pounding or tapping. "It is solid," one of the reporters stated finally, and the others nodded in agreement.

"And empty," the Wizard said. "Completely empty."

"Completely empty."

"Now observe." He took the lock once more and clicked it into place on the closet door, securing the hasp to the metal staple in the frame. The door did not close tightly—there was a quarter-inch crack remaining—but for all practical purposes the closet was not locked securely. The Wizard unlocked it with one of the keys and then clicked it shut again. He passed the keys to one of the reporters and allowed him to repeat his operation. The closet was opened, inspected once more, and finally the padlock was snapped shut by one of the newsmen. The keys were tested one final time to make certain the Wizard had not switched them.

"Keep the keys," the Wizard said with a smile. "And to make certain there is no trickery with the lock, I suggest you put a bit of wax over the keyhole."

The newsmen agreed it was a good idea. With the Wizard's help the padlock's keyhole was plugged with a matchstick, which they broke off flush with the surface of the lock. Then a few drops of candle wax were allowed to drip on to this. It would be impossible to open the lock even with the proper keys. Both of these keys were then placed in a sealed envelope which each reporter in turn initialed across the flap. One of them was assigned to keep it in his office safe until it was needed.

"Now examine the hinges and the screws holding the hasp to the wood," the Wizard said. "Note how they are painted over. They will be the same tomorrow when you return." He gave a little chuckle. "And now—the miracle is yours, gentlemen. What shall the closet contain when you open it tomorrow night? Name anything you desire, and I will accomplish it."

It was a good stunt, one that even Simon couldn't help appreciating. "An elephant," one of the men said.

"Ah, too small a space," the magician answered sadly.

"A girl," I suggested with a laugh. "The most beautiful girl in Cairo."

"Spoken like a true American," the Wizard said with a quick smile. "So be it! Tomorrow night at this same hour—behold, the most beautiful girl in all of Cairo will be locked in my closet. And I challenge Simon Ark to explain how she passed through this locked door and these solid walls."

"It'll be something to see," one of the newsmen agreed, obviously aware that a touch of sex made this an even better story.

I parted from the reporters outside the theater and headed back to my hotel, not entirely convinced that my stunt would locate Simon. It might well be weeks before news of the Wizard's challenge and my part in it reached him, and by that time I would be back at my office in New York. And even if I found him, Simon wouldn't likely jump at the chance to go wandering about the desert in search of a lost plane. Feeling a bit discouraged, I checked at the hotel desk for calls and then went upstairs to my room. I was tired after my first day in Cairo, anxious for the hopeful coolness of my bed.

I unlocked the door and stepped into the room—and froze in the darkness. Someone was there waiting. "Who ...?"

"It is only I," a familiar voice said.

"Simon?" My heart skipped a beat.

"I understand you are looking for me, my friend."

"The United States government is looking for you," I answered, flipping on a light switch, seeing again the tall, stocky frame, the mysterious eyes ever shaded by lowered brows, the face not really old but somehow ancient. "How are you, Simon?"

"Very well." He sighed softly and settled back into his chair. "Excuse me if I startled you, but there are others who seek me for less friendly purposes."

It was good to see him once more, to talk with him again, and for the moment all thought of returning home left my mind. I lit a cigarette and settled down to tell him of my mission. "They want you to find a airplane for them, an army plane that crashed in the desert back in 1945."

He smiled a bit at this. "I search for Satan, not for missing airplanes. And the shifting sands of time would certainly have covered this wreckage long before now."

"Maybe it's uncovered again." I told him about the cigarette case and the rest of it.

"What would be on the plane to cause interest after so long a time?" Simon wondered, half to himself.

"That's a mystery. Nobody's talking."

"You can introduce me to the American agent?"

I nodded. "He's a man named Harry Blake. Seems like a nice enough fellow. Actually, he said he'd call me tonight. Let me ring for a couple of drinks while we're waiting." Simon nodded in agreement and I called downstairs for some scotch. Then I told Simon of my meeting with the Wizard and the trick with the locked closet. "It'll probably be all over the papers in the morning. You really should go there tomorrow night."

He chuckled a bit. "Most interesting."

"You think he'll really produce her inside the closet?"

Simon nodded. "There are at least five ways in which the trick could be accomplished. I only wonder which one he plans to use."

The telephone rang at that point and I picked it up, knowing it must be the unsleeping Blake. I was right. "Harry Blake here. Anything from our man?"

"He's sitting across the room from me right this minute, looking like the Sphinx itself."

"You found him?"

"He found me. Come on over."

And so the post-midnight conference was held in my hotel room, with Simon Ark, Harry Blake and me hunched over a coffee-table studying maps of Egypt and reproductions of yellowed flight charts. Blake told what little they knew of the mysterious crash, and through it all Simon listened intently, sometimes questioning, more often only nodding. And, at the end of it, came the question I'd been awaiting. "Tell me, Mr. Blake, just what is on this plane that makes it suddenly so valuable?"

Blake gave his usual shrug. "Call it gold."

"From what I know of the American government, even a few million dollars in gold would not call for measures such as this."

"I can't tell you any more," Blake said firmly. "Locate the plane and then you'll know for yourself what's inside."

Simon Ark leaned back from the table with a smile. "You awaken my curiosity. Very well, I'll do it."

Blake smiled broadly and turned to me. "Will you be going too?"

"Oh no. I'll be on a plane to New York in the morning!"

Simon wrinkled his brow in my direction. "Might I remind you of the most beautiful girl in Cairo? Surely she is worth waiting for."

"Might I remind you of my wife back in Westchester?"

"It would be like old times, my friend."

"Sure! Out in the desert searching for some damned plane!"

"You must at least remain for the Wizard's trick tomorrow night."

"All right," I agreed. "But then it's back to New York. I'm too old for this chasing around." With that, the meeting broke up. Simon and Blake were to leave by car in some thirty hours, driving to the southern desert area near the place where the plane might be. Where the roads ran out, they would switch to camels.

They left me, and I slept. But the morning's sun brought with it a vaguely troubled feeling which I could not pinpoint. Perhaps it was only the unfamiliar food of this strange land. I spent the afternoon seeing the city, forming my own opinions about its most beautiful girl, finally deciding there was no such thing—at least not in public. Finally, after dinner, I made my way back to the little theater where the Wizard was appearing. Simon was standing in the shadows awaiting me. "Have you seen the show?" I asked him.

He shook his head. "Magic is unchanging, like the climate of Hell. I see magic every day, all about me, and there is no need to see it bartered in the market-place. It is only the Wizard's one trick which interests me."

We moved together down an alley which seemed to circle the building, coming at last to the dimly-lit rear entrance. As I'd expected, the reporters were already waiting inside. There was a brief flurry of excitement as they recognized Simon Ark, and then we headed for the Wizard's dressing-room in a body. He stood in the doorway awaiting us, one hand stroking his pointed beard in a Mephistophelesian gesture. "Ah! The reporters and the American—and the famous Simon Ark! This is surely a pleasure." The accent seemed a little less German tonight, as if he were forgetting about it.

We crowded once more into his dressing-room, as he prepared for his master trick. The closet door was exactly as I remembered it, with padlock in place and keyhole jammed shut. Both the door hinges and the screws of the hasp remained painted over and obviously untouched. Surely the door had not been opened since the previous night. "Here's the key," one of the Egyptian reporters said, producing the familiar envelope with its initialed flap. The others inspected it in turn, and then ripped it open, revealing the two keys which had come with the lock when I purchased it. But of course there was no easy way to undo the padlock now. The wax was scraped away but there was still the broken matchstick to contend with. The keys were useless.

One of the less sedate reporters picked up a sturdy iron bar that the Wizard used for some bit of magic and set to work prying open the locked door. A grunt and a tug from the dark-skinned newsman and the door snapped open, the hasp and its ancient screws pulled loose with a splintering of wood. And there, inside the tiny closet, huddled on the floor against the back wall, was a girl. She might have been the most beautiful in Cairo, but she certainly wasn't Egyptian. She was English or American, a young blonde in her early twenties. "Get her out of there," Simon Ark said suddenly, pushing the others aside. "That girl's sick!"

We helped her out of the closet and into the nearest chair. "What's the matter with her, Simon?" I asked.

"I believe she's been drugged." With these words all eyes turned towards the Wizard. "Was this quite necessary for your little trick, sir?"

"I ..." The Wizard started to speak, then thought better of it.

"But how did he do it?" one of the reporters was asking. "We locked the door ourselves last night. It hasn't been opened since, and yet the girl was inside!" One of the other newsmen was once more inspecting the closet walls and floor and ceiling, but without success.

Simon Ark turned to the bearded magician. "Will you tell them or shall I?"

But the Wizard remained silent. "Tell us," one of the reporters urged, and Simon seemed about to.

But at that moment the girl struggled to regain her senses. She mumbled something and opened her eyes. "Where ... what happened?"

"Are you all right?" I asked, pinpointing her accent as pure Boston.

"I think so. What happened to me?"

"We don't really know. We found you locked in that closet."

"He must have drugged me," she announced firmly. "I feel awful."

Simon Ark's voice boomed once more. "Who drugged you? This man?" His accusing finger pointed in the Wizard's direction.

"No. No, it was someone else, a man I'd never seen before. I was leaving the theater after today's matinee when he called to me from the alley. He wanted me to enter a beauty contest."

"Was he Egyptian?"

"No, he seemed European, perhaps German." She was gaining better control of herself now, and a bit of color was returning to her face.

"Who are you, miss?" one of the reporters asked.

"Rima Jackson. I'm a staff writer for *Fashion Week* magazine in New York. I'm on a vacation."

"Rima as in *Green Mansions*?" I asked.

She nodded with a smile. "My parents liked the book." Looking at her now that she'd partly recovered her composure, I could easily see why the Wizard might have picked her for his trick. Certainly no one could argue the choice. She was blonde, trim, and very very sleek—almost like a cover from *Fashion Week*.

"But what happened to you? Another of the reporters demanded, no doubt aware that his press was fast approaching.

"He must have put something in my drink. We went into this little bar across the street, and that's the last I remember."

And now it was the Wizard's turn to step forward. "Gentlemen," he said in a clear voice, "I assure you I know nothing of this fantastic business, nothing at all."

"You didn't put the girl in your closet?"

"Certainly not! The girl I put there was an Egyptian, and I didn't resort to drugs to accomplish it."

"Then how was it done?" someone asked. "How could two girls have passed through that locked door?"

But before Simon Ark could speak we were interrupted once more, this time by a terrified scream from the direction of the stage. We hurried out, with the bearded Wizard in the lead. Already a circle of performers had gathered in shocked silence about an ancient black woman with a broom, a cleaning woman who had stumbled upon something too horrible to sweep away. There, stretched out on the floor of the stage before one of the Wizard's multi-colored magic cabinet, was the body of a man. His throat had been cut clear across with a single deadly stroke, contorting his face in a final mask of startled pain.

But even more startling was the terrified gasp from the girl, Rima Jackson. "That's him! That's the man who drugged me ..."

By noon the next day, the five of us had found ourselves better than a hundred miles south of the city. That's right—the five of us. Rima Jackson and Harry Blake and the Wizard and Simon Ark and myself. In the middle of the damned desert.

How it happened was simple I suppose. Harry Blake had pulled the right strings to rescue us from the questioning clutches of the Cairo police. By that time the decision had been made for me—either I accompanied Simon and Blake into the desert on their fantastic quest, or I spent the next week or so tied up in Cairo answering a lot of stupid questions about the murder of the nameless man and the cabinet. I chose the desert, and off we went. Five miles outside the city a little French car had overtaken us, and there were the Wizard and Rima, fleeing from police questioning themselves. They refused to turn back, and at this point there was no other course but to take them with us—much as Blake hated to do it. He probably had visions of official Washington popping its lid when the news got around that an American fashion writer and a German magician had accompanied us on a top-secret mission.

So there we were, by car and finally by camel, tramping across the sands of an obscure route that seemed to be known only to Simon. The first night out, we set up our tent on the edge of an oasis, and found a separate place for Rima to sleep among the palm trees. I could imagine the sort of magazine article that was already forming in her mind. Later, while the Wizard tried a few card tricks and Harry Blake checked his maps, Simon and I walked over to look at the camels. I would have gladly settled at that point for one of those trucks that can travel on sand, but we hadn't been lucky enough to obtain one. "Really, Simon, I'm too old to be riding one of these things," I told him. The nearest camel clicked its teeth at me, and I jumped back in alarm. "See what I mean? They hate me."

Simon Ark smiled into the night. "Our search for the lost plane is fast assuming a most complex nature, and the camels are the least of the worries at this point, my friend. It seems quite obvious to me that one of our unexpected companions—either the Wizard or Rima—was most anxious to accompany us on the quest. Certainly it was more than coincidence that they joined us."

"The police were after them."

"The police, even the Cairo police, would have a difficult time proving that Rima Jackson could have slit a man's throat while drugged and unconscious in a locked closet."

"Maybe the guy was killed earlier."

But Simon shook his head. "The magic cabinet was obviously used in the act, so the body wasn't put there till just after the show. Besides the blood indicated that our stranger had been dead only a short time."

"You think the Wizard killed him?"

"I really don't know. At least, not yet. Perhaps the girl was not really drugged."

I threw up my hands. "It's too much for me."

"Then there is the matter of the plane. And its contents. Were you aware of the fact that our Mr. Blake is an expert on Indian affairs? His previous assignment was in Goa, before the recent troubles there."

"Oh?" I found it interesting but not too startling.

"One of the Communists' fondest dreams is to cause a split between the United States and Great Britain, and even now with its decade and more of independence behind it, India is still one place to do it. Are you familiar with a man named Subhas Bose?"

"I don't think so."

"He rates only a single line in Churchill's six-volume history of the Second World War, but he was quite a thorn in the side of the British. Wanted them out of India, even to the extent that he openly collaborated

with the Germans and Japanese. If Japan had conquered India, Subhas
Bose would have been its ruler."

"What happened to him?"

"He was reported killed several times, but always seemed to turn up
alive. The last time was on Formosa, August 18, 1945. His followers in
India were convinced he still lived, but apparently that was the end of it."

"So?"

"My sources tell me that while our friend Blake was in India and Goa,
he was especially interested in the Bose affair."

"It was a long time ago."

Simon nodded. "But the ghost of Subhas Bose may still walk."

"You handle the politics, Simon. I'm just interested in finding the
plane and being done with this business."

Simon Ark stared up at the thousands of twinkling stars, just out of reach.
"Oh, I know where the plane is. I've known since yesterday."

I'd suspected as much from the careful route he seemed to have plotted
for us, but his words still managed to surprise me. "What?"

"When Harry Blake told me about the cigarette case with Lindhurst's
name on it, I naturally investigated the curio shop myself. Perhaps my
ways were more effective than Blake's. In any event, I located the native
who'd found the case. He gave me the location of the plane."

"Where is it?"

Simon stooped to trace some sandy lines with his finger. "Here is the
Nile, running due south to Asyut, where we left the cars. We are now
heading southeast, bypassing Qena and heading generally towards El
Qoseir on the Red Sea. According to my information, the plane lies buried in the sand just north of there, some ten miles inland from the sea."

"Isn't there a great deal of activity in this region, with ships passing
often?"

"Apparently not. And the plane over the years has become almost completely buried by the sand. In any event, another day's travel will bring us
to the spot."

"Then what do we do with the Wizard and Rima?"

"One of them will have to make a move soon, if there is really a move
to be made."

"What about that trick with the locked closet? How did the Wizard do
it?"

In good time I will tell you, my friend. There is a good reason for not telling you quite yet."

We strolled back to the others, who seemed to have retired for the night, and I was about to join them when I heard Rima Jackson call my name. I found my way to her side in the darkness, wondering what she could want at this time of night. She was still dressed in shirt and taper slacks—a *Fashion Week* costume if I ever saw one—and she spoke quite urgently. "Tell me something, please. What is it you're all looking for?"

"Believe me, I have no idea. I do know, though, that this is no place for a girl like you. Why aren't you covering a fashion show at the Waldorf, for God's sake? Or strolling down Fifth Avenue with a hatbox?"

"I'm a reporter, and I smell a story. It may not be a fashion story, but it could be something even bigger. Does that answer your question? After all, don't I have the right to it after being drugged and locked up in a closet?"

I watched the glow of her cigarette for a time in the darkness, and since I had no real answer for her argument, I finally went off to bed. She was a strange one, but then weren't we all?

The morning dawned with a fierce heat that promised to scorch away the chill of the desert night. By the time I'd dressed, the others were outside, fixing a meager breakfast on our little charcoal grill. The camels seemed fresh after the night's rest, and we made good time during the early hours. Simon was indeed leading us now, more obviously than before, and Blake especially seemed to sense that the prize was close at hand. Once during the morning we sighted a distant band of wandering nomads to the north, but otherwise we might have been the only five people on Earth. I wondered if it would seem like this to the first men on the moon.

Presently, as Simon Ark and Harry Blake rode slightly ahead of us, being the most experienced camel-drivers in the group. I dropped back to speak with the Wizard. He looked a bit younger today, even with the false beard which he insisted on wearing. Perhaps it, along with his heavy make-up, kept him free from burning in the sun, but it certainly didn't keep him from sweating. "How much farther?" he asked in the odd German accent.

"Not long now."

"This sun is unbearable."

"Better than a jail cell."

He frowned at that. "You think I killed that stranger?"

"Somebody killed him."

"By now the police have probably solved it."

"Maybe," I said, lighting a cigarette.

"Your brilliant friend Simon Ark—he missed the oddest thing about the murder."

"What was that, Wizard?"

"The stranger's throat was cut, his face contorted and bloody. It is doubtful that his own mother would have recognized him immediately. And yet this girl Rima Jackson named him at once as a man she'd seen for only ten minutes or so. Think of that!"

It was a point, I had to admit. Maybe she'd been a bit too quick and sure with her identification, under the circumstances. "You think she's lying?"

He shrugged, and at that moment Simon Ark called a halt to our weird procession. I rode up to him and he said, "I think we are nearly there. Perhaps just over that next dune." He pointed towards a mound of sand a few miles distant.

The Wizard joined us, but his attention was diverted farther down the valley. "What's that cloud of dust?" he asked, of no one in particular. We followed his gaze and saw indeed that the distant sand was rising, swirling like a minor whirlpool, eddying gradually towards us.

"Sandstorm!" Blake shouted. "Everyone under cover!"

"Where?" I wondered. "Under the camels?"

"Somebody take care of the girl," Blake said, sliding off his animal. "Get these camels sitting down to protect us a little."

"I will help Rima," the Wizard said, but I got to her first.

"No thanks. You might just make her disappear." We were all down then, our faces pressed to the camel's hides, trying not to notice the foul odor. Rima was right next to me, and the Wizard was on the other side of her, the wind already billowing his white robe. Within a minute the sand was swirling around our heads the camels were venting their fright with a queer gasping sob of sound, and nobody could set a thing. I kept a grip on Rima's arm, and I could feel her moving against me, struggling in her own private battle with the storm. I've lost all track of Blake and Simon but I knew they were somewhere near at hand.

As quickly as it came, the sandstorm seemed to subside. "It's letting up," Rima said, and I released my grip on her arm. I was starting to lift my head to verify her observation when it happened.

She gave a slight but audible gasp and that was all. I opened my eyes, shielding them against the dying force of sand, and looked around. Blake and Simon and next to me the Wizard ... *but Rima Jackson had vanished.*

It was impossible. But as the air cleared and the wind died away I saw that it was indeed true. This girl who had been in my hands only a few seconds earlier, who had actually spoken to me, was vanished now as completely as if the sand had swallowed her up. "Simon!" I shouted. "The girl is gone! She was just here and now she's gone!"

"One of the camels is missing too," Harry Blake said.

"Could she be under the sand somewhere?" I suggested, already clawing at the ground around me.

But Simon Ark remained surprisingly calm. "The camel could hardly be under there too," he said quietly, glancing curiously at the Wizard.

Harry Blake drew his gun, a wicked-looking .38 revolver. It was pointing in the Wizard's general direction. "She was her a minute ago," he said. "We all heard her speak. No one could have imitated her voice. And besides the wind has died down enough now to show tracks in the sand. You can see there are no tracks. She couldn't have left."

"The Wizard did it," I accused, knowing this thought was in Blake's mind too. "I said he might make her disappear."

But the bearded man only smiled and said nothing. I took a step towards him, but Simon Ark's hand restrained me. "Careful, my friend. There is no mystery here."

"No mystery! Then where is Rima Jackson?"

Simon turned away, towards the distant dune which might mark our goal. "There is no time to spare. We must hasten to our goal. Explanations can come later."

But Harry Blake was waving his pistol. "This girl is an American citizen, Mr. Ark. We don't move till you tell me where she is."

Simon Ark gave a sigh. "Very well, sir, if you insist." And he took a step towards the Wizard. I thought for a moment he was going to strike out at the bearded magician, but he merely wrapped his long fingers into the hair of the false beard and tugged. There was a gasp of surprise from

Blake and a little screech from the Wizard—and the beard came away and we were looking into the face of Rima Jackson.

"But ... how?" I managed to gasp out. "If this is Rima, where's the Wizard?"

"No more questions," Simon ordered. "We must hurry."

Rima was busy pulling off the false hair and eyebrows she'd used to complete her brief disguise, and I helped her to pull off the loose white robe with which she'd covered her shirt and slacks. "What in hell was the idea of all this?" I asked her.

"I wanted to see if it could be done," she answered simply. "I'm becoming a bit of a detective myself."

"But where's the Wizard?"

"He took off his robe and make-up as soon as the storm started and left with one of the camels. I saw it and decided to try impersonating him. At least I fooled you and Blake."

"But *why?*"

"Ask your friend Simon Ark. I think he knows."

But Simon and Blake had already mounted their camels, and were urging them across the rippled sea of sand. Rima and I followed, with the question unanswered for the moment. Truly this was the day of the Wizard.

Finally we neared the dune Simon had pointed out, our eyes shielded against the blinding glare of the sun, our throats dry with thirst. And through it all Simon would say nothing more of Rima Jackson's strange actions, or the equally strange disappearance of the Wizard, presently, though, we began to make out fresh tracks ahead of us in the sand, indicating the position of a rider at the time the sandstorm passed. "The Wizard?" I asked, pointing them out to Simon.

But he shook his head. "The Wizard is dead, my friend. These are the tracks of his murderer."

"What? Dead? But where is the body?"

"Back in Cairo," he answered quietly, studying the camel tracks in the sand. "The man with the slit throat was the real Wizard."

I started to protest, but Harry Blake had already reached the top of the dune and was urging us forward. There, not a half-mile ahead, was the tail section of a plane, all that remained above the level of the all-engulfing sands. "Is that it?" Rima asked.

Simon nodded, sliding down from his camel. "The final piece of the puzzle, I think."

"Will you tell us now?" Blake demanded. "Who killed that man? How did Miss Jackson get into that closet?"

Bur Simon only smiled. "Will you tell me the contents of that plane? Notice the camel down there, just the other side of the wreckage. Our friend is already on the scene."

"But who is he, if he isn't the Wizard?" I asked.

"Who?" We were moving slowly forward now, on foot, and Blake had drawn his gun once more. "Consider, my friends, and you will know. The Wizard was killed as he stepped off the stage following his act, and this man took his place. It had to be like that, because obviously the impostor could not have gone through a complex magic act. Also, we already established that the body was a fresh one."

"Wait a minute," I protested. "You say he killed the real Wizard, but I talked with the Wizard, both before and after the trick with the locked door. Wouldn't I have realized it was a different person?"

"You might have, my friend, but the fact is you didn't. As Miss Jackson aptly demonstrated just now, the false hair and beard made a most effective disguise. Stage magicians often use trickery involving bearded men. The audiences sees the beard, not the man."

I still wasn't convinced. "But that first time, backstage, I saw the Wizard removing his beard. Why didn't I recognize him as the dead man when I saw the body?"

"Simple. His face was smeared with make-up and such when you first saw him, and quite horribly contorted when you saw him as a dead man. Rima Jackson recognized him because she'd sat and talked with him and seen his natural face, just before he drugged her. Then too, you had no reason to think the dead man might be the Wizard when we all saw the Wizard standing there with us."

"Then just what happened back at the theater?"

"The Wizard, seeking a beautiful girl for his closet trick, drugged Rima and locked her in there. He simply rushed out after the early show, without his beard or make-up, and lured her into having a drink with him. Probably an Egyptian girl would never have fallen for it, but Americans are more foolhardy. It was a shocking thing to do just for publicity, but he probably would have offered to pay her something later. Anyway, he locked her in the closet ..."

"How?"

"What?"

"How did he get through that padlocked door?"

Simon Ark patted his camel's side, never taking his eyes from the remnant of wreckage ahead. "By a trick not even worthy of a good magician. He told you to purchase a common type of padlock. When he saw which make it was, he simply went out and bought another one just like it. He carefully filed off the original padlock without damaging the door, put the drugged girl inside and snapped the new lock into place. With the keyhole jammed and sealed, he knew you wouldn't be able to use your carefully guarded keys, and thus would never realize the switch."

"It seems so simple when you tell it, Simon."

"In the meantime, though, the false Wizard had read the publicity about the search for me and guessed the United States was seeking this missing plane. Unfortunately, I played into his hands by visiting the curio shop, but more about that in a moment. He figured the best way to join our little expedition was to kill the real Wizard and take his place. Remember, he didn't know you'd seen the magician without his beard. The thing must have seemed perfectly safe to him. He arrived at the theater after the evening show, slit the real Wizard's throat backstage among the props, and quickly donned his false hair and beard. Of course he knew nothing about Rima, so he was as surprised as the rest of us when the closet was opened."

"A good story. Mr. Ark," Blake said. "But how did you know all this?"

"There were numerous things. First, why did our Wizard keep his beard on during the entire journey through this heat? It made me suspicious from the start, and my suspicions grew when he didn't once mention the closet trick to me. The real Wizard couldn't have resisted gloating over it. Also, since leaving Cairo the supposed Wizard has amused us only with the simplest of card tricks, because he knew no others. Rima here was suspicious of him, which is why she tried the trickery with his beard after he made his escape."

We were only a hundred yards from the remains of the plane now, but still there was no sign of the man we sought, the man I still thought of as the Wizard. "Who is he, Simon? Who?"

"A man. A man who could do a reasonable imitation of the Wizard's German accent after sitting through just one show—though I believe you noticed a little difference yourself, my friend. He's a man a bit younger than the real Wizard—you noticed that too—and I would guess him to be about forty. He's a man familiar with this small area of desert, or he wouldn't have risked going off alone during the sandstorm. Yet he isn't a native of the country, or he wouldn't have felt it necessary to travel with us as far as he did. I told you the communists were anxious to drive a wedge between America and England. I believe this man is someone who fell in with them during the postwar years, and was sent on a mission now to make sure we don't destroy this plane and its secret. The Communists are just now deciding it's important."

"If he killed the magician, he'll kill us."

Simon Ark nodded. "He would have killed us during the sandstorm if he'd been this certain of finding the plane himself. Now ..."

There was the single crack of a pistol, and next to me Rima screamed. "He's shooting from behind the plane!" I hit the sand, pulling her down on top of me as the others followed.

"We're out of range," Blake said, but a second shot disproved him by kicking up sand a foot from his head.

"What now, Mr. Blake?" Simon asked.

"We've got to take him, before he kills us all." He got to his feet and started down the dune, urging one of the camels before him as a shield.

"Come," Simon told Rima and me, "perhaps we can circle around the other side." But two more shots whistled our way as we started to follow his lead. Ahead and to the right of us, Blake fired once at the unseen target hidden behind the wreckage.

We were still a good distance from the plane when the shooting stopped as suddenly as it had started. Blake must have guessed he was reloading, for he left the shelter of the camel and darted the rest of the distance on foot, running like the wind through the loose, clinging sand. He almost made it. But when he was a scant ten yards from the plane's tail, the enemy's head popped into view. He fired once and Harry Blake went down sliding in the sand.

"Come on!" Simon Ark urged. The killer turned his gun now in our direction and fired again. One of the camels started to go down in a heap before us, filling the air with a strange shrill cry of death.

And then there was nothing else between me and the gun. I looked across the sand and saw death written across the enemy's face. He raised the pistol once more, and a final shot split the desert quiet. The face above the gun shuddered and seemed to dissolve before my eyes. I shifted my gaze and saw Harry Blake on his knees, his .38 held tightly in two quivering hands.

"It is over," Simon Ark said.

"He ... he looks almost like an American without the beard and make-up."

"He was an American," Simon said quietly. "The ways of the gods are strange at times, and the end of the quest is not always a pleasing one. The man before us, the man who killed the real Wizard and took his place, was the pilot of this plane, Major Carey Lindhurst ..."

While Rima bandaged Harry Blake's flesh wound, the government man stared up at the hot and cloudless sky. "They'll be here soon," he said, almost to himself.

"They?"

"Navy helicopters to take us out of here. I've got a transmitter in my gear that's been sending out a radio signal since we started our trip. The Navy's been tracking us from a ship in the Red Sea."

"Why?" Rima asked.

Blake smiled. "In this business you don't take chances. I expected trouble of some sort. With the radio signal they'd have had the location of the wreckage even if we were all killed."

"It was important, wasn't it?" Simon asked.

"Important, yes. I suppose so. Tell me, Ark how did you know Lindhurst was still alive after all these years?"

"He fitted. He was about the right age to take the Wizard's place, and as I said before he knew this part of the desert. He knew where to find the wreckage, once we got him to the general area. That made me suspect one of the crew. And when I saw the plane, buried up to its tail in sand, I knew no wandering native had accidentally come upon that cigarette case of Lindhurst's. And if the case hadn't been buried in that plane, perhaps the pilot hadn't been, either."

"A native could have dug the case up."

But Simon Ark shook his head. "Remember how rusty it was? I doubt if any rust could form in an area of desert as dry as this. No, I know immediately that the cigarette case had spent those seventeen years somewhere else. I suppose the curio shop was linked to the Communists somehow. They felt it was Lindhurst's fault that the cigarette case fell into American hands after all these years, so he had to correct the error. About then they must have started to realize why the plane was important."

"Why did they tell you the location of the plane, Simon?"

"Just to get us out here, where Lindhurst could kill us once he was sure the plane could be located. Of course in the interests of deduction I must admit that our killer could have been some other crew member who was carrying Lindhurst's cigarette case at the time of the crash, but such a possibility was quite remote."

"But the man was an American officer!" Blake said.

"He was. I imagine he felt the plane crash was his fault, and couldn't bring himself to admit that he'd bungled an important mission that cost the lives of everyone but himself. The rest of course must be speculation now. He drifted to Cairo, and somehow during those seventeen years fell in with the Communists."

"Why the Communists?" I asked.

Simon shrugged. "Who else would profit from the secret of the plane?"

"What is the secret?" Rima asked. But no one answered her question. Overhead, distantly, came the beating of a helicopter's blades, and we could see it as a tiny growing speck on the horizon.

"They're coming for us," Blake said. "We'll have to take time to bury Lindhurst. Bury him right where he should have died in the first place."

When the helicopter had landed in the soft sand, and Rima and Blake had gone forward to meet it, I said to Simon, "That Indian you mentioned, Subhas Bose. He was killed in a plane crash, wasn't he?"

Simon smiled a bit and nodded. "In Formosa."

"But the dates were the same! Both plane crashes were on the same day! And you said yourself no one was ever sure of Bose's death on Formosa."

"Who is ever sure of anything on this Earth, my friend?"

"If the plane crash wasn't on Formosa ... if it was here ... if England's most hated enemy in India died on an American plane two days after the war ended ..."

"If."

"But why, Simon? If Bose was on the plane, what was he doing there? Where were the Americans taking him?"

"I can only solve the puzzles of the human mind, my friend. I do not pretend to solve the puzzles of international politics. Let us only hope that Lindhurst did not tell the Communist agents too much about the contents of this plane. It is clear that a confirmation of Bose's death here would give them an advantage."

Blake was deep in conversation with the men from the helicopter as we walked towards them, probably deciding whether a bomb might bury the remains of the plane once and for all. I didn't think much about it, because I was busy thinking about the Wizard, with his beard and his locked closet, who'd died only because I'd picked out his theater on a hot afternoon.

I thought about him, and I thought about Lindhurst, if that was really him stretched out on the sand behind me. He'd travelled a long way to end up back here. A long way through seventeen years we couldn't even imagine, with a rusty cigarette case that had finally in some mysterious way of its own, made the circle complete.

"Come, my friend," Simon Ark said. "It's time to be going back ..."

FUNERAL IN THE FOG

At times Simon Ark was a difficult person to find. He might just as easily be halfway around the world in Egypt or Poland or India as in the little 10th Street apartment he sometimes used. So I wasn't really surprised when my secretary was unable to locate him for me on that misty November morning. I wasn't even surprised when the day ended with her still shaking her head over the telephone.

A day passed, two days, and then Simon Ark returned to New York. He didn't phone the office, but turned up at my home in Westchester on the evening of his return, shaking the rain from the great black coat he always wore when autumn came.

"Simon! My secretary's been trying to reach you everywhere!" I motioned him into the living room where Shelly was catching up on her reading. "Simon Ark's here, honey," I announced.

My wife was always happy to see Simon, perhaps because he had helped to bring us together. But she was a bit frightened of him at times too, as people often were.

"Hello, Simon," she said, rising to greet him. "It's good to see you again."

"You grow younger with every visit," he told Shelly.

She blushed nicely, perhaps considering him something of an expert on the subject of age. "Can I get you fellows something to drink?"

Simon Ark nodded and settled his big frame into a chair. "Anything will do—a little wine, perhaps."

"Just where have you been?" I asked him. "Egypt again?"

"No, only California this time. It's hardly the same, though they do have some interesting *Ra* cults springing up near Los Angeles," He smiled slightly at some memory. "The weather out there makes it difficult to return to New York. But why were you trying to reach me?"

"It's about your book a Satanism," I began as Shelly reappeared with the drinks. "We received an interesting letter about it last week."

"After all this time!" Simon marvelled. "Surely it must be eight years since you published my little study."

"Books on Satanism and witchcraft are big these days. It's one of your stronger backlist items. Of course we always get the usual number of crank letters, and I know you do too, but this one seems more interesting than most. It's from a man upstate who claims the Devil is threatening to kill him."

"Very possible," Simon admitted with a slight frown, "although Satan usually works in a more indirect manner. What is this man's name?"

"Jason Bloomer is what he calls himself."

He nodded as if the name meant something to him. "Oh, yes. He's written a few little pamphlets which he publishes himself. Full of half forgotten incantations and the like. I fear he's a bit obsessed with the subject of Satan."

This seemed an odd criticism for someone as obsessed as Simon to offer, but I let it pass. "Do you think it's worth running up there? He might have an interesting story, at least. He's in Putnam County, across the river from West Point. We could drive it in an hour or so."

"We could drive up on Saturday if you'd like," Simon said, smiling. "Perhaps Shelly would like to come with us."

I glanced at her and she nodded. "It might be fun, if you'll promise there'll be no murders."

"I never promise that," Simon said quietly. He was no longer smiling.

Saturday dawned with a light drizzle of misty November rain. It was a terrible day for a drive up the Hudson, but Simon seemed anxious to go, and after a week of puttering around the house Shelly was eager too. So at ten o'clock we were on our way up the Taconic State Parkway with wheels splashing through shallow puddles. Presently we turned off the Parkway and drove past the gate of a little cemetery shrouded in mist. We continued down the road for about a mile, until we came to an old two-story house surrounded by fields overgrown with brush. Perhaps once it had been a farm, long ago. In the yard a little wooden sign bore the single word *Bloomer*.

"This is the place," I said. "You want to wait for us, Shelly?"

"Never! And miss meeting this Jason Bloomer?" Simon had told us a bit about him on the trip up, about his occasional writings and his interest in Satanism.

We went up the walk, all three of us, and I pressed the bell. After a moment the door was opened by a tall, slim man with a bald head and gray-streaked beard.

"I'm from Neptune Books." I began, extending my card. "You wrote us recently."

"And this would be the famous Simon Ark," he said, ignoring Shelly and me to turn his attention to Simon. "I'm honoured. You must come in."

The living room was in casual disarray, like so many bachelor quarters, but there was a touch of the bizarre in exotic hand carved masks that hung from the walls. There was a small totem pole, too, and an incongruous model of an oil derrick. The crowded bookshelves, which both Simon and I inspected, held well-thumbed copies of witchcraft books by Montague Summers, Willy Ley's *Exotic Zoology*, *The Golden Bough*, Charles Fort, Alister Crowley, and even an ancient bound volume of the *Journal of the Royal Asiatic Society* for 1837.

Jason Bloomer made a slight bow. "You honor my house."

Simon extended his hand. "I am pleased to meet you, Mr. Bloomer. Writings such as yours always interest me, and your letter to my friend here was of special interest."

Jason Bloomer nodded. "Your book was good. When I began to receive these threats, you were the first person I thought to turn to. One does not ring up the police to say that Satan is threatening his life." He stroked his beard as he talked, and Shelly and I could only watch from the sidelines.

"But you think I can help?"

"Certainly," Bloomer insisted. "In your book you state that the devil once appeared to the Duchess of Gloucester while she and the astrologer Bolingbroke were in the midst of bewitching Henry VI to death. That is the sort of knowledge very few men share."

Simon Ark shrugged it off. "The scene is depicted in a painting by Fuseli. My only special knowledge comes in knowing that the scene is a true one."

"Exactly! And your special knowledge can protect me!"

I cleared my throat. "If you want protection from a murder threat, Mr. Bloomer, wouldn't it be easier to hire a private detective?"

He turned on me, eyes blazing. "I could not hire a private detective to protect me from a man—or devil—who can strangle a person without even touching them!"

That was all he needed to hook Simon. I saw the sudden flicker of interest in his eyes. "Really? And the police did nothing?"

"There were no police. It happened on an island halfway around the world—on Java, to be exact. I saw it happen."

"And that's why he wants to kill you?"

"That and other reasons which needn't concern you. But mainly it's because I saw him murder this girl without ever laying a finger on her."

"And how long has he been threatening your life?"

"For a month now, ever since he discovered where I was living."

Beneath the beard and the deep, searching eyes, he was a man afraid. I knew it, and Simon knew it too. "My experience has been that true murderers do not give their victims much warning."

"He—he wants something from me."

"Suppose you tell me the whole story," Simon urged. "That's the only way I can help you."

And the bearded man sank back in his chair, and began to talk.

"I suppose it really started about six years ago, in Vietnam. It was during the early days of the American troop buildup, and with war staring us in the face a good many people like me left the country. I'd been there for several months, studying the modes of devil-worship among the tribesmen back in the hills, but now I knew it was time to get out fast.

"I heard of a small private plane that was flying two passengers south to Java, one of the islands of Indonesia, and I bargained for a seat on the plane. That was when I met Rolf Dagon. I was attracted to the man immediately, for two reasons. His name—Dagon—was that of a fish god of the Philistines. He was, in addition, perhaps the strangest-looking man I had ever seen. Tall, very tall, thinner than me, but with great powerful hands. I could easily imagine him strangling someone, but not, certainly, the girl he was traveling with. Her name was Li Chow, and she was obviously Dagon's mistress.

"We landed on Java at Jogjakarta, a fairly large city near the south coast of the island. They were still having trouble with Communists, and I was a bit timid about being left on my own. So I stuck pretty close to Dagon and Li Chow. He claimed to be French, left over after his country's collapse in Indo-China, but that seemed unlikely to me. I was more willing to believe him a soldier of fortune or a mercenary of some sort. Finally, one night over drinks in a little side street bar, he told me what he was really after. The Japanese had occupied Java during World War II—it was about as far south as they ever got—and he had learned from a Japanese veteran that when the war suddenly ended they'd been forced to leave nearly a million dollars in gold on the island, wealth originally intended for certain island rulers further along.

"Well, Dagon claimed to know the location of this twenty-year-old horde of gold, and the three of us set out for the place. It was said to be in a little valley near the town of Baturetno, deep in the southern jungle.

"It was a strange country, with half-covered patches of volcanic ash and trees that twisted their limbs to the sky while sending off snake-like roots from their braches. We travelled that last part mainly by foot, until at last we reached the place Dagon sought. There was a little hill, a low, grassy mound that stretched upward some thirty feet. It was a hard climb, especially for the little Chinese girl, but finally we reached the top and stood looking down into a circular valley, like a bow, some 300 yards across.

"We found the remains of the Japanese camp along the crest of the hill, and we settled there ourselves. The camp itself was deserted, of course, but down in the lowest point of the valley, in a singularly barren area, we could see two skeletons.

"We inspected them as one would a skeleton in a museum or doctor's office. There is nothing really horrible about a pile of bleached bones, you know. A body with skin still attached is much more horrible than a bare skeleton. There was no sign of violence to the bones, no clue as to how they'd died.

"The next morning I detected a growing tension between Dagon and Li Chow. When he was away, exploring the floor of the valley by himself, the little Chinese girl spoke to me. She said he was a devil, and that he planned to kill us both as soon as he found the gold. She showed me a knife she carried to defend herself, but I doubted it would be much protection against Dagon. He was a full head taller and had a good eighty pounds on her.

"They argued again that afternoon, and he took her for a walk in the valley. I watched them through binoculars from the crest of the hill because I feared what he might do to her. But even with me watching, he still did it. They were walking together in the valley, near where we'd found the skeletons, when suddenly she started to gasp for breath, as if some invisible hands were choking the life from her.

"I looked for a cord or wire of some sort, but there was nothing. After a moment she collapsed to the ground, and seemed to lose consciousness. Rolf Dagon merely stood there watching, unharmed himself. After another moment he began waving his arms slowly in the air above her,

like some ancient high priest summoning the powers of darkness. In that
instant I remembered what Li Chow had said about him being a devil.

"Presently, after he'd stood watching her in the act of dying, he bent
and lifted her body in his arms. He brought her back to the crest of the
hill where I waited, and said that she'd simply died. I looked her over
very closely, but there was not a mark on her body. She'd simply stopped
breathing, as if some giant hand had strangled her without leaving a trace.
Naturally I suspected poison, but all three of us had eaten the same packaged food. I even wondered if he'd killed her with a poison gas of some
sort, but when I walked carefully through the valley myself I found no
traces of it.

"After that, I was anxious to leave. We abandoned our search for the
Japanese gold, and made our way back to the airport at Jogjakarta. We
obtained passage on a commercial airliner to Australia, but at the last
minute I slipped away from Dagon and flew to Hong Kong instead. I was
talking no chances ending up the way Li Chow did."

We'd sat there listening to his story, while the skies outside began to
brighten. I don't think either Shelly or I believed a word of it. But now, as
he finished talking, I saw that Simon Ark was deeply intent on the man's
story.

"And now," he asked, "Rolf Dagon has reappeared?"

"Exactly. The threats began about a month ago. Letters at first, and
then telephone calls."

"Do you have any of the letters?"

Bloomer shook his head. "I threw them away."

"If he's telephoned you must have some idea of his whereabouts."

"Not really, except that he's getting closer. That's why I wrote to Neptune
Books to contact you. I knew if anyone could save me, Simon Ark could."

Simon nodded, thought for a moment, and then asked, "Tell me, sir,
how tall are you?"

"Me? Why, I'm just six feet."

"And you described Rolf Dagon as being quite tall. Just how tall?"

"Oh, he must be six-four or five."

Simon seemed satisfied, but he had one more question. "You said he
was a head taller than the girl, but since she was small and Chinese, she
might have been only about five feet in height. Correct?"

"Yes, I suppose he was more than a head taller."

"As much as sixteen or seventeen inches?"

"That's possible. Why?"

Simon Ark let his breath out slowly. "I believe I can help you, even though you have lied about a very important point in your story."

"I–"

Simon waved a hand. "I will return tomorrow. Perhaps then you will be ready with the truth, Mr. Bloomer."

He would say no more, and we left Jason Bloomer standing in the doorway as we departed. Though the weather had cleared, there was a decided November chill to the air.

I started driving back the way we had come, and Shelly said, "What a strange man! Do you really believe any of that story, Simon?"

"That is the problem," he answered, turning up the collar of his black topcoat. "What to believe and what not to believe. He lies in part, but does he lie entirely? Are we simply the victims of some quite elaborate hoax, or are we up against an evil genius who really threatens Bloomer's life?"

Shelly snorted and took out a cigarette. "Well, I for one don't believe a word of it! There's no reason why we should! How could this Rolf Dagon kill that Chinese girl without touching her or leaving a mark, while Bloomer was watching? And more important, why should he kill her? Just because they had a little argument? It just doesn't make sense."

I joined in then. "But if it's not true, why should Bloomer get us all the way out here just to tell us a crazy story?"

"It may be true," Simon said. "There is one explanation that would fit the facts, provided we assume a single lie on Mr. Bloomer's part."

I turned back onto the parkway and headed for home. "So what do we do now?"

"Would you be willing to bring me up here again tomorrow, when our friend has had time to consider his story and make a slight correction in it?"

"Only if you stop being so mysterious, Simon. What lie did Bloomer tell? What fact would make it all clear?"

"All right," Simon said with a smile. "I won't keep you in the dark. Consider–Why did they abandon their search for the gold after the death of the girl? If Dagon killed her, why did he do so? And most important, when Bloomer saw her dying, why didn't he run down the hill and try to save her?"

"I give up," Shelly said. "Why?"

"Because, my friends, Bloomer left out one little fact. They found the gold."

We were silent for a moment, taking that in, and then Shelly said, "You can't be sure of that."

"I can be sure. They found the gold, and Dagon killed the girl to keep from splitting with her."

"Why didn't he kill Bloomer too?" I asked him.

"Because I think our Mr. Bloomer made good use of the time while Dragon was killing the girl. I think he stayed at the top of the hill so he could do something with the gold—hide it, or dispose of it in some way. When Dagon returned, Bloomer had him just where he wanted him. He must have promised Dagon his share only when they were safely out of that place. Dagon had to agree, but when they reached the airport, Bloomer double-crossed him. He flew off with the gold, or the secret of it. Dagon has been searching for him all these years. Bloomer won't show us his messages because they mention the gold."

"All right," I granted. "It first the facts as we know them, but it still doesn't explain this Satan business, or how Dagon killed the girl."

"That, my friend, has to do with the height of the people involved."

"You mean Dagon used a method of murder that would kill only short people?"

"Exactly."

"Then Jason Bloomer is safe. He's six feet tall." I couldn't help being a bit sarcastic.

"Jason Bloomer is not safe," Simon said quietly. "I only hope he is at least safe until tomorrow."

On Sunday morning Simon and I drove back up the Hudson to the graying house where Jason Bloomer had lived in hiding for all these years. Shelly had not joined us this time. So we went alone, driving over the familiar road through little wind-gathered piles of damp leaves. It was trying hard to be a sunny day, but there was a mist in the air that wouldn't quite give up, casting a sort of haze over everything in sight.

The house seemed deserted when we reached it, and I was beginning to think that the whole thing had been some product of our imaginations. But then Simon tried the door and it opened inward. The main floor was unchanged from our visit of the previous day, except that now a pen and paper lay on a little writing desk in one corner. Jason Bloomer had started to write a letter, or at least a message of some sort.

Rolf—It will do you no good to come here and threaten me. The gold will never be found. If you kill me, I will take it with me to the grave. To settle our accounts once and for all, I offer you a fair share of

The message stopped there, as if Bloomer had been interrupted at that point. "Bloomer!" I shouted. "Bloomer! Are you home?"

"Come on," Simon said, "Quickly!"

We went through the house, every room of it, but there was no sign of Jason Bloomer. There was only more evidence of his strange way of life, the paraphernalia of mysticism, the accessories of the Satanic. Then, from the second-floor bedroom, I happened to spot something out the window.

"Simon! There, across the field, near the woods!"

There were two men, walking. One was certainly Jason Bloomer, and the other was taller—slim and straight and somehow evil. There could be no doubt as to his identity.

"Come on," Simon breathed. We were down the stairs and out of the house in a moment, running across the open field toward the spot where we'd seen the two men. It was a good two hundred yards away, and once on the ground the gently rolling terrain effectively shielded the two figures from our eyes.

But then, topping a small rise, we saw Jason Bloomer once again. He was stretched out on the ground, arms outflung as if to ward off the beat of some giant wings. There was no one else in sight. The tall figure with whom he'd been walking had vanished into the nearby woods.

"He's dead, Simon," I said, moving closer.

Simon bent to feel for a pulse and then rose, nodding. "Dead. And no marks on his body."

I remembered the story Bloomer had told us. "Just like the Chinese girl. My God, Simon; maybe Rolf Dagon really is the devil!"

Jason Bloomer was buried two days later, on a foggy Tuesday morning when even the heavens seemed to be in mourning. Simon and I had spent most of Monday searching the old house, but there was no gold hidden in it anywhere. There was also no evidence of a safe deposit box or any other hiding place large enough to hold a small fortune in gold. All we found was the name of an undertaker with whom Bloomer had made arrangements for his burial, as well as the name of a married sister in New York whom we notified of his death.

The funeral procession was a skimpy one, moving from the undertaking parlor to the little tree-lined cemetery we'd observed on our first visit, Behind a uniformed motorcycle escort, there was only the hearse and three cars—one for the hired pallbearers, one for the sister and her husband, and one for Simon and me. Bloomer had no neighbours close enough, or interested enough, to journey to the cemetery on that foggy morning.

"What do you think, Simon?" I asked as we kept pace with the cars ahead. "Does Rolf Dagon really exist, or did Bloomer make the whole thing up?"

"Oh, he exists, my friend. I spent all day Saturday checking that out. He's a former French mercenary who was indeed in Vietnam six years ago. His description fits what Bloomer told us, too."

"And the Chinese girl?"

"I have no reason to doubt Bloomer's story."

"Then how did Dagon kill her? And how did he kill Bloomer?"

"The medical examiner says that Jason Bloomer died of something as simple as a heart attack."

"Do you believe that, Simon?"

"It seems likely."

"But we saw him with Dagon!" I insisted.

"It could be that Jason Bloomer read too many books on Satanism for his own good," Simon said. Ahead, the motorcycle escort had turned into the cemetery gate, and the little line of mourners followed along. The fog was thicker here, all but obscuring the road at times. When at last the handful of cars halted, Simon did not immediately leave our vehicle. Instead, he sat watching the pallbearers, they unloaded the coffin.

"You seem disappointed," I observed, hearing the sigh escape his lips.

"I am."

"About the funeral?"

"About the height of the pallbearers. They are quite average."

"You expected Dagon to show up here?"

Simon got out of the car without answering, and started up the little hill to the side of the freshly-dug grave. I saw that a gravestone was already in place, with the family name *Bloomer*. The funeral director guided the coffin into place while the dead man's sister and her husband stood to one side. Back on the winding road, the motorcycle driver sat astride his machine, smoking a cigarette.

A minister of some uncertain faith appeared to say a few words, and then the group scattered to move off through the mist to their cars. It had been as simple as that. Later, sometime, the gravediggers would appear to complete to job.

"Ready to go, Simon?" I asked.

"In a moment, my friend."

He waited until the others had departed, their cars swallowed up by fog, and then he acted. "Quickly! Into the grave!"

"Simon! Have you gone mad?"

"We only have a few minutes. Hand me that shovel and use the other one yourself."

"But—"

Moving with more agility than I would have dreamed possible, Simon dropped into the open grave, edging past the waiting coffin. I had no choice but to follow. He drove the shovel down, digging a bit in one spot and then moving to another. Above and around us, all seemed muffled in fog.

"Simon, could you tell me what we're looking for?"

"The gold, my friend. Remember Bloomer's unfinished note to Dagon? He said he'd take the gold to the grave with him, and I think he meant it literally. He'd made funeral arrangements, and even ordered the tomb-stone for this plot in advance. I think—"

He paused, staring up at the great marble block with the word *Bloomer* on its face. "What now, Simon?"

"Help me out of here, quickly!"

"I thought you said the gold was in here."

"He wouldn't have buried it in the earth, where any incautious gravedig-ger might have found it. Much more likely it's hidden in this gravestone."

We tugged and pulled at it, but nothing moved. Then, as we were about to give up, something happened. The upper block edged away from its base, and we saw that the base was hollow. There was a metal box visible inside.

"My God, Simon, I think you're right!"

But he was cluthing my arm. He had heard something, some sound which had not yet reached my fog-muffled ears. "Quiet! He's coming back!"

"Who?"

"Rolf Dagon, unless I'm mistaken."

"But how could he come back when he wasn't even here? Simon. There was no one at the funeral taller than six feet."

And then I heard it. A low, gradually rising sound that at first I couldn't identify. Simon turned to face the fog-laden road, gripping the shovel in his hands.

Suddenly a motorcycle broke through the curtain of mist, heading straight for us. I recognized the uniformed man who'd escorted the funeral procession, only now he seemed different. In a blur of movement almost too fast to follow, I saw the gun in his right hand. Simon shoved me to one side as the shot tore between us into the marble gravestone, then hurled his shovel at the motorcycle's wheels as it tore past us up the hill.

His aim was good. Out of control, with one hand still gripping his pistol, the rider tumbled off his machine as it crashed into a nearby headstone. Before he could rise, Simon and I were on him, disarming him pinning him to the damp earth.

"That's all, Dagon," Simon said.

The tall, thin man under us cursed and tried to roll over. I kicked away his gun and held him fast.

Later, back home over drinks, Shelly said, "But Simon—I still don't understand how you knew Dagon was the motorcycle rider."

Simon Ark took a sip of his wine and replied; "He was the only one there who never stood up, never got off his cycle. If Dagon was at the funeral, as I believed him to be, the motorcycle escort was the only one who could have been tall enough."

"How did you know he'd be at the funeral?"

"If Bloomer really had hidden the gold in or around his grave, I knew Dagon would want to find it. The most likely time was at the funeral, rather than searching through the cemetery at a later date. I imagine he bribed the real motorcycle rider to take his place. Then, after the funeral, he came back for the gold and tried to kill us."

"And the Chinese girl?" Shelly asked. "What about her?"

"That part was simple, really, once I concluded the story was true. You remember Bloomer's mention of volcanic ash? That was the key to it, that and his description of the valley. It was round, remember—like a bowl.

Isn't obvious that the valley was really the long-dead crater of an extinct volcano?"

"Even so," I argued, "it certainly didn't erupt, Simon?"

"No," he agreed, "it didn't erupt. It simply gave off quantities of carbon dioxide gas from time to time. The gas, passing through fissures in the floor of the inactive volcano, accounted for the skeletons of the Japanese soldiers. And it killed the Chinese girl, Li Chow."

"Wait a minute," I objected. "Since when is carbon dioxide gas poisonous? I always thought carbon monoxide was the deadly one."

"And why didn't Dagon die too?" Shelly added.

"Because the carbon dioxide built up only in the valley's low points, displacing the vital oxygen. The soldier and Li Chow simply suffocated for lack of air. She was led to the low spot deliberately, and drowned in a sea of carbon dioxide as surely as she might have drowned in the ocean. Her killer, being a head taller, was able to keep his nose above the deadly layer and breath fresh air."

"I find that hard to believe," Shelly said.

Simon Ark shrugged. "It is true, nevertheless. There is a cave in Italy where a layer of carbon dioxide near the floor makes it fatal to dogs and other small animals, but humans of average height can walk through without feeling a thing."

Shelly still shook her head. "And you mean to tell me that Dagon killed the girl and then killed Bloomer, all for the gold you two found hidden in the tombstone?"

Simon sipped his wine and smiled. "Ah, dear Shelly, I fear I have misled you. There was no gold in the tombstone—only an empty metal box. And Rolf Dagon killed no one, though he came close with us. It was Jason Bloomer who killed the Chinese girl, and Jason Bloomer who would have killed Dagon if fate had not intervened."

I'd heard some of it on the ride down, but I could see that Simon's words were a shock to my wife. "Bloomer? But how could you know that?"

"The key to Bloomer's supposed belief in Dagon's Satanic powers was the death of the girl, which seemed a complete mystery to him. And yet on his bookshelves we saw well-thumbed copies of Willy Ley's *Exotic Zoology* and the *Journal of the Royal Asiatic Society* for 1837—both of which carry detailed accounts of such deadly valleys on Java. Certainly Bloomer knew what really killed the girl, and thus his whole fear of Dagon was a skilful bit of acting."

"But you say he killed Li Chow."

"Quite right. His story had it that Dagon stood over the fallen girl waving his arms. It conjures up quite a Satanic picture, but hardly one in keeping with the facts. If Li Chow was drowning in a sea of carbon dioxide, the last thing her killer would do would be to wave his hands in the air and disperse the deadly layer. If he lied about that, he lied about Dagon killing her. Remember, Bloomer was also a foot taller than the girl. He could have lured her to her death as easily as the taller man."

"And the gold?"

"Could we really believe that Bloomer stole the gold and hid it from Dagon, smuggling it back to America? It was much easier to believe the gold never existed, that it was merely a ploy to lure Dagon to his destruction. Bloomer walked with him in that field, awaiting our arrival. He planned to wait till we were on the scene, and then appear to kill Dagon in self-defense, before witnesses."

"And if we hadn't come?" I asked Simon Ark.

"Then he would have used his graveyard scheme—luring Dagon to the hiding place in the tombstone and then killing him, probably burying his body right there."

"But *why?*" Shelly asked.

"Dagon told us a little of that after we disarmed him. He was a soldier of fortune with whom Bloomer fell in. There was money involved and some talk of Japanese gold, but none ever appeared. Something else did appear, though—evidence of oil deposits. Remember the somewhat incongruous little oil derrick in Bloomer's study? In any event, Bloomer felt he had to kill Dagon and the girl so any oil discovery would be all his. He succeeded with Li Chow. But it was Dagon who escaped from him, rather than the other way around. So the long charade began, to lure Dagon back here to his death. Dagon, for his part, was enough of a mercenary to be attracted by the possibility of gold. Bloomer told him about the gravestone before he died, or hinted at it, and Dagon took part in the funeral to observe it close up. When he returned and saw us, he tried to kill us, thinking we'd been paid by Bloomer to finish him."

"And Bloomer?"

"A simple heart attack in a field, as the medical examiner ruled it. The pressure, the anticipation of killing Dagon, was too much for him. Dagon told me Bloomer actually had the gun out when the seizure hit him. Dagon took the gun himself and ran into the woods."

"Then all this Satanism business was just a ruse to get you up there as a witness, Simon?"

But Simon Ark merely shrugged and reached his wine glass. He might have been a kindly uncle instructing Shelly and me on the proper care of our garden. "That, my friend, we will not ever know. Perhaps, in his twisted mind, Jason Bloomer had truly become Rolf Dagon, the man he intended to kill. Perhaps, in that final moment with the gun, facing the supreme evil which was really himself, all the Satanic trappings became too real for him. Perhaps that is why his heart gave out—because the evil he had to destroy was the evil within himself."

THE AVENGER FROM OUTER SPACE

Neither Simon Ark nor I was in on the beginning of it, but the way we pieced it together later it must have started something like this ...

It was late summer in the *dacha* community outside Moscow, where country homes in the woods served as the state's reward for a job well done. This was a *dacha* of scientists, and Valery Feokarov—long returned from the journey that had made him famous—enjoyed the companionship of these other renowned figures. The country house given him by the state was large by Russian standards, and quite comfortable. The wide expanses of glass in the corner sunroom gave a lovely view of the thick summer greenery outside, making it almost a part of the decor. And Feokarov's wife especially liked the big back yard with its swings and play area for the children.

On this day he had gone out alone to stroll in the woods behind the house, as he often did when he was thinking. He'd reached the top of a small hill and paused beneath a majestic pine tree that was far older than he was. Looking up at its soaring grandeur he was reminded of the Space Exploration Obelisk in Moscow, which he'd helped dedicate in 1964. Those had been the good days before his forced retirement. He missed those days, though he still had the companionship of those who had shared his adventure.

He gazed off toward the horizon, watching the high black cloud moving in. He knew the signs of an approaching storm by now, after all those mornings spent at the launch site in the Ural Mountains. He wondered if he should—

At that instant there was a flash he barely saw, and Valery Feokarov became the first of them to die.

Eight days later, on the Sunday of Labor Day weekend, David Woodword met Lisa Blake at the private marina on the west shore of Galveston Bay. Since the breakup of his marriage three years earlier, Lisa had done more for him than any psychiatrist could have. She had tended to his needs unselfishly, never once asking when he might be free to marry her. She was everything he could ask for, and this day in her white shorts and striped shirt she seemed more lovely than ever before.

He bent to kiss her and then climbed on board the cabin cruiser that was his biggest luxury. "Come on, let's get her out of here. They're predicting scattered thundershowers for later and I'd like to get a couple of hours on the water at least."

"Am I late?" she asked, hopping in beside him.

"No, no! Cast off the line, will you?"

He let the boat drift away from the dock a bit before he switched on the engine. Then they took off, skimming across the waves with a burst of energy that reminded him of the old days on the Cape. Nothing could really match that, of course, but the thrill he felt here on the water came close.

"Did you see Milly and the kids today?" Lisa asked.

"No. She's letting me have them tomorrow for a picnic." He twisted the wheel to starboard. "Shall we head for our cove?"

"Sure!"

They called it their secret cove, though in truth there were no secrets anywhere along the shoreline of Galveston Bay. Still, a stand of trees here shielded them from the nearest house, and it was the closest thing to seclusion to be found anywhere on the industrialized bay. He turned their craft gently toward shore, negotiating the familiar waters until they began to edge smoothly into the cove.

Then suddenly he cursed. "What in hell is this?"

"What is it, David?" she called from the stern.

He bent over the side toward the water. "There's something—"

She saw a blinding flash of light, and David Woodword became the second of them to die.

The first thing I knew about it was a phone call from my brother-in-law, Ray Constance. Shelly's brother was a year older than I, crowding 50, and had a big job in Houston with the National Aeronautics and Space Administration. I hadn't seen him since a family gathering the Christmas before last, and hearing his voice on the phone in my New York office alarmed me a bit. "What is it, Ray? Family all right?"

"What? Oh, sure, they're great. I'm calling on business."

"If you're ready to write your book, Neptune would be happy to publish it." That was a running joke between us.

But Ray was dead-serious. "You remember about twenty years ago, when I was at that guided missile test range in the desert and you brought an old guy named Simon Ark out to solve a murder?"

"I remember."

"Shelly tells me you still see him from time to time. He must be a hundred years old by now!"

"Two thousand, according to him. Why are you asking?"

"I've got something he might help us on, if he's around."

"Sometimes he drops out of sight for years at a time, but I think he's still in New York at the moment. I'll try to reach him."

"Call me back, will you? If he's available the government will fly you both to Houston this afternoon."

"It's that important?"

"We think so."

"I'll see what I can do."

I knew Simon had lingered in New York after our last adventure to pursue some studies into astral projection. I was lucky enough to reach him at the first number I tried. He listened quietly, then said, "I imagine it concerns the deaths of those two astronauts."

"I hadn't thought of that." Yesterday's paper had carried an article on David Woodword, killed by lightning just eight days after Russian cosmonaut Valery Feokarov died in a similar manner.

"The coincidence seems to justify an investigation," Simon remarked. "I might be interested in a trip to Houston."

"This afternoon?"

"My research is not going well. A bit of mental stimulation seems called for. Arrange for the flight, and I will meet you at the airport."

For once my impending absence from home did not upset Shelly. Since Simon and I were going to Houston at her brother's request, there was little she could object to. I promised to phone her that evening, then I called Ray back to say we were coming.

He was waiting at the Houston airport to greet us late that afternoon. Ray was still slim and boyish despite the flecks of gray in his hair, and he asked me at once about Shelly. They'd always been a close family despite the separation of 1600 miles.

"Shelly is fine," I assured him, sliding into the official-looking limousine he'd provided. "We missed seeing you last Christmas."

"This year for sure! If you can't get down here I'll bring the family to New York."

"Tell us what this is all about."

"Wait till we reach my office," he said. "I want our medical officer, Colonel Byers, to sit in on the meeting."

We headed southeast along route 45, then turned off into the sprawling complex of buildings that was the Lyndon B. Johnson Space Center, NASA's Houston headquarters. Ray's office was a plush affair on the top floor of the tallest office building. I didn't need the sign on the door to tell me he'd come a long way from that missile-testing range.

"Sending men to the moon now, are you?"

"*And* bringing them back." He walked over to a model on a desk by the window. "But now we're more interested in the space shuttle."

Simon Ark grew impatient. "About the man who died—"

"David Woodword. He was on the final moon mission. But come, I want Colonel Byers in on this." We walked down the antiseptic hallway to a smaller office on the same floor. An Air Force Colonel in full uniform greeted us, rising from behind a cluttered desk on which I could see color photographs of a wife, two children, and a yacht. Byers was a friendly middle-aged man, one who looked as if he'd gone as far as he ever would in his career.

We shook hands all around and Ray did the introductions. "Colonel Byers, one of our top medical officers and the personal physician to several of the astronauts. He was the first to examine Woodword and the others when they splashed down after the moon flight."

Byers fingered his greying sideburns as he glanced at his notes. "I helped with the autopsy," he explained. "Death was due to electric shock. No doubt about it."

Simon shifted his bulk into one of the chairs and asked, "Were there thunderstorms in the area as the papers reported?"

Ray Constance answered that one. "They were twenty miles away. No one, including the girl in the boat with Woodword, heard any thunder."

Byers went back to his notes. "There was a severe burn on his right hand, obviously caused by electric shock. Something fouled the boat and Woodword reached in with both hands to remove it. He hesitated, then grabbed it with his right hand—and there was a flash of electricity. This woman, Lisa Blake, saw it."

Simon grunted. "So your conclusion is—?"

"He wasn't killed by lightning but by a powerful electric shock."

"Was any wire found in the water?"

Ray shook his head. "Not a thing."

"If it was removed afterward—" I speculated.

Ray nodded, reading my thoughts. "That would imply a deliberate act."

"Murder," Simon Ark said. He was never one to mince words. "What about the Russian?"

"Valery Feokarov, one of their retired cosmonauts. He made seventy-nine orbits of earth on one of the Soyuz missions. The report is that he was struck by lightning while walking in the woods. We're trying to get more details but you know how the Russians are about releasing information."

Simon nodded. "But you must have something besides a phantom wire in the water to fly us out here so urgently. What else is there?"

Colonel Byers looked unhappy and Ray took his time answering, as if choosing his words with care. "The FBI is investigating all this, of course. We called them in yesterday. But there are some aspects of this affair that trouble us. Some aspects which might better be investigated by someone like you, Simon."

"Such as?"

"A man named Conrad Blaze warned us two weeks ago that all of our astronauts were doomed—threatened by an avenger out of space who would destroy them for having ventured too far from earth."

"You certainly didn't listen to that nonsense!" I said.

"Of course not. But yesterday he phoned me at home and repeated the warning. Said that Feokarov and Woodword were only the first two to die. He said by Christmas they'd all be dead—Russians and Americans alike."

"How many would that be?" Simon asked quietly.

"Beginning in 1961, with Gagarin for the Russians and Shepard for us, there have been sixty Russians and forty-four Americans—one-o-four in all. Males, of course, except for Valentina Tereshkova."

"The Russians may have more than sixty," Colonel Byers added. "We think they launched a new Soyuz mission yesterday which they haven't yet announced."

Simon had picked up a pencil and was making marks on a sheet of notepaper. "Over one hundred people who must be guarded, if you believe this man Conrad Blaze."

"If we really believe him," Ray said, "guarding them will do no good. Death will come like a bolt from the blue."

"For David Woodword it may have been more like a bolt from a live wire." Simon put down his pencil. "Is this man Blaze here in Houston?"

"Yes. He imagines himself to be something of a minor prophet, speaking around town on the evils of the space program."

"Does he have any connection with the astronauts?"

"None at all. As far as I can determine, none of them ever laid eyes on him—except maybe on television."

"I will want to see Conrad Blaze," Simon decided suddenly, getting to his feet.

"I was hoping you would," Ray said. "You just might get further than the FBI."

As we were leaving the office I glanced down at the paper Simon had been doodling on. A lightning bolt, made up of three short lines. Underneath, he'd turned it on its side so it resembled the letter Z. Then he'd reassembled the three lines to look like the letter K. I wondered what, if anything, it meant to him.

When we reached a rundown part of Houston populated mainly by Mexican-Americans, it became obvious that the man we sought had acquired no great wealth from his single-minded campaign against space exploration. Conrad Blaze lived in a ramshackle building where the grass out front had long ago been worn away by the playing of children. We passed a few of them on the way in, and Simon paused to pat one brown-skinned girl on the head.

Blaze's apartment was on the top floor and he answered the door at once, almost as if he'd been expecting us. "More FBI?" he asked accusingly. Then, seeing Simon, he pointed a bony finger. "You're too old for FBI. Who are you?"

"Could we talk inside, Mr. Blaze?" Simon suggested.

He turned away from the door and we entered a large loft-like room decorated with colorful banners covered with mystic symbols. I half expected Conrad Blaze to put on a wizard's cape before speaking with us, but he remained as he was—a white-haired man in his late fifties whose deep blue eyes carried a spark that might have been genius or madness.

"You all come to see me now, don't you?" he said, spinning around to sit suddenly facing us on a faded sofa. "No one would listen two weeks ago when I warned NASA. Now the killings have begun, and one hundred shall die before Christmas Day."

Simon Ark sat down opposite him and softly asked, "Who is killing them, Mr. Blaze?"

"The avenger, that's who! Call him what you will—Thor, the thunderer, was the name the Scandinavians gave him. He is the strongest of gods and men, hurling lightning bolts from the heavens at all who would invade his sacred territory."

"Do you worship Thor?" Simon asked.

"On his day, each week, I give an offering."

"Thor's day. Thursday. But these two men did not die on Thursday.'

"The avenger is always with us," Blaze replied.

"Would you kill for him?" Simon asked. "Would you carry out his mission here on earth?"

Conrad Blaze smiled. "Are you asking if I killed those two men? Of course I didn't! Do not try to punish the messenger for the bad news that he carries."

"When will the next killing come?"

"Soon, soon."

"Here or in Russia?"

"Those who rode into space are scattered to all corners of the earth. One is a Senator in Washington. Another heads a large corporation. Thor's bolt could fall anywhere."

"Have you ever met any of the astronauts?" Simon asked.

"I only know them as names in the media. They are our heroes, and every generation has sacrificed its heroes. We will learn, the hard way, that the place for man is only on earth."

I could see we'd get nothing more from this strange man, and I was pleased when Simon finally rose to leave. "Your warnings came at an inappropriate time," he told Conrad Blaze. "They came at a time when they were true."

Outside it had grown dark. Night had slipped up on us without warning.

In the morning, which was the Wednesday after Labor Day, Ray had arranged for us to accompany him to a memorial service for David Woodword. Afterward we went to one of the other astronaut's homes for coffee. Our host was Sky Hardy, who'd been on the Apollo mission along with Woodword when they made the seventh moon landing. He was a tall lanky man with an easygoing personality. Still, it was clear that Woodword's death had deeply disturbed him.

"Imagine going to the moon and back to die in some freak accident on Galveston Bay!" he said as he helped his wife pour the coffee.

"It might not have been a freak accident," Ray told him. "The FBI is looking into it."

"You mean he was killed by someone?"

"We just don't know."

They were interrupted by a moon-faced woman who was introduced as Milly Woodword. She'd been divorced from the dead man since shortly after his moon mission, but she had attended the funeral with his children. Perhaps, I thought, she'd come to see if Woodword's latest woman friend turned up. But according to Ray there was no sign of Lisa Blake at the services.

"He was always foolhardy," Milly Woodword said. "Just the sort to go out on the bay in a thunderstorm."

"The storm was some miles away at the time," Ray reminded her.

She seemed to ignore him and kept right on. "I told him he should never have joined the astronaut program. Astronuts, that's what you all were! I think he joined just to get as far away from me as possible."

"You know that's not true, Milly," a soothing voice insisted. It belonged to another of the astronauts, Pete Saunders. I remembered he'd been the third man aboard Apollo 19, the one who had remained in orbit while Woodword and Hardy walked on the surface of the moon. Saunders was quieter than Sky Hardy, and he had a solemn, pained expression which might have been merely his reaction to Woodword's death.

"You're just another one of them," Milly Woodword told him. "What were you running from, Pete?"

He shook his head and didn't answer. They all seemed to realize she was beyond reason. I gazed out the sliding glass doors at the back-yard pool while Sky Hardy went for more coffee. Milly cornered Ray and started in about Woodword's insurance policy.

"The money goes to his children," Ray explained patiently. "You know he removed you as beneficiary after the divorce."

"What about the things he took along to the moon?" she demanded. "The coins and stamps. They're worth a fortune!"

Ray tried to reason with her. "After the problems on some earlier flights we made a rule. They couldn't carry anything like stamps on which they could make a personal profit. You know that, Milly."

"I don't know anything of the sort! Everyone did it and you know it as well as I do!"

But Ray shook his head. "They showed me their personal kits after splashdown. They had nothing but a few family souvenirs."

Sky Hardy interrupted. "This is hardly the time to be arguing about it. Milly, maybe you'd better leave now."

She started to turn her fury on him. "Are you ordering me out of your house?"

"Milly, how long have we known each other?"

She didn't bother to answer, or to react to his attempt at conciliation. Instead she turned on her heel and strode out of the house. Sky Hardy merely shook his head. "She's a sick woman," he said to Saunders. "Has been, ever since the divorce."

Milly's appearance had dampened the already solemn proceedings even further, and most of the guests departed soon afterward. Driving back into Houston, Ray told Simon and me, "We really live in a little world all our own here. The breakup of a marriage affects everyone."

"What about this woman Woodword was seeing?" Simon asked. "The one who was with him when he died."

"Lisa Blake. She's young and quite attractive. A commercial artist. Never been married, though she's lived with guys off and on. She met Woodword at a party shortly after his divorce."

"I will want to see her," Simon told him.

"Certainly." Ray glanced at his watch. "Look, I have to get back to NASA. We're trying to get a call through to the Russian space agency about this matter. But you two can drive out to see her. I'll give you the address and drop you back at your car." It was NASA's car, really, one that Ray had lent us. "Frankly, I'm a bit surprised she wasn't at the services."

After Ray dropped us off we had a quick lunch and headed into downtown Houston to the Washington Avenue address he'd given us. Lisa Blake's modest apartment also served as the studio for her free-lance art business. We found her hunched over a drawing board when we obeyed the dictum on the door to ring and walk in.

"Be with you in a minute," she called out. We stood there a bit awkwardly, looking over the fashion illustrations and catalogue covers that were pinned to the walls in a haphazard manner.

When she joined us I introduced Simon and myself, telling her I was Ray's brother-in-law. She looked at both of us coolly, studying us with deep blue eyes that could have drowned a man. She was certainly attractive—and talented too, judging by the samples of her artwork.

"It's about David, isn't it?"

"Yes," Simon admitted. "You were not at the memorial services this morning."

"I couldn't face his ex-wife. I preferred to do my mourning in private. Who are you—detectives? I've already talked to the FBI."

"We're helping Ray with NASA's personal investigation," I answered vaguely.

Simon Ark smiled slightly, perhaps to put her at ease, and asked, "Could you tell us everything that happened up to the moment of the tragedy?"

"Very little happened, really. We were out for a cruise in his boat and we headed for a little cove where we often went. Just as we were entering the cove, something in the water seemed to foul the boat. David leaned over the side and—"

"Were there electrical storms in the area?"

She shook her head emphatically. "It was just beginning to cloud up. Whatever killed him came from the water, not from the sky."

"An electrical wire?"

"It could have been, but the police found nothing in the water."

"Could someone have been watching you from the shore and turned on the power when David touched the wire? Then, after he was dead, the power could have been shut off and the wire pulled away."

"I suppose it's possible. We were only about thirty feet from shore. But how would anyone know we were going there?"

"David knew, and you knew," Simon pointed out.

"Do you think I killed him?"

"You said it was a cove where you often went. How many others knew about it?"

"No one."

"Could someone have followed you, or seen you there on a prior occasion?"

"Anything's possible, I suppose," she admitted with a shrug. Before Simon could ask anything else, her telephone rang and she went to answer it. She listened, then handed the phone to me. "It's your brother-in-law, Ray Constance. He wants you."

I wondered what was important enough for him to track us down at Lisa Blake's apartment. "What is it, Ray?"

"Sky Hardy's been killed. Electrocuted in his swimming pool. You and Simon had better get out there right away."

The place was a madhouse by the time we reached it. Ray had beaten us there in his car and he was arguing with a husky motorcycle cop who tried to bar the front door. Finally Sky Hardy's wife appeared from somewhere and allowed us to enter. She'd been crying and looked terrible. Pete Saunders was with her, doing his best to comfort her.

Ray called him aside. "What in hell happened, Pete?"

"Most everyone had gone home and Sky said he needed a swim to relax. He changed into his trunks and dove into the pool. We heard a scream and saw a flash from the water. Somehow a power line that runs overhead broke and fell into the pool. By the time we managed to get him out he was dead. If the shock didn't kill him it probably stunned him enough to drown him."

Simon moved onto the rear terrace, toward the oval in-ground pool we'd only glimpsed before. Several detectives and police officers were there, along with power company linemen. We could see where the wire had fallen, from a wooden pole at the back of the property. It had caught just the edge of the pool, but that had been enough.

"How'd it happen?" Ray asked a detective who seemed to be in charge.

"We think the wire was cut with one of those long poles you use to trim branches. Whoever did it would have been hidden from view behind those bushes. We found a branch trimmer in the next yard, with its shaft wrapped in rubber to insulate it."

"Any suspects?"

The detective nodded. "Picked up somebody on the next street. He doesn't live in the neighborhood and he was acting suspicious."

We followed Ray and the detective around the house to the street. A police car was parked halfway down the block with their prisoner handcuffed in the back seat. It was Conrad Blaze.

"Let me talk to him," Simon suggested. "We got along well last night."

That wasn't precisely true, but the detective seemed agreeable. "Five minutes. And stay in the front seat."

Simon slid awkwardly into the squad car and turned to Blaze. "Hello, Conrad. Remember me from last evening?"

"I remember you."

"Sky Hardy is dead. That's number three."

"There'll be more."

"Did you kill him, Conrad?"

"He was killed by a bolt from Thor, like the others!"

"This time it looks as if Thor had some human assistance down here on earth. What were you doing in the neighborhood?"

Conrad Blaze was silent for a moment. He seemed to be sizing us up. Finally he said, "I wanted to see someone."

"Who?"

"None of your damned business!"

"*Did* you see anyone? Did you see the killer?"

"I saw only Thor, riding the thunderheads. wreaking his vengeance on those below."

Simon sighed and motioned to me to help him out of the front seat. "We must go about this in another way," he said.

"Do you think he's guilty?"

"My friend, each of us is guilty of something. Conrad Blaze is no exception." Then he asked the detective, "Will he be locked up?"

"At least overnight. Then we'll see if we've got anything on him."

"Very well." Simon turned away, as if dismissing all thought of Blaze from his mind. He asked Ray, "Did you manage to speak with the Russians?"

Ray nodded. "Talked with their top man in charge of the Cosmonauts. He speaks English quite well. From what he tells me there's no hint of foul play over there. Feokarov was out walking in the woods. He was on top of a hill, standing beneath a tall pine tree, when the first lightning bolt of an approaching storm hit the tree"

Simon Ark smiled. "Clearly one of Thor's thunderbolts."

"What do you think, seriously?" Ray asked.

"I think there'll be more killings unless we get to the bottom of this quickly."

I imagined that Simon would want to return to our hotel after that, but he fooled me. As soon as we were in the car he said, "We have some unfinished business with Lisa Blake."

"What?"

"I want to see the young woman again. Right now."

She was surprised at our return, and I had the impression she might have been on her way out somewhere. "I thought we were finished with questions," she said.

Simon Ark stepped around her before she could shut the door. "There was one matter we didn't cover earlier."

"What was that?" she asked, suddenly afraid.

"The matter of Conrad Blaze. He's your father, isn't he?"

I was dumbfounded by his accusation. Nothing in the investigation thus far had even hinted at such a relationship, and I was prepared for her instant denial. Instead, she turned pale and stammered, "I—I don't know what you mean."

"I believe you do, Miss Blake." Simon was in command now, crumpling her defenses with his hard, logical words. "You both have the same deep blue eyes, you know. And even before I met either of you was intrigued by the similarity between the names Blake and Blaze. The three strokes of the pen needed for a printed K could easily be shifted to a Z. *Blaze* is the sort of name someone named Blake might choose, especially if he imagined himself a prophet of heavenly fire. Of course he could have been an uncle, or some more distant relative—but then why wouldn't you mention the relationship? I took a chance on calling him your father, and your face tells me I was correct."

"Who are you—some sort of devil?"

"Hardly that," Simon replied. "Only a man who has lived long enough to have witnessed every form of deception. Tell me now, about your father."

"There's nothing to tell."

'The police might feel differently. They're holding him in a cell at this moment, on suspicion of killing Sky Hardy."

"My God!"

"You must tell me what you know about this business. Now!"

She glanced at me, as if seeking some sort of escape, but there was nothing I could offer her. "All right," she said at last. "Conrad Blaze is my father. My mother died in a plane crash and he was always a little crazy on the subject of flying. Living here in Houston, he gradually zeroed in on the space program. He built it into a mystical, religious sort of thing. In a way that was responsible for my meeting David Woodword."

'Tell me about it."

"David was in the papers because of the divorce. Milly was really a shrew and she made life hell for him with the press. My father tried to see David, to tell him the divorce was punishment for having ventured into forbidden space. He never reached David, but some reporters talked to him and splashed the story in the papers. I was so embarrassed by the incident I phoned David to apologize, and a few weeks later I sought him out at a party." She smiled bit at the memory. "He told me I wasn't responsible for the sins of my father and of course he was right. After that I started dating him, and I ignored my father's eccentricities."

"What about last Sunday on the boat? Could your father have been hiding on shore watching you? Could he have charged the wire as David reached out to pluck it from the water?"

"I–I don't know." But something seemed to return to her memory. "Now that I think of it, someone could have been watching us from the shore. David started to reach both hands into the water and then he hesitated, as if seeing something among the trees. Then he reached in with just his right hand–" Her voice broke a bit. "And then I saw the flash. I hadn't remembered that till this minute."

Simon nodded. "A bare electric wire, strung across the entrance to the cove, with the current controlled by someone on shore–someone who knew you'd be coming there. Did your father know?"

"Certainly not! I hadn't even seen him in months."

"But he might have followed you there on an earlier occasion."

"So might anyone else. There were always other boats on the bay. We'd frequently see other NASA people there." She was growing impatient. "Are you going to keep up this questioning all day?"

"No. No, those are all the questions."

When we were outside once more I asked Simon, "Do you think she's telling the truth?"

"Mainly the truth, my friend. The truth as she knows it. Let us return to our hotel."

After the events of the day I expected a quiet evening before our investigation resumed. But the fates conspired against us. We returned from dinner to find a message to phone my brother-in-law.

When I reached him, Ray said, "The police have just released Conrad Blaze."

"So soon? I thought they'd hold him overnight."

"They planned to, but a lawyer showed up and got him out. Said he'd been hired by Blaze's daughter. I didn't know he had a daughter."

"Yes. Well, we just discovered it ourselves." I could imagine Lisa Blake, overcome with guilt, phoning a lawyer as soon as we left her apartment.

Simon, who'd caught the drift of the conversation, reached over to take the phone. "Ray, this is Simon Ark. Where is Conrad Blaze now?"

"We have no idea, Simon," I heard Ray answer.

"Very well. Stay close to the telephone. There may be a break in the case tonight."

Ray started to ask something else, but Simon hung up. "A break?" I asked. "What do you mean by that?"

"I mean that with Blaze out of jail the killer might strike again very quickly."

"You think Blaze did it? But—"

"There's no time for questions now. We must hurry."

I went along with him, as I had so many times in the past, and followed his direction to one of the suburban homes in the tract where many of the astronauts lived. "Whose place is this, Simon?" I asked as we drew up before the house. "We're about a block from Hardy's home."

"If the Houston telephone directory can be relied upon this is the residence of Pete Saunders, the third man on that moon flight."

Saunders himself answered the door and seemed surprised to see us. He was alone in the house and mumbled something about his family being away. "It's you we want to see," Simon told him.

He led us into a large living room with a fireplace that was ablaze despite the moderate temperature. "Ever since Sky was killed this afternoon I've had a chill," he explained. "My God, both of them gone within a few days! Maybe there is something to this idea of a vengeance from outer space."

"Do you believe that Thor cuts power lines?"

"Something sure happened to them."

"I am seeking a more human motive," Simon told him. "Greed. Financial gain."

"What do you mean?" Saunders asked nervously, brushing a hand through his hair. It had grown dark outside, but only the firelight illuminated the room.

"I think you know." Simon seemed to tower above him at that moment, like some Old Testament prophet. "Woodword's ex-wife Milly mentioned something about it earlier today. You carried some coins or stamps to the moon, didn't you? Contrary to regulations."

"I know nothing about it."

"I think you do. You three were in it together and not even your families knew about it—except that Woodword let something slip to Milly before their divorce. Whatever it is you took, it has great value today. That was proved by the stamps brought back by previous astronauts. In your case, as the last moon flight for some decades, the value might be even greater. I believe it was great enough to turn one person to murder."

"But the Russian, Feokarov!" Saunders protested.

"The Russian was killed by lightning. A true accident, but it planted the idea in the killer's head. Astronauts could die too, and even if their deaths didn't pass as accidents, they'd be connected with the Russian somehow. The police would suspect an international conspiracy rather than personal gain. You see, with Woodword dead these valuable objects became yours and Hardy's. With Hardy dead, they're all yours."

"I didn't kill them!" he shouted. "You have no right to accuse me!"

"But you brought back—what?"

He slumped down before the fire, his head bowed. "Coins. One hundred Eisenhower silver dollars with the reverse showing an American eagle landing on the moon. Each was in a sealed packet stating it had been to the moon, and signed by the three of us."

"Where—" Simon began, but he was cut short by the ringing o the doorbell.

"I'll get that," Pete Saunders said, and was on his feet before we realized it.

"No!" Simon shouted. "Don't open that door!"

Saunders hesitated, his hand on the knob, as Simon hurried forward. The flickering firelight made our shadows dance across the opposite wall, and in that moment I might have believed in a demon or a god waiting outside.

"I'm not afraid," Saunders said, and opened it.

Conrad Blaze stood there, pointing his arm at them. "Thor will destroy all who trespass in space! A thunderbolt will claim you as it has the others!"

And then Simon Ark was out there, facing Blaze, as a magician of old might have confronted another. "Get back!" he warned Saunders and me. "Get back if you value your lives!"

"You can't stop me!" Blaze said.

"Yes, I can." Simon shoved him aside with a push of his hand, then walked out beyond him. "Now we meet," he said, speaking into the darkness. "Now, Thor, where are your thunderbolts?"

Saunders found the switch for the outdoor spotlights and turned them on. A man dressed in black stood among the bushes, holding this time not a wire but only a prosaic black pistol which Simon plucked from his hand while the spotlight blinded him. I recognized the man even without his uniform.

It was Colonel Byers.

Though it was nearly midnight by the time we assembled back at Ray's NASA office, I knew we'd be getting no sleep till we heard the story from Simon Ark.

"There's very little to tell," he said, pacing the floor in his best scholarly manner. "One hundred silver dollars were heavy—about five pounds—and they couldn't be easily hidden as those stamps had been on the earlier moon flights. So to avoid detection the three astronauts arranged to pass them to the first person they'd be alone with after splashdown—the doctor who did the preliminary examination on them. Colonel Byers easily carried the coins away in his bag, before they opened their personal kits for you, Ray. The hundred silver dollars—worth thousands of dollars each to collectors—remained in Byers's possession for safekeeping until the astronauts felt the time was right to begin selling them on the world coin markets."

Ray cursed softly. "How could Byers do a thing like that?"

"Better men have done shadier things for money. Perhaps he felt there was nowhere else to go in the military. Perhaps he saw private contractors growing rich and wanted some money for himself. In any event, after Conrad Blaze issued his crazy warning and the Russian cosmonaut was coincidentally killed by lightning, he decided the coins could all be his. With the three astronauts all mysteriously killed, they'd be worth more than ever.

"He'd seen Woodword and his girl in the cove on Galveston Bay, and he must have figured they'd go there sometime ever Labor Day weekend. He rigged a bare electric wire just on the surface of the water and waited to throw the switch. Killing Sky Hardy in his pool couldn't have been planned far in advance. He simply saw his opportunity and took it. With Blaze released from jail I feared he'd try to finish the job tonight by killing Saunders in such a way that Blaze would be accused. He got Blaze out there somehow, but this time he had to settle for a gun as the weapon."

"You didn't seem surprised that it was Byers," I commented.

"Very little surprises me at my age," Simon replied. "There were three things pointing toward Byers. First, if the astronauts brought back something from space and passed it to another person, he was the logical one since he was the first doctor to examine them. Second, the killer had to know Woodword went to that cove. Lisa told us they saw other NASA people out sailing. She didn't say other astronauts but other NASA people. And Byers kept a color photo of a yacht on his desk, leading me to correctly assume he was a yachtsman. Third, and perhaps most important, Byers told us Woodword *started* to reach into the water with both hands. Lisa didn't remember that detail until today. The only way Byers could have known it was if he'd been watching the whole thing. He was watching, and he killed Woodword."

Ray nodded. "I'll get word to the Russians that we've cleared this up. I can't thank you enough for your help, Simon."

There was a full moon out as we drove back to our hotel, and I said to Simon, "It's still up in the sky. There was no avenger out of space after all."

"Not yet, my friend," he agreed, "but some day—who knows?"

THE WEAPON OUT OF THE PAST

"As a student of American history," Simon Ark was saying to me, "you are surely aware of the Battle of Lonely Tree, fought two hundred and twenty-five years ago this week during the first year of the French and Indian War."

"I never pretended to be a student of American history," I protested. "I'm a book editor. If I'm doing a book on history I'm a history expert. Next week it might be gardening or comic strips."

"Nevertheless, I think you should journey with me to southern Pennsylvania, where some local residents plan to reenact the Battle of Lonely Tree at a pageant this week."

I'd known Simon Ark long enough to realize there was something afoot. "What are you investigating this time? Certainly not the French and Indian War?"

"There's an old stone farmhouse which figured in the battle in a most unusual manner. The owners have written me about it and invited me to come out this week during the pageant."

"A mystery," I surmised.

"But one that's two hundred and twenty-five years old."

"A murder?"

"No, my friend. That's the surprising part. The mystery is why the original owner of the house was not killed!"

I knew I was hooked again, and there was no point in fighting it. I phoned my wife Shelly and told her Simon and I would be driving down to Pennsylvania the following morning.

There are times when Simon Ark has claimed to be nearly 2000 years old, but driving with me through New Jersey the following morning he seemed like any vigorous white-haired man in his seventies. I'd known him for 25 years and he hadn't changed in all that time, so I'd stopped trying to guess his real age. All I knew was that I'd probably catch up to him in another quarter-century.

I followed his directions into southern Pennsylvania, through an area of farms and rolling hills, across the Appalachians to our destination.

It was late afternoon by the time we reached the village of Lonely Tree. "This is where the battle was fought?" I asked as we passed the crossroads that seemed the center of activity.

"Near here. It happened shortly before the French and Indian forces from Fort Duquesne defeated Braddock in July of 1755. But the battle itself was preceded by the event at the farmhouse. And an odd sort of event it was!"

"I expect it was odd if it attracted you, Simon."

"I believe this is the road we want," he said suddenly, pointing out a turn to the left that was named Lonely Tree Lane.

The scattering of houses thinned out even more here, and we came at last to a sturdy stone structure that looked more like a country gentleman's residence than my idea of an old farmhouse. We parked in the driveway and Simon led the way up the front walk.

The door was opened by a slim well-dressed man with gray hair who went well with the house. "You must be Simon Ark," he said, extending his hand. "I've enjoyed our correspondence."

Simon introduced him to me as Gregory Cliff, the present owner of the house, and we went inside. Though the place had obviously been remodeled since Colonial days, there was still an aura of early American charm about it. "We've tried to keep the exterior pretty much as it was in the Eighteenth Century," Cliff explained, leading us on a tour of the downstairs rooms. "Though of course it's a private home and we've felt free to modernize the interior. Here's the room you'll be most interested in seeing—the former dining room where the fight took place."

We'd entered a cheery family room with a fireplace at one end and a television set at the other. A handsome middle-aged woman rose to greet us. "Hello, I'm Ada Cliff. So glad to have you in our home."

"I trust it's not an inconvenience," Simon murmured.

"We wouldn't have invited you if it were inconvenient."

"Ada and I are preparing for tomorrow's visitors," Gregory Cliff explained. "The house will be open as part of the pageant."

"It's very kind of you to let us see it a day early," Simon said. "And to invite us to spend the night." He was walking about the room as he spoke, examining the wood-paneled walls and the windows, though I couldn't imagine what he was looking for.

"I'm no historian," I admitted finally. "I guess you'll have to fill me in on what happened here."

Gregory Cliff smiled. "I'm an attorney myself. History is the domain of men like Mr. Ark. But the facts are simply enough stated. A few weeks prior to Braddock's defeat by the French and Indians, a scouting party from Fort Duquesne attempted to take this farmhouse and use it as a forward observation post. I imagine there was a special regard for these thick stone walls, able to withstand musket fire and arrows with ease. Anyway, a French officer named Colonel Muser, who worked closely with the Indian scouts, led a party of them here on that night in June 1755. Today such an operation would be called a commando raid, I suppose, though this was not technically British territory at the time. The raiding party reached this farmhouse shortly before midnight, and—"

Ada Cliff interrupted. "Tell him about the people who lived here at that time."

"The house was owned by a thirty-one-year-old farmer named Ned Feebish who lived here with his widowed mother, Nora Feebish. The people in the area considered Nora Feebish to be a witch."

Suddenly Simon Ark's interest in all this became clear. It wasn't American history that had brought him to this Colonial farmhouse. It was the hint of witches and dark doings. "What did they base this on?" I asked.

"Nothing but local superstition. Enchantments and hex signs have a long history in this region. Old Nora Feebish was probably as harmless as you or I."

The lawyer paused to light his pipe, and Ada Cliff took up the story. "These facts have been known for years, Mr. Ark, as has the fact that Ned Feebish somehow overpowered the French officer in this very room and sounded the alarm. The townspeople, with the help of a British detachment, turned back the French and Indians the following day in a brief skirmish that became known hereabouts as the Battle of Lonely Tree. Of course the defeat of Braddock the following month rendered it all for naught, but at least this old farmhouse had its moment of glory."

Her husband continued the story. "That was all anyone knew until a few months ago, when Ada came upon a remarkable document while cleaning out the attic. It's the document about which I wrote you, Mr. Ark."

"I wiped the centuries of dust from it and couldn't believe what I had," Ada said. "It was a diary or journal for the years 1755 and 1756, containing the planting and financial records of the farm. But more than that, inside the back cover of the book was written an account of that fateful night—an account by the Frenchman, Colonel Muser, himself!"

"You sent me a Xerox copy of that," Simon Ark said. "But perhaps it should be read, for the benefit of my friend here."

Gregory Cliff walked to a desk drawer and removed an ancient ledger with a stained and torn binding. He opened it to the rear and read, "*I have been asked by the occupants of this house to write down my account of what transpired here in the hour before midnight last. Though English is not my native tongue I dictate this to a woman neighbor who takes it down exactly as I speak. When I reached this farmhouse some few minutes before the stroke of twelve, I found the doors and windows locked against the night's roaming savages.*

"*Leaving my band of scouts in the cornfield, I obtained entry by breaking a window in the dining room. I had only just entered when the man of the house, awakened by the breaking glass, confronted me and did battle. We fought in the darkness and he managed to seize my flintlock. My only other weapon was the Indian knife in my belt. My enemy fired once with the flintlock, missing me with the unfamiliar weapon. Before he could reload, I saw his head and shoulders silhouetted against the window and hurled the knife directly at his throat. In the same instant an old woman shouted something from the doorway.*

"*She called upon the Devil, in a tongue I barely understood. The blade of my knife never reached my adversary's throat. It seemed as if the weapon vanished in mid-flight as she shouted her curse. The young man jumped on me, striking me with my own pistol, and I fell to the floor. The alarm was raised and my followers fled by the way they had come. This morning, by daylight, I searched the room for the knife, but it was nowhere to be found. I do believe what they say is true. The old woman is a witch. Signed, Colonel Andre Muser.*"

"An interesting document," I admitted, studying the spidery writing in the book.

"A striking first-person document offering evidence of Colonial witch-craft," was Simon Ark's verdict. "Now you see why I came here, my friend."

Ada Cliff got to her feet. "Well, I think it's time we ate. We have the whole evening to discuss what happened here two hundred and twenty-five years ago."

They showed us to a large spare bedroom upstairs, where we'd be spending the night. As I washed up for dinner, Simon was peering out the window at the garden below. "The cornfield would have been there," he decided. "We're directly over the old dining room where it happened."

"Should we search for secret panels?" I asked.

"I already have," Simon answered quite seriously.

The meal, a pleasant blend of American and French dishes served with California white wine, had barely ended when the Cliffs had another visitor. His name was Milo Bates and he served as the village's part-time mayor. More important, he was the man in charge of the following day's pageant and mock battle.

"We're getting visitors from as far away as New York," he told the Cliffs proudly. "You better be ready for a flock of people goin' through your house."

"The New Yorkers have already arrived," I told the man. He couldn't have been much over thirty, and I wondered what he did when he wasn't being mayor. "We're them."

"Oh! Good to meet you!" He introduced himself all over again and this time answered my unspoken question by adding, "I run the farm-and-garden store down by the crossroads. There's really not much mayorin' to do in Lonely Tree."

"Join us for coffee and dessert," Ada Cliff suggested.

He glanced at her as she urged him into a vacant chair. "Thanks. I could use some coffee, but hold the dessert." He patted his stomach. "Mary says she'll divorce me if I gain another pound."

They ran over the logistics of the following day, with Milo Bates producing timetables and diagrams of the course the mock battle would follow. For the moment the two-hundred-and-twenty-five-year-old witch named Nora Feebish was forgotten.

"I hate having them so close to the house," Ada Cliff interjected. "I can just see my garden getting trampled."

Her husband considered that. "Maybe in the morning I should put up the snow fence along that side of the garden."

"Might be a good idea," Bates agreed. "I put that garden in for you. I wouldn't want to see it damaged."

After Bates had departed, the Cliffs showed us the rest of the house—including the dusty, low-ceilinged attic where Ada had made her discovery. "I notice you didn't mention the daybook in front of the mayor," Simon remarked. "Does he know about it?"

"Only in a vague way," Cliff replied. "Frankly, Mr. Ark, we wanted your opinion before we went public on all the details. I know your reputation for investigating the bizarre. We don't want to be laughed at, and we don't want to yell *witch* about someone who's been dead for more than two centuries."

"You can simply state the facts as you know them," Simon said. "You needn't draw any conclusions. Let the public read this document for what it is."

"Perhaps tomorrow would be a good time to announce the find," Cliff decided. "There'll be some reporters down from Pittsburgh to cover the pageant."

We talked a while longer before deciding to retire. It had been a long drive from New York, and I didn't fight the suggestion that we go to bed at eleven o'clock, even though I rarely turned in before midnight at home. The Cliffs kindly allowed me to phone Shelly back in New York. She was a bit cool at first, as she always was when I went traveling with Simon, but she warmed up quickly enough. After twenty-four years of marriage neither of us stayed angry very long. Even once when she'd nearly divorced me it hadn't lasted. "Is Simon onto one of his weird cases?" she asked.

"It's hard to say. This thing happened so long ago."

When I finished talking, Simon was already in bed. I took the other bed and turned out the light. "We should sleep well in this country air," I said.

He grunted. "It's like sleeping on the eve of battle."

"You mean tomorrow's pageant? I don't suppose that'll do much damage, not even to Ada Cliffs garden."

"I wouldn't be too sure. Bates was talking about devices to fire arrows into the air."

There was a sudden knock at our bedroom door and Ada Cliff came in. "Milo is back again, downstairs. I think he's been drinking and Greg is having some trouble with him. Could you come down?"

"Sure," I agreed, climbing reluctantly out of bed. I heard Simon following, though I doubted that either of us really wanted to get involved. I went quickly down the stairs and found our host with Milo Bates in the front hall. The time was a few minutes before midnight.

"I don't want to go home," Bates was saying, pushing Cliffs hand from his shoulder. "There's nothing for me at home."

Suddenly we heard the breaking of glass from behind the closed door of the family room. Gregory Cliff whirled around. "What's that?" he asked, and even as we were hurrying to the door we heard the scream, brief but chilling.

Cliff opened the door and snapped on the lights. Our eyes went to the broken window, and the figure of a man in Colonial costume slumped on the floor beneath it. His hands were clutched to the knife embedded in his throat. He tried to move, to reach out a hand toward us, but it was a futile gesture. Milo Bates, suddenly sobered by the shocking sight, rushed forward with Cliff. Simon and I followed, while Ada stayed back, hand to her mouth in horror.

"He's dead," Gregory Cliff said, kneeling by the body. "He's been murdered!"

Simon leaned over and pulled the Colonial cap from the head, releasing a mass of long blonde hair. "But it's not a he."

Milo uttered a strangled cry and turned away, sickened.

Cliff stared at the body as if he couldn't believe his eyes. "It's Mary Bates—Milo's wife!"

It was the knife that interested Simon Ark more than the body into which it had been plunged. We hadn't known Mary Bates in life, so her murder didn't affect us with the same shattering force that it struck her husband and the Cliffs. To Simon it was a problem to be solved, and as soon as the state police investigators allowed the knife to be removed from the body and placed in a plastic evidence bag he virtually pounced on it.

"Look at it, my friend. An Indian weapon, surely—and one that's very old. Perhaps it has come to us from the past."

"I'm more interested in where the killer got to in those few seconds it took us to reach the room. Could he have been outside?"

"Doubtful. I believe the knife was hurled from within the room, just as it had been on a previous occasion."

"You're telling me this is the *same knife* that French colonel hurled at Ned Feebish two and a quarter centuries ago? I don't believe it!"

"Believe what you will," Simon said. "It is an old Indian hunting knife—and you'll notice the letter M that has been carved on its hilt."

"M for Muser? No, Simon, I don't buy it. This whole thing is just too pat."

He peered at the knife more closely, and then turned to the state police lieutenant who was handling the investigation. The time was now after two o'clock, but no one had gone back to bed. "Were there any fingerprints on the knife, Lieutenant Falcone?"

"No prints. But if the knife was thrown as you say, I wouldn't expect to find any. It would have been gripped only at the tip of the blade, and that's the part went into her. However, I don't believe we have all the facts here." He was a broad-shouldered, handsome man dressed in civilian clothes, and if the killing had disturbed his night's sleep he showed no sign of it. He knew Gregory Cliff from legal work, and they had shaken hands when he arrived.

"I am certain we don't have all the facts," Simon agreed. "For example, what were we supposed to see, and what did we actually see? Why was Mary Bates dressed up like a man? These matters may be more important than the age of this knife."

The questions, and Simon's whole attitude since his arrival, seemed to intrigue the state police officer. "Are you some sort of investigator?" he asked.

Simon smiled. "I have been known to investigate evidence of the paranormal. Perhaps you would call me a seeker after evil. One day I will surely do battle with Satan himself."

This was a bit too much for Falcone. "Just tell me—are you a detective?"

"I may be of some help on this case."

"Good! I think I'm going to need all the help I can get."

Simon bent to examine the knife again. "In the morning you should get an expert on Indian artifacts to confirm it, but I do believe this is the authentic weapon. It is not a fake."

"How authentic?"

"It is the weapon hurled by a French colonel at the original owner of this farmhouse, in the year 1755."

"You've got to be kidding!"

"It vanished in thin air that night—we have a written account of it. An old witch put some sort of spell on it. The knife traveled two hundred and twenty-five years through time, and stabbed this unfortunate woman tonight."

"You got any proof of that?"

"I believe the knife will be our proof."

A uniformed trooper came to the door. "We've been talking to the dead woman's husband, Mayor Bates. You want to question him?"

Falcone nodded. He motioned to Simon and me. "Come along. You might be of some help."

Milo Bates was a battered hulk compared to the man we'd seen earlier in the evening. His eyes were red from sobbing, and his face was twisted into a mask of despair. "I did it," he told us at once. "I'm responsible for her death! This damned pageant was all my idea, and that's what killed her."

"You'd better explain yourself a bit more clearly," Falcone said. "Exactly how are you responsible?"

"The pageant! I suggested the whole thing—restaging the Battle of Lonely Tree and all! In our early plans there was talk of starting it off with the raid on the farmhouse, but then we decided to skip that part. Mary wanted to do it, and she obviously went ahead with her plan without my knowledge. Good lord, how could it have happened?"

"Weren't you at home tonight, Mr. Bates?"

He shook his head. "I was over on Creed's Hill, making sure everything was ready for morning. I'd had a few drinks," he admitted.

"Alone?"

"Some of the time, yes. I'm running this pageant. I wanted to check the arrangements for myself."

"Had your wife given any hint that she might come here dressed as a man tonight?"

"None whatsoever. But when we first planned the pageant she thought we should include the incident at the Cliffs' house. Ada Cliff had found some sort of handwritten account of Colonel Muser's raid, and Mary thought we should act it out."

Simon Ark interrupted with a question. "Were you aware that the original resident of this house was thought to be a witch?"

"I guess I'd heard talk. But after two centuries what difference did that make?"

"Mr. Bates"—Simon looked at him levelly—"your wife may have been killed by an Indian hunting knife thrown in 1755 and somehow propelled through time to the present day."

"What?" He stared at Simon as if at a madman. "You can't believe that!"

"I don't say I believe it. I only say it is one possibility. If Colonel Muser's account is reliable, his knife somehow vanished that night. Where did it go, and where has it been all these years?"

"Ask Gregory Cliff," Bates lost his control. "It's his house!"

"What were the relations between your wife and the Cliffs?" Lieutenant Falcone asked.

"We were friendly, all four of us. Cliff is my attorney, and I did some landscape work here at the house. We see each other socially."

"No animosity?"

"Why would you think that?"

"Your outburst of a moment ago implied that Gregory Cliff might be a sore point."

"I—you'll have to excuse me. I can't think straight with what happened to Mary."

"Of course," Falcone replied. "I think that'll be all for the present, Mr. Bates. We'll be in touch."

But as the youthful mayor was leaving the room, Simon asked, "Will the pageant go on as scheduled?"

Milo Bates nodded. "But without me, I'm afraid. My heart's gone out of it."

When he had left, the state police investigator settled back in his chair. "Now suppose we go over the whole thing one more time."

I finally got to bed and drifted into a fitful sleep shortly before six o'clock, only to be awakened a few hours later by the sound of a booming cannon. It took me a moment to remember where I was, and another moment to remember the pageant. Obviously the mock battle between the British and the French had begun.

I slid out of bed and discovered that Simon was already at the window watching them. "Ah, my friend, you're awake."

"How could I sleep through cannons? What time is it, anyway?"

"Just nine o'clock. They seem to be right on schedule."

We dressed and went downstairs where Ada was preparing a quick breakfast. "Nothing fancy, I'm afraid," she apologized. "After last night it's a wonder I can make a cup of coffee. Greg and I were awake all night."

And her husband, when he appeared, was red-eyed and irritable. "They're behaving like a bunch of overgrown boys, running around out there with their muskets and arrows! Most of them aren't even from town—they've come here from all over the state! And even from Maryland and West Virginia."

"Sit down and eat your breakfast, Greg."

He stared at his plate, blinking his eyes as if it was difficult to focus them. "You seem to forget there was a killing in this house last night, Ada. I can't just carry on as if nothing happened! Mary Bates was a friend of ours."

"Greg, we have guests."

The reminder seemed to surprise him. He turned to Simon and me with a half-hearted smile. "Sorry. Did you sleep well?"

"The cannon woke us," I admitted.

"Well, after breakfast I'll show you around the battle scene. We have a couple of clever special effects, like a machine for firing rubber-tipped arrows, that add to the authenticity."

A machine for firing arrows didn't sound very authentic to me, but I let it pass. "The newspapers may be more interested in the real killing here than in the mock battle out there," I pointed out.

"We're closing the house," Cliff decided. "We can't have it open to the public after what's happened."

"Of course not," Ada quickly agreed.

When we went out after breakfast a few people had already gathered on the road, looking and pointing toward the house. Gregory Cliff explained that the police had requested the public not be admitted. It was a lie, but an acceptable one under the circumstances. We followed the attorney around the side of the garden, where I noticed that no snow fence had been erected after all. Ahead, at the edge of a small woods, a handful of men dressed as Indians were loading arrows into some sort of device. Three or four others could be seen nearby.

"Look here," Cliff said. "It's my own invention. The French and Indians might have won the war if they'd had it. Basically it's a modification of the traps used to launch clay targets in skeet shooting. The arrow is placed in this groove, the arm pulled back against the spring until it locks, and when the cord is pulled—"

He demonstrated as he spoke, and the spring-propelled arm swung instantly in a half circle, propelling the arrow upward at an angle. We watched it travel about 250 feet before it curved back to earth. "Just rubber tips, of course," Cliff said, showing off one of the arrows. "We don't want anyone injured."

"Why not use bows?" I asked. "Seems it would be just as fast."

"Even with rubber-tipped arrows we felt there'd be a danger in having inexperienced people running around using bows. You can see the spectators wander quite close. The muskets are using powder only—no balls—and by firing the arrows with these modified traps we can exactly control their flight path and landing area. It gives the effect of arrows flying through the air without any danger at all to spectators or participants."

While we spoke I noticed that Simon seemed unusually interested in the device.

"Can the elevation be regulated?" he asked.

"Certainly." Cliff demonstrated it for us. "It's really just like a skeet trap. All I had to do was make certain it would hold the arrow. We're using a dozen of them here today."

Someone came running up with a problem, pointing out that spectators were edging near the garden area. Cliff sighed. "Guess I'll have to put up that snow fence after all."

A group in British Colonial uniforms ran by us, chasing Indians. "That one looks like he's supposed to be George Washington," I remarked.

Cliff nodded. "Washington took part in the battle, but he was a bit younger-looking than that. Excuse me, will you? I have to see about the snow fence."

Simon waited till the arrows had been fired and then picked up one of the traps, moving it on its heavy metal base until it was pointed at a nearby tree. He caught one of the Indians running by. "Here, let me borrow that knife for a minute," he asked.

"Be careful of it. I borrowed it from my son." The man smiled behind his Indian warpaint.

Simon knelt to place the knife on the arm of the trap, then pulled back against the spring to cock it. When he released the cord the knife was propelled at a slight upward angle, striking the tree about four feet off the ground. The impact at this close range was enough to drive the blade into the trunk.

"Good, good!" Simon was pleased with himself.

"You think that's how she was killed?"

"Let us return to the house and see, my friend."

"Do you think Cliff—"

"Do not jump to conclusions," he cautioned.

We went at once to the family room, where Simon stood in the approximate position occupied by Mary Bates when the knife hit her. We both said it at the same instant. "The fireplace!"

It was a large gaping hole, lower than the level of a person's neck, but we'd seen the trap adjusted to fire upward at any angle. "The screen is closed," I pointed out.

"But it could have been open last night." He bent to open it now and looked inside. The random pattern of ashes had been disturbed, and there were unmistakable traces of something having rested in the dust. "I think so," Simon said softly. "I really think so."

That was when Ada came into the room with Lieutenant Falcone. "I thought I heard you. The lieutenant's been looking for you."

Falcone was obviously excited. "You were right, damn it! I had somebody from the University check out this knife. It's Eighteenth Century, without a doubt. That's enough to start me believing in the supernatural!"

"Too bad," I said. "Simon was about to demonstrate how the killing could have been worked by quite natural means."

"What?"

"With one of the modified skeet traps being used to hurl arrows," Simon explained. "It could have been hidden here in the fireplace, and aimed at a proper elevation to hit the throat of anyone who tripped the cord."

Lieutenant Falcone smiled. "This is the first time I've met one of you hot-shot investigators. I'll admit we don't get many supernatural killings out this way, but I'd believe in the supernatural as quickly as I'd believe in a mechanical device for hurling a knife at someone's throat. How would the machine know the height of the victim?"

"The machine wouldn't, but the person who set it would."

"And what happened to the cord and trap after the killing? None of you mentioned noticing them."

"We didn't look for anything like that," Simon said. "We especially didn't look in the fireplace."

"The fireplace?"

"Let us bring one of the traps down from the hill and I'll demonstrate."

A skeptical Falcone helped me carry one into the house and set it deep inside the large fieldstone fireplace. Simon cocked the arm and placed a small steak knife in position. We placed a board on a chair to represent the target. Then Simon ran a cord from the triggering mechanism. "Ready?" he asked.

"Ready," I responded, moving well out of the way.

He tugged the cord and the arm shot forward, propelling the knife up from the fireplace toward the board. It hit, clung momentarily, and then fell to the floor. "Satisfied it could be done?" Simon asked Falcone.

"Maybe," he admitted. "But that cord would have been seen."

"A thin wire would do the job and remain virtually invisible."

"What about that?"

He pointed to the released throwing arm of the skeet trap, now in its forward position, clearly visible in the fireplace opening. "He's right, Simon," I agreed. "Why didn't we notice it?"

But Simon Ark was not to be sidetracked by our objections. "I agree that it's visible, but you'll note that the arm does not extend beyond the fireplace opening. If I close the screen—like this—the incriminating device all but disappears from view."

"The screen must have been closed in those first few minutes," I agreed, "while our attention was diverted by the body."

"There were five of you who entered the room together," Falcone observed. "You two, Mr. and Mrs. Cliff, and Milo Bates."

Simon nodded. "And I am prepared to name the murderer, and to tell you what happened on the night two and a quarter centuries ago when Colonel Muser hurled his knife."

It took us a while to gather them together, and when we did the mock battle was still raging on the distant hill. We could see the smoke from the cannons drifting slowly over the landscape as Simon Ark stood before the windows and began his explanation.

"Our problem, if we accept the murder weapon as a genuine Eighteenth Century Indian knife, is its location during the intervening two hundred and twenty-five years. I have studied the handwritten account left by Colonel Muser, describing the events in this room on that fateful night— the eve of the Battle of Lonely Tree. You're all familiar with it. You know that, by Colonel Muser's account, the knife he hurled at Ned Feebish seemed to vanish into thin air when the man's mother shouted a curse of some sort from the doorway. What happened to that knife? Did it really travel through time to kill Mary Bates in this room last night?"

Gregory Cliff and his wife exchanged glances, while Milo Bates shifted uneasily in his chair. No one spoke.

"I have already demonstrated to Lieutenant Falcone here," Simon continued, "how the knife could have been fired in this room last night—fired from a skeet trap like those that were modified for the mock battle today. But the real mystery remained. What fate befell the knife all those years ago? If it did not vanish as a result of a witch's curse, what happened to it? Well, Colonel Muser hurled it, in a darkened room. The knife disappeared and though he searched the room in the morning he could not find it. In the dark it's reasonable to assume he might have missed his target, but where did the knife go? Remember now two things about his account: he'd broken a window to gain entrance to the house, and Ned Feebish was silhouetted against the window when the French officer hurled the knife."

"The window!" Ada gasped. "Of course!"

"Of course," Simon agreed. "It's the only possibility. The colonel, perhaps unnerved by the unexpected shout of the old woman, missed the young man's head and the knife went through the broken window. In the dark he never would have noticed it. It landed out there on the ground, and was probably trampled and buried during the following day's battle activities."

"Then how did it reappear?" Falcone wanted to know.

"It was found, of course. Dug up when the present garden was put in. And who was it who put in that garden for the Cliffs?"

Gregory's mouth had dropped open. "It was—"

Simon nodded. "Milo Bates."

Milo was out of his chair. "No! I didn't kill her? You can't say I did it! I loved her!"

But Lieutenant Falcone already had his handcuffs out.

Later, as they were leaving for town with Milo Bates in the state police car, Simon found time to speak with Falcone. "I think we've got a case," the detective said. "It would have been easy enough for him to talk his wife into the stunt, and he could have rigged the trap for her to spring. He hasn't broken yet, but a few hours of questioning should do it. And we have you to thank."

"Yes," Simon agreed with a sigh. "You have me to thank."

We watched the state police car pull away and I asked, "What is it, Simon? What's wrong?" I'd known him long enough to catch the nuances of his mood.

"My friend, I've just sent an innocent man to prison. It's not something I do lightly."

"Innocent! But I thought—"

"Let us go back inside. The battle, I see, is almost over."

The smoke from the cannons had cleared on the hill, and the men in their British and French and Indian costumes were coming back from their games. Someone had started singing an old English carol and others along the line of march took up the tune. Ada Cliff came out on the porch to watch them as we mounted the steps.

"A colorful sight, isn't it?" I said.

"It certainly is! To think that Milo Bates planned it all and then didn't get to see it. I still can't bring myself to believe that he killed poor Mary."

"The ways of the human heart are strange indeed," Simon remarked.

He was staring at her and I could see it made her uneasy. "Is that remark meant for me?" she asked.

"It is," Simon replied. "You see, I expected you to confess when I accused your lover of murdering his wife."

"Lover! What are you talking about? Are you insane?"

"You set the death trap for Mary Bates, Ada. There was never any weapon out of time because that entire account by Colonel Muser was a crude hoax."

"That's not true!"

"Yes, it is. First, there was no old-fashioned spelling in the journal entry, and if it had really been written in 1755, there would have been Eighteenth Century usage and flavor. Second, there was one glaring error. A Frenchman like Muser might well have used the French word silhouette, but he couldn't have used it in 1755. The word came from the surname of Etienne de Silhouette, the French finance minister for a brief eight months in 1757. His taxation program proved so unpopular that the public attached his name to the little shadow portraits of the time, indicating the shadowy and unsubstantial nature of his financial policies. So you see the word itself simply didn't exist prior to 1757."

She closed her eyes and steadied herself. "Why would I make it up?"

"Why! I believe you found that journal while cleaning the attic. That much was true. I believe you found the old knife at the same time. The idea came to you to use it to kill Mary Bates, your rival for Milo's affections. You invented Muser's account and wrote it in the old journal yourself, using what was known of actual history. It wasn't difficult to persuade Mary to don a Colonial costume and break the window to gain entry to the house. She'd wanted to be part of her husband's pageant and was looking for a way. You set a thin wire where she'd be sure to hit it coming through the window. By chance Milo had arrived at the same time and roused us all. That must have given you a fright. Of course the knife might have missed her or only wounded her, but that was a gamble you were willing to take."

"Why me?" she asked. "Why not Greg or Milo?"

"The killer had to be able to yank in the wire and close the fireplace screen in those first moments after we entered the room. Both men ran to the body but you held back, afraid to look. That's when you closed the screen behind our backs."

"But...you knew about Milo and me?"

"That you were lovers? It was only a guess, based on a glance exchanged when you urged him into a chair last night. But I have come to notice such things, and to weigh their import. Tell me something—would you have killed your husband too, in order to be with Milo?"

"Greg would have divorced me. He wasn't the problem."

"Then I repeat my first statement. I expected you to confess when I accused Milo Bates of the killing. You must have known when you lured me here with that fake journal entry that I would investigate the killing, that I would try to fix the blame."

"I expected you to bolster the supernatural angle," she admitted. "If Milo hadn't arrived when he did last night, I would have gone downstairs first when the window was broken. I'd have made sure she was dead, and hidden the trap before I raised the alarm. I wanted a house full of witnesses."

"And Milo?" Simon asked quietly.

She was silent for a moment, staring off at the hill where the battle was ended and the warriors gone. "No," she said at last. "Milo won't have to take the blame. I'll tell them everything."

Later, as Simon and I drove back across the hills toward home, I said, "There was nothing for you in this case, Simon. No witches or magic. If old Nora Feebish really was a witch we found no evidence of it."

"But perhaps we did, my friend. Perhaps the strongest evidence of all was the fate that befell those who lived in her house. Perhaps her real curse was the love she brought to Ada Cliff and Milo Bates."

I had no answer for that.

THE SORCERESS OF THE SEA

"The sea is a woman," Simon Ark said, gazing out at the gently rolling waves as they drifted in to shore along the west coast of Florida "At least that is what the poets tell us. A sorceress who lures the hapless mariner with waving locks of green."

"I know—like mermaids." I settled back in the car seat and watched a two-masted fishing schooner sailing far out on the Gulf. Do you think it was a mermaid that killed Hans Belkor, Simon?"

"Stranger things have happened, my friend. I once knew a man who lived his entire life by the sea and then died by stepping on a fish. It was a stonefish, one of the deadliest of God's little creatures."

"But a mermaid—"

"I believe the term used in Belkor's log was *sorceress*."

"All right then sorceress. Do you honestly believe a sorceress or siren or mermaid strangled Hans Belkor with her own hair?"

"That is what we're here to determine."   .

I'd been vacationing at Palm Beach with my wife Shelly when I received the urgent summons from Simon Ark. He was in Sarasota, not much more than one hundred fifty miles away, and he needed my help. Shelly grumbled about it, as she so often did when I went off somewhere with Simon but in the end she agreed that I could make the side trip to meet Simon while she went off on a two-day visit to an aging aunt in Key West.

I arrived in Sarasota on a Monday morning in early September, having promised Shelly that I'd be back in Palm Beach by Wednesday evening. I picked up Simon in my rented car and we drove north along the Florida coast, past the beaches and marinas that were so much a part of the region's economy. Presently we came to a high-rise condominium fronting on the water, and we sat in the parking lot while Simon finished filling me in on the details.

He'd been summoned to Florida by Regina Belkor, wife of the dead man—a woman Simon had encountered at various Manhattan meetings of assorted psychic research societies. "Her husband was strangled to death while alone on his ketch. He left a sort of log mentioning a sorceress who came from the sea to tempt him. And he was strangled with a twist of long blonde hair."

That was what he told me as we sat staring out at the sea—or at the Gulf of Mexico, to be more exact. Even without my flip comment about mermaids, it was obvious this was the sort of case that Simon Ark thrived on. He claimed to have traveled the earth for close to 2000 years in search of Satan, and some nights when the moon was full and the drinks were strong I almost believed him.

We took the elevator to the eleventh floor of the condominium and were admitted to a spacious apartment with a wide picture window over-looking the Gulf. Mrs. Belkor was the first surprise. I'd heard Simon mention her on occasion and had an image of a fat middle-aged woman whose whims ran to the otherworldly fascination of psychic research. The reality was quite different. She was no more than thirty five with a trim figure and deep blue eyes that went well with her short blonde hair and deep suntan. She greeted Simon with a handshake and then turned to me.

"You're Simon's publisher friend. I've heard him mention you."

"Actually I'm an editor at Neptune Books," I said, correcting her. "I'm sorry to meet you under such tragic circumstances."

"Hans always did everything with style. His death was no exception." She suddenly remembered the fourth person in the room, which was the next surprise. "Gentlemen, this is Ronald Hanagan, an old family friend. He also happens to be investigating my husband's murder—for the local police."

Hanagan, a tall gray-haired man who'd stood in the background till now, stepped forward to shake hands. "I'm here mainly as a family friend," he insisted. "I'm an investigator for the District Attorney's office, but we're not usually called in until the police make an arrest."

"Is an arrest imminent in this case?" Simon asked.

"Not that I know of."

"Has the funeral been held yet?" Simon asked Mrs. Belkor.

"Hans desired to be cremated. We're holding a memorial service on Friday."

"Suppose you tell me just what happened."

She started to speak, but her voice broke almost at once. Hanagan rested a gentle hand on her arm and took over. "We know very little, Mr Ark, which is why Regina asked your help in the first place. Hans went out alone in his ketch late Saturday afternoon."

"Was that unusual?"

"No, sometimes he liked sailing alone after a day at the office. The ketch has an auxiliary engine and he didn't bother putting up the sails when he took it out alone. He was due back for a late dinner but he never returned. The Coast Guard spotted his running lights and just before midnight they found the ketch drifting three miles off shore. Hans was dead. He'd been strangled with a long tress of blonde hair that had been twisted into a garrote."

"Human hair?" Simon murmured. "An extraordinary murder weapon."

"Then he hadn't gone sailing alone after all," I said.

"The marina owner swears no one else was on the boat. He filled the gas tank and helped cast off the mooring lines, and Hans was alone. The killer must have intercepted him in another boat."

"Or come out of the sea," Regina Belkor said.

Simon Ark turned to her. "You used the word *sorceress* to me on the telephone, Mrs. Belkor. Just what did you mean?"

She reached over to pick up a large slim book from the end table. It appeared to be bound in sailcloth and had the single word *Log* printed on its cover. "I gave Hans this ship's log for Christmas last year and he kept it on board the *Miranda*. I never had occasion to read it till after his death. This was the entry for last Wednesday—three days before he was killed: *Sighted strange glow in the sea just after sunset. As I approached I saw the water bubbling and steaming. From the very center of the glowing water a beautiful woman with long blonde hair came to the surface. I brought her aboard. Her name is Doris, and I believe she is some kind of sorceress.*

"Interesting," Simon admitted. "Is that all of it?"

"That's all for Wednesday. But he went out on Thursday and Friday too. I thought it was odd, because he didn't usually go sailing alone every night. On Thursday he wrote: *Doris again, rising from the glowing bubbles at sunset. I feel I am enchanted.*"

"Why was he alone on these nights? Why didn't you go with him?"

"He had a brokerage business. He usually drove to the marina directly from the office. I often went sailing on weekends, though on Saturday he said he wanted to go alone."

"I see. What else does the logbook say?"

"On Friday: *Doris visited me again. Where does she come from? Where does she go? Is this sorceress of the sea to be my damnation?*"

Simon took the logbook and glanced at the neat, precise handwriting while I looked over his shoulder. He turned back a few pages. The writing was exactly the same, but the comments were far less interesting: *Heavy seas*, or *Clear sailing, many gulls.*

"He must have expected you to see this log sooner or later," Simon commented. "Didn't he tell you anything about this woman from the sea?"

"He never mentioned a word about her. He came in late each night after eleven, but when I asked him where he'd been he only said 'Out on the boat.' From about six till nearly eleven each night."

"There's no entry for Saturday, the day he was killed."

"No," Hanagan said. "Obviously she killed him before he could write it."

"What do the police think about all this?"

"Not much," he admitted. "They don't like the idea of people rising from the glowing water of the Gulf of Mexico."

"We have only his word for it, of course," Regina said. "But his death—and the manner of his death—seems to give some weight to what he wrote."

"Where was the logbook found?"

"He kept it in a locked drawer on board the *Miranda*. I'd seen it only once or twice since I gave it to him, and I might never have seen it again if he hadn't died."

"Did he seem different in any way last week?"

"A bit edgy, perhaps. More excited than usual. But he said nothing." She poured herself a glass of wine without offering us any. "I assumed he was under some sort of pressure at work, and we never discussed that."

It didn't sound to me as if they discussed much of anything, but I didn't put my thoughts into words. Simon turned to me at that moment and asked, "Do you have any ideas about all this?"

"Only that Doris is a fairly prosaic name for a sorceress."

"On the contrary, my friend, it is a perfect name. Doris was the mother of Amphitrite, who was the wife of Neptune. Doris was King Neptune's mother-in-law. What better name for a sorceress of the sea?"

Ronald Hanagan cleared his throat. "You can see why Regina was anxious to get your opinion, Mr. Ark. She tells me you're an expert on this sort of parapsychological happening. It's certainly more in your field than in mine."

Simon was running his fingers over the cover of the logbook. "Perhaps. In any event I will want to see the boat. And also the murder weapon. Today, if possible."

"That can be arranged," Hanagan said. "We'll stop by police headquarters and then I'll take you down to the marina."

"Fine."

Hanagan turned to the woman. "Want to come along, Regina?"

"No, I've seen enough of that ketch to last me a lifetime."

"Will you be all right alone?"

"Of course. I'm getting used to it now."

We left my rented car in the parking lot and drove to the police station in Hanagan's black sports car. It was an effort for Simon to bend his old bones into the small vehicle, but once we were on our way he seemed comfortable enough. "How well did you know Hans Belkor?" he asked Hanagan.

"Socially. Dinner parties and such. This is the sort of community where lawyers and brokers just naturally travel in the same circles."

"Did you know them in New York?"

"No, just since they moved to Florida last year."

Hanagan seemed to know everyone at police headquarters. A detective in charge of the case unlocked a filing cabinet and showed us a plastic bag containing a two-foot length of blonde hair, nearly an inch thick even though it had been twisted and tightened with use.

"It would take someone strong to strangle a man with that," Simon observed.

"Belkor had a little bump on his head," Hanagan told us. "If he'd been knocked out first it would have been easier. Our lab boys will check it today to see if the hair was freshly cut or not."

The idea appalled me. "Do you actually think this so-called sorceress strangled Belkor with her own hair and then cut it off and left it knotted around his throat?"

"Stranger things have happened," Hanagan said. "Where do you think the hair came from?"

"Human hair can be purchased," I said. "Especially blonde hair, which is finer than black. It's sometimes used in delicate scientific instruments."

Simon held the hair close to his eyes, studying it as he might read the fine print in the newspaper. "Your lab should have checked this immediately," he told Hanagan.

The lawyer was obviously embarrassed. "We only have a small department here. No real lab," he admitted. "The Sarasota police are sending someone up to look at it this afternoon."

"While we're on the subject, will you be running lab tests of that handwriting in the logbook too, to make certain Belkor wrote it?"

"Oh, there's no doubt he wrote it. I'd know that neat little handwriting of his anywhere. Regina and I are certain he wrote it, but I'm having it checked against handwriting samples from his brokerage office, just to make sure I have an airtight case if we ever go to trial."

"Who do you think might be accused?"

"This sorceress person, of course. We'll see how her magic works on a jury."

Simon smiled. "You have to find her first."

Hanagan drove us to the marina next. He left the car in a parking lot and walked with us to one of the docks. "Here we are. That's Belkor's ketch straight ahead."

The boat Hanagan indicated was perhaps 30 feet long, with a tall forward mast and a shorter one near the stern. Between them was an enclosed cabin area with four little windows on each side. I followed Hanagan on board and then helped Simon negotiate the shaky gangplank.

"Have you ever gone sailing with Belkor?" Simon asked him.

"Not really. I've been to small parties on board, but we usually stayed close to shore."

"Where was the body lying when the Coast Guard found it?"

"As I understand it, Hans was sprawled by the cabin entrance here."

"And the log?"

"Was locked in this drawer. Regina found it when we were looking over the boat yesterday. That's when she decided to phone you."

Simon ran his fingers over the polished brass fittings. "Would it be possible to take the boat out, to the area where it was found?"

Hanagan smiled. "Just what do you expect to find, Mr. Ark? There are no footprints in the sea."

"There may be a sorceress, though. I'd like to find out."

"I have an appointment this afternoon, but maybe Sam from the marina could run you out. I'll ask him."

He left us and returned in a few minutes with a balding, weatherbeaten man named Sam Linter. "Always glad to help the law," he said, coming on board while Hanagan waved goodbye from the dock.

"This here's my marina now. Mr. Belkor helped me buy it earlier this year. He was a fine gentleman."

He produced a ring of keys from his pocket, chose one, and inserted it into the boat's ignition. The engine came to life and the Miranda edged away from the dock.

"Thank you for taking us out," Simon said.

"Wouldn't do it if Hanagan hadn't given his okay. The police were still here yesterday searching for clues. But he's with the D.A.'s office and if he says you're okay I guess you're okay."

"I gather you knew the dead man quite well."

Sam Linter scratched at a day-old stubble of gray beard. "Sure, everybody around the marina knew Mr. Belkor."

"How old was he?"

"Fifty-five, the paper said. I would have figured him younger than that. A vigorous man, in good physical shape."

They cleared the harbor and headed into the open waters of the Gulf. "Do you know Mrs. Belkor too?"

"Met her a few times, but mostly he liked to take the ketch out alone. Sometimes he was late getting back, after dark, and I'd watch for him at the dock, help him moor it."

"Did you meet him any nights last week?"

"Sure did. He was late every time. Almost eleven o'clock one night. I should have guessed something was wrong."

"Did he ever mention meeting someone out on the water?"

"Not a word. We chatted about the weather, and if the water was smooth—you know the sort of thing."

"What about when he sailed out in the afternoons? Did you see him then too?"

"Sure. I was usually checking his fuel tanks and stuff. And I'd help him cast off. When you're sailing alone it helps to have somebody handle the mooring lines."

"Did he ever show you his logbook?"

Linter looked blank. "Log? No, I never saw it. Not many owners of small pleasure boats keep a log."

"This was more a diary of his impressions on the trips," Simon explained. "There were no compass points or navigational details." Then Simon was staring out at the sky, where only a few fluffy white clouds dotted the horizon. "Was Regina Belkor his second wife, by any chance?"

"Don't know," Linter replied. "What makes you ask?"

"There's an age difference of twenty years, and the boat is named Miranda."

"I asked him about that once. It's his daughter's name. She's away at college in England." He thought about that for a few seconds. "Say, I guess he musta had another wife if he's got a daughter old enough to be in college."

"Unless he married Regina while she was in her teens, which is possible." Simon seemed unwilling to leave the subject of Regina Belkor. "When I knew her in New York her hair was much longer. It hung halfway down her back. Did she cut it recently?"

"Not that I know of. The few times I seen her she looked pretty much the same."

"What about Ronald Hanagan? Did he come around often?"

"Occasionally, not often. Usually when Mr. Belkor had a few people on board for a party."

They headed north for another twenty minutes before Linter told us, "This is the area where the Coast Guard found the boat drifting. They told me it was just south of those keys at the entrance to Tampa Bay."

"Are there any other islands near here?"

"We have lots of keys all along the coast here, but most of them are within sight of land. There's nothing out very far."

"So if someone boarded the Miranda out here they had to come from another boat?"

"Sure."

"If he didn't use his sails you could tell how far he went by the amount of fuel he used, couldn't you?"

"Roughly. But most evenings he just went out and sailed in circles for a few hours. It relaxed him, you know—like some businessmen play tennis or golf after a day at the office."

Simon stood staring at the sea a few moments longer, then sighed and decided, "Let's go back in."

We ate dinner at a little seafood place by the water, and over dessert I said to Simon, "You think Regina killed him, don't you? Strangled him with the hair she'd cut off her own head."

"No, no," he insisted with a smile. "It's much too soon to accuse anyone."

"Hanagan drives a sports car. He's got young ideas which might have included Belkor's wife."

"My friend, you are too quick to make a love triangle out of this. Are you unwilling to accept the possibility of a sorceress out of the sea?"

"Rising from a glowing bubble? Simon, that's exactly why these people got you down here in the first place—because they knew you'd take that logbook seriously! I think the whole thing is a fake."

"You are too much the realist, my friend."

"The sorceress of the sea has a nice ring to it, but as a book editor I can even tell you where they came up with that. In 1903 a British publisher brought out a collection of short mysteries about a woman murderer called *The Sorceress of the Strand* by L. T. Meade. I suppose if you wanted to invent a murderess at sea *The Sorceress of the Sea* would be a likely phrase."

Simon rarely chided my reasoning but he did so now. "I am familiar with the Meade book. But I am also familiar with a far older work—*The Sorceress of the Sea*, a poem signed only by *W.*, which appeared in a Boston magazine, *The Memorial*, back in 1827."

"My God, Simon, how could you remember that?"

"The poem is quite long and deals with a woman who rises from the waves at midnight to tempt and finally kill a young mariner."

"Which proves what?"

"Which proves that this idea of a beautiful temptress rising from the water is not a new one. It is a legend perhaps traceable back to the Sirens who tempted Odysseus and his crew."

"You mean you actually believe it?"

Simon smiled and returned to his dessert. "As always, I believe until there is reason to disbelieve."

"In a sorceress named Doris?"

"Which reminds me—I would certainly think that as editor of Neptune Books you would be familiar with the names of the sea god's family. His wife was Amphitrite and her parents were Nereus and Doris. Amphitrite, in turn, was the mother of Triton—"

I cut him off with a wave of my hand. "Too much, Simon." I was beginning to wish I'd gone with Shelly to visit her aunt.

"All right," he agreed. "It's time we got down to business. You watched Sam Linter handle that boat this afternoon. Do you think you could take it out tonight? With me along?"

"Who—me?" I was astounded by the question. "Back home I've got only a twelve-foot runabout, Simon."

"Could you take it out?" he repeated.

"Well, sure, I suppose I could. But I wouldn't guarantee getting either of us back alive."

"I'll attempt to guarantee that part."

"But the Coast Guard will arrest us for stealing the boat," I protested.

"Not if we have Regina Belkor's permission. Come on."

She opened the door of her condominium wearing a bright red lounging robe that didn't exactly look as if she were in mourning for her late husband. "Oh—Simon Ark! I wasn't expecting you again this evening."

"We'll only be a minute," he assured her. "We'd like permission to take the ketch out tonight."

"But—but Ronald said you were out this afternoon."

"That was with Sam Linter. We wish to go out alone tonight. My friend here is an expert yachtsman, so there's no danger."

"Are you making progress?"

"Perhaps."

"Is there really something out there that killed Hans?"

"There was on Saturday night. I'm hoping it will be back tonight."

"All right," she decided. "Take the boat. But be careful."

"We'll need the key," Simon reminded her. "I know Linter has one, but it will be more legitimate if we have your key."

"Very well." She disappeared into the bedroom and returned with it.

"I'd also like the key to the drawer where the logbook was kept."

"The ignition key opens that too. My husband didn't believe in lots of different keys."

Simon paused at the door. "You never mentioned having a daughter named Miranda."

"What? Oh, the boat's name! She's Hans's daughter by his first marriage. She's studying at Cambridge, in England. That's why we delayed the service until Friday—so she can be here for it."

"What happened to the former Mrs. Belkor?"

Regina Belkor seemed to grow pale at the question. "She was killed in a boating accident, while Hans was still living in New York. A sudden storm came up and she was swept overboard. He wasn't able to rescue her."

"I see."

If he saw, it was more than I did. When we were back in the car I asked him, "What was all that business about the daughter, and Belkor's first wife? Do you think she came back from a watery grave a thousand miles away to kill her former husband?"

"If the sorceress was the first Mrs. Belkor I'm sure he would have recognized her," Simon said.

"Then what—?"

"We are still gathering information. Tonight, with a bit of luck we shall gather the most important piece of all."

"What do you expect to find out there, Simon?"

"What Hans Belkor found."

Sam Linter obviously thought it strange that we were taking the ketch out alone when a few hours earlier we'd needed him to run it. But he turned on the dock lights for us and cast off the mooring lines and we were on our way. It was the biggest craft I'd ever handled, but once we were free of the crowded marina area I felt more at ease with it.

"Just don't ask me to run up the sails," I told Simon.

"You're doing very well."

"Which way should I go?" It was almost sundown and I was anxious to complete most of our journey before dark.

"South, I think," he decided after some thought.

"But the boat was found drifting to the north."

"That's why we're heading south."

I shrugged and did as I was told. Simon busied himself by puttering around the cabin, looking in drawers and searching shelves. At one point he unlocked the drawer where the logbook had been, but now it was empty.

"What are you searching for?" I asked finally.

"I'll know when I find it."

He went over to a navigation chart that was unrolled on one of the bunks. I'd glanced at it as we made our way out of the harbor, to familiarize myself with the location of the fixed and flashing lights along the shoreline at night.

"Here's something," he said suddenly.

I followed his pointing finger. "That's nothing but a pencil mark."

"He would have had to mark the location some way, if he returned to it three nights in a row."

"Maybe she found him, in a different location each time."

Simon ignored my suggestion and told me to steer for the spot indicated on the chart. Though there were shore lights to guide me, I was no navigator. A half hour later, when the sun had dipped below the western horizon, all I could say was, "This is the general area. It's as close as I can get."

In the twilight we could make out a long narrow key between us and the shore. "What's our depth here?" he asked.

I glanced at the chart. "We're right around the six-fathom line."

"All right. Don't go out any farther. We want fairly shallow water."

We headed south for another few moments. Simon had found a pair of binoculars and was studying the shore of the island as we passed.

He swung the binoculars and suddenly tapped my shoulder. "Cut your engine."

I did as I was told. "What do you see?"

"I'm not sure. Take a look."

"Is it—a glow of some sort in the water?" My heart was racing.

"That's what it seems to be."

"Do we go closer?"

"Of course. We're drifting in the right direction. Don't start the engine again unless you have to. And kill your running lights."

"That's against the law." But I did it anyway.

In the stillness of the night I thought I could hear distant voices. There was something else—perhaps another darkened boat—ahead of us. But as we drew nearer, the thing that held me fascinated was a glow of light from beneath the water. It flickered, grew, died, then came to life again. And all around it the water of the Gulf seemed to bubble and hiss. Then, when we were perhaps 50 feet away, someone broke the surface of the water—a woman, her sleek young body outlined by the glow from beneath the surface. I waited no longer. I pointed our spotlight at her and turned it on.

In that instant, as she rose in the water with her long blonde hair trailing behind her, I thought she was the most beautiful woman I'd ever seen. Here indeed was a sorceress who could lure Hans Belkor to his doom.

Then she shouted, "Kill that damn light or we'll put a bullet through it!"

And the illusion was shattered.

The other boat came alongside and a young bearded man covered Simon and me with an automatic shotgun. The woman hoisted herself on board, water streaming from her long legs and one-piece bathing suit. She unhooked the scuba gear from her back and stared at us. "This is Hans's ketch," she said suddenly. "I thought I recognized it."

"Hans is dead," Simon told her. "As you may already know."

"Dead?" She pondered that. "I didn't know. We don't read the papers out here."

"Who are they?" the bearded man called out. "Should I get Larry out of the water?"

"Shut up a minute!" she called back. The other boat had drifted away from us, but the bearded man was still within shotgun range. I'd killed our spotlight as the woman had demanded, though there was still enough light for us to see each other. Some of it came from the flickering glow which was now directly next to our boat. The young woman turned her attention back to us and repeated his question. "Who are you? What are you doing with this boat?"

"We came to find you, Doris," Simon told her

"How'd you know my name?"

"Hans told us," he replied, and I suppose that was true in a way. "He spoke very highly of you."

"How'd he die?" she asked. "Quickly."

I couldn't take any more of their sparring. Pointing to the water I asked, "Will someone please tell me what's going on down there?"

Simon smiled and answered before Doris could. "They're after something on a sunken yacht, of course. Not too large a craft in this relatively shallow water. I'd guess some sort of narcotics. The lights we see are their underwater lamps and welding equipment."

"Welding equipment!"

"You know a great deal," Doris said. "Did Hans tell you all that before he died?"

"He told me nothing," Simon admitted. "But he left a logbook about his three meetings with you. I should have realized the first time I read it that its slightly poetic allusions were merely the ramblings of a middle-aged man in love with a lovely young woman."

"What did he say?"

"He called you the sorceress of the sea, and I'll admit you do make a spectacular entrance, rising out of that glowing, bubbling water."

"What's causing all that?" I asked.

"It's from the welding," she replied indifferently. "You need compressed air for underwater welding, to keep the water away from the flame. It naturally churns up the surface a bit. Larry's an expert at it. He used to work for a Florida firm that specializes in underwater welding."

The man with the shotgun was growing impatient. "For Pete's sake, Doris, cut the chatter and find out what they want!"

"Jake's right," she said. "What do you want?"

"We're investigating the murder of Hans Belkor," Simon told her.

"You didn't say he was murdered!"

"I thought you knew. He was strangled with a two-foot length of blonde hair. The police have the logbook that mentions you, and they naturally suspect that you're involved."

"That's crazy! He came out here one night last week and found us at work. I had a few drinks with him on the boat while the boys kept working. He liked my company and came back twice more."

Simon nodded. "On Thursday and Friday. What about Saturday?"

"We didn't see him Saturday. Is that when he was killed?"

"Yes. The ketch was found drifting several miles north of here, but that doesn't prove anything. You've got something to keep secret here and Belkor found out about it. That could have been reason enough to kill him."

She stood with hands on hips, staring at Simon Ark. Suddenly she turned to the man in the other boat. "Jake, get Larry up here. We have to talk."

"But—"

"And put down that damn shotgun before someone gets hurt!"

He did as he was told and tugged at a group of hoses that ran beneath the surface from three large tanks on the deck of the boat. Almost at once the underwater activity ceased and the glow was extinguished. A young sandy-haired man in bathing trunks and scuba gear rose to the surface and climbed aboard the other craft.

"What's going on?" he asked. "Who's the old guy?"

"My name is Simon Ark. I am investigating the unfortunate death of Hans Belkor last Saturday night."

"Is that true?" the welder asked Doris.

"It's true. Somebody killed him. We could be in big trouble."

"Hell, we didn't do it," the one called Larry said.

"You're already in big trouble," Simon advised them. "The Coast Guard will be searching these waters, and they're bound to uncover your little scheme soon. What is it? Something connected with drug smuggling, I'd guess. That's Florida's main growth industry these days."

"You know a lot for an old guy," Jake said. He glanced down at the shotgun.

"An unwise move," Simon cautioned before he could act. "Why make your troubles worse than they are."

"What do you want of us?" Doris asked.

"Proof that you didn't kill Belkor. You can start by explaining what you're building here."

"We're not building anything," she said with a sigh. "There's a sunken yacht down there. It's been there for ten years or more. It's on all the charts."

Simon smiled slightly. "I see. And with welded watertight compartments I imagine it would make a perfect way station for smuggled drugs. They could be unloaded here, possibly through a flexible hose, and stored in that sunken yacht for days or weeks. The smugglers' ship would avoid the danger of landing their cargo on the beach, and you could come out at your leisure and pick it up."

"He knows too much!" Larry grumbled. "Belkor must have told him."

"Belkor told me nothing."

"We didn't kill him," Doris insisted. "If we had, we'd certainly kill the two of you for what you've guessed. My God, the man was in love with me! He was older than my father and he was in love with me!"

"You saw him only on those three nights?"

She nodded. "Wednesday, Thursday, and Friday. He found us working out here, and he called me a sorceress. I told him I wasn't anything special, only a girl trying to make a buck, but he didn't care."

"He lost his first wife to the sea," Simon explained. "Somehow he must have thought the sea was giving her back, in you."

A light evening breeze had come up off the Gulf and the boats swayed gently as we stood there facing each other. Finally Doris asked, "What will you do now?"

"Go back to shore," he said. "What you do here doesn't concern us."

The other boat pulled alongside and she jumped onto it. Then the two crafts drifted apart and I switched on the engine. The three of them stood watching us in the darkness as we pulled away.

Ronald Hanagan was standing on the dock as we eased the ketch into its berth at the marina. I was thankful for having got it back in one piece, and was unprepared for Hanagan's blustering. "Regina told me you took the boat out again. I think it was very unwise, especially after dark. This is a valuable ketch, and needs to be handled properly."

Simon Ark merely smiled. "My friend was quite skillful at the wheel. You needn't have worried. I trust you haven't been waiting here long."

"Long enough." He was still unhappy, but our safe return seemed to have calmed him a bit. "Look, we've got a lab report on that hair. It's not real."

"Oh?"

"It probably came out of a wig, they say. A fairly expensive one, because of the length of the hair. In the morning they're going to check some costume and theatrical supply shops in the larger cities."

"That's a good idea," Simon agreed. "You may need the evidence for the trial, after I tell you who the killer is."

"You know?"

"Yes, I know."

"You found something out in the Gulf?"

"You might say that."

"The sorceress of the sea?"

"No, only a breeze that rocked the boat gently on the water."

"A breeze told you who killed Hans?"

"Yes."

"I can't believe that!"

I also found it hard to believe, even though I was familiar with the intuitive nature of his deductions at times. I finished tying the ketch to its moorings and joined them on the dock. "It was a small clue," Simon began, "but an essential one. It had to do with the logbook in which Hans Belkor wrote about his encounter with the sorceress."

"It's his handwriting. We've verified that."

"I don't doubt it. Now it was the logbook, plus the use of the hair as a murder weapon, that led to a belief in this so-called sorceress. My friend and I found the sorceress tonight, and the fact that we are alive is the best evidence of her innocence."

"You found her?" Hanagan said, his mouth gaping open.

"That's another story for another time. We're concerned here with the strangling of Hans Belkor. There's no doubt that he wrote the logbook, and I can carry it one step further. If the so-called sorceress didn't kill him, the real murderer must have been familiar with his logbook entries. Otherwise why strangle him with that twist of hair, a difficult weapon at best? And why kill him on his boat, necessitating a second boat for the escape? The killing was made to seem the work of this sorceress, and thus the murderer must have known about the logbook. Who had this knowledge?"

Hanagan shrugged. "Regina gave it to him as a gift. But she never saw the entries till after his death."

"But *when* did Belkor make the entries in his logbook? Certainly within a day of his journeys, because when he died Saturday there was an entry for Friday. Did he make them on the boat or at home? Obviously on the boat. The log was kept there in a locked drawer. We can't believe he would remove it from the drawer, take it home to write in it—without his wife seeing it—and then return it to the boat. No, the entries must have been made on the boat."

"Well, of course," Hanagan blustered. "That's obvious."

"But *when*, on the boat? While it was out on the water?" Simon drew a deep breath and answered his own question "Hardly, because you'll remember the handwriting was all neat and precise. But as the breeze reminded me tonight, the water on the Gulf is not uniformly smooth. In fact, one of the logbook entries actually describes *heavy seas*. It's impossible to believe Belkor could have written so neatly under those conditions. No, my friends, the only remaining possibility is that he wrote the entries each evening after the ketch returned to its moorings, but before he left the dock and returned home."

"How does that tell us who killed him?" Hanagan asked.

"There is one person who met the ketch most nights when it returned late, who helped moor it and filled its fuel tanks. A person who holds an ignition key that also opens the logbook drawer. A person who *must have seen* Hans Belkor writing in his logbook, yet denied it."

"Sam Linter," I said.

"Exactly. Why would he lie about the logbook? Only if he'd unlocked the drawer and stolen a look at it, and learned about the sorceress of the sea and how he could kill Hans Belkor. He cut some long blonde hair from a wig and followed Belkor out on the Gulf on Saturday evening. He hailed the ketch, came aboard, hit Belkor over the head, then strangled him."

"But why?" Hanagan wanted to know. "What was his motive?"

"He mentioned Belkor helping him buy this marina. They had a business deal together, and I think we'll find it was to Linter's financial advantage to kill his partner."

Suddenly there was the sound of a car gunning its engine. It shot out of the parking lot, heading toward where we stood on the dock "It's Linter!" I shouted. "He overheard us!"

"Yes," Simon Ark said, as if he'd known it all along.

Hanagan and I dove for cover, but Simon stood his ground. It was as if he knew Sam Linter was beyond harming anyone but himself.

The car shot across the wooden dock and through a guard rail. Then it hit the water between two yachts, sinking almost out of view before we could do anything. Sam Linter made no effort to escape, and when Hanagan and I dove into the chilly water we found the car doors locked. By the time we broke through the window and dragged Linter to the surface he was dead. He'd chosen his own peculiar punishment.

I drove Simon to the airport the next day, on my way back to Palm Beach. "What about that girl, Doris?" I asked as he was boarding his plane.

"To Hans Belkor she was indeed a sorceress," he said. "Perhaps she loved him for a brief time, coming up from the sea like a goddess. But in a way she destroyed him. The words he wrote about her gave Sam Linter the idea how to kill him."

I watched until his plane was out of sight. Then, standing beside my car, I thought about Doris and that spot in the Gulf where the sea glowed and bubbled. I still had a day before Shelly expected me back. Perhaps...

But I shook my head sadly and drove on to Palm Beach.

THE HOUSE OF A HUNDRED BIRDS

M y wife Shelly had just learned I was going off again on a trip with Simon Ark, and we were having our usual quarrel. "Where is it this time?" she asked. "India? North Africa?"

"London, actually. We've been there before a couple of times."

"I remember. The first time was right after our marriage."

"Look, Shelly," I pleaded, "why not come along with us? You could shop and see the sights while I'm involved with Simon."

She shook her graying blonde head and I knew it was hopeless. "I can't get away this week. The committee dinner is on Thursday and mother's coming for a visit on the weekend."

"I'll bring you a gift from London," I said.

"The last time it was a bottle of perfume from the airport gift shop."

"I'll do better this time," I promised.

Her face relaxed into a tired smile. "I suppose it could be worse. You could be running off with another woman instead of Simon."

"That would never happen," I assured her. "Not unless she looked just like you."

That evening Simon and I were on the plane to London.

The trip began badly for me. At Heathrow Airport a mousy little man bumped into me and stole my wallet. Luckily my traveler's checks and credit cards were in another pocket, but I still resented the loss. In the cab to London I grumbled all the way. "If you're such a great detective, Simon, why can't you catch the guy who stole my wallet?"

"My friend, a pickpocket is hardly the kind of challenge I seek."

He seemed about to drill into his philosophical ramblings about pursuing Satan for nearly two thousand years, and I was in no mood for it just then. I changed the subject "Would you mind telling me just what it is that brought us to London? On the plane all you would say was that it involved Chauncey Rideout."

Rideout was a friend of Simon's whom I'd met once or twice in New York. He ran a large London travel agency, and was a garrulous man who seemed to fascinate Simon with his endless stories of faraway places.

"We're seeing Chauncey this afternoon. Perhaps it's better if he tells us himself. He did mention some intriguing aspects on the transatlantic phone, though. A murder, for one thing, and a house of a hundred birds."

"A house of—"

But Simon motioned toward the taxi driver's back and would say no more. I settled down and contented myself with the passing scene. Rideout had arranged for our airline tickets and hotel through his travel agency, and he'd booked us into a luxurious Park Lane place we could ill afford. Happily he was paying the expenses.

Chauncey Rideout was never overlooked when he entered a room. His large stomach, always covered by a bright red vest, announced his presence even before his booming voice. Seeing him later that day in his fancy London office I found him more subdued than I remembered, but still wearing the red vest.

"There were two sisters." he began after the usual preliminaries about our trip. "Anna and Gertrude Stigner. Retired civil servants, both in their sixties, never married. Lived in a big old family house in the north of London. I got to know them through the travel agency. Booked them on a two-week tour every spring, regular as clock work. They liked the Mediterranean—the Greek islands and such—and I sort of took them under my wing."

You speak of them in the past tense," I observed.

Chauncey Rideout nodded. "Gertrude was killed four days ago—last Friday night. Stabbed to death by an intruder in her own kitchen. About six months back they asked my advice about taking in a boarder. I suggested they advertise for one, and next thing I knew they'd rented to a chap named Irving. Now Anna fears he might be involved in the murder. She's scared stiff and I can't console her. I couldn't begin to tell her if this mysterious boarder might have killed her sister."

Simon Ark smiled slightly. "So you telephoned me across the ocean."

"You were the only one I knew who might be able to help," Chauncey said. "And you didn't seem very interested until I mentioned the birds."

"Yes, tell us about the birds," I urged. They seemed to be the key to Simon's interest in the affair, and I wanted to learn more.

"There's not much to tell, really. The sisters kept a great many caged birds in the big house. Canaries, doves, songbirds of various sorts. In every room Anna told me once there were a hundred all together."

"A hundred birds!" I glanced over at Simon. "Is there any significance in one hundred caged birds?"

"Not in the number. But their presence suggests—"

We were interrupted by Rideout's secretary who entered the office with the afternoon's correspondence requiring his signature. She was a comely brunette named Thelma Bok and she flashed me a broad smile as we were introduced. "We were just talking about the birds out at the Stigner house," Rideout told her.

Thelma nodded. "I went there once last year to deliver their plane tickets for a tour. You wouldn't believe that many birds!"

"Are they quite noisy?" Simon asked.

"Noisy enough! Though she did cover their cages when they got too bad."

"She? Gertrude or Anna?"

"Gertrude—the one who died." She lowered her voice on the final word, as if in respect. "The birds were hers, really, though I think Anna cared for them too."

"I see." Simon turned back to Chauncey as his secretary left with the signed letters. "Would it be possible for us to meet Anna Stigner?"

"Certainly. Today was the funeral, so maybe tomorrow morning might be best. I'm sure she'll tell you whatever she knows."

"This boarder—have you ever met him?"

"I caught a glimpse of him the other day when I went out there. Young chap, with a beard and long hair. Don't know why they rented the space to that type in the first place. I suppose they needed the money, but they have some valuable pieces of furniture downstairs."

"One other question," Simon said as he stood up. "Did the hundred birds come before or after this boarder?"

"Oh, before. They've had the birds as long as I've known them, and Irving has only been there about six months. Since around the time they both retired. Douglas Irving—that's his name. He's a baker, which is supposed to explain why he's out all night and home during the day."

"I'll look forward to meeting him," Simon said. "In the morning."

A misty drizzle was falling the next day as we drove out to a residential section in the north of London. It was an area of big old houses, many of them now cut up into apartments for young working people. But even in such surroundings the Stigner house stood out. It was a rambling three-story monster, with little porches and gables everywhere. I suppose it was the perfect place to house a hundred birds.

Chauncey Rideout led the way up the steps to the porch, where, dusty rockers creaked in the breeze just beyond the reach of the rain. He let the heavy knocker fall three times and presently the door was opened by a pale woman in black. She had once been beautiful, I thought, though age had played its usual unkind tricks. "This is Anna Stigner," Chauncey said, introducing us.

"Please come in." Her voice was soft and cultured.

She led us through a dim hallway into a pleasant sitting room at the front of the house, and I saw at once what all the bird fuss was about. There were cages everywhere—hanging from the ceiling in the outer hall, on standards in the sitting room, even resting on a table in an adjoining room. Some cages held a single bird, but many had pairs of doves or love-birds. Their chirping, soft but constant, seemed to fill the house.

"I see you are a lover of birds," Simon remarked to the woman as he seated himself by the fireplace. I took a chair on the other side, grateful for the warmth after the chill drizzle outdoors.

"They were really Gertrude's," Anna Stigner explained, "but I may keep most of them. I couldn't imagine living here without them."

Chauncey shifted uneasily in his chair. "Tell him about Gertrude's death, Anna, and about your boarder."

Her thin hands moved on her lap as she spoke. I hope you can help me, Mr. Ark. I just don't know what to do now. Gertrude was older and she always made the decisions for both of us. It was her thought that we should get a boarder for the downstairs after we both retired and our income dropped off. Douglas Irving seemed a nice enough chap at first."

"At first?" Simon questioned.

"Well, he simply appeared at our door one morning about the room, before we'd even had a chance to run an advertisement. He's a baker and works from two a.m. till ten in the morning. He baked cakes and pies for us, and even built a special table in the kitchen for mixing his dough. But he began having a strange visitors a few months back. They'd drive up at night in fancy cars. Always men—he never had women visitors. My sister was bothered by it."

Simon Ark nodded. "Tell me about last Friday."

"It was late in the evening, a little before midnight. I hadn't been feel-ing well and I'd gone to bed early. I was awakened by a sound. It might have been Gertrude screaming for help. I called to her and there was no response." She hung her head, as if in silent prayer. "I put on my robe and slippers and went downstairs—and found her stabbed to death on the kitchen floor. Stabbed with one of our own knives."

"Was there any sign of forced entry?"

"No. I called the police at once, of course, but they could find no signs either. Gertrude and I each had keys and of course Mr. Irving has one too. The police believe the intruder entered with a duplicate key."

"Did Douglas Irving have an alibi for the time of the murder?"

"He claims he'd stopped at a pub before work. The bartender remembers seeing him just before they closed, which was eleven o'clock. Of course the killing wasn't till a bit later than that, but the police don't seem to consider him a serious suspect."

"You do, though."

She looked away. "He just acts strange. If Gertrude surprised him doing something bad he might have killed her."

"Had she ever surprised him at anything in the past?"

"Once she told me she came downstairs around midnight and he was in the kitchen with some men. They had flour spread out on the table and Douglas said they were making dough for bread."

Simon Ark asked, "Could we see this kitchen where your sister was stabbed?"

She led us through a dim back hall and a large pantry, with caged songbirds hanging overhead. Pausing at one of the cages she covered it with a fancy satin drape. "Time you were sleeping now!" she told the birds. But I noticed she did not cover all the cages.

The kitchen itself was large and roomy, with a big double-door refrigerator and modern sink and stove. But Simon's attention was drawn to a large square table with closed sides, closed from table top to floor, standing against one wall. It seemed almost like an altar to some ancient kitchen god. Simon ran his hand over the smooth knotted wood surface and commented, "Very good workmanship. Is this the table Irving built for his baking?"

"Yes. He said we could have it if he ever moved out."

"I think Douglas Irving is a man worth meeting."

"He should be home from work very soon."

"While we wait, Miss Stigner, suppose you tell me the real reason for all these birds."

She shot a glance at Chauncey Rideout, as if suspecting he had told us some secret. "I don't know what you mean. My sister liked—"

"You covered only some of the cages," Simon Ark said. "I'll venture a guess you have so many birds so that some may be left uncovered in each room day and night. It is believed in certain parts of the world that caged birds keep ghosts and evil spirits away from a house that may be haunted."

"I don't—"

"Isn't that what you really fear, Miss Stigner? That your sister was killed by a ghost?"

Anna Stigner had steadied herself against the table, her face suddenly white as chalk. She might have been seeing one of those ghosts herself in that moment. Rideout went quickly to her side, and turned quickly to scowl at Simon. "I asked you to help the poor woman, not frighten her."

"If I am to help, I need to know the truth. I believe she wishes to blame her boarder for the crime to free herself from the terror of the unknown, from the possibility of evil spirits lurking in this house she loves so much."

"I do love it," Anna Stigner gasped.

"Of course you do, or you would have moved long ago rather than fill the place with birds to keep away the spirits." Simon's voice turned unusually gentle. "Now tell me why a ghost may have killed your sister."

"Could I have a glass of water, please?"

Rideout ran the cold water and brought her a glassful. She drunk it down and then straightened to face us, hands gripping the edge of the table behind her. "I didn't tell the whole truth about Friday. Gertrude had always been afraid the house was haunted. Our mother had told us years back of seeing ghosts here. That was the reason for the birds, and it was the reason we took in a male boarder. We believed it would give us some sort of protection. We traveled frequently when we could, just to be away from here, but it is a lovely house and we couldn't bear to sell it. So we put up with the creaks and crashes in the night—"

"The wind," Chauncey Rideout insisted. "Nothing more."

"—and we brought in all the birds, because they seemed to offer some protection. Then we took in Douglas Irving, to have a man on the premises. For a time it was good, despite his odd hours and strange companions. But then came last Friday. I was ill, as I've said, and had retired early. But about half past eleven Gertrude came and wakened me. She said she heard a noise downstairs. though we both knew Irving had not returned. His car was not in the driveway."

She paused and Simon had to urge her on. "What happened next?'

"Gertrude went downstairs while I waited in my bedroom. I heard her say something unintelligible and then she screamed. It was the most terrible sound I've ever heard in my life! I hurried downstairs and found her stabbed to death here on the kitchen floor."

"And the ghost?"

"Mr. Ark, I will swear that I heard not a sound after Gertrude screamed. There were no running footsteps, there was no slamming door. The killer never left, and yet there was no one here!"

"There are many explanations," Rideout insisted, trying to calm her. "A thief may have been in his stocking feet to avoid making noise. He could have slipped out unnoticed as you came downstairs."

Then we heard the front door open and footsteps approaching. We all turned toward the doorway as a slim young man entered. He must have been in his mid-twenties, with hair just over his ears and a dark fringe of beard across his chin. He seemed surprised to find us all gathered in the kitchen. "What's this?" he asked Anna Stigner. "More police?"

"This is my boarder, Douglas Irving," Anna said, and introduced Simon and me. Apparently Rideout had met him at the funeral.

"If you're not police, who are you?" the young man asked.

Simon answered for us. "I am an investigator of unusual phenomena. It's possible the death of Miss Stigner's sister was not caused by a human agency."

"Not caused—? You gotta be kidding, mate! I don't believe in ghosts!"

His arrival had set the kitchen birds to chirping and Anna Stigner covered their cages. Chauncey Rideout cleared his throat. "It's not a matter of believing in ghosts, Mr. Irving. But there was a crime committed here and the police seem unable to get to the bottom of it. If my old friend Simon Ark can shed some light on the matter, I believe we should listen to him."

"Sure, sure," Doug Irving agreed. "So long as you don't try and pin this thing on me. I was down at the Cross and Anchor and I got witnesses to prove it."

"The Cross and Anchor closes at eleven o'clock," Rideout pointed out. "The police checked on it."

"The bartender let me stay later, in the back room. We were drinking till past midnight. I couldn't have been here killing anybody."

"We'll see about that," Chauncey Rideout turned to us. "I have to get back to the office now. Can I drop you anywhere?"

"Our hotel, I think," Simon decided. "Goodbye for now, Miss Stigner, Mr. Irving. We'll be talking to you again."

As we were leaving the house Simon saw the rubbish men removing the Stigner's week's trash. Something in one of the cans attracted him and he walked over to examine it. The trash collector looked annoyed as Simon pulled out a large folded sheet of thin clear plastic and held it up.

"What's that?" Rideout asked, turning up his coat collar. The morning's drizzle had stopped but there was still a chill in the air.

"A plastic sheet," Simon remarked, stating the obvious. "There seems to be a small hole near the center." He put his finger through it.

"About the size of a knife blade," I suggested. "But wouldn't the police have found it?"

Chauncey Rideout was excited. "You mean the killer stabbed her through this to keep the blood off his clothes?"

"Such things have happened," Simon agreed. He tucked the folded plastic under his arm as the trash man went away grumbling.

Simon would say no more about his find, and when Rideout dropped us at the hotel I asked what we were going to do next. "I want to get this analyzed at a private lab," Simon said, patting the sheet.

"For traces of blood?"

"For whatever is to be found."

"How did you happen to notice it in the trash?"

"It seemed an odd thing for Miss Stigner to have—and odder still to be discarding, since it's still as good as new."

"Except for the hole."

"Except for the hole," he agreed. "While I'm doing that, I wish you would go to this pub, the Cross and Anchor, and speak with the bartender. It's increasingly important that we verify Irving's alibi for the night of the killing."

"Then you don't believe in ghosts?"

"Not unless I see one."

The Cross and Anchor was a typical London pub, located on the corner of a well-traveled street a few blocks from the Stigner house. The bar area had a number of afternoon drinkers, and I had to edge between them to order a pint of bitter. When the barman served me I asked, "Know a fellow named Doug Irving? He's a baker."

The barman, a burly fellow with muscular arms, wiped some moisture from the bar. "Oh, sure—Doug's in here evenings, before he goes to work."

"Was he in here last Friday evening?" I took a sip of my beer.

The barman turned away. "I already talked about last Friday to the police. You more of them, or are you a reporter?'"

"Neither one. I'm just looking for information." I slipped a pound note across the bar.

"What do you want to know?"

"Were you on duty last Friday night?"

"Sure, I was on. I'm on most of the time. My brother and I own the place. I'm Ike Dalton."

"Glad to know you, Ike." I shook his hand. "You know Irving pretty well, then?"

"Sure, I know him. Known him for years."

"Where'd he used to live before he moved in with the Stigner sisters?"

"Oh, he had an apartment over on Buckley Terrace. But he said his girl friend told him about the Stigner place and he took it. Said it was cheaper rent and closer to the bakery where he works."

"What about Friday night? He said he was drinking with you after the place closed."

Ike Dalton eyed me suspiciously. "You're not checking my hours, are you? I don't want no trouble on that."

"No, I just want to know about Doug Irving."

"Yeah, we were drinking in back. I told the police that, off the record. Nothing wrong with it. The drinks were on the house. Just a sociable thing."

"Till midnight?"

"Somewhat past, I'd say."

"He kept drinking till it was nearly time to go to work?"

"Hell, he don't work on Fridays! The other baker comes in then."

"You sure of that?"

"Pretty sure. I know he wasn't working last Friday. He was going back to his place to meet some people."

I slipped him another pound. "You've been a great help. Do you know the names of any of these people he hung around with?"

"No, he usually comes in here alone. I don't know much about his friends, except what he tells me."

"Thanks, Mr. Dalton. You've been a big help."

"Come again. And call me Ike. Everybody does."

I finished my pint of bitter and started for the door. I hadn't even noticed the woman in the booth until she spoke. "Buy me a pint, honey?" she asked.

I glanced down at her, ready to walk on, and then stopped dead. It wasn't her voice, with its accent verging on Cockney, that stunned me. It was her face.

It was the face of Shelly, my wife.

For just an instant I thought it might really be Shelly, following me across the Atlantic to surprise me like this, but then I realized the face was not quite right. It was a younger Shelly for one thing looking the way I remembered her from a decade earlier. And even then the nose was not exactly hers. But the resemblances was still remarkable.

I sat down in the booth opposite her. "You look exactly like my wife."

She gave a bit of a chuckle. "Now that's a new line, mister."

"No, no, it's absolutely true! I simply can't believe it."

"Maybe, I'm her sister."

"No, she's back in America."

"Does that win me a pint?"

"I think so." I stepped back to the bar and ordered two pints. Dalton grinned a bit but said nothing. He'd seen it all before.

When I returned to the booth the woman introduced herself. "Mine's Milly Yeats. What's yours?"

I told her my name, still half stunned by the resemblances to Shelly. "Do you come here often?" I asked.

"This is my first time. I'm in West Kensington. I don't get up this way very often."

"What brought you here today?"

She smiled coolly. "Maybe I was following you."

"Oh, come now!" but I felt an uneasiness at the thought. I remembered the birds at Anna Stigner's house and wondered if ghosts ever walked by daylight, in English pubs.

"Why did you come to London?" Milly Yeats asked.

"I'm here with a friend."

"Girl friend?"

"Hardly! I told you I was married."

"Handsome chap like you can still have a girl friend."

We talked on like that for some time, and I wanted to get away but I couldn't. We had more beers, and presently the pub closed for its three-hour afternoon break. I was having trouble standing then, and someone helped me outside. I'd never felt that way from beer before.

Presently I remember I was in the back seat of someone's car, and Milly Yeats was leaning over me and asking, "Why did you come here? What are you after?"

I answered something, hardly able to concentrate on my words.

"Who is Simon Ark?" someone else asked me.

Presently I remembered nothing except the car starting. We drove for a long time and I heard more voices. I opened my eyes and saw it was dark.

"We'd better finish the job," a man said quietly.

Then Milly's voice seemed to swim at me out of the darkness. "No, you don't! I didn't agree to anything like that! Dump him out if you want, but you're not killing him!"

"He could tell the police—"

"He won't remember a thing! Dump him out!"

The car slowed and I closed my eyes, trying not to move. The rear door opened and rough hands grabbed me under the shoulders, yanking me out. I tensed as I hit the ground, still not certain which of them had won the argument. But after a moment the doors slammed and the car drove away.

I started to get up but then fell back onto the roadway. That was the last I knew for some time . . .

When I came to I was in a hospital and Simon Ark was standing by my bed with Chauncey Rideout. "Can you talk? What happened, my friend?"

I struggled to sit up in bed. "It was Shelly—"

"Shelly?"

"A woman who looked like Shelly. I think she drugged me. They were going to kill me but she wouldn't let them."

Simon took a deep breath. "Try to tell us everything that happened."

I did that, repeating what the bartender, Ike Dalton, had said. Then I went on to my meeting with Milly Yeats. When I'd finished, Rideout could only shake his head. "You're lucky to be alive."

"Indeed," Simon agreed. "Do you think this bartender, Dalton, put them on you because you were asking questions?"

"Maybe. But the girl—she looked so much like Shelly!"

"This is some sort of gang," Rideout said, "but what are they up to? And why did they kill Gertrude Stigner?"

"Do not jump to hasty conclusions," Simon Ark told him. "If this so-called gang had committed one murder, they'd hardly have stopped at a second." He turned to me. "The doctors say you can be released after the drug wears off. How are you feeling?"

"Better every minute. Let's get out of here."

I tried to stand but was still wobbly. Simon helped to steady me. "You say they were questioning you. I suspect this woman slipped a knockout drug into your beer and then they injected you with one of the truth drugs like amobarbital or thiopental."

"Why? What were they after?"

"Information. They're worried we might have discovered something."

Finally I was feeling steadier, and as I slipped into my clothes. Rideout phoned his secretary at the office. "Thelma, I'm at Charing Cross Hospital. I'll be in shortly. Are there any messages?"

If his secretary was in the office it had to be morning I realized for the first time that I'd been unconscious all night I pulled open the drapes and squinted against the morning sun. "What time is it?" I asked Simon.

"Just after nine. The hospital found your room key and called the hotel. I contacted Chauncey and we came right over."

Rideout hung up the phone. "I'm glad I called Thelma. She says that Anna Stigner phoned first thing this morning, very agitated. She wants to see us as soon as possible."

Simon rested an arm on my shoulder. "Are you up to it? Can you manage it?"

"Of course!"

But on the drive to the Stigner house I was still bothered by what had happened to me. "Put it out of your mind for the present," Simon advised.

"She looked just like Shelly—the way Shelly looked ten years ago. Even her hair was the way Shelly wore it! How is that possible Simon?" And when he said nothing I asked, "You do believe me, don't you?"

"All in good time, my friend."

We arrived at the house to find a distraught Anna waiting to greet us at the door. "What in heaven's name is it?" Rideout asked.

"My birds! Three of them are dead!"

The news didn't seem to surprise Simon Ark. "Kitchen birds?" he asked.

"Yes, they were some of the ones I kept in the kitchen."

"And I imagine you let them fly around the room occasionally while you clean their cages?"

"Yes, but—"

"I should have warned you," he said, almost to himself.

"Was it the ghost? Did the ghost kill them? There's something evil in the kitchen, isn't there?"

"Yes, but it is not a ghost."

We followed her into the kitchen and she showed us the dead birds. But Simon was more interested in the rest of the room. It didn't seem to have changed from our visit the day before, although he obviously had spotted something. He got down on his knees very gingerly and inspected the floor near the table at close range.

"What is it, Simon?" I asked.

"Nothing that I didn't expect to find." He got to his feet and I put out a hand to help him. "Miss Stigner, I need to ask a favor. I want you to tell your boarder when he comes in from work this morning that the past week's events have upset you so much you're going away for a few days' rest. Tell him you're going up to Harrogate to relax at one of the resort hotels."

"How long will I really have to be away?"

"Only a few hours if we're lucky. Chauncey, could she stay at your house, just for this evening?"

"Certainly!"

"But not a word of this to anyone! We're very close to finding the killer now, and getting to the bottom of this entire business."

"I hope so," I said. "Where will we be going, Simon?"

He smiled. "We'll be staying right here. I don't want anyone who's watching the house to see us enter later in the day."

"You mean—"

"I mean we'll be here tonight to see what happens in Miss Stigner's absence."

We hid ourselves in an upstairs bedroom as soon as Douglas Irving made his appearance. It was a long afternoon and once Anna Stigner had departed, the big house seemed strangely desolate. The constantly chirping birds did nothing to dispel the feeling, at least for me.

"We're to remain here until evening?" I asked Simon quietly, munching on a sandwich Anna had left for us.

"Correct. Irving must be convinced he's perfectly safe and alone in the house."

"Then you believe him to be the killer?"

"I didn't say that. I believe him to be in charge of the strange happenings in the kitchen."

"What are they—ghosts, devil worship? That table he built could be an altar." I took another bite of the thin sandwich. "And what killed the birds?"

"Freedom, in a sense."

"Stop talking in riddles, Simon! If I'm going to stuck here all day you can at least give me a few facts."

"Very well," he agreed with a sigh. "What do you want to know?"

"That woman, Milly Yeats—the one who looks like Shelly. How was it possible that one of the gang—if there is a gang—could so resemble my wife?"

Simon leaned back in his chair. "Nothing supernatural about that. Many men carry a picture of their wives in their wallet."

"My wallet!" I started to reach for it and then remembered it was gone. "You mean the man who stole my wallet at the airport was—"

"Part of this so-called gang? Yes, I think so. You said her appearance and hair style were the way Shelly looked years ago. The way she looked in the photo you carried in your wallet—correct?"

"My God, Simon, I never thought of that!"

"They stole your wallet to find out who you were, what you were doing here. But the wallet contained no incriminating identification—only a picture of your wife. By chance they knew someone who resembled her, and with some makeup and a change in hair styling they made her look like the picture of Shelly. It was enough to grab your attention so this Milly could drug you and they could question you further. I suspect Milly will prove to be a prostitute or some sort of shady character."

"I think she saved my life, Simon They wanted to kill me but she wouldn't let them."

There was a creaking on the stairs and Simon motioned silence. We waited, barely breathing, as we heard doors opening down the hall. "He's checking the room," Simon whispered. "Quickly, into the closet."

We huddled in the darkness, up against some musty coats, as our bed-room door opened and then closed again After a time we heard steps going back downstairs. "He's not taking any chances," I whispered.

"We may not have much longer to wait."

About an hour later the doorbell rang and we heard low voices in the downstairs hall. Then there was a silence again, for nearly another hour. It was almost evening when a car pulled up across the street and we saw three shadowy figures emerge. They came quickly toward the house and the doorbell sounded again.

"This is it," Simon said. "Come on—but very quietly!"

We left our hiding place and crept out to the top of the stairs. As the evening shadows lengthened in the house, the birds had quieted down. In the upper hall Simon covered their cages so our presence wouldn't stir them up again. The downstairs seemed almost dark now, though there was a glow of light from the hallway leading to the kitchen.

We moved slowly down the stairs, well aware of their tendency to creak. I tested each tread lightly and stepped over the worst of them, helping Simon to do likewise. Finally we were at the bottom, and made our way down the hall to the kitchen.

I'd expected some devilish rites, or a sinister meeting at the very least. But what we saw was prosaic in the extreme—four men in bakers' whites standing around the kitchen table. A sheet of clear plastic had been spread across the table, and several small mounds of flour emptied on it. I might have been standing in the back room of the corner bakery.

It was Irving who whirled around and saw us. For just an instant there was a trace of panic on his face. Then he relaxed and said, "Simon Ark, isn't it? And your friend. What are you doing here? I thought the house was empty."

"We came to watch," Simon explained simply. "And to solve a murder."

The other three men were older than Irving, and one of them was a mousy little fellow who looked familiar. "Simon," I said, suddenly remem-bering, "he looks like the fellow who bumped into me at the airport when my wallet was stolen?"

"I never—" the man began, but Simon cut him short.

"I'm sure it's the same person. They needed to know what we'd come for. They must have suspected we were drug-enforcement agents of some sort."

"Drugs?"

"Of course. Did you suppose merely because they are dressed like bakers that is flour on the table? It is pure cocaine, waiting to be cut and no doubt distributed through Irving's bakery."

That was when the mousy little man drew a pistol from beneath his white jacket. "We should have killed them earlier," he said. "This time I'll do it myself."

Simon Ark held up his hands, as if to deflect the bullets. "It would be unwise to shoot us until you hear what I have to say. It should be very important to you."

I was dumbfounded by the turn of events. "How did you know it was cocaine, Simon?"

"There were traces of it on that plastic sheet I had analyzed, as the death of the birds confirmed my belief it was cut here in the kitchen. Out of their cages, the birds found bits of the drug on the floor, ate the bits, and died. You'll remember Anna told us, her sister surprised these men once with flour on the table. Only it wasn't flour that time either."

"So she found them again Friday night and they killed her," I suggested.

The mousy man cursed and raised his gun "We've had enough talk."

"If you kill us," Simon said, speaking quickly, "the police will be certain you killed Gertrude Stigner as well. Put down your gun and I'll tell you who really killed her."

The man hesitated and Irving said, "He's trying to trick us, Harry."

Simon pressed his advantage, like an elderly schoolmaster making his point to an unruly class. "Listen to me, Harry. You're been cheated. Mr. Irving here has very cleverly connived to steal some of your cocaine."

"Don't listen to him!" Irving shouted, in full panic now. "He's crazy! He's a cop!"

But one of the men with Harry ordered, "Let him talk."

Simon strode carefully past the pointed gun and pushed aside the pile of cocaine from the center of the big wooden table. "Let me tell you a story—about bakers in Fourteenth Century London. Not many people know this story, but I imagine it's well known to London bakers like Douglas Irving here. It seems there was a baker named John Brid who often invited neighbors and others to bake their bread in his oven. They would come with their flour and put it on his table. But in the top of this special table was a small hole which could be opened from below—perhaps about the size of one of these knots in the wood. John Brid had a servant hidden beneath the table, to open the hole and steal the flour, little by little. It was said he and other London bakers stole a large quantity of flour from their neighbours in this manner."

The man named Harry peered more closely at the table top. "You mean he's been stealing my pure cocaine through a hole in the table?"

"If you need any more evidence, here's a tear in the plastic sheet just over this knot. When the hole was opened the sheet had to be cut from below to get at the cocaine."

Harry swung the pistol on Doug Irving. "You dirty crook! I'll—"

"And," Simon hurried on, "that was what caused Gertrude Signer's death. She didn't come upon you mixing your so-called dough. After all, that had happened before without her realizing the truth. No, this time she came downstairs to discover Irving's confederate crawling into position beneath the table. And for that she was killed."

The wooden panel hiding the end of the table suddenly swung open, and a black-clad figure tried to scamper to freedom. But Simon grabbed at it and I helped, catching a leg and holding firm. "Let me introduce Irving's accomplice, and the killer of Gertrude Stigner," Simon Ark said.

It was Chauncey Rideout's secretary, Thelma Bok.

Then a great many things happened at once. Irving dove for Harry's gun and wrestled him to the floor while Simon and I clung to our captive. The other two men decided to run, and they were at the front door when we heard the sound of police whistles. In a few moments it was all over. There were police and detectives everywhere, and in their midst was Chauncey Rideout looking aghast at his secretary. "Thelma, what in hell are you doing here?"

"I'm sorry, Chauncey," Simon informed him. "She killed Gertrude Stigner."

"I can't believe it! Did you know this all the time?"

"I had a strong suspicion," Simon admitted. "My friend's pocket was picked on our arrival at the London airport, by this man Harry who was seeking more information about us. He later had my friend drugged for the same purpose. But who knew we were arriving in London? Only you, Chauncey, because you made our reservations. Only you, and of course your secretary who always handles the actual arrangements.

"We heard from Anna Stigner that Doug Irving came looking for a room before she'd even had a chance to advertise for a boarder. Again, only you—and Thelma here—knew of the Stigner sisters' intentions.

"The bartender at the Cross and Anchor informed my friend that Irving's girlfriend told Irving about the Stigner house. Who could the girlfriend be, other than our Thelma here? There was confirmation in the fact that Anna told us Irving never had women visitors. Why should his girl friend stay away after suggesting Irving move here, unless it was because she was known to the Stigner sisters and didn't want to be connected with Irving."

"That told you she was his girl, but what about the murder?" I asked.

"Remember the hole in that plastic sheet I found yesterday? That plus the look of the table Irving built suggested to me that he might be familiar with John Brid's old baker's trick. Of course the scheme called for an accomplice hidden under the table to steal the flour—or cocaine in this case. Irving's girl seemed the likely person. She would enter the house with a duplicate key before Irving arrived with the rest of the gang to cut the cocaine. They probably worked the scheme several times before Gertrude caught Thelma sneaking in into the kitchen.

"Thelma stabbed her with a kitchen knife and hid under the table when Anna came to investigate. That's why Anna didn't hear anyone leaving the house. Then Thelma no doubt sneaked out while Anna was on the phone to the police. You see? Thelma was Irving's likely girlfriend, and supplied the information about our arrival The girlfriend was most likely Irving's accomplice in the cocaine stealing. And the accomplice was the most likely killer, because Irving had an alibi and the accomplice knew a natural place to hide after the killing when Anna heard no one. Therefore, Thelma Bok is the most likely killer."

"But you weren't sure until she came out from under the table."

Simon Ark smiled. "No, I wasn't sure," he admitted.

One of the Scotland Yard men came in from outside, leading Milly Yeats by the arm. "I found this one waiting in a car down the street," he announced.

Simon stared at the face that was so much like Shelly's. "Is the one who drugged you?" he asked.

I looked into Milly's eyes. "She's the one," I said quietly. And then to the detectives, "Go easy on her. She wouldn't let them kill me."

Milly stood for a moment staring at me "I swear I didn't know what was going on. Harry just hired me to do a job. I was waiting to get paid now." Her voice softened a bit. "You got some lucky wife, fella. I envy her. You know, you and I could have had some great times together."

The birds were still chattering as Simon and I left the house. Maybe they were keeping the ghosts away.

PRISONER OF ZERFALL

S imon Ark and I had not met in some months, but his absences from New York were nothing unusual. I knew one day I'd hear from him again, but when the call came I hardly expected it to be while I was attending an international book fair in Berlin. The annual event had long attracted American and British publishers, and this year the powers-that-be at Neptune Books had decided I should undertake the trip to Berlin alone.

The book fair was a friendly place, and although several Eastern Bloc nations were represented there was none of the mutual suspicion so often present at international conferences. I returned to my hotel after the first full day's events, assured that I'd bagged a couple of good translations for American publication.

That was when I heard from Simon Ark. "How'd you know where to find me?" I asked, recognizing his voice at once. "I've only been in Berlin a day."

"There are people who know of your presence. I was kept informed."

"What do you mean? Where are you calling from, Simon?"

"Here in Berlin. I am at the American embassy at present. Would you be so good as to join me here?"

I couldn't imagine what Simon Ark could possibly be doing at the American Embassy unless he was in some sort of trouble. Although his voice sounded calm, his request was more like a summons. A mixture of friendship and curiosity made me reply, "I'll be there as soon as possible."

The Marine guards at the embassy seemed to be expecting me, and I was admitted at once by way of the private entrance. A blonde young woman in a tailored suit was waiting to escort me to the ambassador's office on the second floor. Where I found Simon Ark ensconced in a large leather armchair.

"My friend!" he greeted me, partly rising to shake my hand. It is so good to see you again!" He seemed older than I remembered, with a gaunt look to his face that emphasized his nose and cheekbones. But then, how do you judge the age of someone, who seriously claims to have lived for nearly two thousand years?

"This is a real surprise," I admitted. "I hadn't expected we'd meet in Berlin." He introduced me to the ambassador and an official-looking person named John Rengate.

"I must say I opposed calling in another person on this," Rengate told me sourly, "especially a New York publisher. But when Mr. Ark learned you were here in Berlin he insisted."

"We're old friends," I explained. "What's the trouble here?" If our government had enlisted Simon's aid there had to be trouble of a most unusual nature.

The ambassador looked uncomfortable. "You realize what you hear in this room is top secret. We're dealing with a very serious matter."

"Of course."

John Rengate took over the conversation. "I was just filling in Mr. Ark on our problem. Does the name Erwin Witterberg mean anything to you?"

I dredged through my memory and came up with it. "A convicted Nazi war criminal, wasn't he? I suppose he's dead by now."

"He's not dead," Rengate insisted. "Or at least we don't think he is. He's been imprisoned here in West Berlin for nearly forty years, since the Nuremberg trials."

"Like Rudolph Hess," I said, remembering the name of another famous prisoner.

"Exactly like Hess," Rengate agreed. "Hess is imprisoned at Spandau, while Erwin Witterberg is at Zerfall Castle, in the Tegeler Forest area in the northwest sector of the city. Like Hess, he is guarded by a joint force of American, British, French and Russian military police."

"Isn't that awfully expensive for just one prisoner?"

"It is indeed. Some $400,000 a year. But the cost is paid by the Berlin city government. Like Hess, his imprisonment has become something of a political symbol. No one wants him pardoned, least of all the Russians. Their small guard force at the castle gives them a toehold in the western part of the city."

"Why don't you at least imprison Witterberg and Hess together?" I suggested.

"In the beginning, immediately after the trials, there were seven Nazi leaders at Spandau and ten at Zerfall. It just happened that these two are the last survivors. To put them together now, in their old age, would no doubt upset the men, as well as the careful balance of the four-power agreement. Hess is over ninety and Witterberg is seventy-six, so the arrangement will be over soon."

"Maybe sooner than we want," the ambassador remarked.

"Yes," Rengate said. This castle—it's an Eighteenth Century structure, much older than Spandau, with all the usual stories of hauntings and secret passageways. Some claim it was used by devil worshipers in the early 1700s. That's why someone suggested we call in Simon Ark."

Simon smiled slightly. "My fame precedes me."

"I still don't understand," I told them. "Why are you worried about something that happened nearly three hundred years ago, and how is it connected with your prisoner?"

John Rengate and the ambassador exchanged glances, sharing a reluctance to unveil their final secret. Then Rengate spoke. "Erwin Witterberg has vanished from his prison. The guards insist it couldn't have happened, but it did. He has simply disappeared."

It was only the lateness of the hour that kept us from visiting the castle that evening. In the morning, at an hour so early I barely had time for a quick breakfast, an embassy limousine picked me up at my hotel. Simon Ark was already in the back seat looking fit and rested. I'd seen the look before at the start of an investigation. It was as if the prospect of a puzzle to be solved delivered new vigor to his aging body.

The Tegeler Forest was a large tract of public woodland along the shore of the Tegeler See, a lovely lake that was actually part of the Havel River and its canal systems. The waterway wandered through East Germany and eventually connected with the North Sea, providing employment for river nomads who braved the stringent security regulations of the East German police to bring goods in and out of the city on barges. On the edge of the Tegeler See, within sight of its picturesque islands, was a service club and restaurant for the French garrison in Berlin. Just up the shore from the club was the 280-year-old Zerfall Castle. Now, driving up to the massive front door in the morning sun, the castle seemed more like some quaint movie set than an actual relic of the eighteenth Century.

"It's fairly modern, as castles go," Rengate explained after he'd greeted us at the door. I wondered if he'd spent the night at the place. "It was built by a wealthy German named Zerfall, who had a fondness for the esoteric. Legend has it he built the place, with a number of secret rooms and hidden passageways where Black Masses and other rites of devil worship could be practiced in safety."

Simon Ark looked up at the dank stone walls. "My experience is that the devil rarely bothers with those he already owns. But what purpose did the building serve in the intervening centuries?"

"It was a library for a time, and a place for German studies. The Nazis erected a flak tower on the roof during the war. Then it was converted into a small prison. As I mentioned, Erwin Witterberg is the last prisoner left. Though only in his mid-thirties when the war ended, he was convicted of various war crimes. He played an important part in the transportation of Jews to the death camps."

"He disappeared from his cell?" Simon asked.

"They aren't cells as such—more like small apartments in which the prisoners were locked each night. Witterberg's has a bedroom and bathroom."

"I assume the rooms were inspected for hidden passages?" Simon asked.

"Certainly. But he didn't disappear from his room. He vanished while taking his daily exercise in the enclosed courtyard."

I saw Simon's eyes brighten at the words. Before Rengate could tell us more we were joined by an American army officer. "I'm Colonel Kayman, the acting commander of the prison. Happy to meet you, Mr. Ark."

Simon bowed slightly. "I understood there was four-power control ..."

Kayman, a middle-aged man with a square jaw and the look of a fighter, spoke in sharp, brisk sentences. "The position of commander rotates monthly. This is my month, unfortunately."

John Rengate cleared his throat. "Colonel Kayman, we've brought in Simon Ark because he knows a great deal about the history and practices of devil-worship cults. If there's anything about this castle we haven't discovered in forty years, Mr. Ark will find it."

"You're welcome to try," the colonel told Simon. "However, no secret passageway could explain the prisoner's disappearance from the exercise yard."

"Sometimes," Simon told him, "there are unseen doors which exist only in the minds of man."

Colonel Kayman grunted. "What's that supposed to mean?"

"The colonel is a practical man," Rengate said. "And this is a very practical matter. Shortly you'll be meeting the Russian officer stationed here—Colonel Vladimov. We've long suspected that Vladimov is a KGB man in addition to his army duties."

"You believe the Russians spirited Witterberg away?" Simon asked. "But why?"

Colonel Kayman shrugged. "To embarrass us. That's why we've kept it secret thus far. But Vladimov knows, of course, and we expect the Russians to leak the news to the press at any time."

"How would it embarrass the Americans any more than the Russians?"

"Because an American is in command this month," Rengate explained patiently. "They look for whatever propaganda victories they can score."

It seemed like an elaborate plot for such a minor victory, and I could see that Simon was dubious, too. "I'd like to know exactly what happened," he said.

They led us through a large central room of the castle which had been converted to an office, its row of metal file cabinets standing out incongruously against the rough stone arch of the wall design. Colonel Kayman used a key to unlock a metal door at the far end of the room, and we passed through it into a corridor. "This is the way to the individual confinement rooms. Ah—and here is Colonel Vladimov!"

The Russian was taller than Kayman, and younger. His sharp eyes seemed to take in everything at a glance, and he gave the impression of a shrewdness beyond that necessary for the job he held. Perhaps Rengate was correct about his connection with the KGB.

"You have brought in more Americans to assist you," he told Rengate and Colonel Kayman with a trace of accusation in his voice. "I understood we had agreed to absolute secrecy in this matter!"

"I am not an American," Simon Ark corrected him.

The Russian peered at him more intently. "Jewish?"

"I come from Egypt, though I have lived in America in recent years."

"He's an expert on parapsychology," Colonel Kayman told Vladimov. "We're investigating every possibility. I'm taking him to see the exercise yard now."

"The other two should be present," Vladimov decided, "I'll summon them."

While the Russian was gone, Rengate explained, "Only the four unit commanders have stayed on here to help with the investigation. Office staff and guards were returned to their units in the interest of security."

"You have kitchen facilities here?" Simon asked.

"No, all meals are supplied by the French service club nearby. It's good food. They have one of the finest chefs in the city."

We continued down the corridor to an enclosed courtyard about fifty feet square. There was grass in the center, but along the walls it had been worn thin by the trudging of feet. Colonel Kayman walked to the very center of the yard and stood for a moment pondering the blank walls that enclosed three sides of it. Then he turned back toward the doorway in the fourth wall as Vladimov returned with the others.

The Frenchman was also a colonel, and his name was Serrer. A small man with a neatly trimmed mustache, he shook hands and then stood by silently. It was the British representative who provided the morning's surprise, at least for me. Colonel Kayman explained that the regular colonel was on leave this month, back in England. His place was being filled by the second-in-command, Captain Rachel Easton, an attractive red-haired woman who filled her uniform very nicely.

"Captain Easton can tell you what happened," Vladimov said. "She was on duty at the time." The tone of his voice suggested it would never have happened if he'd been on duty.

"Well," she began, directing her remarks to Simon and me, "we have regular guards on the night shift, but in order to keep the complement as low as possible, one of us usually relieves them in the morning for breakfast. The prisoner eats in his quarters and then is allowed an hour alone in the exercise yard. I took him there yesterday morning and left him."

"Is that standard practice?" Simon Ark asked.

It was Kayman who answered. "More or less. These walls are twenty feet high and quite smooth. Where is a seventy-six-year-old man to go? When there were more prisoners, things were done differently, of course."

"Continue," Simon told her.

"There's little more to tell. I was at my desk just inside the door, with a view of a portion of the yard from the window. I saw Witterberg pass by the window several times as he circled the yard. After twenty minutes or so, I didn't see him. I thought he might have been resting on that bench over there, but after a time I decided I should check on him, in the event he was ill. I went into the courtyard and found it empty."

I volunteered an opinion. "Sounds to me as if someone threw a rope over the wall for him."

"Quite out of the question," the Frenchman said, joining the conversation for the first time. "He was far too feeble to climb a rope. And two of these walls are still within the walls of the castle. Scaling them would provide no escape at all."

"And the third wail?' Simon asked.

"The wall, opposite the building here overlooks the lake. There's a drop of perhaps sixty feet to the water. So that way is impossible, too."

"Perhaps," Simon commented.

"There was a prison break back in America where a helicopter was used," I told them.

It was Captain Rachel Easton who spoke again. "Impossible! I was at my desk right inside, that window. A helicopter landing or even hovering overhead would certainly have attracted my attention, to say nothing of everyone else in the castle."

Simon was deep in thought. "You remember nothing unusual yesterday morning? Nothing out of the ordinary?"

"Nothing."

The loud honking of a ship's klaxon reached us from beyond the wall. "What's that?" I asked.

"Sometimes the cargo barges blow their horns when they pass through the lake. Many of the crew are French, and they have friends working at the service club."

"Have you searched the shore of the lake for a body?" Simon asked, "He may have tried to scale the wall and fallen to his death."

"We've been all over it," Kayman said. "We found nothing. And we searched the rest of the castle, too, before you ask. Erwin Witterberg didn't merely move from one courtyard to another. He vanished from Zerfall Castle."

Simon and I took some time to examine the castle on our own, after viewing the missing man's meager possessions in his quarters. The occasional modern touches—the radio room for quick communication with the four-power governments, the searchlights on the roof—stood out in sharp contrast to the suits of armor in the halls and the decorative broadswords on the stone walls.

"What do you think really happened, Simon?" I asked as we descended the wide staircase.

"I think there are four people here who do not trust one another."

"Do you think Witterberg escaped on his own?"

"Highly unlikely at his age. But we must speak with his doctor."

"Then he was rescued."

"Or kidnapped."

"But why? And how?"

"There are several possibilities."

"I don't see any," I admitted. "I've never heard of a case like this."

"There is very little new under the sun, my friend. In 1815, at a Prussian prison at Weichselmunde, a valet named Diderici, imprisoned for impersonating his master after the latter died of a stroke, vanished while walking in chains in a walled exercise yard. Other prisoners walking behind him say he simply faded from sight, and his chains fell to the ground, nothing more was ever seen of him."

"My God, Simon! That's impossible!"

"It is if you believe it happened that way, if you believe the testimony of the other convicts."

"Can you explain what happened?"

"Anything can be explained, my friend."

"Try it."

"The convicts were lying. They fell upon the man and hacked him to pieces with home-made knives, letting the chains fall free to the ground. The pieces of the body were thrown over the walls, and the blood on the ground was covered with dirt."

I was speechless at the thought of it. The horror of his theory was only surpassed by the awful thought that it just might have been true. Finally I managed to ask, "Do you believe something like that might have happened here?"

"Hardly, my friend. Witterberg was alone in the exercise yard. If Captain Easton lied about that, she would surely have concocted a more convincing lie about the entire affair."

We'd left the main building and were strolling through one of the walled courtyards that flanked the exercise yard. Simon paused to stare up at the top of the wall. "What do you see now?" I asked.

"A fresh scratch in the masonry."

"As if a ladder might have rested there?"

He studied the ground at our feet. The soft earth of a rose garden ran along the wall, and the imprint of a ladder would surely have left marks. "No," he decided with a sigh. "There was no ladder. Even if there had been, Witterberg would not be free on this side of the wall. We're still within the castle grounds."

"Did you find anything?" a voice called. It was the Frenchman, Serrer, and he came into the courtyard with his hands behind his back as if he were about to inspect the place.

"Nothing," Simon assured him. "You have a most baffling case here."

"And one which cannot be kept secret much longer, no matter what the Americans want."

"It was Colonel Kayman's decision to withhold an announcement?"

"Of course. I don't have to tell you that the other man, John Rengate, is the resident CIA agent at the American embassy here."

"I suspected as much," Simon admitted, though the thought hadn't occurred to me.

"Whenever anything unusual happens, they convince themselves it is a Russian plot. Believe me, Colonel Vladimov is as baffled by this affair as the others are."

"And yourself?" Simon Ark asked. "Do you have a theory, Colonel Serrer?"

"Neo-Nazis!" The Frenchman barked the word, like a tasteless obscenity. "I believe they rescued him somehow and plan to use him as a symbol of their revival."

"It's possible," Simon admitted. "But how did they penetrate the castle? It is a prison, after all."

"From the river," Serrer decided. "The river holds the key."

"You mean the Tegeler See?"

"I think of it as a river. The barges pass by and sound their klaxons."

"But the barge crews, many of them, are your countrymen," Simon pointed out. "They are French."

"Only a few. Many are German. Whole families live on the barges—wives, children, dogs and cats. They are nomads, like gypsies. The East German river police keep a close eye on them during the thirty-six hours it takes to reach Berlin by boat, but here security is much more lax."

"I was told there were hidden passageways and secret rooms within the castle. Could we see them?"

"They are in no way connected with the disappearance. If you wish to see them you must speak with Captain Easton. She has made a special study of the place."

We found Rachel Easton in the communications room, taking a coded message from London. "It's only routine," she explained. "We usually have someone on duty here, but Serrer suggested to Colonel Kayman that everyone be sent back to their units during the investigation."

"How many men are usually here?"

"It varies from month to month. The month's acting commander, on a rotating basis, sometimes brings in a dozen or so of his people for house-keeping chores. As a rule, we have about twenty people here. We rely upon the nearby French service club for meals and medical personnel."

"I was wondering about that," Simon told her. "I'd like to speak with the physician who last examined Erwin Witterberg."

"Dr. Felix. I believe that can be arranged."

"And now the secret rooms."

She stuffed the London message into her jacket pocket. "Come this way. They're fun to see."

The first of them was a stairway concealed behind a wall near the main entrance. It led to the upper hall, and from there Rachel Easton showed us a pair of closet-like chambers and a larger room that was used for storage. "Interesting," Simon Ark remarked. "This one could have been used for small meetings."

"Zerfall seems to have had that in mind when he built the place. But I assure you there are no secret passageways in the area used for our prison, and nothing at all in the courtyard. I understand they had the walls x-rayed back in 1946, before Zerfall Castle was converted for use as a prison."

"Tell me about Witterberg," Simon suggested. "Did you have many conversations with him?"

"Virtually none. He'd grown quiet in recent months. Quiet and old. I think he was waiting to die."

"Or escape," I suggested.

She gave me an appraising look, as if suddenly wondering what I was doing there. "Or escape," she agreed.

"Serrer thinks the Neo-Nazis helped him."

"Anything is possible, I suppose, in a situation where nothing seems possible."

We were descending the main staircase once more when Simon had a thought. "The suits of armor in the main hall here—did you look inside them?"

Rachel Easton chuckled. "Of course! I was brought up on the same books you were. They're all empty. I assure you we searched everywhere—the hidden rooms, passageways, the grounds. Every inch of the place was covered."

"I'd like to have another look at Witterberg's quarters, if I may."

"Certainly."

She led us to the lower level and through the metal door to the prisoners' wing. The door to Witterberg's cell was still kept locked and she used her key to open it. The first thing I saw was the figure rolled up in a blanket on the bed. "He's come back!" I said, startled at the sight.

Captain Easton ran to the bed and snatched back the blanket. It wasn't Erwin Witterberg. It was the CIA agent, John Rengate, and his throat had been cut.

Colonel Kayman abandoned hope of keeping their secret any longer. He telephoned the American Embassy and then summoned Dr. Felix from the nearby service club. The Military Police were notified. His former inaction was suddenly changed to a burst of activity. Serrer and Easton looked on, allowing Kayman to exercise his command authority, but the Russian was far from docile. When Colonel Vladimov joined us, towering over everyone, he was quick with his demands.

"I will bring in KGB experts from East Berlin to conduct the investigation," he decided.

"Like hell you will!" Kayman barked. "I'm the commanding officer this month, and I'll be in charge of the investigation."

The tall Russian pressed his point a bit longer, but finally went off to sulk, or to contact Moscow for further instructions. Meanwhile, Dr. Felix had arrived to examine the body. He was a brisk young man who spoke good English.

"Throat cut, as you can see," he told us. "Dead about an hour."

"I'm certain Vladimov did it," Kayman said, "That's why he wanted his own people handling the investigation."

"But why?" Simon asked quietly. "What was his motive?"

"Maybe Rengate found something in this room," I suggested.

"Perhaps." When the doctor had finished, Simon knelt on the hard stone floor to conduct his own examination. He was especially interested in Rengate s right hand. "A sticky, gummy substance here." He sniffed the dead man's hand. "Some attempt has been made to wipe it off, but there are still traces."

"What does that mean?"

"I have no idea," Simon told me. Then he called after the departing doctor. "Dr. Felix, do you have a minute?"

"Certainly."

"I understood you examined Erwin Witterberg regularly and kept his medical records."

"I examined him every three months, more often when he was ill."

"Could I see those records?"

The doctor glanced at Colonel Kayman for approval. "Show him," Kayman agreed with a wave of his hand.

We drove the short distance to the French service club in Dr. Felix's car, and he conducted us around the back to his office. Some of the French officers were beginning to arrive for lunch, and I noticed that a number of civilian officials were among them. "Some say we have the best food in Berlin," the doctor explained. "It's a popular place."

He opened his file drawer and took out the thick medical records of Erwin Witterberg. "Here you are—nearly forty years."

Simon flipped through the records, with their periodic photographs, cardiograms, x-rays and blood pressure data. It was like watching the man age before our eyes. The earliest photos were mere black-and-white mug shots. The later ones were in color. The lines of age appeared, then a mustache which turned gray gradually, finally a beard which seemed to become more unkempt with the passage of time. The hair on the top of the head thinned to the point of virtual disappearance.

"He lost weight over the years," Simon remarked. "When did you examine him last?"

"Two months ago. He was virtually the same as on the previous examination. Perhaps a bit more feeble, but holding his own."

Simon read a few paragraphs of the latest report. "He had arthritis?"

"His hands and feet were very bad."

"Could he have climbed a ladder?"

"Not without great difficulty. He had to be helped on any sort of stairs."

"You're aware that he's disappeared?"

"I was informed by Colonel Kayman."

"Do you have any theories?"

He shrugged. "Not unless you accept a massive conspiracy involving all four of the commanding officers and some of their men."

"Is there any physical way in which he could have left that exercise yard without being seen?"

"None. He was too feeble to dig or climb, and what is there left?"

"Thank you, Doctor," Simon told him. "You've been a great help." We were about to start back when another thought struck him. "One more thing, Dr. Felix. What determines the order in which the four powers supervise the prison at Zerfall Castle?"

"It's been alphabetical since the beginning—France, Great Britain, the Soviet Union and the United States."

"I see. Thank you again."

Dr. Felix had a driver run us back to the castle. Simon Ark seemed encouraged by the conversation, but I could find no grounds for it. "Simon, when the doctor said he couldn't have left that exercise yard without being seen, you positively glowed."

"Perhaps I did, my friend. You see, it is the impossibility which points the way to the possible."

"You know what happened to Witterberg?"

"Almost everything. But we must speak again with Captain Easton, about the coded message she received from London."

We found Rachel Easton in her office by the exercise yard. As Simon spoke with her about general matters, I tried to visualize how someone might have plucked Witterberg from the courtyard unseen. The opposite wall and the right-hand wall were clearly in view from her window, and she had only to shift her chair a foot to see the left-hand wall as well. Could she have been lying? Was that what Simon had meant about the impossibility pointing the way to the possible? A klaxon sounded from the Tegeler See, and my mind came back to the present.

"... the message you received earlier today," Simon was saying.

Rachel Easton pushed back her red hair nervously. "That was top secret, of course. I cannot discuss it."

"I believe you can, Captain. You were anxious to keep it out of our sight—I believe, you decoded it, and the message carried information vital to our investigation."

"It carried a piece of information. I don't know the meaning of it but it could damage an innocent person."

"Or a guilty one. Captain Easton, you know Rengate was murdered because he discovered something about the disappearance. You could be the next victim."

"But there's no one I can trust until my commander returns from his holiday" she insisted. "Any of the three of them might be."

"You can trust me," Simon assured her.

She thought about it for a minute or two, while staring out the window at the empty exercise yard. Finally, she said, "It may have no bearing upon the disappearance at all."

"Tell me."

She glanced uncertainly at me, and then back at Simon Ark. "London reports that Paris shifted a large sum of money to a Swiss bank account sometimes used to pay for clandestine activities on behalf of the French government. The money, about $500,000 American, was then transferred to a second account in the name of Colonel Serrer."

"When did this happen?"

"Three days ago."

Simon nodded. "Thank you. I believe that's the last piece of the puzzle I need."

"You mean Serrer ..."

"I mean nothing. The truth about this affair cannot be expressed in a single glib sentence."

Without warning, Colonel Kayman entered the office. "The American ambassador has arrived, along with a couple of CIA men, I'm afraid. They want to question everyone about Rengate's murder."

We went upstairs to the big central room, and I saw that Vladimov and Serrer were already seated. The two men who flanked the ambassador were grim-faced and silent. For the moment they were letting the ambassador do the talking. "What happened here, Mr. Ark? I asked your assistance. I didn't ask for another killing."

"Another?"

"If Witterberg was killed yesterday ..."

"He was not."

"Then he escaped? You know how he escaped?"

"I know what happened here yesterday morning. In an odd way, it bears some resemblance to the disappearance of a man named Diderici from a prison exercise yard in 1815."

I remembered his bizarre theory of the other prisoners hacking Diderici to death with home-made knives. "Simon, you can't mean ..."

"I mean that Diderici was a valet imprisoned for impersonating his master after the latter's death from a stroke. The man who disappeared from here yesterday was impersonating Erwin Witterberg."

Colonel Vladimov spoke up. "That's preposterous!"

"Not at all. When John Rengate discovered it today, you killed him."

The Russian was the first to draw his gun, but the CIA man on the ambassador's right was the first to fire. Colonel Vladimov's expression was one of surprise as a bullet hit him in the chest.

"He's dead," the ambassador announced, straightening up from the body. "Now we really have a mess."

"Not at all," Simon Ark told them. "You will merely announce that Vladimov and Rengate killed each other during a personal quarrel. The Russians will not dispute it, not unless they want the entire scheme made public."

"You'd better tell us just what the scheme involved," the ambassador said. He glanced sharply at the CIA man who'd fired his weapon. "Kindly do not draw that gun again in my presence, Rogers. Not ever."

Simon Ark took the center of the floor, clearly enjoying himself. "The real Erwin Witterberg died last month, probably of a stroke or other natural causes."

"How do you know that?" Colonel Kayman demanded.

"For the moment, accept my word that the man who disappeared yesterday was an imposter. We know the real Witterberg was alive two months ago because Dr. Felix gave him a periodic examination. It's difficult to believe that the death and substitution could have happened without the knowledge of the acting commander, who generally had additional members of his command present during his month in charge. Under the usual rotation plan, Vladimov would have been in charge last month. Correct?"

"Correct," Colonel Kayman agreed. "But if Witterberg died, why did he keep it a secret?"

"Because, as we heard earlier, this castle—along with Spandau—represents the Russians' only toehold in West Berlin. It was especially valuable to Vladimov because, I believe, he was running some sort of illicit trade by means of the barges which pass here daily. That part is for others to investigate. In any event, this location was so important as a gateway to West Berlin that the Russians had to maintain it at any cost. They prepared for the eventuality of Witterberg's demise by recruiting someone—a much younger man, I imagine—who could be made up to pass as the German's double. Luckily, the real Witterberg died during Vladimov's tour of duty and the substitute was spirited in here the same day the body was removed. All that would have been simple with the Russians in charge."

Colonel Kayman shook his head. "You've only substituted one impossibility for another. Whether it was Witterberg or an imposter, the man still vanished from the exercise yard."

"I believe the imposter wore a rope around his waist with a grappling hook on one end. He snagged the top of the wall with it and climbed to the top. I found a fresh scratch on the other side of the wall which could have been caused by such a hook. Once on top of the wall, he was agile enough to leap to the ground, beyond the flower bed. He left no footprints, and after removing his disguise he passed for one of the younger men assigned to duty here. When they were sent back to their units, he merely left the castle with the others. With four nationalities involved, I doubt if they all knew each other that well."

"How do you know there was an imposter?" Rachel Easton asked. "He seemed like the same man to me."

"Only in physical appearance," Simon reminded her. "You told us yourself that he'd grown quiet of late and rarely talked. When I found that scratch on the wall, I immediately thought of a hook of some sort, and a rope for him to climb over. Dr. Felix assured me his age and arthritis made that impossible. But one impossibility pointed out a possible solution. If Witterberg couldn't have escaped that way, perhaps the escaped man wasn't Witterberg at all. I went over our facts, looking for confirmation, and I found it. The sticky substance on Rengate's hand was spirit gum, used by actors to attach false beards and mustaches. Rengate found it in Witterberg's cell and began to suspect the truth. That's when Vladimov killed him, but he couldn't quite wipe off all the gum from his hand."

"I suppose it wouldn't have been that difficult to fool us," Rachel Easton admitted. "A shuffling old man, the baldness, the beard and mustache—that's what we all saw. I'm a bit surprised none of us noticed the substitution, though."

"One of you did," Simon assured her. "The imposter certainly didn't climb that wall because Vladimov wanted him to escape! It ruined his entire scheme to keep the Russian contingent at Zerfall Castle. Someone did indeed notice the substitution, and in a masterful stroke of counterintelligence, paid the imposter to defect. Paid him to escape from here."

"Who?" Kayman asked.

Colonel Serrer cleared his throat. "I did. My government put up 300,000 American dollars when I informed them of the situation"

Kayman couldn't believe it. "My God! Why didn't you just tell me?"

"We didn't want another American-Russian confrontation over it, but at the same time we wanted the Russians out of here. For the false Witterberg to disappear was the simplest solution. And now that we have him, he just might provide valuable information."

"You'll have to give him to us," the CIA man said.

"We won't *give* him to anyone. We may consider selling him, if your price is high enough to cover our expenses."

"We found out about the money transfer," Simon explained, without going into detail. "And I remembered it was you, Serrer, who suggested the other men assigned here be returned to their units. That was so the imposter could exit with them, once he was over the courtyard wall. Of course you supplied him with the rope and grappling hook."

The Frenchman nodded. "I don't think Vladimov ever knew, or he would have killed me, too."

I missed the rest of the book fair; Simon and I flew home to New York the following day. The announced death of Erwin Witterberg and the closing of Zerfall Castle brought only mild notice in the press. Even the deaths of Vladimov and Rengate were treated with as little sensationalism as possible. Someday, I imagine a reporter will dig up the true facts, but until then the book has been closed on the prisoner of Zerfall.

THE S.S.S.

The regular Wednesday morning editorial meetings at Neptune Books were not among my favorite gatherings. In theory each of Neptune's senior editors was free to buy and publish whatever books he or she liked, but in practice it was these weekly editorial meetings that finally decided the company's list.

Much of the discussion was routine and boring, leading me to speculate on whether or not there would be any great difference to corporate profits or literary history if we published book A or book B. Rosa Bland, our mystery and fantasy editor, was especially time-consuming at these meetings, insisting upon quoting at length from readers' reports on various manuscripts whose plots seemed almost interchangeable to me.

It was after one of Rosa Bland's more soporific sessions that Neptune's president, Baynard Skyvos, turned to me and asked, "Are you still in contact with that odd friend of yours—the man who searches for Satan and claims to be a couple thousand years old?"

"You mean Simon Ark. We published a book of his on Satanism about ten years ago. Sure, I still see him occasionally. He gives talks and lectures at area colleges."

"We've got some nutty religious group that's after us because of our colophon. I was thinking Ark might be able to help."

I turned to look at the statue behind me. "You mean Neptune?"

"Yes, only they insist it's really the devil because he's holding a pitchfork."

"It's not a pitchfork," Rosa Bland insisted. "It's a trident!"

"I know, but how do you reason with people like that?" Skyvos slid a neatly typed letter across the table to me. "You'll remember all the trouble that soap company had last year with a similar thing."

I skimmed over the letter with growing amazement. "They're talking about organizing a boycott of Neptune publications unless we change our colophon! I don't believe this!"

The letter was passed around the table while Baynard Skyvos brushed back his thin gray hair and continued speaking. "You'll note the letter is dated over a week ago. I ignored it at first as the work of some cranks. But yesterday this fellow Rappoport telephoned me and repeated the boycott threat."

Vincent Frawley, a senior editor in charge of nonfiction, scoffed. "You can't take this seriously, Baynard! To equate the sea god Neptune with Satan shows an utter lack of fundamental knowledge."

"Still, these people must be given an answer. I trust the consensus is against changing the colophon to a drawing of some innocuous waves?"

"Certainly!" I agreed.

"Then would you ask your friend Simon Ark to meet with these people? He's something of a theologian and a scholar. Maybe he can explain it in language they'll understand."

It seemed like a simple enough request, and I carried it to Simon Ark the following afternoon. He was ensconced in an armchair at the college library, pouring over a volume of Frazer's *The Golden Bough*, when I arrived. "My friend!" he greeted me. "You've been absent too long! Have a seat here and tell me your problem."

Simon was a tall man who generally dressed in priestly black, although today—perhaps in deference to the balmy summer weather—he wore an unaccustomed pair of blue slacks and a white sport shirt. "Good to see you again, Simon. Sorry I haven't called sooner, but Shelley's brother was visiting us and things were a bit hectic."

"It's good to see you in any event! But on the telephone you spoke of a problem."

I showed him the letter from Jacob Rappoport. Its basic accusation was that our colophon of King Neptune was a cleverly disguised representation of Satan, and that Neptune was a cleverly disguised representation of Satan, and that Neptune Books was secretly in league with the devil. It threatened a nationwide boycott against our publications unless we stopped using the offending colophon. Simon read it in silence and then passed it back to me. "What do you thing?" I asked. "Could you try reasoning with these people?"

He glanced at the letterhead. "*The Society for the Suppression of Satan.* I'd hardly think a society was needed! This modern age has done the job quite well. Even the sermons in our churches rarely mention Satan any more. The devil has been replaced by the computer as the cause of our everyday problems."

"This group could be a nuisance, Simon."

"The headquarters of the S.S.S., as they call themselves, is only a few miles from here. If you wish to phone them for an appointment I could accompany you there this afternoon."

"Do you have some good arguments ready?"

He held up the book he'd been reading. "Frazer gives some examples of human sacrifice to the sea gods. I suppose, in other times, the line between gods and demons was sometimes blurred. Both demanded human sacrifice, and both could bring down their wrath upon mere humans. The near-naked Neptune with his beard and trident might well be mistaken for a representation of Satan, especially in your little black-and-white colophon."

"You're siding with them!" I said in alarm.

He chuckled. "Not at all, my friend. I'm merely pointing out that these people could be sincere. They may not be simple cranks."

"We'll see."

I telephoned the number on the letterhead of the S.S.S., and the girl who answered connected me with Jacob Rappoport. He was a deep-voiced man who immediately agreed to a meeting with Simon and me. We were there forty minutes later.

The Society for the Suppression of Satan had its modest offices on the second floor of a shopping mall in lower Westchester County. We took the escalator up and passed through a curtained glass door that simply read SSS. The receptionist, who'd answered the phone, smiled at us and said Mr. Rappoport would be just a moment. We sat down behind a coffee table heaped with the sort of old magazines one found in dentists' offices.

Ten minutes later she ushered us into the inner office. Like the rest of the place it was sparsely furnished, with a plain oak desk and three chairs. Jacob Rappoport, a husky bald man wearing glasses, rose to shake hands. "Glad you could come in. We find it much more sensible when the principals are willing to sit down and chat about the problem, rather than go running to their lawyers." He glanced uncertainly at Simon Ark. "Or is Mr. Ark a lawyer?"

"No, he's an expert on religion. And on Satanism."

"I see." Jacob Rappoport looked unhappy. "Well, I don't really think we need to get into a discussion of theology."

Simon smiled. "By definition, Mr. Rappoport, theology is a study of God, not Satan. You seem to be confusing your terms."

The bald man reached onto a shelf behind him and produced one of Neptune's latest best-selling novels. "All I know is that this trademark—"

"Colophon."

"What?"

"It's called a colophon," I said.

"All right. This colophone is a clear representation of Satan."

"It's King Neptune," I said with a sigh. "The name of the company is Neptune Books."

The bald man stared at me with a bland expression. "Let me put it this way. We are dedicated to the suppression of Satan and his works, wherever they are found. We have found them here."

Simon Ark cleared his throat. "I remember an old story by M.P. Shiel titled 'The S.S.', about a secret organization called the Society of Sparta. Its members were dedicated to making the world a better place by murdering those with illnesses or infirmities. Perhaps your group is a modern counterpart—destroying everything that is morally ill."

"You could put it that way," Rappoport answered carefully, "though we violate no laws. We use persuasion, not violence."

"What is the nature of your financial support?" Simon asked.

"We exist entirely upon donations. Several far-sighted companies have made corporate contributions to further our cause."

I started to say something but Simon interrupted. "Would Neptune be allowed to make a small contribution to your work?"

Jacob Rappoport smiled. "Well, certainly."

"Wait a minute!" I objected. "How could you take money from us when you accuse us of being in league with the devil?"

"Obviously a contribution by Neptune Books to our work would be overwhelming proof of your innocence. It would cause us to re-evaluate our original conclusions." He picked up the book again. "King Neptune, you say?"

"What is the usual corporate contribution to your group?" Simon asked.

"I believe $25,000 is a suitable sum, though of course larger companies sometimes contribute more."

Simon nodded. "If Neptune were to contribute $25,000 to the S.S.S., would that end the threat of a boycott?"

"It would certainly cause us to reconsider our position. It would be a show of good faith that would purge the company of any hint of Satanic practice. Yes, I think I could safely say that the threat of boycott would be lifted."

The anger was building quickly inside me, and I think I would have let loose if it had not been for the expression on Simon's face. I'd seen that look too many times before. He was baiting the trap coaxing Jacob Rappoport just a little bit further with each sentence. "Would you want a check or cash?" Simon asked innocently.

"Whichever is best for you. Certainly cash is acceptable if it is easier on your bookkeeping."

Simon nodded. "I think we can promise it by tomorrow, can we?"

That was my cue and I took it, almost choking on the words. "We certainly can."

Simon Ark stood up. "Suppose we make it for the same time tomorrow afternoon?"

"Very good." Rappoport shook hands and showed us to the door.

I could barely contain myself until we were out of the building and back in my car. "Simon, the guy's nothing but a con man—an extortionist!"

"Exactly, my friend."

"But how did you know that?"

"I've had my share of dealings with the legitimate ones. They invariably surround themselves with the trappings of their obsession: religious icons, charms against Satan and the like. Rappoport has none of these. His two-room office with bare furniture and a few old magazines—not even a filing cabinet—seems more the lair of someone prepared to close down operations and flee at a moment's notice. As soon as I established that, it was a simple matter to lead him into requesting a donation."

"And in cash!"

"You don't need my services any longer. Simply contact the police and they'll mark the bills used in the payoff."

But Simon agreed to come back to the office with me while I explained it all to Skyvos, and before the afternoon was over he'd consented to be present when the money was delivered the following morning.

I arrived at the Neptune office early the next day, and our controller a snort, intense man named Walter Muller, suggested I go to the bank and withdraw the $25,000 in hundred-dollar bills from the operating account.

Back at the office, Lieutenant Graves of the New York Police Department watched while one of his men carefully marked each bill with a trace of invisible ink.

Graves was a graying man in his late forties, beginning to develop a pot belly on an otherwise well-kept body. "I'll be waiting outside with someone from the Westchester police," he explained. "As soon as you two leave the office we'll move in and make the arrest. It's as simple as that."

Rose Bland came into the conference room to watch the marking of the money. "It's all in hundreds," she said, surprised. "Didn't he want it in tens and twenties?"

"He wasn't quite that open about it," I explained. "In fact, Simon is the one who suggested cash in the first place."

Simon Ark nodded. "His acceptance of a check would have proved nothing until he cashed it. This way the police can arrest him on the spot."

Lieutenant Graves smiled. "You'd make a good man in the department, Ark. Ever think of going into police work?"

"I have helped the police on some occasions," he admitted. "Informally, of course."

The detective finished marking the last of the stack of hundred-dollar bills, and Baynard Skyvos stared at them with something like apprehension. "I don't like using our money for this," he said. "What if something goes wrong and he escapes with it?"

"He won't escape," Lieutenant Graves assured him.

"Doesn't the police department maintain a fund for this sort of thing?"

"Not really. We have money available for paid informants and certain types of narcotics buys, but not for extortion or confidence games."

The two hundred fifty bills made a stack little more than an inch thick. We placed rubber bands around it and Muller said, "Rosa, can you get me a small manilla envelope?"

Vincent Frawley, the notification editor, came in then and watched the preparations. "You're not really going to give him the money?" he asked.

Lieutenant Graves smiled. "We're going to give it and take it back." Rosa brought an envelope and he slid the banded currency inside. I took it, found it was a bit large for my pocket, and decided I'd have to carry it in my briefcase. I left it on the conference table and went in search of the case.

Graves followed me to my office. "I don't want you taking any unnecessary risks, sir. If you'd feel better I can have one of my men pose as an employee and accompany you."

But I shook my head. "No, I think Simon and I should call on him, just like yesterday. Otherwise he might be suspicious it's a setup."

I got out the briefcase and went back to the conference room where Rosa Bland and Frawley were standing by the window with Simon Ark. Baynard Skyvos had gone back to his office. The envelope of cash fit easily into the briefcase and I told Simon we were ready.

"Good luck." Rosa said. "Don't let the devil get you."

We drove up through the Bronx to Westchester County. I saw no sign of Lieutenant Graves and his men, but he'd said they would follow us and I assumed they were doing just that. Or maybe he'd taken a faster route to the shopping mall where the S.S.S. had its office. When we pulled into the massive parking lot it was impossible to pick out his car.

This time the outer office was empty. Rappoport had dispensed with his receptionist to greet us alone. "You're right on time," he said, smiling and shaking hands.

We followed him into the inner office while I make a pretense of last-minute resistance. "I feel a bit odd about turning over this much money in cash. It's certainly not the way Neptune usually transacts business."

Jacob Rappoport merely smiled. "Think of it as your contribution to fighting Satan. It's a never-ending battle—"

His words were interrupted by the sudden opening of the office door. I saw the startled expression of Rappoport's face and my instant thought was that Lieutenant Graves had moved in too soon. But it was not Graves who stood in the doorway. It was a tall man with flowing gray hair that reached to his shoulders. "What are you doing, Jacob?" he demanded.

"I—Proctor! I didn't expect you!"

"That is obvious." He turned to Simon and me. "Has he asked you for money?"

Before I could respond, Rappoport sputtered defensively. "It has nothing to do with the organization, Proctor. It's a private business deal. Please leave us alone!"

The man called Proctor would have none of it. "If this man asked you for money he was going against the basic tenets of the S.S.S."

"He wrote us a letter," I started to explain.

"Who are you?"

I handed him my business card and introduced Simon Ark. "Your Mr. Rappoport wrote us and later telephoned our president, Baynard Skyvos. He said the Society for the Suppression of Satan felt that our colophon of King Neptune bore a marked resemblance to the devil. He threatened a nationwide boycott of Neptune Books, but withdrew the threat after Simon here offered to contribute $25,000 to the Society."

Proctor glanced down at my briefcase. "And you have the money with you?"

"Yes."

"In cash?" When I nodded he turned his full fury loose on the hapless Rappoport. "You idiot! Do you want to bring the police down on our heads? Do you want to ruin everything I've built here?"

I could see our plan for arresting Rappoport growing dimmer every minute. "He wasn't trying to shake us down," I insisted. "We offered the donation in good faith."

Proctor snorted. "Give me the money!"

I took the small manilla envelope from my briefcase and handed it over. Proctor took it and turned his back on Simon and me, facing Rappoport across the desk. "Take it and count it," he demanded. "Then return every cent of it to these men and get a receipt for it, you understand? If you're involved in anything crooked, may the devil take you!" He tossed the envelope on the desk between them.

"Yes," the bald man quickly agreed. "I'll just count it and give it back."

Proctor whirled with a flourish and strode through the outer door as Rappoport picked up the envelope and opened it.

After that I saw only a blinding flash and I felt myself hurled backward against the wall.

Then everything went black.

The first thing I knew after that was a sharp prick in my arm that brought my eyes open. A young man in a white coat had just jabbed me with a hypodermic needle. I saw Lieutenant Graves bending down next to him, looking concerned.

"Bomb," I managed to mumble. "In the envelope."

"We know," he said. "Try to rest now. We're getting you to a hospital."

"Simon?"

"He's all right."

I closed my eyes and felt them lifting me. That was the last thing I knew for a long time.

When I opened my eyes again Simon Ark was standing at the foot of my bed. "It's all right, Simon," I managed to say. "I'm alive."

"Thank heaven for that!"

I tried to move, but my head hurt. "What's the matter with me?"

"Not too much, we hope," a doctor said, stepping into my line of vision. "You've slept for almost seven hours, but your vital signs are good. You may have a mild concussion, and there was some bleeding from cuts and scrapes, but nothing worse than that."

My memory focused on the explosion. "Tell me what happened, Simon. What about Rappoport?"

"He's dead. Killed instantly. The man named Proctor was unhurt."

I sat up a bit straighter in the bed. "But how could it happen, Simon?"

He shrugged. "Someone switched envelopes on you."

"But how? And when?"

"There are only two possibilities—either back at the Neptune office or in the S.S.S. office just before the explosion."

"Before?" I thought about that. "You mean Proctor?"

"It's a possibility. His back was turned for just an instant. He might have switched envelopes."

"I've got to get out of here," I decided, starting to lift the covers.

But the doctor managed to restrain me. "We'd like to keep you overnight. If your head seems all right in the morning you can go home."

That was the best I could bargain for. Simon comforted me and promised to be there for my morning release. "And Shelly is waiting outside. I'll send her in."

"Where are you going now, Simon?"

"To do a little more investigating into the nature of the S.S.S."

I was released in the morning as promised, and Shelly arrived promptly at ten to drive me home. "I should be going into the office," I protested without much real enthusiasm.

"Rubbish!" Shelly overruled me. "You almost gave your life for Neptune Books yesterday. That's enough for this week. Besides, you're all cut up. Authors don't want to see you like that."

As we were getting into the car Simon Ark appeared, walking solemnly along the pavement toward us. "There's Simon! He said he'd be here."

"Let's pretend we don't see him," Shelly suggested. "He's nothing but trouble."

But I'd already waved and motioned him to join us in the back seat of the car. "What did you find out, Simon?"

"A great deal, my friend. The Society for the Suppression of Satan is not what it first appeared."

"You mean it's an extortion racket. We already know that."

"No, I mean it's not an extortion racket. The S.S.S. is exactly what it claims to be."

"But Rappoport—"

"Rappoport was a renegade member who decided to make a little money on the side. He set up that office on his own and sent the letter to Neptune Books. Proctor is the key to the real organization—and by the way, Proctor is his title, not his name. He's actually a man named Milton Wanger. As the group's Proctor his mission is to keep order and otherwise supervise the members."

"And punish them for their wrongdoings?" I asked.

"Perhaps. Last night I was able to infiltrate an emergency meeting of the S.S.S."

From behind the wheel Shelly snorted. She'd come to take a dim view of Simon's activities in recent years. "What'd you do, learn the secret password?"

"Nothing so complicated. I have earned a certain respect among the anti-Satanists. They realize our goals are the same."

"But—"

"In any event I was able to attend the meeting. Proctor himself seems to be second in command. The leader, whom they spoke of as the George, did not appear."

"An obvious reference to St. George, who defeated evil by slaying the dragon."

"It's all prime foolishness if you ask me," Shelly said.

"Not completely," Simon argued. "Perhaps our modern world has become too indifferent to the nature of evil. The S.S.S. may serve a useful purpose in reminding us."

"If they're not behind the extortion, what do they do?" I wanted to know.

"Battle Satan, but in a most unusual manner. If you're well enough I'll take you to see it tonight."

Shelly would hear none of it. "He's just out of the hospital, Simon! Are you trying to get him killed?"

"Let's see how I feel," I said, trying to mediate the dispute.

There was a surprise waiting for me at home. Rosa Bland had come up from the office, bringing flowers and good wishes from my co-workers. "Thank heaven you're all right!" she said, showing more emotion than I'd ever seen at the office.

"I suppose Skyvos is worried about his twenty-five thousand."

"He thinks the insurance covers it; he has Mr. Muller checking on it."

I glanced at Simon and said, "Rosa, that bomb had to be substituted for the money either at the office before I left or in Rappoport's office just before it went off."

"How could it have happened at our office?"

"Remember I left an envelope with the money inside on the conference room table while I went for my briefcase? That's when the switch could have been made. I returned to the room and you were standing by the window with Vincent Frawley."

"Yes?" Her face wore a puzzled expression, waiting to see what I was getting at.

"Who else came into the room in that minute or so while I was gone?"

"I don't know..."

"Skyvos was there when I left," I said, jogging her memory.

He went back to his office, but I think one or two other people stuck their heads in to see what was happening. The whole office was buzzing with rumors."

"Were you and Vince facing the table all the time?"

"Well, it as only a minute or so, as you say. We looked out the window some, at that big construction crane across the street. I suppose anyone might have switched the envelope without our noticing."

I persisted in the questioning. "Could Vince have done it?"

"Well, I suppose so. But I can't believe he did. Why would anyone do such a thing?"

"For twenty-five thousand dollars."

"That, yes—but why the bomb?"

"I don't know," I admitted. "There was a man called Proctor at Rappoport's office just before the explosion. It's possible he made the switch. He seemed to dislike Rappoport."

Rosa hopped up from her chair, as she often did at the conclusion of editorial meetings. "Well, I must be going. Take care of yourself. We all want you back soon."

"Thanks for coming, Rosa."

After she was gone, Simon said, "An odd little woman. Is she a good editor?"

"She's good with genre fiction. Her books generally show only small profits, but it all adds up."

Shelly tried to get me into bed but I resisted with vigor. My head was feeling better all the time and I was anxious to accompany Simon to the S.S.S. meeting that night. After all those years of being married to me, Shelly knew when it was hopeless. She sulked a bit but finally fixed us a good meal before we started off.

I had no idea where Simon was directing me, and I was surprised when we turned at last into the parking lot of a discount toy store. "This is where Proctor works," Simon explained. "He's the store manager and they meet here after hours."

There were a dozen or so cars there ahead of us, and another followed us in. The back door to the toy store was unlocked. As we entered, a young man in a blue business suit handed us light-weight white cotton robes to put on over our clothes.

"He didn't ask for any sign or password," I whispered to Simon when we had gone by him.

"It is not a secret society, my friend. Not in the strictest sense, at least. They assume anyone who knows about this meeting is a friend and believer."

"But these robes! Are you sure it's not like a Black Mass, with someone dressed like the devil?"

"It is something far worse, I fear."

"What could be worse than a man posing as Satan?" I asked, but Simon Ark did not answer me.

At the front of the store was a little raised platform, apparently for toy demonstrations. The Proctor stood upon it, addressing perhaps fifteen other white-robed figures. "... regret to report that Brother Rappoport has been taken from us. His sin is great, against our Society and against his fellow man. We can only believe that in the end he was in league with

Satan while pretending to oppose him. And he died in a fiery blast, like one of Satan's own."

Another white-robed figure, shorter than the Proctor, had stepped onto the stage. I couldn't see the face beneath the cowl, but a low murmur ran through the assembly. "The George has honored us by taking part in our assembly tonight. Come—step forward and drink the wine of fellowship that we may be united in the suppression of Satan."

A glass goblet three-quarters full of red wine was produced, and the George drank from it in silence. Then the Proctor held it as the others approached. Each in turn took a long drink from it, but the level of the liquid seen through the glass did not seem to diminish. Finally our turn came to approach the platform. The Proctor himself sipped from the cup and then held it out to us. It was still almost filled with wine. Simon and I both drank, and others came after us, but when we returned to our former positions on the floor I could see that the level of the liquid was constant. After everyone had drunk his fill, the George took the goblet and tipped it, allowing the remaining wine to run onto the floor. By the time the goblet was truly empty, a large puddle had collected on the platform.

"Is that some sort of miracle?" I asked Simon in a whisper.

"You asked what was worse than someone posing as Satan, and now I will tell you. It is someone posing as God."

And with those words Simon threw back his cowl and strode forward. The Proctor was just beginning to speak again. "Our campaign against Satan and his works needs your support as never before. I will now pass among you for any donation you may wish to—"

Simon was on the platform with him then, and his uncovered face was like a fury. "Do not listen to him. The Proctor is no saint, nor is the George any sort of god. They oppose Satan by using the devil's own weapons. This person—the George—caused the death of Jacob Rappoport!"

That was when the other figure on the platform moved, pushing the Proctor off balance so he fell against Simon. I saw in a flash what was happening—the George was attempting to escape through the back door. At the same instant I saw the reason for this sudden panic. Lieutenant Graves had appeared at the door of the toy store, just in time to hear Simon's words of accusation.

I had only a moment to act. The George would pass not ten feet from me, on the other side of a high pile of toy boxes. I pushed as hard as I could, and the pile began to topple. The George paused, looked up, and was lost. As the boxes toppled all around him, Simon Ark came at him from the rear while Graves moved in from the front.

"This is your killer," Simon said, yanking the white cowl away to expose the face of their captive.

It was the face of Neptune's controller, Walter Muller.

I was shocked by the unmasking of Muller, but for some strange reason I wanted to know first about the seemingly bottomless goblet of wine. "It was like the loaves and fishes, Simon! How did he do it?"

"A variation on a simple magic trick, my friend. When I saw how easily he gulled these people, I had to expose him. See, here is the goblet. The thick glass conceals a double-walled construction that traps a quantity of the wine within the sides of the glass itself. That wine is what one sees from a distance, distinct from the wine actually held in the goblet and able to be drunk. Each of the spectators drank from the glass itself, and when it was almost empty the Proctor pretended to drink while actually refilling the glass from a tube beneath his cowl. After everyone had drunk, the George removed this concealed wax plug from the opposite lip of the goblet and allowed the wine to run out from within the double-walled glass. I imagine it was one of several so-called miracles he used to impress his followers."

"But what is the S.S.S.? And who are its members?"

"As I told you before, they are sincere—if somewhat misguided—in their aim of suppressing the devil and his works. They are the people who in another location or another era might have joined the Ku Klux Klan or any number of other organizations. There is no need to prosecute them. The Proctor, of course, may be held as an accessory, but somehow I doubt that he had advance knowledge of Muller's plan for the bombing. He would have not risked entering the office at that moment had he known. Rather, he would have been far away concocting an alibi."

"How did you know Proctor didn't switch the envelopes?"

Simon merely smiled. Then he asked, "How would he have known what size to make the bomb?"

"Huh?"

"Bombs, like packages of currency, come in all sizes, my friend. Rappoport never specified the denominations of the currency, and I never told him what we would bring. We might have had an envelope, or a cigar box, or even a bread box to hold that much money. Proctor could not have known, and therefore he could not have made the substitution.

It was done at the Neptune office. But even there, the killer must have had advance knowledge. One does not keep the makings of a bomb in his desk drawer, to tinker with on coffee breaks. The bomb and its detonator had to be already assembled by someone who knew exactly the size and weight and appearance of your package."

"Yes," I said softly. "I see."

"Now could Rosa Bland have had that knowledge in advance? Could Vincent Frawley, or even your president, Baynard Skyvos? No, none of them could have known in advance what denominations of bills you would bring back from the bank, and thus none of them could have known in advance the size of the package. Only Neptune's controller, Walter Muller, could have known—Walter Muller, Muller, who instructed you to obtain the money in hundred-dollar bills, and even suggested putting it in a small manila envelope."

"But why did Rappoport try to extort money from Muller's own company?"

"Perhaps he didn't know Muller worked there. It might have been a bizarre coincidence. But more likely he decided to challenge Muller on his home ground, hoping that Muller would agree to pay the money for the sake of his organization. Certainly the S.S.S. was important to Muller, but his reaction was not what Rappoport had expected."

"What will happen to the organization now, Simon?"

"I would like to think that its members have seen the foolishness of their pursuit. One does not suppress Satan by evil deeds—nor by foolishness."

"We should be getting back," I said. "Shelly will be worried. But one last question—how did Lieutenant Graves find his way here at just the right moment?"

"I may have told him of the meeting," Simon Ark admitted. "There are times when we can all use a little help."

THE WAY UP TO HADES

My wife Shelly has often claimed that I would go anywhere with Simon Ark, and it's true that I've journeyed with him to exotic places like India and Egypt and Brazil. Still, I used to think there was a limit to my patience with Simon. I would not go anywhere he asked, would I?

"It's right here in New York, my friend, at Madison Square Garden."

"Simon, you're asking me to attend a rock concert with you? Have you lost your mind?"

"Rager claims to summon the Devil during his concerts. There is fire on stage."

"Believe me, Simon, it's all part of the act. There are a dozen others just like him, and some a lot better. Why should we waste an evening listening to some punk kid try to burst our eardrums?"

But I went, as Simon must have known I would. The place was jammed with shouting, stomping teenagers. The few older members of the audience like Simon and myself seemed distinctly out of place, and I noticed one youth drop a hand-rolled cigarette to the floor and grind it underfoot when he noticed us. There was a warm-up act of a hard-rock trio and then after a suitable intermission Rager himself took the stage, appearing through the smoke and sparks of a spectacular electrical display. He danced around the stage while thumping on his electric guitar, looking exactly like the life-sized cutout in the lobby. Frequently during his act he hurled balls of fire at the floor of the stage, reminding me of a magician I'd seen in my youth. Perhaps rock stars like Rager were the magicians of a new generation.

The morning paper had told me all I needed to know about Rager. Born in London twenty-two years ago with the rather prosaic name of Roger Jones, he'd changed it to Rager when he broke away from a rock group three years ago and started recording and touring as a single. Sitting there watching him for the better part of an hour while he held the stage alone—his back-up singers and instrumentalists concealed by a curtain—I began to wonder what all the excitement was about. Then, as the act came to a gratifying conclusion, I noticed Simon Ark lean forward in his seat.

Rager dropped his guitar, threw his hands to the heavens, and cried out, *"Satan, take me! If there is a Lord of the Underworld, let me be with you this day in Hades!"*

Then he vanished in a burst of flames and smoke. The kids went wild.

"I hope you're satisfied," I told Simon as we threaded our way toward the exit.

"I would like to go backstage," he told me.

"Simon, I'm sure no one gets backstage except a few nubile groupies."

He insisted, but I was right. We got no farther than a dapper young Englishman at the stage door who announced himself as Rager's personal manager, "Les Fenton's the name. You got any messages for Rager, they go through me."

"I need to speak with the young man personally," Simon Ark persisted.

Fenton looked him over, taking in Simon's black suit and white hair. "What are you—his grandpa or his preacher?"

"Neither one," I interjected, offering my card.

Fenton saw the name NEPTUNE BOOKS and shifted his gaze to me. "A publisher? Want to talk about a book? Rager's autobiography would sell millions of copies."

"He's only twenty-two. Has he had that much of a life?"

"You'd be surprised. Look, there's a reception for Rager tomorrow afternoon at the Millbrook Manor Hotel in Times Square. Come early, about one o'clock, and we can have lunch first."

A young woman in a black leather miniskirt and too much makeup appeared in the corridor behind him. "Les, Rager needs you."

"Be right there." He shook hands with both of us. "One o'clock at the Millbrook Manor."

When we were alone I said to Simon, "I have no intention of publishing Rager's autobiography. We're an old-line quality house."

"You can tell him that later. I'd like very much to meet Mr. Rager and this looks like our best opportunity."

"Simon, he's just a kid trying to shock other kids. All this business about Satan in his act is so much window-dressing."

"We shall see," Simon Ark said.

Millbrook Manor was a hotel chain that had gotten its start in national parks and recreation areas. It kept the name when it expanded into the cities, and even when it built a sixty-story glass and steel luxury hotel with a huge indoor atrium in the heart of Times Square. Neither the name nor the building seemed out of place in a city that sees everything. Somehow it went well with the Marriott Marquis across the street and the two other hotels under construction in the area.

Like the Marriott, the main feature of the atrium was the bank of glass elevators which rose in full view of the lobby, carrying guests to all sixty floors. A few of the elevators even continued on, seemingly through the roof, transporting visitors to the Skytop Restaurant with its magnificent view of the city. That was where the reception for Rager would be held to introduce his latest record album.

"Stay for the reception," Les Fenton urged Simon and me over lunch the following day. "When you see the sort of important people flocking around Rager, I know you'll agree the chap is much more than another fad performer."

We weren't alone at lunch. Fenton had brought along a stunningly dressed young woman named Clare Goddard who handled Rager's publicity. She was American rather than British and spoke with a slight southern accent. I wasn't surprised when she revealed she was from North Carolina. "I've been up here five years, but Rager is the first client who's really excited me. The kids go crazy over him."

"They're interested in doing his book," Fenton told her.

"Wait a minute. I didn't go that far." They were ready to sign a contract before we finished lunch. "Actually, it's my friend Simon here who's really interested in Rager."

"It would be a great book," Clare Goddard insisted, warming to her sales pitch. "And I'm certain he'd help promote it."

"I understand he's quite aloof," Simon said. "Insists on riding alone in his limousine and even in elevators, never waves to fans or signs autographs."

"They love it," Fenton replied. "They love that manner of his."

"At the conclusion of his act, when he calls upon Satan to take him to Hades, has anything unusual ever happened?"

The manager laughed. "What do you expect, some great horned monster to appear and snatch him away? Might not be a bad gimmick, I suppose, but we haven't done it yet."

Clare Goddard tapped Fenton on the arm. "I think Mr. Ark is a believer, Les."

"Hell, no one believes in Satan any more. He's got even less of a following than God. You think Rager'd be doing that act if he really thought
there was a Devil?"

After lunch we all went down to the lobby to meet Rager when he
arrived. Actually we went to the floor below the lobby, where the cars
pulled in off the street. Les Fenton hurried along the bank of elevators,
checking the arrangements for the rock star's arrival, making certain there
were no groupies hidden behind the potted palms. I followed him, noting
there were a dozen elevators in all, arranged around a central core. Down
here in their closed shafts they appeared perfectly ordinary. It was not
until they rose above the lobby level that the glass sides revealed the splen-
dor of the entire atrium with its revolving fountain and full-sized trees.
There was even a small waterfall illuminated by colored lights.

Rager arrived alone in his limousine shortly before two thirty. There
were police officers to keep back the crowd, and we could only watch
from a distance as Fenton and Clare Goddard greeted him. As usual
Rager refused to wave or acknowledge his fans. He said a few words to
Les Fenton and then followed his manager to the elevator marked Skytop
Express. He was wearing the same silver vest with bare arms that had been
his on-stage costume the previous night. Obviously he didn't believe in
more formal dress for promotional appearances.

A teenaged girl broke through the police line and ran up to the elevator, but Fenton waved her away. "No autographs," he said sharply. "Rager
doesn't sign autographs." Then the elevator doors slid shut as a red arrow
pointed upward. Fenton was left waiting for the next car. Even he didn't
get to share an elevator with Rager.

Simon and I took an escalator to the lobby floor directly above and
we were in time to see Rager's glass elevator emerge from below and rise
quickly up the entire height of the sixty-story atrium. He stood away from
the glass with his back to the elevator door and never moved, refusing to
acknowledge the waves from fans clustered in the lobby. "The young man
has some ego," Simon remarked.

"It's all part of the act." As the express elevator disappeared through
the ceiling of the atrium far above our heads we boarded a local with some
hotel guests for the ride to the Skytop Restaurant.

I recognized one of the passengers as the leather-clad young woman
we'd observed in the backstage corridor the previous night. "You're a
friend of Rager's, aren't you?" I asked her.

I introduced myself and Simon Ark. "We're to see Rager about a book idea," I explained, not bothering to tell her the idea was Fenton's rather than mine.

She warmed up a bit as the elevator stopped to discharge the last of the hotel guests at their floor. "I'm Susan Yantz. I met Rager on his first American tour last year, and I've been with him ever since."

Beneath the layers of makeup I could detect the face of a young woman barely out of her teens. She had the voice of a native New Yorker and she still wore the black leather miniskirt or its twin. "Are you from here?" I asked.

"Yeah. It's good to be back for a week. We've been touring all over the world—Australia, even!"

The elevator came to a stop and we got out at the restaurant. The luncheon crowd was gone, replaced by the invited guests for the record launch. But I saw at once that something was wrong. There was no sign of Rager and television crews seemed confused. One cameraman even aimed at us as we emerged from the elevator.

"Where's Rager?" a bald man asked, fighting his way through the crowd to Susan Yantz's side. "Isn't he with you?"

"No, stupid. You know he always rides alone in elevators. He's already up here."

"No, he isn't."

"He came up on the express elevator. I saw him get on it myself. Everyone saw him."

"We were waiting for that elevator. But when the doors opened it was empty, except for one of his fireballs burning a hole in the carpet."

Simon Ark moved then, pushing past me. "Take me to this elevator at once."

I followed along. "We're holding it here until the hotel people can assess the damage," the bald man told us. "I know it's a damn foolish stunt—"

"It may not be a stunt," Simon said.

He opened the elevator door with a key from outside. It was still full of smoke, and a large scorched area was visible just inside the doors where we'd seen Rager standing. "What's that odd smell?" I asked Simon.

His face was very calm, but his words were thunderous. "I suspect it is the odor of brimstone, my friend. Rager has finally had his wish granted. Satan has taken him to Hades."

No one else was ready to accept Simon's assessment of the situation. The bald man, who identified himself as Thomas Robock from the record company, ushered us quickly into a private room. Susan Yantz was left outside. "We don't need that little tramp," he muttered. "There's enough trouble already."

"We were to meet with Rager," I said lamely. "His manager, Les Fenton, was arranging it."

"Where the hell is Fenton?"

"No doubt on his way up from the lobby," Simon said. "Tell me exactly what happened."

"Nothing happened," Thomas Robock said. "We were all waiting here to welcome Rager when he stepped off the elevator. Fenton was holding it downstairs for his arrival. As soon as the light went on showing it was coming up, we got ready. Then the doors slid open and there was no one inside—just one of his damned fireballs."

Simon Ark nodded. "No chance he could have slipped past you, hidden by the smoke?"

"None. The smoke wasn't that thick"

"What about the escape hatch that's in the top of every elevator?"

"This one has hidden bolts that can be worked from inside or outside the car. But they do have to be opened. These were still tightly closed."

"There would have been no time for that anyway," I hastened to point out. "Rager was in full view in that glass elevator all the way up to the sixtieth floor. He was only hidden for the last floor, a matter of a few seconds."

"The people in the lobby couldn't see him, up that high."

"No, but the bank of glass elevators is surrounded by terraces leading to each floor's guest rooms. Any number of guests might have observed him all the way to the sixtieth floor."

There was a knock on the door and Les Fenton entered. "Where is he, Robock? What's happened?"

The recording executive went through his brief story again. "Tell me it's a publicity stunt, Les. Tell me he'll turn up any minute."

"If it's a publicity stunt, it was done without my knowledge. Find Clare Goddard and get her in here. She's in charge of publicity."

She was outside talking with the press, trying to calm them down. She came in shaking her head, looking a bit less cool and collected than when I'd first seen her. "If this is one of Rager's tricks—"

"You mean you don't know where he is?"

"Of course I don't know," she told Fenton. "If I knew, I'd have him out there with the press this minute. He's had his fun with this elevator business. I hope he comes to his senses and reappears."

"There may be no way back from where Rager has gone," Simon Ark said quietly. They all stared at him. "He called upon Satan to take him, you'll remember."

"He did that every night," Les Fenton scoffed. "It was part of the act. The kids love that weird stuff."

"If his disappearance was a trick," I asked, "how was it done?"

"Maybe he was never on the elevator in the first place," Robock said.

Fenton and Clare Goddard were quick to rule that out. "Fifty people saw him board that elevator, including fans and police guards," Fenton said.

"And I saw him rising through the lobby myself," Clare confirmed. "The elevator doesn't go anywhere but up here. It doesn't even make a lobby stop. It's strictly an express for Skytop customers who aren't staying at the hotel."

Robock pondered for a moment. Then he said, "This has gone far enough. I'm calling the police."

A missing persons report in New York City rarely brings out a detective with the rank of lieutenant. But Rager was someone special, and so in a way was Lieutenant Fisk. He was tall, with steel gray hair and a manner that could change from friendly to tenacious in an instant.

"The missing man's name is Roger Jones?" he asked, making careful notes of everything said.

"Rager is his stage name," Les Fenton said. "That's the name everyone knows him by."

"All right. Roger Jones, alias Rager."

"It's not really an alias. The man's not a criminal."

"That remains to be seen," Fisk told them. He glanced over at Simon and me. "Who did you say you were?"

"We came to see Rager about doing a book. I'm the senior editor at Neptune Books, and this is Simon Ark, an author and investigator of unusual phenomena." I made a point of not mentioning Satanism.

The detective glanced at Simon. "You solved this one yet, Pop?"

Simon started to speak, but I cut him short. "We can show you the elevator where it happened."

Lieutenant Fisk took the trouble to get down on his knees and examine the scorched carpeting. He even took an evidence envelope from his pocket and scooped some of the remaining ash into it. When he stood up he said, "This looks like some sort of con game to me. Was Rager into you people for any money?"

"It's no con game," Robock said. "The young man earns better than a million dollars a year with concerts and record albums."

"Is that so?" Fisk opened his notebook again. "I'll want to talk to each of you individually. Let's start with Miss Goddard here."

He led her into a private room while Fenton and Robock went out to confront the waiting guests. I was content to enjoy the Manhattan skyline, but Simon had other ideas. He spotted Susan Yantz, Rager's girlfriend, across the room and headed toward her. I tailed along.

"Any sign of him yet?" Simon asked.

Susan was beginning to look distraught. "I think something bad has happened to him. If it was some sort of stunt he'd have told me in advance."

"It certainly seems he would have told someone," Simon agreed, "either yourself or his manager or his publicity agent or his record producer. Tell me, were there any other women in his life?"

"Not since he met me," she said with the supreme confidence of the young. "He didn't need anyone else."

"Did he have any enemies, anyone who threatened him?"

"Not really. He got into a fight in a bar in Australia—"

"But nothing here, in New York?"

"No."

"Were there ever any unexplained mystical experiences, especially after his nightly shows when he issued his challenge to the Devil?"

Susan Yantz shook her head. "You're taking that whole Devil thing too seriously. Lots of performers do something like that for a big closing. You know, with lightning bolts and all the—"

She was was cut short in mid-sentence by the sudden appearance of Lieutenant Fisk. He burst from the private room and dashed toward the elevators, with Clare Goddard trailing behind. "What is it?" I asked her.

"Something's happened downstairs. He just got a call."

We started toward an open elevator, but Fisk chose the one from which Rager had vanished. "The express is faster," he told us, jabbing his finger at the bottom button.

Simon and Clare and I managed to crowd in with him before the door closed, but Susan was left behind. "Has Rager reappeared?" Simon asked.

"Maybe," Fisk told him. "There's a fire on the lower level, in the parking garage."

The elevator deposited us in the garage itself, below the street level, and we saw at once that the fire had been confined to a service area close to the ramp. A line of several Dumpsters collected each day's rubbish from the hotel and were in turn emptied by daily service from a private contractor. Two fire hoses led down the ramp from the street, and the firemen had made short work of the blaze in one of the Dumpsters. Now only a pall of smoke hung in the air.

I was still wondering about the detective's hurried trip down here when I saw him approach the fire chief. "Lieutenant Fisk, I was upstairs on a related investigation when the precinct relayed your call to me."

"Here's what we got, lieutenant. A body in the Dumpster. Pretty badly burned, but it looks like a young Caucasian male."

"Oh my God!" Clare Goddard gasped at my side. I steadied her with my hand.

A fireman produced a short ladder, and Fisk climbed up to take a look. "We'll want someone to identify him, if possible." He glanced across the garage and saw Fenton and Robock coming from the elevators, with Susan close behind.

"We heard there was a body," Robock began.

"Which one of you can identify him?"

Les Fenton stepped forward, running a tongue over his dry lips. "I can."

He climbed up on the ladder, took one look and started to retch. "I—I think so. He's so badly burned I can't be sure."

"It's Rager?" Susan asked.

"I think so," Fenton repeated. She let out a low scream that grew in volume. Clare hurried to her side and led her away.

"What do you think now, Simon?" I asked.

"It would seem that Satan gave him a very brief view of Hades, and then tossed him back with the rest of the rubbish."

It was late in the afternoon, nearly six o'clock, before Lieutenant Fisk got around to questioning Simon and me. "I'm sorry you had to wait so long, but I've been busy following up leads," he told us. The hotel had reclaimed its Skytop Restaurant and the questioning sessions had been transfered to a small meeting room on the third floor. Now, however, the Millbrook Manor seemed to be swarming with uniformed police and detectives. Fisk was no longer alone.

"Has the body been positively identified?" Simon asked.

"It's Rager, all right. We haven't completed the fingerprint and dental checks, but Thomas Robock has also identified him, in addition to Fenton. And Susan Yantz has described a small strawberry birthmark on the back of his neck that matches one on the body. If she's feeling better tomorrow, she'll view the body, too."

Fisk's attitude seemed to have changed completely from the earlier session. What he'd viewed as a publicity stunt had turned into a particularly ugly death. Now he was even willing to admit he knew who Rager was. "With rock stars," he went on, "the first thought is always that the death could be drug-related in some way. Maybe he was high and set himself on fire. Maybe he had a fight with a dealer over money. We're looking into everything."

"At the close of his act he called upon Satan to take him to Hades," Simon pointed out.

"Yeah, well, that's more in your line than mine, Mr. Ark. There's no way I can hang this on Satan, so I'm looking for a more down-to-earth explanation."

"Have you looked into those fireballs of his?" I asked.

"Yeah. His manager says they're purchased from a magicians' supply house. It's a fast-burning sulfur compound, though Rager was always fooling around with variations for his act. The idea is, it burns fast and goes out quickly, before there's any danger of the fire spreading."

"One of them could have ignited in his pocket, though," I said.

"After he conveniently climbed into that Dumpster?"

Simon Ark stirred restlessly. "You two are concentrating on the death of Rager rather than his disappearance from that elevator. The disappearance is the key to the case. If he was not transported to Hades, what did happen to him?"

The detective turned back to me. He seemed uncomfortable conversing with Simon. "You're a publisher or editor, or whatever. Are there any books about disappearances from elevators?"

"Not that come to mind. Certainly there have been murders in elevators. *Fatal Descent* by John Rhode and Carter Dickson is one such novel, and James Yaffe's first short story, "Department of Impossible Crimes," is another example. Both use entirely different solutions. Ronald Dahl's "The Way Up to Heaven" does not have an impossible crime, but in a sense it too is about a murder in an elevator. Cornell Woolrich's "After Dinner Story" has a murder among several people trapped in an elevator at the bottom of the shaft. Unfortunately none of these fictional situations applies to the present circumstances."

Lieutenant Fisk shook his head. "A man is seen by several witnesses to enter a glass elevator which takes him up sixty floors and makes no stops on the way. He is observed inside the elevator. Yet when it reaches its destination he has vanished, replaced by a ball of fire. Can such things be, or is everyone in this case lying?"

"The ways of the Devil—" Simon began, but Fisk immediately interrupted.

"Let's rule out the Devil as a suspect for the moment. He's beyond my jurisdiction. Any idea why someone might want to kill Rager, assuming it wasn't drug-related?"

"None," I said. "But then we never even got to meet the man."

"We don't really know Rager, do we?" Fisk fretted. "Maybe if we knew him better this whole thing wouldn't be so much of a mystery."

He was finished with us, but as we were about to leave, Thomas Robock came into the room unannounced. "I have to speak with you, lieutenant. It's about Rager."

Fisk motioned the bald man to a chair. Robock barely glanced in our direction, and since Fisk didn't order us out I could see Simon was intent on remaining. "All right, what is it?" the detective asked.

"There's a great deal of money involved here. I made contract payments to Rager last week, advances on his next album. I believe I may have been swindled."

"How could Rager swindle you if he's dead?"

"That's just the point. Are you certain that body is his?"

"Reasonably certain. His dental records are in England, but Fenton identified him and so did you."

"I wasn't that sure. The face was badly burned."

"The clothing seemed to be his, what was left of it. He had a birthmark in the right place on his neck. Physically the body was the right size."

"The clothing could have been switched. And you could find someone that age and size any time of the day right over on 42nd Street."

"Let me get this straight, Mr. Robock. You believe Rager faked his own death as part of a plot to swindle you out of some money?"

"It wouldn't be the first time such a thing has happened."

Simon Ark spoke up from the sidelines. "Mr. Robock, does your company carry an insurance policy on the lives of your recording artists?"

"What? Well, yes, on some of the biggest stars. Quite often our projections of sales are based upon the star's continuing to perform and promote the album. Not everyone is Elvis Presley or the Beatles. If they die or stop performing, they can be quickly forgotten by today's kids."

"Did you insure Rager's life?"

"I think so, yes."

"For how much?"

"A million dollars," he said quietly.

"So Rager was worth more to you dead than alive?"

"Hardly. His records had a potential for making five times that much. If I was after the insurance money, would I be sitting here trying to convince you Rager might be still alive?"

"We'll know soon enough whether it's him or not," Fisk promised. "His fingerprints are on file, and Susan Yantz is going to view the body in the morning."

The disappearance and apparent murder of Rager was all over the TV news that night, and was still good for front-page headlines in the following morning's papers. Shelly knew of Simon's interest in the case, but she didn't ask me too many questions. Perhaps she thought by not talking about it the whole thing—and Simon Ark—would simply go away.

"Will you be home for dinner tonight?" she asked as I was leaving.

"I hope so. Earlier than last night, at least. I'll call you later."

I had arranged to meet Simon at police headquarters, where Lieutenant Fisk planned to bring Susan Yantz after she'd viewed the body. Simon said very little while we waited, but as soon as we saw Susan I knew the results. She was red-eyed from crying and Fisk had his arm around her shoulders.

"It's him," she said, replying to our unspoken question.

"Come into my office," Fisk told us.

"What about the fingerprints?" I asked him.

"They match. There's no doubt."

Simon had another question. "I saw you take samples of the ash on the elevator floor yesterday. What was it?"

"No bones or anything spectacular, Mr. Ark. Just cardboard. Probably the container for the fireball."

Simon leaned forward in his chair toward Susan Yantz, so close that I think he frightened her. "I have just one further question. This one is for you, Miss Yantz. What vest was Rager wearing when he disappeared?"

She blinked, looking surprised. Whatever question she'd been expecting, this wasn't it. "Why, his silver one. I remember being surprised when he was dressing for the reception because he'd worn the same outfit on stage the night before."

"He had many different costumes?"

"Certainly. He usually wore the tight black pants, but the vests were always different. He traveled with a dozen or more."

"I suspected as much," Simon said with a gentle nod.

"What has his jacket got to do with any of this?" Fisk demanded.

"Oh, the jacket has everything to do with it. Now I know how Rager vanished from that elevator. Unfortunately, it doesn't tell me who killed him."

In typical fashion, Simon refused to give us an explanation, saying only that he could not reveal anything until we had the murderer in hand. Susan Yantz sat through it all with wide eyes, finally bursting out with, "Point him out to me and give me a gun, and I'll save you the trouble of a trial. Anyone who could burn Rager like that—"

"He was killed before he was burned," Fisk told her. "The autopsy shows he was strangled."

"Has the Devil ever been known to strangle people?" I asked Simon.

"Once I solved the elevator mystery, it was clear Satan was no longer involved. However that doesn't get us any closer to the actual murderer."

"There's a lot of pressure on us to wrap this one up quick," Fisk admitted. "I'll take any help I can get."

"Then let us have a reenactment of the crime," Simon decided. "Perhaps we'll see something we didn't notice the first time."

Lieutenant Fisk reluctantly agreed to the scheme and the principal actors from the previous day were again assembled. There were only four—Susan Yantz, Les Fenton, Thomas Robock and Clare Goddard—and when we were assembled on the ground floor of the hotel, near the bank of elevators, Simon explained his reasoning for this.

"I am about to demonstrate, with Lieutenant Fisk's kind permission, how it was possible for Rager to vanish from a glass elevator between here and the Skytop Restaurant when the elevator makes no stops on the way. It could only have been done with his cooperation, whether the original idea was his or someone else's. That is my first point. My second point is that the killer had to know of the plan in advance so he would know where to find Rager and murder him. As was pointed out earlier, you four are the only people in this city he is likely to have told. His girlfriend and traveling companion, his business manager, his publicity director, and the record magnate who was sponsoring the reception he was supposed to attend. He would not have carried out his intended stunt without telling at least one of you."

"He never said a word to me," Les Fenton said, and the others joined in agreement.

"I want each of you to take up the position you were in at the time Rager entered the elevator," Simon instructed.

"I was upstairs waiting for the elevator," Robock said

"Then go up there—but take a different elevator, not the express one."

Lieutenant Fisk was watching it all from the sidelines with two of his officers. He seemed willing to give Simon as much leeway as he needed. "Go up there with Robock," he told one of the officers, "I want you there when the elevator arrives. Call me on the house phone and tell me what's happening."

"I was with him at the elevator," Fenton said. "Where do I stand? Who's playing the part of Rager?"

Simon Ark stepped forward, "I am."

The idea of Simon's standing in for a twenty-two-year-old rock singer seemed ludicrous to me, but no one laughed. Fenton went to his side, ready to accompany him to the elevator, Susan Yantz announced that she had taken a separate cab to the hotel because of Rager's quirk of riding alone, and hadn't quite arrived when Rager boarded his elevator. "Remember?" she reminded Simon and me. "I rode up on the elevator with you."

"That's right," I confirmed.

"I was with Les and Rager," Clare Goddard said. "We'd come down after lunch to meet him. After Rager went up alone, Les and I followed."

"Together?" Simon asked.

"No. I believe Les went up first, right after Rager. He had to use a local, of course. They held the elevator up there when Rager wasn't on it."

"All right." Simon pressed the express button. "I will board the elevator. Each of you should behave exactly as you did yesterday, but I want someone to accompany you." I got the job of riding up with Fenton, while the other officer went up with Clare. Fisk would remain with Susan Yantz.

The express elevator arrived and Simon stepped into its interior alone, giving a little bow like a stage magician entering a magic cabinet. He pressed a button and the doors slid shut, the lighted arrow pointing up.

The house phone rang almost at once and Fisk took the receiver from its wall compartment. "Yes, Mr. Robock. He's just started up. He should be there soon. I'll hang on." He glanced over at me and smiled indulgently. No one really expected Simon Ark to vanish as Rager had done.

The time seemed to drag by. A minute, two minutes. How long did it take an elevator to travel up sixty stories?

"Yes," Fisk said into the phone. "It's arrived? What? What are you saying? Where's Simon Ark?"

I shouldn't have been surprised but somehow I was. Damned if he hadn't pulled it off, just like Rager.

Fisk and the others stood there dumbfounded, not knowing what to do next. Then from behind us came a familiar voice. "Are you satisfied now?" It was Simon Ark.

"All right," Fisk said. "How'd you do it? The elevator makes no stops between here and the Skytop Restaurant, not even in the lobby. You got on here—we all saw you—but the elevator was empty when it arrived. How?"

"Rager's method can be explained in three simple words. All the rest is mere window-dressing."

"Three words? Where did he go if he didn't go up?"

"He went down," Simon Ark said simply. "Isn't that right, Mr. Fenton?"

Les Fenton would have made a terrible poker player. I knew Simon was bluffing, and he should have known it, too. But I'm not one to judge the pressures of a murderer's conscience. Simon's words broke him down completely, and Fisk was reading him his rights as he got out the hand-cuffs. Then it was time for Simon's explanation.

"It's true that the express elevator only goes to one place, the Skytop Restaurant, when it's going up. But it also goes to the parking garage on the floor below this. How do I know? Because we took it with Lieutenant Fisk when he was notified of the fire. Remember him saying, 'The express is faster,' as he jabbed the button?"

I shook my head in disagreement. "It won't wash, Simon. The lit arrow above the elevator doors was pointing up."

"Fenton could have fixed that with a ladder and a screwdriver, which I imagine is what he did. He came here to the hotel several hours early, probably dressed as a workman. He unscrewed the face plate from those indicator lights and rewired them so the up arrow came on whether the elevator was going up or down. It was probably Rager's idea, but he needed Fenton to carry out the details."

"No one noticed it?"

"Why would they? The elevator still arrived sooner or later. I'll admit I checked my theory earlier this morning, before meeting you at police headquarters. It was simple enough for me to duplicate the trick, cover-ing the buttons with my hand so you couldn't really be sure which one I pushed. I got out of the elevator in the garage and then sent it back upstairs empty, adding only about ten seconds to its trip. Then I took the stairs up to surprise you."

"You're forgetting one thing," I reminded him. "You and I were in the lobby. We actually saw Rager going up inside that glass elevator."

"Consider the timing, my friend. We watched the elevator doors close on Rager and then took the escalator up to the lobby. His elevator was just coming into view. Certainly an elevator travels much faster than an escala-tor. That should have told us the elevator had been delayed somehow for several seconds. Rager left the elevator at the garage level and replaced himself with—"

"With what?" Fisk asked.

"—with a lifesized cardboard cutout of himself like the ones in the lobby of Madison Square Garden."

"He was holding a guitar in those," I objected.

"The part over his body could be easily covered with black paper or painted out. Both ends of the guitar could be cut away, leaving a color duplicate of Rager alone. He probably hid it under a car parked by the

elevator, pulled it out, stood it up in the glass elevator, near the door so
its two-dimensional flatness wouldn't be visible from the lobby, and sent
it on its way. He'd coated the back with the fast-burning sulfur compound
used in his fireballs. The sulfur was the brimstone odor in the air. A short
fuse on the back ignited the cardboard just as it passed from view, and
when the doors opened at the Skytop Restaurant only the last of the cardboard was still burning. Again, a test run in the elevator would have told
Rager—or Fenton—how long a fuse was needed. They may have tested the
burning time of the cardboard as well."

"When did Fenton kill him?' the detective asked.

"Right after he left the elevator, I imagine. Fenton hurried downstairs,
strangled him in the garage, and hid his body in the Dumpster with
another fuse that would start the fire later. Once I established what had
happened, I pretty much ruled out the two women. The killer had to
strangle his victim, a twenty-two-year-old man in good health, carry his
body across the garage to the Dumpster, and then hoist it over the edge.
Certainly a woman could have done it, but a man seemed far more likely.
Robock was upstairs all the time, from the discovery of the empty elevator
to the discovery of the body. That left Fenton as the most likely killer, the
only one among the suspects with the physical means and the opportunity. It was guesswork, of course, but it paid off."

Lieutenant Fisk said, "Lucky for you he seems to have cracked. Once
you confronted him he just went to pieces."

"I think you'll discover the motive lies in the financial manipula-
tion of Rager's various assets. Robock mentioned advance payments
to Rager, but I think you'll find the payments were actually made to
Les Fenton as Rager's business manager. He may have felt Rager had
to die before he and Robock got together and compared notes on the
transactions."

"What about Rager's jacket?" I asked. "Why was that so important?"

"At the performance the other night we noticed he looked just like the
lifesized cutout in the lobby, meaning he was wearing the same costume.
Susan told us it was unusual for him to wear that silver vest two days in a
row. Why did he wear it yesterday? Because he needed to be dressed like
the cutout again, to make the disappearance work. I suppose it was meant
as a publicity stunt, but Fenton turned it to his own ends."

We went away from there then, and Simon and I walked for a time among the crowds in Times Square. "The Devil didn't take Rager after all," I said at one point.

But Simon wasn't ready to admit that. "Perhaps he did, my friend. Perhaps he only works in devious ways. Perhaps he has taken both Rager and Les Fenton. It's something we shall never know."

THE VIRGINS OF VALENTINE

The town of Valentine is nestled in the hills of northern Pennsylvania not far from the New York State line, about a four-hour drive from Manhattan. I know because I drove Simon Ark there on a blustery February weekend during the worst winter the East Coast had experienced in a decade.

"Is this trip really necessary, Simon?" I asked as I edged the car around a lumbering snowplow from the state Department of Transportation.

He sat beside me in the front seat, staring out at the snow. "It seems to be letting up," he decided, no doubt trying to raise my spirits.

I had to admit that the snowfall had lessened as we moved away from the coast, but I still wondered how I'd allowed myself to be talked into this expedition in the first place. My wife, Shelly, who never harbored any great warmth for Simon, had denounced it as sheer foolishness—driving over two hundred miles in a snowstorm to visit a graveyard in a Pennsylvania town no one had ever heard of.

Somehow, as Simon Ark's voice droned on, he made the journey seem both necessary and desirable. "My friend, we will not see such a conjunction of lunar and calendar events again for decades. Tonight is Friday the thirteenth, the first night of the full moon, and the eve of St. Valentine's Day."

"So we have to go to a cemetery in Valentine, Pennsylvania?"

"The only other towns named Valentine are in Nebraska and Texas, both too far south for a proper positioning of the full moon at midnight."

For as long as I'd known him, Simon Ark had been engaged in a tireless quest for Satan, seeking him on the voodoo beaches of Rio and in the burial pits of Bombay. Simon claimed to have been a Coptic priest in Egypt nearly two thousand years ago, and who was I to argue with him? Whatever he was, he knew a great deal about Satanism, witchcraft, and allied subjects. A decade ago my firm had even published a book by him which attracted a moderate degree of attention. Over the years Simon often called upon me to serve as his companion during periodic investigations into the strange—and occasionally Satanic—events in the world around us. It was a role I accepted with mixed feelings, though I had to admit the company of Simon Ark was rarely dull.

By the time we passed through Scranton, heading northwest on Route 6, the snow had stopped. And when we reached the little town of Valentine in midafternoon, there were actually a few bare spots of grass showing through the mantle of white. The temperature was into the low thirties and some sun had broken through the clouds.

"You made our reservations?" Simon asked.

"At the Village Inn. There's not much choice in a town this size."

The Village Inn was a quaint little place on Main Street, freshly painted in an obvious effort at restoration. A sign in the shape of a large red heart was tacked to a pillar by the front steps, announcing in big black letters: *Welcome to Valentine! We'll Steal Your Heart Away!* Simon merely grunted at that as I helped him up the icy steps and into the lobby.

A fresh-faced young woman, short and small-boned, appeared from somewhere to greet us, wearing jeans and an old shirt. "You must be Mr. Ark and Mr.—"

"That's right," I confirmed. "From New York."

"Have you come for our Valentine's Day celebration?"

"More or less."

She smiled and gave us registration cards to sign. "I'm Kate Summers. We have a nice room reserved for you on the second floor, with double beds. It gets lots of morning sunshine."

"I'm sure it'll be satisfactory."

"You'll be with us two nights?"

"We expect so, yes."

She took out a fancy lighter and cigarettes and lit one as she studied our cards. "Come, I'll show you the room."

It was as homey as I'd expected, with bright flowery spreads on both beds. The big bay window looked out onto Main Street and I could see my car at the curb. "Do you have parking for guests?"

"It's around back. Turn right at the next corner and you'll see the driveway."

Simon Ark was testing out the bed nearest the window. "Tell me, Miss Summers—"

"It's Mrs. Summers. My husband Herb runs the place with me. You'll see him at dinner. We start serving at five."

"Which way is it to the Methodist church and the cemetery?"

"Oh, I'm afraid the church is closed now. The minister only comes through once a month to conduct services here, on the last Sunday. Most people drive into Sayre where they have Catholic and Baptist churches."

"We were only interested in the cemetery," Simon explained.

"Oh! Well, you drive straight out Main and it's on your left, about a mile. But I certainly never noticed anything special about that old place."

I cleared my throat. "We do tombstone rubbings sometimes."

"You'd better not go out there tonight. The place'll be full of teenage girls."

"What?"

"Here in Valentine we follow all the old customs," she explained. "Girls used to believe that they would eventually marry the first eligible male they saw on Valentine's Day. In England two hundred years ago it was customary for the braver girls to go to the local graveyard at midnight on St. Valentine's Eve. They would sing a prescribed chant and run around the church twelve times. Each girl was supposed to conjure up the appearance of her future spouse. Here in Valentine the boys don't leave anything to chance. They usually drive out to the cemetery themselves and manage to put in an appearance at the magical moment. Then everyone goes off to a party."

"That's quite a beginning for Valentine's Day," Simon admitted. "What happens tomorrow?"

"We have a little parade and the general store has a sale. The post office is kept busy, of course. Everyone wants a letter or card postmarked from Valentine on February fourteenth."

"It doesn't bother the girls that it'll still be Friday the thirteenth when they arrive at the cemetery?" I asked.

"Goodness, no! We're not superstitious here."

After she went back downstairs I started to unpack my overnight duffel. "I doubt if you'll have any success encountering Satan in a graveyard full of screaming teenage girls," I told Simon.

"Stranger things have happened, my friend. Virgins are often used at black masses where the devil is said to preside."

"We'll see."

Kate's husband Herb Summers helped serve dinner in the Village Inn's small dining room. He was a handsome, soft-spoken man around thirty, and it was obvious he was quite content to let his wife take charge of running the inn.

"I'm just the handyman around here," he explained with a pleasant smile. "It's all Kate's place. She inherited it from her dad. I always imagined I'd be a farmer and here I end up as an innkeeper." He glanced around at the empty tables and added, "Not much of one, though, at least in the winter."

"Doesn't anyone else come for your Valentine festival?" I asked.

"A few people drive in for the day, but we don't get many staying overnight."

We finished our dinner and went for a walk around the town. There were stores and a movie theater, though upon closer examination this proved to be shut down. A few bars dotted the center of town, and there was a small bank with a lawyer's office upstairs. Near the edge of the retail area was a farm implement dealer, and farther out in the growing darkness we could just make out the steeple of the Methodist church.

"Do you want to take a ride out there now," I asked Simon, "while there's still a little light?"

"That's a good idea."

It was after six by that time, and practically night, but we went anyway. I parked in front of the church, close to the graveyard, and we managed to avoid some of the deeper snowdrifts to walk where the ground was almost bare. We studied some of the tombstones.

"These inscriptions are all pretty old," I observed. "I wonder if the place is still used."

"It doesn't matter for our purposes."

"Suppose you tell me just what our purposes are, Simon. What do you think is going to happen here at the conjunction of the full moon, Friday the thirteenth and Valentine's Day?"

"It may be that Satan will walk, as on Hallowe'en when that day precedes the feast of All Saints. If he is to appear anywhere, the graveyard in a town named Valentine seems the most likely place."

"Some doubt St. Valentine ever existed. It's merely a legend, Simon."

"These days some doubt that Satan ever existed, but it does not prevent the evil done in his name. If I were to see him now, striding toward us between the gravestones—"

"Simon! What's that?"

There was indeed someone out there in the night, outlined against the snow, moving toward us. A man dressed in black, wearing a full-length cape that showed flashes of a red lining as he drew near. A man who,

God help us, even had a devilish little beard coming to a point beneath his chin.

"Stop there!" Simon Ark called out. "Who are you?"

"I might ask the same of you," the man answered, coming a bit nearer. "I'm Oliver Martin. I live in the next house down. I was out walking my dog when I saw someone in here." As if on cue, a large golden retriever bounded over a snowbank to join him.

"My name is Simon Ark and this is my friend. We're traveling through and decided to spend the night at the Village Inn. Valentine seemed a likely place in view of the date."

"Sightseers, are you? Not many sights to see in a cemetery at night. Come, Rex, we're going home." He turned without another word and returned the way he had come, the dog following at his feet.

"Not very friendly," I observed, "but then I don't suppose the devil has a sense of humor."

"Appearances can be deceptive, my friend."

"I suppose you're right. Satan would have had a black cat, not a golden retriever."

"There is nothing more to be seen here. Let us return to the inn until it is close to midnight."

"You're really serious about this whole thing, aren't you, Simon?"

"I am indeed. We will be back at midnight."

We spent some time browsing in the Valentine general store until it closed at nine. It was more of a modern supermarket than a traditional general store, and scores of hearts dangled from the ceiling to announce the Valentine Sale. I bought a couple of magazines to read and Simon purchased a box of dog biscuits.

"Are you that hungry so soon after dinner?" I chided.

"They might prove useful."

We stopped in one of the bars along Main Street for a beer, sitting at a little table while a few men argued over the merits of some hockey players on the television screen.

"You think Oliver Martin will return at midnight?" I asked Simon. "Is that what the dog biscuits are for?"

"We'll see. I had imagined we would have the cemetery to ourselves at that hour, but if we must have virginal chanting and running about, who knows what else might turn up?"

The temperature had dropped back below freezing and the night chill prompted a return to our room at the inn for warm sweaters to wear under our coats. Kate Summers was not in sight, but Herb was behind the desk in the lobby. Simon struck up a conversation with him, the motive of which quickly became obvious. "We were out by the graveyard and we met a man named Oliver Martin, walking his dog."

"Martin is something of a town character," Herb Summers explained. "He does have a sinister air about him. Some people think he looks like the devil, but he's harmless enough. He worked for a big electronics company up in Syracuse, but he moved down here with his wife a couple of years ago. They've been active in the town affairs, and in fact Amy Martin is the one who revived the custom of girls going to the graveyard on Valentine's Eve to conjure up visions of their future husbands."

"Is that so? It seems a harmless enough custom," Simon remarked.

"Keeps the kids off the streets. The boys usually drive out there too, and take the girls off to a party afterwards. Chaperoned, of course."

"By the Martins?"

"Yeah, how'd you know?"

"It seemed likely," Simon Ark replied.

We drove out to the graveyard at the Methodist church around eleven-thirty. Simon was quiet most of the way, but as we approached I could see a number of girls arriving, bundled in parkas and ski jackets, many with scarves wrapped around their heads and faces against the February cold. "There will be twelve of them," Simon said quietly. "Twelve virgins. The traditional number of witches in a coven."

"You're really convinced that Oliver Martin is the devil? After meeting the man for all of two minutes, Simon?" But even as I spoke I saw Oliver Martin approaching down the road, accompanied now by a tall handsome woman wearing an expensive white mink coat. The retriever trailed at their heels.

We got out of the car and approached them. Martin scowled in our direction and said, "You two back again? What are you, big-city reporters?" The promised full moon glowed behind him in the eastern sky.

I introduced myself and passed him my card. "A publisher, actually. But we're only driving through. What's going on here?"

"My wife will tell you. It's her project. Come, Rex!" He hurried along the road, leaving Amy Martin to make excuses for him. I suspected it wasn't the first time.

"He'll be back," she told us. "He just wants to exercise Rex. His bark is worse than his bite."

"Rex's, or your husband's?" I asked.

"Both of them," she answered with a smile.

Simon gestured to the cemetery, where more girls were arriving. "I understand this is an annual tradition."

Amy Martin laughed. "Only for the past two years. It's an old English custom, and I thought it went well with the town's attempts to revive the traditions of Valentine's Day. The teenagers love it."

"Just what do they do?"

"I wrote a little chant for them to sing, and then they're supposed to run around the church twelve times and see a vision of their future husbands. The boys arrive about that time to make sure the visions are of flesh and blood. Come along and watch."

I could see a few other townsfolk pulled up along the side of the road as midnight approached, but the cold night air kept most of them in their cars. I assumed they were the parents of some of the girls. A few cars had their headlights on, but much of the cemetery and churchyard was in darkness. Just before midnight Oliver Martin returned with his dog and wandered around to the side of the church where his wife was passing out song sheets.

I did a quick count and told Simon, "Only eleven virgins. You were off by one."

Exactly at midnight the chanting began with a musical but slightly off-key rendering calling upon St. Valentine to lift the veil from the future and reveal the girls' true loves. A car pulled up by the church and two tardy virgins jumped out, running bareheaded across the snow to join the others. "Now it's thirteen," I chided Simon. "You're still off by one."

"Twelve times around the church," Amy Martin announced in a loud voice as the chanting ended, "and then you will see your future love!"

The girls set off, more at a trot than a run, conserving their energy. Oliver Martin stood in their path, counting off the laps as they passed him. Suddenly I realized we were not the only spectators who'd left our car to brave the cold. Herb Summers from the Village Inn had joined us with a tall, beefy man wearing a wide mustache. "Mr. Ark, this here's Sheriff Aikens. He keeps things lawful in Valentine."

The sheriff shook hands with us. "Always happy to see tourists in for Valentine's Day. You be staying for the parade tomorrow?"

"We hope to," I said. I heard Martin call off the third lap.

"I suppose this seems silly to people from New York—"

"No, no," Simon assured him. "It is in rural America that the folk customs of an earlier period are preserved. Some say Valentine's Day is the date on which birds mate. It is a pleasant holiday, given over to love and romantic notions."

Summers drifted away but Sheriff Aikens stayed to chat. "I been telling folks for years that we should do more to cash in on the name of Valentine. Before the Martins moved here we didn't do anything, except for the special postmark. Now we've got this thing for the kids and the parade and sale tomorrow. That usually brings them in from the surrounding towns. Hell, if Punxsutawney can become famous every Groundhog's Day, I guess we should be able to do the same on Valentine's Day!"

Oliver Martin was already up to lap number seven and the girls were still running through the night. To me it looked more like an exercise class than a Valentine's Day ritual. But presently I saw the lights of two more cars arriving down the line, and several teenage boys piled out of each. I had to admit the thing was being well orchestrated.

"Lap number ten!" Martin called out as the girls ran by in a group, a few stragglers trailing some feet behind.

The boys were creeping along the road, staying behind the parked car so they'd come into view just as the girls finished their laps. Sheriff Aikens left us, saying, "I'd better keep those kids in line."

As the bevy of teenagers rounded the Methodist church for the last time, they converged on Oliver Martin. He held up his hands, signaling the end of the event. At my side Simon started forward, disturbed by something I couldn't see. "That fiend!" he muttered.

"Do you still believe he's the devil, Simon?"

"Don't you see what he's done? Don't you realize—?"

One of the girls screamed, and the tight little circle around Martin suddenly parted. There was another scream, and another, and then blind panic. The boys had run forward on cue, but no one was paying the least attention to them. All eyes were on Oliver Martin, who'd toppled over onto the snow-covered ground. His black cape had fallen open and as we hurried forward I could see the knife protruding from his chest.

Sheriff Aikens was no small-town bumpkin, and I had to admire the manner in which he immediately took charge. The state police were notified, an ambulance was summoned from the volunteer fire department, and he started taking down the names of everyone who was on the scene. "We don't get many murders here in Valentine," he told us as he copied down our names and addresses. "I guess this'll put us on the front pages if nothing else will."

Amy Martin had remained remarkably composed during the moments after her husband's death, but now I noticed her in tears as some of the other women led her away. The golden retriever, Rex, was forgotten for the moment, and Simon Ark found a use for the pocket full of dog biscuits he'd brought along.

Most of the girls were near hysteria in the moments after the killing, and there was only one to whom the sheriff could speak. She was a bit taller and older than the rest, an eighteen-year-old named Laurie Enright. She wore a red down ski jacket and earmuffs, and was pretty enough to have modeled the garments in a magazine ad. "I don't know what happened," she told the sheriff while Simon and I stood nearby. "We ran up to Mr. Martin, just as we did last year, and crowded around him. All of a sudden he gasped and his body seemed to stiffen. One of the girls screamed and I felt him falling over, right on top of me."

"Did you see the knife then?"

"Not till he was on the ground. Then everyone was screaming."

"Who would want to kill Mr. Martin?" the sheriff asked.

"I don't know."

"Did any of the girls ever talk about him?"

"Not really. Jennifer thought he was really sinister, but that was about all."

"Jennifer?"

"Jennifer MacDonald, over there."

"Oh, yes," the sheriff agreed. "I know her."

But Jennifer was in no state to be questioned at the moment, and Sheriff Aikens wisely arranged for her mother to bring her to his office first thing in the morning. Then he turned his attention to Simon and me.

"You fellows are the only strangers here. I got to consider you as suspects."

"We were twenty feet away when he was stabbed," I pointed out. "How could either of us have done it?"

"The knife could have been thrown just as the girls crowded in around Martin. The pressure of their bodies would have kept him upright for a few seconds. In the darkness no one would have noticed."

"There was enough moonlight to see that," I argued.

"Well, you're planning to stay around tomorrow anyway, aren't you? Come down to my office in the morning and we can talk about it. I'll need statements from everyone here, and I'm not going to get anywhere with these hysterical girls tonight."

The Valentine celebration had turned to horror, and as Simon and I returned to our car we could still see groups of girls comforting one another as anxious parents attempted to locate their daughters. The ambulance had arrived and so had the state police, and photographs of the body were taken before it was covered and moved away. The quiet graveyard seemed alive with flashing red lights and the crackle of police radios. I saw Herb Summers grab hold of Rex's collar and lead him down the road toward the Martin house.

"I guess he wasn't the devil after all," I told Simon as we drove away. "Only a mortal human like the rest of us."

"But perhaps one who engaged in devilish pursuits."

"Why do you say that? And what was it that so upset you the instant before he was killed?"

"Didn't you realize what you were seeing, my friend? After circling the church twelve times, the virgins were supposed to have a vision of their lover, their future mate. Yet they all flocked around Oliver Martin. He was the first male any of these impressionable young girls saw after their chanting and running. And don't you think Martin arranged it that way?"

"You make him sound like a Svengali with some sort of harem, Simon. I think you're letting your imagination run wild."

"We shall see, my friend. If one of those girls stabbed him, she must have had a reason."

We were up in the morning after only five hours' sleep, awakened by a loudspeaker in front of the general store playing "My Funny Valentine" and other suitable love songs. Obviously the celebration was progressing in spite of the murder. Simon and I had the dining room all to ourselves for breakfast, served with a preoccupied frown by Kate Summers.

"Herb told me what happened last night," she said. "It's all over town this morning. God, I can't believe it!"

"The sheriff wants a statement from us," I told her. "We're on our way over there now."

"You know, just about midnight I looked out the back window here and saw that full moon, and I knew something awful was going to happen. It was a premonition."

"Did you know Oliver Martin well?"

"Hardly at all. I'd see him around town, but I probably spoke more to his wife than to him. Amy's a lovely person, always wanting to help people."

"She seemed nice," I agreed. "I understand this business at the cemetery was all her idea."

"That's right. She got it going two years ago, shortly after they moved here. She was supposed to be in the parade this morning, too." She walked with us out to the counter as we talked.

"What time does that start?"

"Around ten o'clock." She finally managed a smile. "It won't take long. A parade in Valentine's not like New York City."

We reached the sheriffs office around nine-thirty. A state police investigator was with him and they were questioning the MacDonald girl and her mother. A half dozen other girls were in the waiting room with their parents. Most were red-eyed and silent.

When the sheriff saw us waiting he excused himself and ushered us into an adjoining office. "He can handle the interviews alone. After the first two, I could see they're all going to be the same. The girls saw nothing and they know nothing. It's as if Oliver Martin was struck down by the hand of God."

"Perhaps he was," Simon speculated.

Sheriff Aikens showed us a plastic evidence bag with the murder weapon inside. "Since when does the hand of God wield a wooden-handled boning knife with a five-inch blade?"

"Fingerprints?" I asked.

"None. And we'll never be able to trace it. It probably comes from a set of kitchen knives that most any home might possess."

"Did he die instantly?"

"Right to the heart. Probably didn't live more than a few seconds."

Simon looked thoughtful, picking up a list of the girls to be interviewed, as if the names themselves might tell him something. I glanced over his shoulder and read along:

Catherine Brophey
Shannon Cinelli
Kathy Clark
Laurie Enright
Julie Foley
Christine Hawkes
Jennifer MacDonald
Jamie Morey
Lisa Russo
Yvonne Sojak
Kristan White
Amanda Williams

I wondered what had happened to all the Marys and Janes I grew up with. Simon grunted and returned the list to the desk.

"Of course, everyone was wearing gloves out there last night," the sheriff said, "so the lack of fingerprints is no surprise."

I tapped the evidence bag with my finger. "This boning knife couldn't have been thrown with any sort of accuracy."

"Possibly not," Sheriff Aikens agreed, "but we'll try it out. I find it hard to believe one of those girls killed him."

We dictated our statements, describing what little we'd seen. When we left the sheriff's office there were still several girls waiting to give their statements. They all shared an expression of fear and bewilderment.

Outside, the parade was starting. A float decorated with valentine hearts led the way, with a small boy in woolen underwear pretending to fire cupid's arrow at a pair of young lovers. This was followed by a carload of town officials and a high school marching band. A few more cars and trucks completed the parade. Kate Summers had been right. A parade in Valentine didn't take long.

"Seen enough?" I asked Simon.

He nodded. "Let's drive out to the Martin place."

"It might be a bad time to intrude."

"Sheriff Aikens is a smart man, but he's out of his depth here. He clearly needs our help."

"Against Satan?"

"Against a clever murderer."

We drove out Main Street to the house next to the cemetery. I pulled in the driveway and the door was opened at once by Amy Martin. "Oh!" she said, frowning at us. "I was expecting the funeral director. I have to go over the arrangements."

"We're sorry to intrude at such a time, Mrs. Martin," Simon Ark said. "If we could just have a word with you—"

She studied us for a moment and then said, "All right. Come in." Again she seemed in control of herself, as she had been immediately after the murder.

The house was large and richly decorated. I could see she took pride in it. Simon and I took seats in the living room and she sat opposite us. "It's about your husband," Simon began.

"You're dressed in black. Are you a priest?"

"I was once, a long time ago. But then, your husband dressed in black, too. What was he?"

"Only a poor deluded man."

"Mrs. Martin, was Oliver having an affair with one of those girls?"

The audacity of such a question to the grieving widow startled me, but perhaps Simon had a better insight into her feelings than I did. She hesitated a few seconds and then replied, "I think he was having an affair, yes, but I never dreamed it was with a high school girl. I still can't believe that. There was some evidence recently—mysterious phone calls at night, little notes that he managed to hide before I could read them. You get to know the signs, especially if you've been through it before. When we were living in Syracuse he was quite friendly with his secretary. I guess I thought he'd grown out of it at his age."

"Did you accuse him of it?"

"Yes. We had a stormy session about two weeks ago. He told me he'd already broken it off, but of course I had no way of knowing if that was true."

"Did he mention her name?"

"No. He told me nothing about her."

Simon Ark drew a deep breath. "Did you hate your husband enough to kill him, Mrs. Martin?"

"Yes, I think I did," she said after a moment's consideration.

"Did you kill him last night?"

"No, Mr. Ark, I did not."

Simon stood up to go and I followed his lead. "Thank you for your frankness."

"Will there be an end to this nightmare?"

"I believe so, very soon."

On the drive back to the Village Inn, I asked Simon, "What will you do now?"

"Perhaps I will buy a Valentine at the general store. Have you sent Shelly one?"

I had to admit it had slipped my mind during the preparations for our trip. When we returned to our room I telephoned the florist we used back home and ordered a dozen long-stemmed roses delivered to my house. "Thanks for reminding me, Simon. I'm in enough trouble for taking this trip in the first place. Now what? Do you still want that Valentine?"

"No, no. We will relax a bit this afternoon, and return to the cemetery after dark."

"Are you still expecting the devil to appear there?"

"Either the devil or a murderer. You might telephone Sheriff Aikens and invite him to join us."

Simon's vagueness with the sheriff was a problem, but finally he agreed to join us at the cemetery just after dark. We sat in his car, which was parked behind the Methodist church, where it couldn't be seen from the road. When we first arrived, Simon had walked out a bit to where the tracks of the previous night's runners came around the corner, and dropped something on a bare spot of ground. I couldn't see what it was.

When he returned to the car, Sheriff Aikens asked, "What are you up to? What's this all about?"

"A theory I have, nothing more. We may unmask a murderer, or we may lose a night's sleep. Only time will tell."

Around eight o'clock a carful of teenage boys came by to inspect the murder scene. They stayed about ten minutes and then drove off. Another car came about an hour later. We could see there was a boy and girl in that one, but they didn't get out. By ten o'clock we were all a bit discouraged. "I could be questioning those girls again," Sheriff Aikens grumbled. "Or getting some sleep."

"Did you get anywhere with them today?" I asked.

"No," he admitted. "One of the young ones, Julie Foley, thinks she saw the flash of the knife in the moonlight, but with everyone clustered around she couldn't tell who was holding it. The other girls didn't see a thing until he started to fall."

"Were any of them especially friendly with him?"

"One of the seventeen-year-olds, Amanda Williams, had spoken to him a few times on her way home from school, but that was all."

We heard the barking of a dog on the road, and the sheriff slipped out of the car for a look. He came back to tell us, "It's Mrs. Martin walking Rex, but she stayed out on the road."

We settled down to wait some more.

I was half dozing when Simon touched my shoulder lightly. "There! It's the beam of a flashlight moving along the ground!"

I felt Sheriff Aikens grow tense beside me as a small figure in scarf and ski jacket came into view. "What's she looking for?" he whispered.

"Something she thinks she dropped last night, when she stabbed Oliver Martin. Come on!"

Simon Ark slipped noiselessly out of the car without closing the door behind him. We followed along. The figure with the flashlight had just reached the bare spot when the beam of light must have picked up whatever Simon had dropped earlier. She bent over to retrieve it as we moved in.

"Hold it there, miss," the sheriff said.

She whirled around, her face still covered by the scarf, and ran for the road. We were after her in an instant, and Sheriff Aikens grabbed her around the waist, spinning her off her feet. The scarf fell away.

"Let me go!" she shouted. "Damn it, let me go!" It was Kate Summers from the Village Inn.

We went down to the sheriff's office after that, while Simon Ark explained it all. "My friend and I counted thirteen girls last night," he said, "but there were only twelve names on your list. That simple fact told the whole story. The killer had mingled with the girls and then escaped in the darkness and confusion after the murder. Dressed for winter, with scarves around some of then-heads and faces, it was easy enough to pass undetected while they were running around the church. The fact that the killer chose to escape rather than stay and identify herself told me she wasn't a teenager. She was someone who would have seemed out of place with the others, which is why she couldn't stay."

"It could have been a man or boy," I pointed out.

"True enough, though the one necessity was that the killer has small stature. That pretty much eliminated men, and a boy probably would have been noticed by the girls around him, especially during the chanting that preceded the run. Also there's the question of motive. If Oliver Martin really had broken off an affair with one of the women in town, that might have given her a motive to kill him. A spurned love, especially on Valentine's Day in a town like this, might have been too much to bear."

"But why Kate Summers?"

"Remember earlier today at breakfast when Mrs. Summers mentioned seeing the full moon out the back window at midnight? We saw it rising in the eastern sky at about that same time, out at the cemetery. But our room at the Village Inn, facing Main Street in the front, is on the eastern side. Kate Summers herself told us it got the morning sun. If the front of the inn looks east, the back must face west. She couldn't have seen the moon out the rear window at midnight. She was lying."

"Why would she lie about a thing like that?" the sheriff wanted to know.

"She was trying to establish her presence at the inn around midnight, the time of the murder. I suppose she saw the full moon in the western sky much later, when she returned from the cemetery. By placing the time at midnight she implicated herself. Then when I really looked at her, I saw a short, small-boned woman who could easily double as a teenage girl. This was even before I saw your list with only twelve names on it. On a hunch I stole her cigarette lighter which she'd left on the counter, and I dropped it out at the churchyard tonight. She was so preoccupied this morning I took a chance that she wouldn't remember when she'd last had it. The lighter was distinctive enough that she couldn't take a chance on having dropped it in the snow while running around the church. She came out tonight to search for it, and we had her."

The sheriff nodded. "She's with her lawyer now. I think she's going to make a confession."

Later, as we drove out of Valentine and headed back toward New York, I told Simon, "There was nothing very romantic about this Valentine's Day."

"I disagree," Simon Ark said. "After all, my friend, she killed Oliver Martin because she loved him too much to let him go. And she stabbed him through the heart. In its own way it was a fitting Valentine's Day crime."

THE STALKER OF SOULS

There's an old horror story that I read once, by an author I've forgotten, about a man who kept hearing footsteps behind him. Whenever he turned to look, there was no one in sight. I thought of that story while I was talking on the telephone to Arno Blackmoor in Stockholm. I met Blackmoor the previous October at the Frankfort Book Fair and we'd become fast friends, the way people sometimes do when thrown together far from home at a convention or trade show.

Blackmoor was 38, a native of Stockholm, and senior editor at a small publishing house that specialized in "new age" books, a term that has come to mean anything from reincarnation and the occult to flying saucers and pyramidology. We'd spent a few evenings together in Frankfort over drinks, discussing the publishing problems of New York and Stockholm, and he'd phoned me once at Christmastime to impart season's greeting and casually inquire as to my opinion of a certain Manhattan literary agent.

Now, in February, he was on the phone again. When we'd disposed of the small talk he came to the point. "In one of our conversations at the Book Fair you mentioned a close friend, a man named Simon Ark. You pictured him as something of an exorcist."

I had to laugh at his choice of words. "Oh, Simon may be a seeker after the devil, but I'd hardly call him an exorcist."

"Nevertheless, I may be in need of his services. I'm having some very peculiar experiences."

It was not the sort of conversation I usually held with a business acquaintance nearly half a world away, but his voice was clear and the concern was evident. "What's the trouble?" I asked.

"I live in the Old Town section of the city, as I've told you. My wife and I have a quite modern home behind one of the medieval housefronts at Stortorget. I work downtown, near the Royal Opera, and it's only a brief walk across the bridge to Old Town. These nights, of course, darkness comes so early that it's night when I arrive home. Old Town can be an eerie place at night."

He paused, and I could only urge him to continue. I'd become caught up in those words coming to me from so far away. "Go on. What happened?"

"For the past three nights someone has followed me on the way home. I hear these sounds behind me, like hoofbeats on the cobblestones, but when I look there is no one in sight."

"I'll mention it to my friend," I promised, "but I don't really think he can be of much help. Perhaps you're hearing a dog or some other animal."

"Not an animal, no." His voice changed, as if someone had entered the office. "It's been good talking to you," he told me. "My thanks for the information. If you can handle this matter for me it would be greatly appreciated."

"I'll speak to my friend," I promised him.

At that time I had not seen Simon Ark in nearly a year, but we'd spoken a few times on the telephone and I knew he was in the city, pursuing some research of his own involving the unicorn tapestries. I had every intention of calling him about my Swedish friend, but as it happened my good intentions came to naught. Arno Blackmoor was dead within twenty-four hours.

It was a cablegram from his wife that brought me the sad news. *Arno died suddenly Thursday,* she informed me. *Memorial service on Tuesday.* The terse message seemed to take for granted the possibility that I would attend, though I had no real excuse to make the trip. The man had been a casual friend of a few nights and some subsequent telephone calls, a good deal younger than me and living in a different world.

"You're not thinking of going, are you?" my wife Shelly asked when I told her of the message that evening.

"I don't know. I think I should call Simon Ark."

Shelly sighed and went into the kitchen, and she may have feared then that I'd be making the journey.

When I reached Simon on the phone later that evening he seemed pleased to hear my voice. "I hope I'm not interrupting your research."

"No, no, my friend. I was merely writing a brief paper on the age-old controversy about unicorns' hoofs—whether they are solid or cloven. The descriptions of early writers were split about evenly, you know. I visited the Metropolitan this afternoon to view *The Unicorn in Captivity,* which definitely shows the hoofs to be cloven."

"Like the devil's," I suggested, unable to resist a little dig at Simon Ark's main area of interest.

"Well, yes," he admitted. "But the unicorn has always been a symbol of good."

"Simon, I'm calling because a friend of mine in Stockholm has died. He called me earlier in the week and wanted me to get in touch with you. I didn't do it soon enough." I told him Blackmoor's story.

"His wife didn't tell you how he died?"

"No."

"I believe I saw a small item in the London *Times*. The New York papers didn't carry it. Ah, here it is, in this morning's edition. A shop near the University receives it by air every afternoon. *Swedish Editor Slain*.

The fact of his murder didn't surprise me. "Does it give any details?"

"Only that he was killed on the way home from his office, shortly after six p.m. yesterday. That would have been shortly after noon New York time. The police suspect robbery was the motive."

"Is there any indication what sort of weapon was used?"

"No. It's a brief article. The second paragraph tells of his publishing career. There's to be a memorial service on Tuesday. Do you plan to attend?"

"It's a long journey all the way to Stockholm, and he wasn't that close a friend," I said, repeating the arguments I'd made to myself earlier.

"I would be willing to accompany you, my friend. The man thought I could help him. Perhaps I still can."

"But he's dead, Simon!"

"Nevertheless—"

I think Shelly had known I'd be going as soon as she heard Simon Ark was involved. In my younger days when I saw more of him he was often taking me off to some exotic locale, much to her dismay. This time I tried to reassure her. "We'll only be gone a few days. I'll bring you back some Swedish crystal."

"You'd better!"

The flight from New York to Stockholm was long and uneventful. When I wasn't dozing I listened to Simon's account of his activities during the past year. Much of it could be viewed as pseudoscientific hogwash, but occasionally he'd spark my interest with some bit of arcane knowledge. He was just launching into a discussion of Sanskrit grammar when the plane came in for a perfect landing at Arlanda Airport, some twenty-three miles north of the city. It was mid-morning on a sunny February weekend, though the air was brisk and the temperature near freezing. Here and there we could see patches of snow on the ground.

I had never met Greta Blackmoor, though I'd sent her a cable advising her of our plans. We'd taken a large room at the Grand Hotel, overlooking the water and only a few steps from the bridge to the Old Town section where the Blackmoors lived. I telephoned Greta to tell her we'd arrived, and she immediately invited us to her home that afternoon. Some of Arno's old friends would be stopping by later, she explained, and it would be an opportunity to meet them before the memorial service on Tuesday. I accepted, but told her we'd have Sunday dinner first at our hotel.

While we dined Simon was regretting his poor knowledge of the Swedish language. "You won't need it today," I assured him. "Mrs. Blackmoor speaks perfect English and I'm sure Blackmoor's friends do too. Swedish schoolchildren learn English from the age of nine, and have done so since shortly after World War II. Almost everyone under the age of fifty speaks it well. When I spent that time with Blackmoor at the Book Fair he told me Swedish bookstores all have an English-language section. They import a great many books from Britain and some from America."

We found the Blackmoor home with little difficulty, after only one false turn among the narrow medieval streets of *Gamla Stan* or Old Town. It was a three-story building overlooking a small square where round wooden tubs obviously held flowers in the warm weather. Greta Blackmoor opened the big wooden door herself in response to our ring. "Come in," she said. "I am Greta." She was a pretty woman in her mid-thirties, wearing a black dress with white trim that went well with her golden hair and healthy complexion. "It's such a pleasure to meet you. My husband spoke of you often after meeting you in Frankfort."

I shook her hand gently. "It was a pleasure knowing him. In New York we have a habit of forgetting that book publishing is carried on in other cities as well. And this is my old friend Simon Ark."

The smile faded for just an instant and then reappeared. "I only wish you could have come sooner. My husband believed you might have saved his life."

"Then his death was not merely a street crime?" Simon asked, shedding his topcoat.

"Someone had been following him for days, stalking him, he said. He could hear their steps behind him but he never saw who it was."

"He told me that on the telephone," I said.

She led us into the living room, and I saw now that the entire inside of the building had been gutted and rebuilt. The cathedral ceiling rose all the way to the building's roof, where skylights admitted the light of the day. Balconies on the second and third floors led to bedrooms and baths, Greta Blackmoor informed us, along with a room where Arno had worked when at home. She mentioned his name without emotion, seemingly resigned to what had happened.

As we sat around a large glass coffee table, I asked for details of his death. "He phoned me on Wednesday afternoon," I told her. "It would have been evening here and I suppose he was calling from home."

She confirmed that with a nod. "He was very upset about being followed for three straight nights and he remembered your mention of your friend Simon Ark."

Simon shifted his position on the leather-covered couch. "Why me? Had he been to the police?"

"He did not believe the police could help him."

"But wasn't it a robbery?" I asked.

"In a sense. My husband believed someone was trying to steal his soul. His body was—almost decapitated when they found it."

Simon Ark stared up at the skylight in silence, and for a moment nobody spoke.

It was the ringing of the doorbell that broke the spell, and Greta Blackmoor hurried to answer it. She returned with two men who reminded me vaguely of Arno. Both were in their thirties, blond, and with the appearance of successful businessmen. Mrs. Blackmoor introduced them as two of her late husband's oldest and dearest friends. The taller of the two was Bertil Millman, assistant director of the Museum of Antiquities at the Royal Palace. The other man, both shorter and stouter, was Carl Kiruna, a designer of computer chips.

"You've come all the way from New York?" Kiruna asked, finding this little short of amazing. "Did you know Arno well?"

"Not really," I admitted. "A few days at the Frankfort Book Fair last October, and some telephone calls since then. But I spoke with him just a day before he was killed."

"A terrible crime," Bertil Millman said, seating himself next to me. "Simply terrible! To die like that—"

"The police have no clues?" Simon asked.

"Apparently not. They think it was a random thing." Millman took out a pipe and nervously began to fill it. "Just some madman on the prowl who happened upon poor Arno."

"He was followed for three nights," I pointed out. "He told me so on the phone. It was as if he was being stalked."

"Perhaps the killer was waiting for an opportunity," Carl Kiruna suggested.

Greta was growing impatient. "I didn't invite you here to discuss Arno's death, but his life. Bertil and Carl, would you both be willing to say a few words at the service on Tuesday?"

"Certainly."

"Of course." Millman lit his pipe and drew on it. "What about Wahlstrom? Will he be there?"

Greta Blackmoor hesitated. "I don't know. He was one of the original crowd at the university, wasn't he? The four of you—"

"Five," Kiruna corrected, "but of course Semlor is dead now."

"My God!" Greta put a hand to her mouth and I saw the color drain from her face. "I just remembered!"

"What is it?" Simon Ark asked.

"When Semlor died in that motorcycle accident last year, Arno told me he'd been decapitated in the crash. He died the same way as Arno. Did someone steal his soul too?"

Simon Ark stood against the mantel of the fireplace, looking like a commanding elder statesman in his black suit and tie. "I have heard enough about this stealer of souls. Will someone please tell me what it's all about?"

Millman and Kiruna exchanged glances. "Nothing serious," Kiruna replied finally. "Schoolboy foolishness."

"Arno told me about it once, shortly after we were married," Greta said, ignoring her late husband's friends. "It was when they were all at the University together, nearly twenty years ago. They had a foolish ceremony and sold their souls to the devil."

I let out my breath. "And that's why your husband wanted Simon Ark. That's why he spoke of an exorcist. He feared the devil was coming to collect."

"It's true, isn't it?" she challenged the others, but they remained guiltily silent.

"Why the head?" Simon asked softly. "Why would Satan cut off the head, if that is what you believe happened."

"I don't know what to believe," she admitted. "There was a story by Poe in which a man bet the devil his head."

I smiled slightly. "Poe meant that story to be humorous, though perhaps something was lost in the translation to Swedish."

Finally Millman said it. "Go talk to Hans Wahlstrom if you need to. He'll tell you all about it. He even mentioned it once in a newspaper interview."

I could feel the tension in the room, and I knew Simon and I were partly the cause of it. When I suggested we leave, Greta Blackmoor seemed almost relieved. She went off for our coats and then saw us out. "I'll look for you at the service on Tuesday morning," she said. "It will be ten o'clock at St. Jacob's Church near your hotel."

"If we decide to visit Hans Wahlstrom, where can he be found?" Simon asked.

She hesitated, her hand on the big wooden door. "Wahlstrom was no friend of my husband's. They had a falling-out some years ago over a book he'd written. Arno refused to publish it and Wahlstrom barely spoke to him after that. He lives on Karlavagen. You can find the number in the phone book."

"Thank you," Simon Ark said. "We will do what we can."

As we strolled back to the hotel the late afternoon air seemed to chill our bodies. It was already growing dark and I increased the pace. "There aren't many people in this area of the city, especially when the shops are closed."

"Never fear, my friend. The devil does not want our heads."

"What would the head have to do with the soul, Simon?"

"Some cultures believe the soul exits the body through the mouth after death. I suppose some might feel that decapitation speeds up the process."

"That's insane."

"Let us visit Hans Wahlstrom tomorrow and see what he thinks of the matter."

"Those other two certainly didn't want to talk about it."

"Wahlstrom may be more willing."

I was awakened early in our hotel room by the sound of Monday morning commuters coming off the small ferry boats that docked regularly just outside our windows. I watched for a time as they came off in the near-darkness and hurried up the streets to their offices and shops. As the sky gradually brightened I saw there were a few flurries of snow in the morning air.

Simon Ark came out of the bathroom and began to dress. I hadn't even realized he was up. "What is the weather, my friend?"

"Some snow flurries. I don't think it'll amount to much."

After breakfast at the hotel I looked up Hans Wahlstrom's number and telephoned him. He agreed to see us at his home that afternoon. We were about to go off for some sightseeing when a tall, gaunt man in a topcoat and hat intercepted us in the lobby. He greeted us by name and then identified himself. "Superintendent Frowler of the Stockholm Police. I wonder if I might have a few words with you gentlemen."

We sat down in a lounge area of the lobby while I explained my casual friendship with Arno Blackmoor. He questioned Simon too, and seemed unconvinced by the answers he got. "You see, gentlemen, my department is investigating a very serious crime here. Arno Blackmoor was a highly respected citizen. To be killed like that on a dark street in Old Town, virtually decapitated by some madman, is more than we can tolerate. His widow told me you arrived yesterday, and she told me he spoke to you by telephone the day before his death."

"That's correct." I described the call as best I could remember it.

"He felt he was being stalked by someone or something?"

"He did."

"But he gave no hint of what it might be?"

I hesitated. "Well, he had the misapprehension that my friend Simon here was an exorcist. He wanted his help. I suppose that implies a fear of satanic possession."

"Come, now! Mr. Blackmoor was an intelligent, educated man. Why would he believe he was possessed of demons?"

"I have no idea. Perhaps his widow might know."

"I've spoken to her twice. She seems unable or unwilling to tell us more. That's why I was hoping you gentlemen might be of help."

"We may be," Simon Ark told him, "but not yet. Sometimes puzzles must await the proper moment for their solution."

"The proper moment? When there's another killing?"

"There may have been another killing already," Simon told him. "You might investigate the death of a man named Semlor in a motorcycle accident last year. I understand he was decapitated in the crash."

The detective frowned. Obviously this information was new to him and he made a note of the name. "How long will you be staying in our city?" he asked as he prepared to leave them.

"Through tomorrow, at least," I told him. "After the memorial service we'll see how long we're needed."

"I hope you won't leave without contacting me."

I promised we'd be in touch, but I had the distinct feeling there'd be little chance of our slipping away without his knowing about it.

It was early afternoon when we reached the address on Karlavagen where Hans Wahlstrom lived. It was an elaborate apartment building, no more than ten years old, with a uniformed doorman to announce our arrival. Wahlstrom was waiting to greet us when we stepped from the elevator. "Come in, gentlemen. I don't really know how I can help you, though. I have not been close to Arno Blackmoor in recent years."

He seated himself near the windows, with the light to his back. A large man with a middle-aged stomach, he hardly seemed like a classmate of the others we'd met. He brushed back the thinning hair from his deep brown eyes and asked, "First off, who told you about me?"

"A man named Bertil Millman, actually."

"Ah, Millman!"

"He said you'd tell us about some sort of pact with the devil you all made when you were at the University together."

"You want to know about that?" He leaned back and laughed.

"He said you mentioned it once in an interview."

"As a writer perhaps I viewed the whole episode with more humor than they did."

"You were a writer in your university days?" Simon asked.

"Short stories for our literary magazine."

"Did you ever write about this so-called pact with Satan?"

"No, no—I would never use friends in my fiction. That was one of the reasons for my falling-out with Arno. His firm had published two novels of mine with a fair degree of success. Then I submitted a third book and Arno himself rejected it. He claimed I had introduced real people into my fiction and he feared they could be identified. I told him that was foolish, but his mind was set. The book was finally published by a rival firm after I'd shortened it a bit. But I've wandered off the subject, as I often do. You asked about the pact with Satan. I never wrote about it, but I mentioned it last year in an interview in connection with this book. Since it dealt with young people in their university days, the interviewer asked if I'd ever done anything wild during my own time at the University. I told him there were no sex orgies, but some friends and I once sold our souls to the devil."

He seemed to treat it an an enormous joke, and Simon carefully entered into the spirit of it. "How did that happen to come about?" he asked with a rare smile.

"Oh, there were five of us and we'd been drinking. Semlor and Millman shared a room, as I remember it, and that's where we were. I was a couple of years older than the other four. Maybe that's why I didn't take it quite so seriously as they did. We were sitting around on the floor finishing off a bottle, probably passing around a joint, and talking about the future. About our careers. This was in the early 70s, remember, when the country was full of Americans fleeing the Vietnam draft. Jobs weren't that easy to find. Someone suggested we should make a pact with the devil, selling our souls for success in our chosen fields."

"Who suggested it?" Simon wanted to know.

"I'm not certain. It could have been Arno."

"Go on."

"Someone drew a chalk pentagram on the wooden floor and we took turns reading passages backwards out of the Bible. There were candles burning and it was an eerie setting, especially after a few drags of pot. Carl Kiruna claimed he actually saw something, but no one really believed him."

"Was any time limit placed on this soul-selling?"

"No, I don't think so. We simply said we would sell our souls to the devil in exchange for success in our chosen careers. You know something? We all did succeed too—Blackmoor as an editor, myself as a writer, Kiruna in computers, Millman at the museum, and Semlor as an actor. None of us were huge successes yet, but we achieved a great deal while still under forty."

"Semlor was killed," I reminded him.

"I know." He turned serious for a moment. "It was Carl Kiruna who phoned to tell me about it last year. He even mentioned the pact with

Satan, which I hadn't thought of in years. He wondered if the devil was starting to collect."

"His head—"

"It was a motorcycle accident, at dusk. He didn't see a steel construction cable stretched across the road at one point. There were warning signs, but he ignored them. He told me once that riding the motorcycle gave him a feeling of immortality."

"He was wrong," Simon said dryly. "What about the others?"

"I haven't seen any of them since my breakup with Arno over the book. Carl phoned me that one time, and Bertil Millman phoned, quite upset, after that interview appeared about the pact with Satan. No one took it seriously, though."

"And yet Arno Blackmoor is dead now too, and he also lost his head."

"A coincidence. This was murder, the first was an accident."

"Perhaps. Did anyone see Semlor's accident?"

"I—no, I suppose not. He was said to be alone at the time."

We left shortly after that, and Wahlstrom rode down in the elevator with us. Perhaps he was being a good host in seeing us to the outer door, perhaps he just wanted to make certain we were really gone.

The following morning was sunny, but with a chill wind from the sea that had us turning up our coat collars as we walked the few blocks to the memorial service at the nearby church. It was an old building, dating from the seventeenth century, and so spacious that the mourners seemed lost among its columns and shadows. The brief memorial service was in Swedish, so Simon and I could understand little of it, but when it was over we gathered outside.

"Please come back to the house with the others," Greta Blackmoor urged us. "I so appreciate your traveling all this distance."

As we walked across one of the other bridges to the Old Town section, further down from our hotel, Bertil Millman from the Museum of Antiquities fell into step with us. "You must visit my museum at the Royal Palace before you depart," he urged.

"There is so much to see here," I agreed. "What's that modern building to our right?"

"Stadshuset, our handsome city hall. It's where the Nobel Prize receptions are held each December."

As we left the bridge and entered the streets of Old Town, Simon Ark said, "Blackmoor could have been beheaded with a sword. I imagine there are many such ceremonial weapons in your museum, Mr. Millman."

"Not so many as you'd think. The city contains several statues of St. George and the Dragon, but none in which the sword is easily removable. However, if the stalker of Arno Blackmoor's soul was a supernatural being, it would not have needed a sword from my museum or anywhere else."

"Surely you don't believe in this supernatural business!" I said, surprised by his words.

"I don't really know," he answered in all seriousness. "I too have heard recently the footsteps behind me."

"Tell us about it," Simon Ark urged, immediately interested.

"It was only that, a sound behind me that was not quite footsteps."

"More like hoofbeats?"

"Perhaps, or only the beating of my own heart."

"Distant, or close?"

"Close, and gaining on me. I turned to look, of course, but there was nothing in sight."

"When was this?"

"Sunday evening, on the way home from Greta's house, and again last night after I left work at the museum.

"Have you told the police?"

He shrugged. "What can they do? It may be all my imagination."

"You seem to be a sensible person, Mr. Millman. If you heard steps behind you, I doubt if they were your imagination."

"We saw Hans Wahlstrom yesterday," I told him.

"Oh?"

"He told us about the pact with the devil."

"Mere adolescent foolishness. It meant nothing and no one believed in it. I'd quite forgotten it until that fool Wahlstrom mentioned it in his interview."

"Yet two of the five who made the pact are now dead, and both were decapitated."

"There was nothing suspicious about Semlor's death. It was a motorcycle accident."

"Maybe he heard something behind him too," I suggested. "Maybe he was fleeing from something and didn't see the steel cable that killed him."

We had reached the Blackmoor home by that time and the conversation ceased as we entered. Greta took our coats off to another room and Carl Kiruna performed the introductions, leading us among small groups of relatives and friends. At one point I looked around for Millman, but he'd gone into one of the other rooms.

When Greta Blackmoor rejoined us, Simon asked, "Didn't Hans Wahlstrom attend the service?"

She shook her head. "I didn't invite him. He was no friend of Arno's."

"We saw him yesterday."

"Bertil already told me."

"Did he also tell you he has heard the sound of feet or hoofs behind him, as your husband did?"

She seemed startled by this. "When?"

"The last two nights."

"Arno heard them for three nights before he died."

"Do you believe—?" Simon began, but was halted in mid-sentence by the expression on her face. She was looking over his shoulder and when I followed her line of sight I saw that Superintendent Frowler was standing at the door, just admitted by one of the neighbors who'd apparently heard his knock. Greta moved away from us to greet him.

"Excuse me for coming at such a time," the police official told her. "We've found the murder weapon dropped down one of the sewers. I was wondering if you might step outside and tell us if you've ever seen it before."

The color had drained from her face at his request. "I'll go with you," I offered.

"Thank you," she said, accepting my arm. Simon Ark trailed along after us.

Frowler's official car was parked at the curb. He opened the trunk and showed us a carefully sealed plastic evidence packet. Inside was a long-handled ax, its blade dirty and stained. Greta Blackmoor gasped and looked away. "I've never seen it before," she managed to say.

"Your husband had no such tool?"

"No. We buy our firewood already cut. There is no use in the city for a woodsman's ax."

"It's a large weapon for someone to carry through the streets," I pointed out.

The superintendent shrugged. "But one easily concealed beneath a long winter coat."

Mrs. Blackmoor excused herself and went back inside. "A powerful man must have swung that ax," I suggested.

"Not necessarily. There were two or more blows. We believe the first one tore through the back of his coat collar and probably knocked him down. Then the killer stood over him and delivered the fatal blow or blows."

"And no one saw this?"

"These streets are narrow and some of them are not well lighted. Street crime is not common in Stockholm but it does happen. Our own prime minister was assassinated in the street a few years ago."

"They may not have seen him because he was invisible," Simon Ark suggested.

"Invisible?"

"Arno Blackmoor told my friend of the footsteps or hoofbeats behind him, yet he saw nothing. I understand someone else has had the same experience."

"Who would that be?" the superintendent asked.

But Simon ignored the question. "It's chilly out here. We must get back inside."

"When will you be going back to America?" he asked.

I answered for both of us. "Tomorrow, I think. Tomorrow, if we can get a flight."

From our room that evening Simon phoned Bertil Millman at home. "Ah, Mr. Millman. I wanted to be certain you arrived home safely and without incident. Good! Perhaps the sounds you heard were merely a trick of the wind. Are you in for the evening now? Oh, a meeting of the Antiquarian Society. Where would that be—at the Museum? I see. Well, good night, Mr. Millman."

"What was all that?" I asked.

"He heard no sounds this evening, but he must return to the museum for an eight o'clock meeting."

"Do you really think he's in danger?"

"There was a gap of several months between the first two deaths. It hardly seems likely that the stalker of souls would be on the prowl so soon. And yet—"

"I know. You want to go out, just to be certain he's safe."

"If I am wrong in my theory, it may truly be the devil who pursues him, and who can say what sort of calendar the devil uses?"

That night, as we crossed the bridge and prowled once more through the narrow streets of Old Town, I felt the way Simon Ark might have, if he'd really been pursuing Satan for the past two thousand years. I felt like someone prowling these very streets seven hundred years ago, searching for whatever evil might have lurked here then.

"It will happen on the way home, if it happens at all," Simon decided.

"Why is that?"

"The full moon is directly overhead now, bathing these narrow streets in its glow. An hour from now, after the meeting, the shadows will once again reign here."

We watched a little of the meeting from the back row, but left before it was over. Simon didn't want Millman to know we were following him. But as we waited outside and the small crowd filed out, he grew increasingly nervous.

"Something is wrong, my friend." He stopped a stocky woman who'd been on the platform with Millman. "Pardon me, has the assistant director left yet?"

She was startled at being addressed in English but managed to reply, "Yes. He went out the back door."

"You take that street," Simon told me, really alarmed now. "I will go to the left. Hurry!"

I trotted about a half-block until I became winded and slowed to a fast walk. The street ahead was in semi-darkness and I could see no one. I was alone.

Except that I could hear something very close behind me. It was like an echo of my own footsteps. I whirled around quickly and saw—

Nothing.

I started walking again, and heard it again.

Were those the sounds of hoofs on the stone paving? Or were they the sounds of the stalker of souls prowling the night with his ax? I started running.

At the next corner I turned left, hoping to encounter Simon Ark, but there was only another empty street. Far ahead I could see a well-lit square with people but I knew I would never reach it in time. The footsteps behind me seemed louder now.

And then I reached the next corner, and saw the three men locked in a deadly struggle not twenty feet away.

"Simon!"

I ran forward, forgetting my invisible pursuer, and threw myself on them, going for the man with the ax in his hand. Simon pulled Millman free and in a moment we had the assailant down in the street. I yanked the ax from his grip and then reached up to pull away the scarf that hid his features.

"It is Mr. Carl Kiruna, of course," Simon Ark said. "Our designer of computer chips. If you two will continue holding him, I will summon the police."

An hour later, Simon and I sat with Bertil Millman in Greta Blackmoor's living room, listening to Superintendent Frowler outline the case. He'd asked us to assemble there so he could take statements to wrap up the investigation. Millman told of the footsteps he'd heard, and Simon and I recounted our chase after him through the streets of Old Town.

"I was nearly to the corner when I heard the steps behind me again," Millman said. "I looked back, but of course no one was there. As I increased my pace a bit, this figure stepped suddenly from a doorway on my right. I saw him raise the ax, and then Mr. Ark shouted at him from down the block. The three of us tussled, and Mr. Ark's friend ran up to join in. When we got the assailant down on the ground, we saw that it was Carl—Carl Kiruna. I couldn't believe it."

"He's admitted killing your husband, Mrs. Blackmoor, but he'll say nothing about his motive." Frowler was reviewing his notes as he spoke. "He denies any part in the death of Mr. Semlor, however. I expect by tomorrow he may be willing to make a fuller statement."

Greta Blackmoor tried to pour us some coffee but her hand was shaking. I took the pot from her. "Was he carrying anything unusual in his coat pocket?" Simon asked.

"He was, now that you mention it." The superintendent unzipped his briefcase and removed a black plastic gadget somewhat larger than a pack of cigarettes. "Looks a bit like one of those devices that automatically opens your garage doors."

"I believe that's exactly what it is," Simon Ark told him, "though in this case it served a different purpose. As soon as I heard the description of these so-called hoofbeats or footsteps where there was no person or animal present, the thought occurred to me that they might be some sort of electronic sounds. Mr. Kiruna was introduced as a designer of computer chips and my interest immediately focused on him. We've all seen greeting cards that play a simple tune when opened." He turned to me. "My friend—"

I knew what was coming and I handed over my coat, which I'd kept folded on my lap.

"Both Mr. Millman and my friend here heard the mysterious sounds tonight, shortly before Mr. Millman was attacked." He turned up the collar of my coat and cut a few threads in back, where the collar was sewn to the body of the coat. From inside the collar he extracted a tiny plastic disk about the size of a penny. He pressed the button on the black box Kiruna had been carrying, and the disk immediately began to emit electronic sounds exactly like footsteps. Simon Ark smiled. "When muffled by the fabric of the wearer's coat, they sounded just far enough away to be mistaken for a follower. Yet the street remained empty. Kiruna was watching from a distance, of course, and only activated the device when no one else was nearby. There's an identical one in Mr. Millman's coat collar. Tonight, when he turned it on, my friend on the next street was also within range and his device was activated accidentally."

"What was the purpose of it?" Millman wanted to know.

"To frighten the intended victim. He would speak of it to others, even phoning New York in the case of Arno Blackmoor, and when he was later killed the murder would take on a supernatural aspect. Decapitation with an ax was chosen in hopes it would be linked to Semlor's earlier accidental death, and the so-called pact with the devil."

I still didn't understand it all. "Simon, how could that thing have been placed in my coat, and why? I wasn't connected with these others. Why would Kiruna want to kill me?"

"He didn't, my friend. The disk was placed there only to frighten you and me away, if that became necessary later. As I said, it was triggered by accident tonight. As to how it was placed there, that could only have been done in this house, probably earlier today when Greta Blackmoor solicitously carried our coats to the other room. Cutting the thread, inserting the disk and resewing the seam could have been accomplished in a moment's time."

The blood had drained from Greta's face, and now the coffee cup dropped from her fingers, bouncing on the carpet. "I—I didn't mean to—I didn't know he'd try to kill you too, Bertil! It was only supposed to be Arno—"

The following afternoon, as we arrived at the airport, I said, "No pact with the devil, no stalker of souls, only the eternal triangle and a woman who wanted her husband out of the way."

Simon Ark nodded. "Kiruna would have killed Millman to further the illusion. Perhaps he'd have gotten around to Hans Wahlstrom too. As for Greta, she wasn't all that innocent. Remember she was the one who sewed the disks into the coat collars of her husband, Millman and yourself. And she was the one who brought up that pact with Satan, and the similarity to Semlor's death, in case the police missed the point. The disk had to be ripped from Arno's coat after he was killed, of course. That was why the police thought the first blow of the ax had hit his collar. Kiruna and Greta were both stalkers of souls, doing the devil's work."

I remembered the crystal I'd promised Shelly and bought it at the duty-free shop. Then we boarded the plane for a peaceful flight home.

THE SOCIETY OF THE SCAR

Istanbul from the air is a city like few others, divided into three distinct parts by busy waterways. "Below us is the inlet of the Golden Horn," Simon Ark explained over my shoulder as we peered out the window of the wide-bodied jet aircraft that had brought us from London. "Off to the left are the straits of Bosphorus, separating the European continent from Asia, and the Bosphorus Bridge is the first to link two continents."

It seemed like a very old city from the air, filled with an Arabian Nights mixture of mosques, bazaars, and palaces, though here and there clusters of taller, more modern office buildings could be seen. My business in Istanbul would take me to one of those buildings, while for Simon the journey was a return to a city in which he'd lived many years ago, before I knew him.

"It was called Constantinople then," he told me in his sonorous voice, "and they wrote popular songs about it. But that was before you were born."

The plane turned west after passing over the city and made a perfect landing at Yesilkoy Airport. This was the way most travelers came to Istanbul since it was no longer the eastern terminus of the fabled Orient Express. I'd never been here before, but Simon's unceasing description of the landmarks made me feel as if I were returning to an old friend.

My New York firm, Neptune Books, had sent me to the city to complete arrangements for the acquisition of three novels by Mustafa Byzas, rumored to be a favorite for the next Nobel Prize. Simon Ark had come along strictly for pleasure, he claimed, and to renew his acquaintance with the city. "While you are dealing with Byzas's agent in the morning, my friend, I shall be visiting one of the city's great art museums."

"Are there many art treasures in the city?" I asked with just a touch of irony.

"It has fabled treasures, but I am more interested in the modern Turkish painters like Guran and Calli. There are, however, some elegant Ottoman miniatures which I remember from my last visit."

Our hotel was comfortable enough, one of a large American chain that had circled the globe. We slept soundly after our flight across seven time zones, and in the morning after breakfast we parted to make our calls. The literary agent who handled Mustafa Byzas had an office in a disappointingly plain building just a few blocks from Topkapi Palace, within sight of the railway station. In the days of the Orient Express, Simon had told me, it was an area of fine and fashionable hotels. Now most were cracked and tottering, if they hadn't already given way to car parks and fruit stalls.

The literary agent was named Celebi Karpat, and he shared a large single-room office with a young secretary named Dasha, a dark-haired beauty who wore too much lipstick and pancake makeup. Their desks were separated by a bookcase that gave the illusion of some privacy as I spoke with Karpat and Dasha typed correspondence in her cubicle.

"We are very pleased that Mustafa Byzas is to be published in America," the agent told me. He was a short, balding man whose gray suit had food stains on the sleeve. "Your contract terms are agreeable, as amended."

"Is Mr. Byzas in the city at present?" I asked. "It would be a pleasure to meet him during my visit."

"He lives outside the city," the agent answered vaguely, "but a meeting might be arranged. How long will you be here?"

"I'd planned on just two days, but I might stretch it a bit if there were a chance of meeting Mr. Byzas. I'm here with a friend who is renewing his acquaintance with the city and touring some of your art museums. He's visiting with Professor Metzger this morning."

"Ah, we have many artistic treasures in Istanbul."

I glanced through the contracts and affixed my signature. "My friend Simon Ark is an admirer of the modern painters as well as some from the Ottoman era. He lived in the city back in the 1920s."

"If I can arrange a meeting with Mustafa Byzas, he is certainly welcome to join us. Byzas himself has some interest in art."

"Will you let me know?"

"I will phone you at your hotel this afternoon. I will try to arrange something for tomorrow so as not to disrupt your travel plans."

We shook hands and I left the building, walking back across the Galata Bridge to my hotel.

It was just after noon when Simon Ark returned from the museum, and I could see at once that something had agitated him. "My friend, I have seen my old acquaintance at the museum. He has presented me with a mystery to be solved."

"You have not been here in nearly sixty years, Simon! How can this man Metzger still be working?"

"He is elderly, to be sure," Simon Ark agreed. "I knew him as a young man. Now he is a retired professor of art, and is acting curator at the museum, called back from retirement by the trustees."

"What's the mystery?"

"Someone has been slashing the paintings on exhibit at that museum, and elsewhere in the city. Nearly a dozen have been defaced over the past three months, despite stepped-up security precautions. My old friend, Professor Metzger, is most concerned. He's asked me to meet with the museum's chief of security this afternoon."

"Protecting valuable paintings is a bit out of your line, Simon, unless they think the Devil is slashing them with his barbed tail."

"The motive for the slashings might be nearly as bizarre," Simon murmured, but would say no more.

Later, as Simon prepared to leave for his meeting, Karpat phoned with the news that we could meet with Mustafa Byzas for lunch the following day. He mentioned a restaurant near his office and we arranged a meeting for the following noon. "Maybe we can get out of here by Thursday after all," I told Simon.

"I must be going," Simon Ark said. "If you are free now, why not accompany me? I must offer you something in return for meeting a future Nobel Prize winner."

I had nothing better to do, and I'd learned in other cities that an afternoon with Simon often proved more enlightening than the standard round of haphazard sightseeing. "Let's go," I agreed.

We set off by taxi for his meeting at the museum.

Professor Metzger was an elderly man who walked with a slight stoop. I had pictured him with a beard, but he was clean shaven, with bright eyes that he only covered occasionally with reading glasses. "I never thought I would live long enough to see Simon Ark back in Istanbul," he confided to me.

"What was he like in the Twenties?" I had to ask.

"Much as he is today. He has changed very little."

"But that was over sixty years ago!"

"A mere afternoon to one who claims he has lived thousands."

"Then you believe Simon's claim?"

"When one is as old as I am, one begins to hope it is true."

We entered the office of the museum security chief in the basement of the old building. Even here, partly hidden by shadows, was a mosaic of a sad-eyed Christ, a reminder of the last flowering of Byzantine art. The security chief, an overweight man named Plaque, puffed on a thick cigar and seemed oblivious to the tarnished beauty of his surroundings.

He shook hands with Simon and me and came right to the point. "I am told you could be of some help in apprehending the slasher, Mr. Ark."

"I have had some experience with criminal oddities."

"This is no oddity, only a madman who seems to be invisible to my guards." We had taken seats across the desk from him and he offered each of us a cigar. We all declined, and he continued with his account. "Eleven paintings slashed within three months' time. Nine in this building, plus two that happened to be on loan to other museums in the city."

"Did the paintings have anything in common?" Simon asked.

"They were all portraits, mainly of Turkish noblemen or their wives. Nineteenth century, for the most part."

"It sounds to me like a deranged person," Simon decided. "I'm sure you'll apprehend him sooner or later."

But Plaque shook his head. "Not when he can perform his act of vandalism right in front of me without being seen."

"What do you mean?"

"Last week, at the time of the latest incident, I was patrolling in the main gallery myself. One of our paintings is a portrait of the mother of Sultan Selim III. A young woman and a few schoolgirls were painting copies of it, as they often do in art galleries. A man with a limp was across the room, examining some of the other paintings. No one else was in the gallery. I passed the painting and it was completely intact. Within a minute, before I'd reached the doorway to the adjoining gallery, one of the children screamed. I hurried back and saw that the portrait had been slashed across the face of the lady."

"No one saw it happen?" I asked.

"No one."

"Those children—"

"Of course, it was my first thought! We searched the children, the man and the woman for any sign of a weapon. There was nothing that could have sliced the canvas like that—no knife, no razor, not even a nail scissors.

It had to be done in a split second, remember, and I still find it strange that no one noticed."

"An interesting problem," Simon Ark murmured.

I could see that the seeming impossibility of it had caught his attention. He asked a few more routine questions about the number of guards and their hours on duty. Then he told Professor Metzger and the security man, "We have a limited time in your city. I will do what I can." We returned to the main floor.

The professor saw us to the door. "How much do you trust Plaque?" I asked. "Is his account reliable?"

"I would believe anything he said. Plaque is an honorable man."

We left him at the door and went down the outside steps to the street. I noticed a young man with a slight limp walking in our direction, as if to intercept us, and tried to remember who else had mentioned a limping man just recently. Before it came to me, the man crossed directly in front of us, almost bumping into Simon. He was close enough for me to see the tiny scar on his left cheek.

"Are you all right?" I asked. "He almost knocked you over."

"Quite all right, my friend." The man had hurried on, and Simon stood looking at a piece of folded paper that had been slipped into his hand. "Let us go for a stroll."

When we were a few blocks away in a tree-lined square, he unfolded the paper and read: *Learn about the Society of the Scar, Grand Hamam, four o'clock.*

"What does it mean, Simon?"

"I don't know."

"What is the Grand Hamam?"

"Hamams are public steam baths, or Turkish baths as they're known in other countries. The Grand Hamam is a very old one that has been here for years."

"This person wants to meet you there? What is the Society of the Scar?"

"I believe we will learn that by appearing at the bath. It could be tied in with the slashing of the paintings."

"Why do you think so?"

"Because a slash across the face of a portrait is something like a scar, and because that security man, Plaque, told us there was a limping man in the gallery at the time of the most recent slashing."

The Grand Hamam was a beautiful old building filled with elaborate marble basins and baths. Checking our clothes as we entered, Simon and I made our way down a curving flight of marble stairs to the steamy lower level, clad only in generous blue towels that circled our middles.

"Turkish towels, I'll bet," I commented to Simon.

"Of course!" he agreed, exchanging a smile with me. His chest was virtually hairless, with skin so smooth it suggested that of an adolescent boy rather than an elderly man.

Downstairs, a fully clothed painter with brush in hand, wearing overalls and a paint-spotted cap, seemed out of place among all the naked men. We made our way from one steamy room to the next, seeking out the limping man, but he was nowhere to be found. "It's just four o'clock now," I pointed out. "We were a bit early."

We sat in a big circular room where marble slabs were heated from below as shafts of sunlight from a cluster of ceiling portholes cut through the steam. The room seemed twice as high as the others, and then I remembered we were in the basement.

"It's hot in here," I commented, staring at the room's only other occupant, a sleeping man who lay on the heated marble with a red towel over his face.

"That is the idea, my friend. The Romans enjoyed it even before the Turks. One of their many contributions to modern civilization."

We waited, and presently a stout bearded man entered the room to join us in silence. There was still no sign of the limping man. "It's twenty after four, Simon. I don't think he's coming."

"Let's wait another ten minutes." He was staring at the sleeping man, who hadn't moved since we entered the steam room.

I sensed that something had caught his interest. "What is it, Simon?"

"Does it strike you as odd that he has a red towel over his face when all the other towels are blue?"

"He probably brought it with him from home," I suggested. "Why would he do that?"

Simon got to his feet and walked over to the man. He stared down at him for a moment and then lifted the towel from his face.

It was the man we'd come to meet. Where his throat had been, there was only a gaping red wound.

The police questioning was fairly routine. The lieutenant in charge seemed to dismiss the whole thing as a homosexual killing in a bathhouse. When Simon Ark alluded to the Society of the Scar, the lieutenant looked blank. He copied down our passport numbers and then dismissed us.

"The killer draped him with a red towel so the blood soaking through wouldn't reveal the crime too soon," Simon theorized as we taxied back to the hotel. "A crime so premeditated hardly sounds like a routine spur-of-the-moment killing."

I had to admit he made sense. The unknown man who'd come to meet us was dead, almost certainly killed to keep him from telling us what he knew. "We seem to be at a dead end," I told Simon.

He was silent when we got back to our hotel, and said very little about the affair over dinner that evening. In the morning, however, his spirits seemed to have returned and he was still looking forward to lunch with Byzas and his agent. The restaurant where we'd agreed to meet was the Bosphorus, a fine old place with dark woodwork and yellowed newspaper clippings framed on the entranceway wall.

The first surprising thing about Mustafa Byzas was his perfect command of the English language. It shouldn't have surprised me, of course, because his biography clearly stated that he spent a year at Oxford. Still, I was unprepared for the gentle British tones of his voice, just as I was unprepared for the woman who accompanied him. She was taller than Byzas by several inches, and seemed to tower over him there in the entranceway. She was dark, probably Turkish, but slimmer than most Turkish women I'd seen on the streets. Her clothes appeared to be the latest in fashionable Paris design, and she wore them well.

"This is my wife, Margurita," Byzas said after he'd been introduced by Karpat and shaken hands all around. She too spoke good English, though not so perfectly as her husband. I judged her to be in her early thirties, perhaps twenty years younger than Byzas. So she would not feel ill at ease as the only woman at lunch, Karpat had invited his secretary, Dasha, to join us too. She seemed to know Margurita from previous visits, and as we were escorted to the table they chatted together in Turkish.

I was seated next to my author, and I told him how pleased I was that Neptune Books would be publishing him in America. "I've always admired your first novel, *Ataturk*. I intend to lead off with that title early next year."

"Very good," Byzas said. "My books have a fair success in England and I have always hoped to have them published in America as well."

"He wants to visit New York," his wife confided with a smile. "That is the dream of every Turkish author."

"Have you been to America?"

"Once, briefly. I have done some modeling. The Western nations are so free and open, especially for women. It is very difficult living in a Muslim nation."

"Turkey is hardly Iran," I pointed out.

"Still, you must see the Muslim schoolgirls with their long coats and scarves over their heads. It is so different from the Western ways."

"Margurita would like it if I moved to London or Paris," Byzas said with an indulgent smile. "But I am a Turkish writer. This is my place."

Karpat still felt the need to praise his client, even though the contracts had already been signed. "He knows this country better than any living man. Dasha, tell them about the professor."

His secretary smiled and launched into a story she'd obviously told many times before. "This professor from England was doing research on brothels around the world. At least he called it research. He asked Mr. Byzas to put him in touch with a local expert in this area. We knew of no one, of course, and I telephoned Mr. Byzas to see if he might have an acquaintance who could help. He came down to the office and took the professor off on a personal tour of the brothels that very night!" She glanced sideways at Margurita. "Of course this was before he had remarried."

"I've heard the story before," Margurita assured her. "I thought you were going to tell the one about the professor at the art museum."

"Which one was that?" Simon Ark asked, joining the conversation for the first time.

"I've forgotten the details," Dasha admitted, brushing a stray wisp of hair from her eyes.

The memory of the incident was obviously clear in Margurita's mind. "This little old man, Professor Metzger—" I shot a glance at Simon but he didn't react "—contacted the office nearly four months ago. He needed information about some incident in World War II. Naturally Mustafa could help him, and the man met us at Mr. Karpat's office. He was quite ancient and stooped over. I had nothing against his appearance, of course, but my dears, I thought he would never leave. He stayed all afternoon, till after five!"

"About four-thirty, as I remember it," her husband corrected with a tolerant grin. "He wanted to know about a rumor which has persisted over the years regarding Turkey's involvement in the war. As you know, our nation was an ally of Germany during the First World War, but we were neutral during the Second. This city was occupied by the Allied powers in 1918, which led to the overthrow of the last sultan by Ataturk."

I nodded, smiling. "I've read your novel."

"Of course. To cut the story short, Professor Metzger believed some outlaw factions in Turkey might have helped Nazi war criminals escape from Europe in 1945. One of them might even have been a prior curator at the museum, now long dead."

"Interesting," Simon Ark agreed.

"The point of all this," Karpat told us, "is simply that Mustafa Byzas is perhaps the most knowledgeable person you'll ever find about our city and our nation—in addition to being a superb novelist."

"You don't have to convince me," I said. Our drinks had arrived and the conversation paused while the red-coated waiter took our luncheon orders.

When the conversation resumed, the agent turned to Simon Ark. "You must have a question about our city, even though our friend tells me you lived here during the 1920s."

Simon turned his gaze toward Byzas and addressed the author directly. "Yes, there is one question."

"Ask it!"

"What is the Society of the Scar?"

It seemed for an instant as if a cone of silence had descended over our table. Perhaps it lasted no more than a few seconds, but as I sat there waiting for an answer it might have been half a lifetime. Then Mustafa Byzas cleared his throat and began to speak.

"The Society of the Scar was an informal group of rebels within the harem of Topkapi Palace. Young women sent there against their will would sometimes cut a scar on their cheek deliberately, to make themselves less attractive to the sultans. Some say the custom has continued down to the present day, in an ultra-rightist organization whose members include men as well as women. Metzger asked about it too."

"See?" his wife asked. "Didn't we tell you he knows everything?"

"I find that very interesting," Simon told him. "Thank you for the information."

The waiter wheeled in a serving cart with our food and conversation ceased again. When it resumed, Dasha was inquiring about the sights we'd seen, and no further mention was made of the Society of the Scar. I had not felt it necessary to tell any of them about the dead man in the Turkish bath.

Later, when I finally parted from Mustafa Byzas and his wife, there was much handshaking and even a kiss from the tall slim woman. "I'll phone you with the first reviews," I promised. "But you'll be getting proofs long before that, probably by September."

It was a lovely warm afternoon so Simon and I took the long way back to the hotel, pausing to watch the commuter ferryboats docking near the Yeni Mosque. "What could be the connection between a harem society dating to the turn of the century or earlier, and that dead man who was trying to tell you something?" I asked as we enjoyed the breeze off the water.

"A rightist group, Byzas said. And we learn that Professor Metzger has been asking about possible secret involvement in helping Nazi war criminals flee Europe after the war." Simon mused about this as we set off across the Galata Bridge toward our hotel.

"Remember our flight home leaves tomorrow noon."

He turned to me with a smile. "Then there is just time for another visit to the art museum. Come, my friend. Let us get a taxi."

Professor Metzger was in his office when we arrived, and he rose from his desk to greet us. "It's so good to see you both! I'd thought you would have been busy with Mr. Byzas this afternoon."

"We finished early," I explained. "And Simon wanted to see you again."

Simon Ark moved about the office, as if carefully choosing a chair that would position him properly. I realized he wanted to have a good view of Metzger's face, instead of a mere silhouette outlined by the glow from outside.

"Karpat, Byzas's agent, tells us you called on him recently with an unusual question."

"Question? I remember no question."

"About a prior curator of this museum who might have had right-wing ties with Nazis after the war."

"Oh, yes," he answered, a bit flustered. "A great many things changed in this city after you left, Simon."

"In what way?"

"The country remained neutral during the war, of course, but there were people old enough to remember the First World War who thought we should be fighting with Germany once again. One of them was Goknil, the curator here."

"What sort of man was he?"

Metzger rose from his desk and walked to a large cabinet with flat, horizontal drawers for storing paintings and prints. He pulled open the third drawer from the top and removed a large framed photograph. "This used to hang on my wall. I got tired of looking at it."

"Mr. Goknil?" Simon asked, studying the picture.

"The very same."

"He has a small scar on his cheek, like a dueling scar."

"You see many people with scars."

"I have heard they belong to a society."

Professor Metzger smiled. "That was in the old days of the sultans' harems."

"Yet you were curious enough to contact Byzas about it, through his agent."

Metzger hesitated and then nodded. "Yes, I was. I see you've been checking up on me, Simon. After Goknil's death I inherited a filing cabinet full of his personal correspondence. Though he was very discreet, I found some odd messages from 1945 that hinted he had a hand in helping war criminals escape to South America. They would make their way from Germany to the Balkans and then here, where Goknil arranged transportation for them, usually in the guise of museum representatives seeking art objects for sale in Latin America. They would arrive in Rio or Buenos Aires and simply never return."

"Byzas provided this information?"

"He simply confirmed what I'd already suspected. I met with him one day at his agent's office. He pointed out the scar in a photograph of Goknil and told me about the Society of the Scar, a right-wing organization descended from the old harem days."

"Why didn't you tell us all this earlier?"

"It can have no bearing—"

"Ah, but it can!" Simon insisted. "Has it not occurred to you that the slasher of paintings may be searching for something, rather than merely trying to vandalize the pictures?"

"What gives you that idea?"

"A vandal would not concentrate merely on portraits of people. And if he struck at other museums as this one has, he would not limit himself to a pair of portraits on loan from this museum. He is searching for something specific."

"Something hidden on the back of the paintings?"

"More likely something hidden between the canvas itself and the paper backing."

"Nothing larger than a sheet of paper could be hidden there," I pointed out.

"Exactly," said Simon Ark. "A sheet of paper. And what sheet of paper, long hidden behind the canvas of one of those portraits, might be valuable enough to lead someone to slash eleven paintings in a search for it?"

"Something about Goknil and the war criminals?" I ventured.

"No doubt! Goknil listed the names of those he helped, and perhaps even where he sent them. Of course it was more than forty years ago and most of them would be dead now, but in the hands of a right-wing organization the list could still be valuable. The survivors, their children, those who hid them, might easily make generous contributions to a right-wing cause to keep their secret."

"Why deface the paintings merely to find the list?" the professor wondered.

"Because it was the only way, at least for an obsessed killer who would stop at nothing."

"Killer? Who has been killed?"

"One of the Scar members who tried to tell us what he knew." Simon told him about the murdered man.

"That's terrible! I live in fear that it might be one of our guards next time, but what can we do to prevent it?"

Simon reached over suddenly and plucked a thick catalogue from the top of the professor's desk. "What's this?"

"A catalogue of our acquisitions and permanent collection. All museums publish them."

"Each painting lists the year in which it was acquired?"

"Of course, along with a brief description."

Simon quickly turned the pages to the beginning of the list. "The slasher has to be using a system of some sort, even if it's a crazy one. Otherwise why would he leave this museum to attack two paintings on loan and then return here? Help me with this, Professor. We know he attacks only portraits. What year did Goknil die?"

"I'm not certain, but he retired as curator in 1949 and lived the rest of his life in quiet luxury."

"No doubt." Simon ran his finger down the list. "So we will limit ourselves to portraits acquired prior to his retirement, when he would have been in a position to hide that list of names. Here is the first one, a portrait of Ataturk as a young man."

"It was the first painting to be damaged, three months ago!"

"Excellent!"

It took them only five minutes to establish that the eleven paintings had been slashed according to their order in the catalogue, omitting non-portraits and portraits acquired after 1949. "That's it," I agreed. "He's using a copy of this catalogue."

"Then the next painting to be slashed," Professor Metzger said, "will be—"

"—This portrait of Sultan Mehmet II, with the ruins of the Sacred Palace in the background. Acquired in 1934," Simon announced.

Metzger scooped up the telephone and dialed the security office. "Plaque! We think the next slasher vandalism will be in the west wing, ground floor—the Scanda portrait of Mehmet. Could you place an extra guard in the room? *What?*" He looked up at us. "Someone just pulled the emergency alarm in that very room!"

"Quickly—how many exits are there from the building?"

"Only one for the public."

"Seal it! Don't let anyone in or out," Simon ordered. "We may have our vandal trapped inside."

"What about the guards?" I asked. "It could be an inside job."

Simon shook his head. "No, the guards and employees can be trusted."

I had no idea how he'd determined this, but I followed along as we left Professor Metzger's office and hurried down the marble steps to the ground floor. Plaque, the security chief, was in the west wing gallery, looking distraught. "There's been another one, Professor. We're too late! My guard pulled the alarm when he found it."

"The Scanda portrait?"

"Yes. See—it's been slashed like the others."

Simon Ark hurried over to examine it. "There was nothing hidden here. The search is not over yet."

"But who—?"

Simon hurried through to the next gallery. He seemed to know exactly what or who he was seeking. I followed, seeing him pause two rooms over, where a young woman was seated at a small canvas, copying a landscape by Sisley. She was wearing a smock and beret.

He went up to her and spoke. "Pardon me, I believe we've met before."

She turned and sprang at him with a thin camel's-hair brush. It seemed the most innocent of weapons for an attack, but Simon fended her off, finally managing to grab hold of her wrist as Plaque and the professor hurried up. "Be careful of the brush," he told the security man. "She's got part of a razor blade hidden in the bristles."

Even before her beret fell off in the struggle I had recognized her. It was Dasha, the agent's secretary.

Before they led her away, Simon Ark took a damp cloth and wiped it across Dasha's cheeks, removing some of the heavy pancake makeup she always wore. It was then that we saw the small scar and knew that he was right.

"It was mainly a process of elimination," he told us a little later, back in Professor Metzger's office. "You, Professor, and Plaque and everyone else who worked here were pretty much removed from suspicion by a simple fact. If the slasher were merely trying to find that piece of paper, and he were an employee of the museum, there would have been no need for slashing. He or she could have examined the paintings one at a time, removing them from the walls at leisure. The paper backing might get torn a little, but there certainly would be no need to slash the canvas. No, the slasher had to be an outsider. But who? Almost certainly a member of the Society of the Scar, since it was the scar-faced man who offered us information and was killed for that. Now when did the slashings begin?"

"Three months ago," I volunteered. "We were told that twice."

"Exactly! And that would have been shortly after Professor Metzger's meeting with Byzas, which was nearly four months ago. It certainly seems as if that conversation may have triggered the slashings, since it dealt with the activities of the museum's previous curator. We never heard who was present, but surely in that small office there could have been no one but Byzas, the professor, Karpat and his secretary Dasha, and Byzas's wife Margurita."

Professor Metzger nodded. "That was all."

"Dasha must have already known that a list had been hidden inside a portrait at some museum. When she overheard the mention of Goknil it told her which museum, and she started her search. You told me, my friend, that only a bookcase separated her desk from Karpat's office space, so overhearing conversations would have been easy. Likewise, yesterday she heard you tell the agent I was visiting Professor Metzger. She picked up my trail outside the museum and saw the limping man slip the note to me. She followed him to the Grand Hamam and killed him there."

"Karpat had all the knowledge Dasha did," I protested. "Couldn't he have been the slasher and killer?"

"When Mr. Plaque described the vandalism that took place virtually under his eyes, he told us who was present in the gallery—some children, a young woman copying a painting, and the limping young man who later became the victim. None of those could have been Karpat, but the young woman might have been Dasha, especially since her heavy makeup could have been hiding a scar. A piece of razor blade hidden among the bristles of her brush made a perfect slashing weapon, enabling her to vandalize the portrait virtually in plain sight. I believe she used a similar weapon at the baths yesterday, dressing as a painter and hiding a knife blade among the bristles of a much larger brush."

"She was that painter we saw?"

"Of course! What would a painter be doing there, in that steamy, moist atmosphere which would make painting impossible? It seemed likely the painter was the killer, but then I had to ask myself why he bothered with that attention-getting costume. By removing one's clothes and being nearly naked like everyone else, the killer would have been virtually invisible. But was there someone who could not remove their clothes in a Turkish bath without attracting attention? Yes—a woman!"

Professor Metzger nodded. "She had to speed up her search by striking again today, and that was what did her in. I trust the police will track down the other members of her group. And I will begin an immediate search of the other portraits for any list or document. I can only thank you for all you've done, Simon."

Simon Ark smiled. "Perhaps we'll meet again in another sixty years."

We flew home the next day as scheduled. Metzger wrote Simon a month later, telling him the police had indeed rounded up other members of the Society of the Scar. Goknil's list had been found and various international agencies were studying it with great interest. As for Dasha, she never came to trial. One night in her cell she bled to death after slashing her wrists.

NO BLOOD FOR A VAMPIRE

I'd found myself in many strange places with my friend Simon Ark, but none quite so strange as this. Crowded in among spectators of every possible skin pigment, we were watching a staged combat between a pair of large warthogs, each weighing more than two hundred pounds. The corrugated metal warehouse into which a hundred or more spectators had jammed was steaming with foul, humid air that no one else seemed to notice. Even after the fight started and the beasts had locked tusks for the first time, an Arab with a canvas purse tied around his waist still moved among the spectators, taking bets on the outcome.

"It is a bit close in here," Simon Ark admitted when I expressed my discomfort. "Perhaps we could stand nearer the door if we return tomorrow evening."

"Tomorrow!" I was aghast at the thought of it.

The two ugly warthogs came apart, circled, and then charged again, this time butting heads as they attempted to jab each other with their incurving tusks. The large facial warts that gave the beasts their name served as some protection, and they soon broke off the encounter as the partisan roaring of the crowd increased. I tried to block out the sight of it and recall what had brought me here to a humid, stinking warehouse on the coast of Madagascar.

It had been a warm August afternoon in Manhattan when my secretary at Neptune Books had buzzed me to announce quietly, "Mr. Simon Ark—a tall old man in a black suit. He has no appointment. Is he one of our authors?"

She'd been with me only a few months, and anyone's first encounter with Simon could be a bit unnerving. "He did a book on Satanism some years back," I explained. "Send him in."

Simon's vigor was undiminished since I'd last seen him six months earlier. As soon as he'd greeted me, he unfolded a map of Africa and pointed to the large island of Madagascar off the eastern coast. "Vampires," he announced dramatically in the harsh voice I'd grown to know so well.

Like most people I was vaguely aware of Madagascar's existence, but it wasn't high on my tourist agenda. "I didn't think you believed in vampires, Simon."

"I believe in them only as a manifestation of a greater evil. Men do not turn into bats and flit through the night air, but they do indeed commit murder and drink the blood of their victims upon occasion. There are many well-documented cases, as you know. A person named Mano Ratki believes such a killer is loose in Madagascar."

"Surely it's a matter for the local police."

"They scoff at the very idea, because no blood has been spilled. The victims have all been strangled. Ratki has read that old book of mine and thinks I can help."

"How could you find what the police can't?"

"He says only that he recognized this person from another country, where the person was forced to leave because of charges of vampirism. My correspondent knows the same thing is happening again, even if he doesn't know how. Madagascar is a strange country in many ways. The people open the tombs of the dead, and sometimes dance with the corpses of departed relatives."

"What? Can such things be, Simon? This is practically the twenty-first century!"

"Come with me, my friend, and see for yourself."

So I had come, risking yet another scene with my wife Shelly, who'd never quite approved of Simon Ark. In her younger days she could joke about his claim of wandering the earth for two thousand years seeking battle with Satan. Now, with both of us well into middle age and Simon looking much the same, the jokes had grown tired.

It was Simon's correspondent, Mano Ratki, who met us at the airport in Madagascar's centrally located capital city of Antananarivo. He was a small brown-skinned man of uncertain ancestry, but I judged him to be mainly Malayan-Indonesian like the bulk of the nation's population. "I thank you for coming this distance," he said, speaking English with a trace of French accent. Madagascar had been a French colony until its independence in 1960.

"I have read your letters with interest," Simon told him. "Are we to see the person you claim is a vampire?"

"All in good time," the small man told us, smiling to reveal a gap-toothed grin. "First we will drive to the coastal town of Brickaville, about a hundred miles from here. There is a warthog fight tonight which you may find interesting."

"Warthogs?" I repeated, catching Simon's eye to signal my distaste.

We stowed our luggage in the back of his battered Land Rover and set off down the highway. The temperature in the low eighties was quite pleasant and Simon remarked on it, trying to encourage conversation with this man who'd summoned us nearly halfway around the world.

"I fear it will be more humid on the coast," Mano Ratki said, keeping his eyes on the road.

"Are there a great many warthogs in Madagascar?" I asked finally.

Ratki gave a snort. "There are no warthogs on the entire island! They are imported from Mozambique on the African mainland. Our poor country has only second-best—a similar animal called a bushpig. They fight head-to-head, much like the warthogs, but they lack those impressive tusks. People come to Nafud's fights to see those tusks in action."

"Who is Nafud?" Simon asked.

"An Arab trader. He runs the fights and takes bets on the outcome."

"And the vampire?"

"Ah! You shall see!"

Later, as we maneuvered a steep jungle road, I asked, "Is the entire country as hilly as this?"

"There is a flat plain to the west on the Mozambique Channel. The rest is rough, but hardly impassable."

Presently we drove down onto a narrow coastal plain near the village of Brickaville. A decidedly European influence was visible here, and I assumed that the docking facilities and warehousing had been left by the French when they departed. A small hotel called the Seaman's Rest could be seen a bit farther along the shore.

We made at once for one of the corrugated metal warehouses, joining a crowd that was already gathering. Here, on the shore of the Indian Ocean, the diversity of race and ethnic origin seemed even greater than I'd observed during our overland journey. Some, like our companion, seemed to have Far Eastern roots, but Arabs and Africans were present, too. There was even a Frenchman named Dr. Creux who might have remained as a child when his countrymen pulled out in 1960.

I asked him about this, when Ratki had introduced us, but he smiled and shook his head. "No, I was born and educated in France. But French doctors remained here after the country gained its independence, and there was always a need for more. A great many French-speaking people remain, though Malagasy is the official language."

He was a man in his forties, graying at the temples, who seemed somehow at home among this mixture of races and nationalities. "Do you actually come here to see the warthog fights?" I asked.

Dr. Creux smiled. "This is not an exciting place. We must make the best of the few amusements available. If Nafud wants to hold warthog fights, I will come and watch."

Simon Ark let his gaze sweep over the spectators as they filled the place. "Which one is Nafud?"

"The Arab with the canvas purse," Ratki replied. "You'll meet him later. We'd better get inside."

I noticed the French doctor pause to speak with a strikingly handsome young woman with a camera around her neck. It was an expensive camera and I suspected she was more than a tourist. As the crush of spectators increased, I lost sight of them and we were pressed against a cage full of noisy lemurs awaiting shipment.

The warthog duel ended after some fifteen minutes when one of the animals drew blood. It was none too soon for me. Both animals were taken away while the Arab with the canvas purse paid off the winners.

Ratki led us through the crowd to Nafud's side. When he'd finished his gambling transactions we were introduced. "I welcome visitors from America," he said formally, shaking our hands. Then he peered more closely at Simon's chiseled features. "You have some Hamite or Berber ancestry in your blood, Mr. Ark. I see it in the lines of your face."

"I trace my lineage back to Egypt some two millennia ago," Simon answered a bit vaguely. Then, changing the subject, he gestured back toward the lemur cages where we'd been standing. "Are you responsible for those creatures?"

"They are awaiting shipment to zoos."

"Lemurs are nocturnal. Their cages should be covered."

"In this hot place it is better they get some air. And lemurs are evolving into daytime creatures anyway, Mr. Ark."

"It is a profitable export," Mano Ratki explained. "Lemurs are found nowhere else on earth."

A late bettor came up to claim his winnings and we continued outside. I realized we hadn't eaten since a meager snack on the plane some hours earlier and Mano Ratki apologized for his neglect. He led us through the gathering darkness to a cafe in the small hotel I'd noticed earlier. "It is not very good," he cautioned, "but it is the best we can offer."

The spicy East Indian food was filling, at least for the moment, and that was all we asked. After dinner, relaxing with an American soft drink, I saw Dr. Creux enter with the attractive brunette woman I'd observed earlier, "Enjoying our local cuisine?" the doctor asked with a smile. "May I present Madame Desladas, a visitor to our shores."

"Carla Desladas," she corrected with a smile, extending a hand to Simon and me. She was a tall, slender woman in her thirties, and her jet-black hair was loose to her shoulders. The expensive Japanese camera still hung from her neck by a strap. She was wearing an old plaid shirt and tapered jeans, for which she immediately apologized. "After all, what do you wear to a warthog fight?"

"It is a man's sport," Ratki admitted. "Here, join us for a drink."

He pulled up extra chairs to our table and Dr. Creux and the woman sat down. "Only for a moment," the doctor said. "I must get back to my clinic."

"It's here, in Brickaville?" Simon asked.

"Just a mile up the coast. We are well equipped for all the usual ills and even some unusual ones. The clinic has the only kidney dialysis machine in this part of the country, and full surgical facilities as well. This evening, as we do once a week, we are offering free tests for AIDS."

"It's a problem in Madagascar, too?" Carla Desladas asked.

The doctor nodded. "On the African mainland it is very serious. We try to keep it from our island, but that is impossible."

Before long Simon had struck up a conversation with the Frenchwoman. "I'm a journalist," she was explaining. "I've been here on the coast for a few weeks and tomorrow I head inland for the season of *famadihana*."

Simon Ark nodded. "The turning of the bones."

She seemed surprised. "You are familiar with the local custom?"

"I know that ancestor worship here is as strong today as it was hundreds of years ago. Even the Catholic Church has come to terms with it."

"You'd better explain it," I said.

"In August and September, when the crops are in and the weather begins to cool, the people feast and often bring the dead from their tombs to be wrapped in new shrouds."

"All this and warthogs, too!" Madagascar seemed farther from Manhattan with each new revelation.

Dr. Creux dismissed that with a wave of his hand. The warthogs are strictly Nafud's scheme to make a little money. They have nothing to do with the reality of life in this country. Up in the hills, at villages like Imerina where men dance with the dead one last time—that is reality here."

"I will take you there tomorrow morning," Mano Ratki promised Simon and me.

"You're actually going there?" Carla asked. "Would you have room for an extra passenger?"

Ratki eyed her for a moment before responding. "I suppose so," he agreed. "If you don't have luggage."

"Only me. And my camera."

"We leave promptly at nine, from the hotel."

I'd been hoping that we'd be spending the night back in the capital, where a few modern buildings seen from the air had led me to imagine a first-class hotel. Instead we ended up at the Seaman's Rest, upstairs over the cafe. "Merchant seamen often like a night ashore," Ratki explained, "with a woman. This fills a need."

I could hear comings and goings in the hall half the night, before finally drifting into a restless sleep in the lumpy bed. I awakened shortly after six to find Simon standing by the shutters, fully dressed, observing the street below. "You're up early," I muttered before burying my face in the pillow.

"Get dressed, my friend. There seems to be an altercation in front of the hotel, between Mano Ratki and a police officer."

"All right," I gave in, knowing that further sleep was impossible. "I want to shower first. I'll meet you downstairs."

He hadn't told me that the trickle from the shower head was luke-warm at best. I dressed quickly and joined Simon on the street. The dark-skinned police officer, Captain Billy Lightly, wore a braided shirt and a large gold badge. He was questioning them about a murder that had occurred during the night, down by the docks. "You are always on the scene when there is a killing, Mano," he told our friend. "I have my eye on you." Finally he turned and crossed the street to a waiting police car, removing his sun helmet to wipe his forehead.

"What happened?" I asked Ratki.

The small man wrinkled his brow, seeming genuinely concerned. "Another man strangled with a cord, down by the dock."

"A seaman?" I asked.

"No, one of the workmen at Nafud's warehouse. They are never seamen."

Simon raised his eyes. "The victims of your so-called vampire? They are never seamen?"

"That is correct."

"Interesting. Why does the captain think you are involved?"

"He looks for a scapegoat. I am on the scene because of my suspicions, but he scoffs when I mention vampires. 'There is no blood for vampires,' he says. 'There are no teeth marks on the throat.' But he sees too many films."

"What do the autopsies show?"

"No noticeable blood loss. But that is why I summoned you, Mr. Ark. You must find out how it is being done."

I wondered whether the heat of this place had gotten to Ratki, obsessing him with visions of black-caped stalkers.

"What does it matter to you?" I asked. "Why do you care so much?"

He led the way to his Land Rover and opened the door. "I care because the first victim was my brother," he said. "Far away, in a different country. I have followed his killer here."

"Name him for me," Simon urged.

"In due time."

Later that morning, after a breakfast of native fruit, we set off for the interior, first stopping to pick up Carla Desladas as promised. She was dressed today in a khaki bush jacket with matching shirt and pants, her long black hair pulled into a bun in back. She carried a camera bag in one hand.

Carla joined me in the back seat for our journey, and as we drove past the warehouse we saw Nafud and two of his helpers lugging a large burlap sack. "Looks as if he has a body in there," Carla joked.

"Stranger things have happened here," Ratki said from behind the wheel.

I knew Simon was as frustrated as I was by the man's frequent hints of dark doings, never once naming the person he suspected. At one point on the journey I remembered the lemurs and said, "With all the odd animals in Madagascar, surely you have vampire bats."

"No, true vampire bats are found, only in Central and South America. Here there is only the false vampire bat. Like the bushpig, we are second best." He lapsed again into silence.

"Have you done much African photography?" I asked Carla after another few miles of driving.

"Some. My ex-husband and I used to shoot large animals—elephants, giraffes, hippos."

"What happened to him?"

"We split up, and after that he got involved in some nasty business. Poachers were killing elephants for their ivory tusks. Ron photographed them, but they bought him off. He was always something of a weakling. The last I heard he was serving a short prison sentence."

"Is ivory poaching still a problem?"

"Your country and some others now ban the importation of African elephant ivory. That has helped a great deal. Of course there are no elephants in Madagascar so it has never been a problem here."

Suddenly we topped a rise in the road and came upon a small village surrounded by rice fields. "This is our destination," Ratki told us. "A festival is in progress. They will open the tomb later today."

He'd barely parked the Land Rover when a black man wearing a jacket and headband approached us. He was a member of the village council named Ramajiso and he greeted Ratki warmly. "You arrive in good time for the feast," he told us. "We will open the tomb soon and later the council will read out the names of the dead to be brought up."

"Is this a family tomb?" Simon Ark asked.

"Yes, my family is there—nearly two hundred of them, stretching back for generations."

"I would like to see it. Your customs here are strange to us."

"But first you must eat," Ramajiso insisted.

The feast was indeed under way, and we gorged ourselves on helpings of beef, pork, and rice, washing it down with a locally brewed alcohol. "I won't want to eat for a week," Carla announced when we'd consumed all that we could. I glanced around for Mano Ratki, but he seemed to have disappeared.

"If you wish to see the tomb," Ramajiso told Simon, "I will take you now. Once the names are read out, the male relatives will enter immediately to bring forth the bodies."

Though I was included in the invitation, it was explained that women never entered the tomb. Carla reluctantly stayed behind, clicking off shots of the tomb entrance as the heavy granite door was opened for us. It was built into the side of a grassy knoll some distance from the center of the village, and the door was not locked now, if it ever was. Ramajiso handed us candles and lit them, revealing a flight of wooden stairs leading to the underground tomb. "This is my family resting place," he said with quiet dignity.

I had expected a typical mausoleum with rows of coffins in niches. Instead we found slabs of granite upon which rested some two hundred bodies wrapped in white cloth and sheathed in straw mats. "You don't use coffins?" I asked.

"Only to carry the body to the tomb. Then it is removed and borne inside. This has been so in my family for one hundred fifty years."

"Some of these will be removed today?" Simon asked.

"Eleven names will be read, and we will bring the bodies up. My family will dance and there will be more feasting. The dead will be rewrapped in fresh white cloths before being returned here."

The odor of the place was beginning to reach me, and I was grateful when we were back above ground. Already we could see the villagers gathering for the reading of names. Carla Desladas stood near the fringe of the crowd, her camera humming with each click of the shutter.

As Ramajiso had predicted, all eleven names were members of his extended family who had died during the past decade. The wrapped bodies were carried from the tomb by celebrating male relatives who might have been enjoying a Mardi Gras. In most cases the dried dead skin had separated from the bones and the effect was gruesome in the extreme. The dancing, singing family members seemed not to notice.

Then it happened without warning. As Carla edged closer with her camera, one of the straw mats was unrolled, revealing a white cloth that seemed cleaner and fresher than the others. Ramajiso himself bent to uncover the body, then leaped back with a gasp of horror. This was not one of his family.

It was the body of Mano Ratki, and he'd been strangled like the other victims.

When the village police arrived to investigate the killing, Simon Ark and I stood off to one side. "I couldn't have known," he said quietly, staring down at the body under its white covering.

"Of course not," I agreed. "Don't blame yourself. Anyway, this can't be the work of any vampire. There's not a drop of blood anywhere. That white cloth is spotless." We both saw that it wasn't completely true, and Simon bent to examine a dark brown smudge in one corner. He rubbed a bit and most of it came off on his hand.

"Interesting," he said.

"What is it? Not blood, certainly."

He sniffed his fingers. "It appears to be greasepaint."

"But why—?"

We were interrupted by a native police officer in charge of the investigation. He bore little resemblance to the dapper figure of Captain Lightly back in Brickaville. "Which of you is Simon Ark?"

"I am."

"I have communicated by telephone with Billy Lightly. He encountered you this morning while investigating another murder. This dead man, Mano Ratki, was also questioned about it."

"That's correct," Simon agreed.

"Murder seems to follow you around, Mr. Ark. May I ask what you are doing here?"

"The dead man, Mr. Ratki, brought us to witness the festival."

Carla was standing nearby, holding her camera, but she'd made no effort to take a picture since the arrival of the police. The officer asked why she was there. "I'm a news photographer," she answered, not altogether truthfully. It seemed to satisfy him.

The villagers had been in a turmoil since the uncovering of the unwelcome body, and I couldn't blame them. Ramajiso and his brothers had immediately searched the tomb by candlelight, taking inventory of the bodies. All were accounted for. Ratki's corpse had merely been added to the collection, shoved onto a slab near the tomb entrance. If it had not been found before the tomb was closed again, it might have gone undiscovered for a decade.

"A perfect hiding place," Simon observed. "Down among the dead men and women."

"Why did no one see it happen?" I asked.

"The tomb is some distance from the village center, hidden by that knoll. Someone could easily have lured Ratki away during the feast and strangled him. The fresh winding sheets and mats are laid out nearby. And he was a small man, easily carried."

"Who were his enemies here?" the officer asked.

"There were none," Ramajiso insisted. "He came here occasionally, but I knew him best from my own trips into Brickaville for supplies."

"Have there been any other murders or unexplained deaths recently?" Simon asked.

"Not a one!" Ramajiso insisted. "We are a peaceful people."

Carla agreed to drive Ratki's Land Rover back to Brickaville. On the way, I could see Simon was deep in thought, puzzling over events of the past twenty-four hours. Mano Ratki had summoned him because he suspected a vampire killer had come to Madagascar. There were mysterious deaths, but none seemed to involve the spilling of blood. The only blood I'd seen had been spilled by that warthog's gouging tusks, and even vampires didn't resort to warthog blood.

Simon broke the silence only once. "Ratki would have introduced us to the person he suspected. I feel certain we have met the killer."

Captain Lightly was waiting for us back at the docks in Brickaville. He wore a fresh, neatly pressed uniform, but was without his sun helmet. "You are a great detective, Mr. Ark," he said by way of greeting. "Do you know who strangled our good friend Ratki?"

He hadn't seemed so friendly with Ratki earlier that day, but I didn't bother to remind him. The question had been directed to Simon and he answered it. "Not yet, but I will know in time. Has the autopsy been completed on last night's victim?"

"The body was sent to the capital. The preliminary report gives strangulation as the cause of death."

"No wounds of any sort?"

Captain Lightly smiled slightly, revealing teeth stained with betel juice. "Nothing unusual. Men who work in the warehouse always have a few cuts and scrapes on their arms."

"What about his blood?"

Billy Lightly sighed. "The medical authorities in Anananarivo are not bothered by fine points. This man, like the others, had the proper volume of blood in his body. That is all I can tell you. The body has been released for embalming."

Simon had a sudden thought. "Embalming? He's not one of those to be buried in a native village like Imerina, his body wrapped in a mat and placed in a family tomb?"

The captain smiled again. "Once people leave their native villages they rarely return. The dead are usually buried where they die. Ratki was born here but he has lived in Marseille and Rome." He eyed Simon and asked, "Will you be returning to America soon?"

"Perhaps tomorrow."

"Ah, then I may see you at Nafud's warehouse tonight."

"Tonight?"

"There is to be another of his warthog fights."

Carla went off to take a bath, claiming the odor of death still clung to her. I felt like doing the same thing, but Simon insisted we visit the dock area while it was still daylight. "After the fight it will be getting dark," he said, remembering the previous evening.

I followed him out to the docks, past bags of coffee, rice, and peanuts waiting to be loaded onto the next ship. A few workmen turned to stare as Simon's tall, black-garbed figure moved among them, but most ignored him. Finally he found what he was seeking—the burlap sack we'd seen Nafud and his men carrying earlier in the day. "Do you have a knife?" he asked me.

I unfolded a penknife and handed it to him. He made a quick cut in the burlap and we stood back. On the shore people were beginning to gather at Nafud's warehouse. It was almost time for the match to begin.

"It's as I thought," Simon told me.

I stared into the burlap sack. "A dead warthog. Probably the loser in last night's battle. What was he going to do, heave it into the ocean?"

"The cargo ship would dump it for him, well offshore." He used my penknife to poke at the head. "Notice that the tusks are missing."

"The tusks?"

"Ivory, my friend. Not as large as elephant tusks, but better than nothing."

"My God! Is that why Nafud imports them from the mainland?"

"It seems so."

I bent to examine the wounds where the tusks had been cut out. "I'm surprised there aren't more bloodstains," I commented.

Simon felt of the dead animal and made another incision on its under-side, where the force of gravity should have drawn the blood after death. "There is no blood," he said quietly.

"Simon—!"

He glanced quickly toward shore. "Come my friend. We have not a moment to lose!"

I followed him off the dock and into the milling crowd. The first person we recognized was Captain Lightly, busily conversing with a couple of sailors off one of the freighters. But Simon didn't stop to speak until we encountered Carla, looking fresh and cool in a clean shirt and jeans. "Have you seen Nafud?" Simon asked.

She nodded. "He's taking bets over on the other side. His men are bringing in the animals now. You'd better sit down."

I could read the anxiety on Simon's face as he struggled to break free of the press of spectators and reach Nafud. We saw the Arab now, moving among the late arrivals near the big warehouse doors, accepting currency in return for betting slips. But it was useless. I placed a hand on his shoulder and cautioned, "You'll be trampled in this crowd. Wait till it's over. He's not going anywhere."

He settled down reluctantly between Carla and me as the warthogs were brought in. I could see that the crowd was larger than the previous evening, possibly because there was one more freighter in port. But it seemed that some of the natives from nearby villages had made the trip in, too. "Isn't that Ramajiso?" I pointed out to Simon. "What's he doing here?"

The council member from Imerina was easily recognizable by his jacket and colored headband. "I've seen him in Brickaville before," Carla said. "He told us he came here for supplies."

"On the day of their festival?"

"Ratki's murder and the desecration of the family tomb may have put a damper on the festival," Simon Ark suggested.

There was a roar from the crowd as the warthogs faced each other and were released by their handlers. I spotted Dr. Creux at ringside, forced backward into the crowd as the animals locked tusks virtually in his lap. The battle dragged on longer than the previous night's fray, indicating the large animals were more evenly matched. Watching two ugly creatures batter and slam at one another was not my idea of a sport or prize contest, and I was relieved when one of them finally toppled over from exhaustion. Nafud stepped forward to declare a winner, amidst cheers and boos.

"At least it's not quite as humid as last evening," I said as the crowd began to flow toward the door.

But Simon had other things on his mind. "We must reach Nafud at once. Follow me," he urged.

Carla started to trail along, but we were separated by the warthog handlers. I was about to return and try to rescue her when I saw Dr. Creux reach out and offer his hand as she stepped around the collapsed animal. I noticed what looked like a brown birthmark on his arm.

Apparently the favorite had lost and there were few bettors to be paid off. The Arab finished with them, closed the purse at his waist and beat a hasty retreat toward the rear of the warehouse. "This way!" Simon urged, trying to head him off.

If Nafud saw us, he wasn't about to stop. A rear door stood open and he was nowhere to be seen. "Nafud!" Simon shouted, but there was no reply.

"I guess he doesn't want to see us," I suggested.

"We must find him before there is another murder."

"You mean Nafud is the vam—?"

"Quiet!" He stood by the door with one foot outside.

There was a movement nearby, in the darkness. No one had come out the door with us, but almost anyone could have slipped around from the dispersing crowd at the front of the building.

There was a sudden gasp, and the sound of a tussle. My fingers, running down the door frame, found a fight switch and I snapped it on. The sudden overhead light spilled out into the tall grass behind the building, revealing two men locked in a struggle. Simon and I sprang forward together to pull them apart.

"Thank heaven you were there!" Dr. Creux gasped. "Nafud was trying to strangle me."

I had the Arab in my grasp, but it was Simon Ark who loosened my grip and turned to Dr. Creux instead. "You've killed your last man, Doctor. And drunk your last beaker of blood."

Doctor Creux protested his innocence right up until the moment Captain Lightly opened the locked refrigerator at the clinic and discovered three and a half gallons of human blood in carefully labeled jugs. Then he fell silent and refused to speak at all.

"He was drinking human blood?" Billy Lightly asked, still unable to believe the evidence before him. "You mean like a vampire?"

"Exactly like a vampire," Simon Ark confirmed. The doctor had been taken away, but we were still at his clinic listening to Simon explain it all.

"His criminal madness manifested itself in a craving for human blood—large quantities of human blood. His problem was in obtaining the blood from his victims in a manner that would not be discovered. He succeeded in this quite well. I believe Mano Ratki knew the doctor back in Marseille where his brother was killed. When Creux fled here to Madagascar, Ratki followed him. He became aware of the mysterious stranglings, and summoned me to investigate. Unfortunately, Dr. Creux decided he had to die before he could voice his suspicions."

"How could he have killed Ratki?" I asked. "He wasn't even at the village."

"Ah, but he was, my friend. The smear of brown greasepaint on that white winding sheet hinted that the killer might have darkened his skin color to pass as a native."

"I noticed the same sort of brown mark on Creux's arm this evening," I admitted. "I thought it was a birthmark."

"He simply hadn't had time to wash it all off. He probably parked his car some distance away, mingled with the villagers and got Ratki aside to kill him, hiding his body in that tomb. He was unlucky that it was discovered before the tomb was sealed again."

Captain Lightly gestured toward the gallon jugs of dark red liquid. "If we are to believe the labels, there is none of Ratki's blood here."

"Of course not. Creux had neither the time nor the equipment to extract it, away from his clinic."

"But the others died away from the clinic," the officer protested.

"They died here. Nafud was to be another exception tonight. Dr. Creux saw us on the pier earlier, examining the body of a dead warthog. He knew he had to kill the Arab before we questioned him."

"What could Nafud tell you?"

"He was bringing the warthogs over for the gambling matches, then killing them for their ivory tusks."

Captain Lightly shrugged. "It's not illegal. Only elephant ivory is protected."

"I know that," Simon replied. "But Creux cut out the tusks for him, to obtain the maximum amount of ivory. And while he was at it he drained the warthog's blood."

"What? Why would he do that?"

Suddenly I realized the horror of it before Simon Ark uttered the words. "Don't you see, Captain? The doctor replaced his victims blood with that of a warthog."

Lightly's reaction at his words was a disbelieving snort. "That's impossible!"

"Is it? The warthogs weigh around two hundred pounds, so their bodies would have roughly the same amount of blood as an adult human. You'll remember that the doctor offered free AIDS testing here one night a week. When the patients returned for the results, he chose one who was free of AIDS and other diseases, strangled him, and immediately hooked up his body to the kidney dialysis machine he mentioned to us. The dead man's blood supply was removed and replaced with warthog blood. The needle marks on the body passed unnoticed on a dark-skinned workman whose arms already had a number of cuts and scrapes."

"An autopsy would certainly reveal that it was animal blood," I argued.

"It probably would if anyone suspected. The test is a simple one. But why would they test? The victims were strangled, remember, without a drop of blood being spilled. It may be that Creux came to Madagascar for the very reason that autopsies here might be less thorough than back in France, and animal blood was more readily available."

Captain Lightly examined the labels on the jugs. "How much from each victim?"

"Probably about six quarts," Simon answered, "depending upon the body weight."

"It's a strange world."

"It is indeed."

We flew home the following day, shortly after learning that Dr. Creux had committed suicide in his cell by biting through his wrists and bleeding to death.

THE GRAVEYARD GHOUL

"**M**y friend," Simon Ark told me as we sat waiting for our host's arrival. "it has been said that everyone has three lives—the public one, the private one, and the secret one. Certainly the secret life is the most interesting, especially in a person of some renown."

"You're thinking of government leaders, statesmen, generals?"

"Or mere poets and essayists like Ralph Waldo Emerson."

The idea made me chuckle. "I'm sure a preacher and philosopher like Emerson had no secret life. He was a very open man."

"Open indeed! Are you aware that his first wife, Ellen, died of tuberculosis at the age of nineteen? He took to walking to her tomb every morning, and one day after she'd been dead for thirteen months, he opened her coffin."

"My God! What did he find?"

Simon Ark shook his head sadly. "We can be thankful he didn't tell us. His journal for March of 1832 records only that, 'I visited Ellen's tomb & opened the coffin.' After thirteen months in her coffin, even the most beautiful of young women would have been terrifying to behold, especially by the young man who had loved her so deeply."

"Why would he have done that? Why would he replace the living memory of her with—"

My question went unfinished, for at that moment our host walked through the wide double doors of the club library. He was a slender gray-haired man named George Mitchner, and after shaking hands with them he led the way to the dining room. "I thought my club would be the best place to dine, gentlemen. We won't be disturbed here."

I knew Mitchner slightly because our firm, Neptune Books, had published a slender volume of his on old cemeteries. It hadn't been a big seller, and another editor had handled it, but I'd met him once when he was in the office. It was this fact, and my well-known friendship with Simon Ark, that led to the present dinner invitation at one of Manhattan's more exclusive clubs.

After the drinks had been ordered he turned to Simon, openly examining his black suit and aged face. "I understand you're something of a psychic detective."

Simon Ark smiled slightly. "Only to those who must categorize everything. I am merely a mortal in search of evil—in search of the devil, if you will. Sometimes I find traces of him in the most unexpected places."

"Be that as it may, I need your advice about some unexplained events on my estate."

"Grave robbers," I said, getting right to the point. I'd already told Simon that much, which had brought to mind his story about Emerson.

"Let us wait until after dinner." George Mitchner said with a gesture of his muscular hands. "It is not a topic to discuss before eating."

Over dinner Mitchner went at his food with determination, his angular brow dipped toward the thick steak on his plate. When he spoke at all, it was of other meals he'd eaten in distant places. "The best food in Cairo, you know, wasn't at Shepheard's Hotel but at a little café off Ramses Street."

Simon perked up at mention of Cairo. "You lived there?"

"During the war—World War II. I was very young then. I helped the British build a wall of bricks and sandbags under the chin of the Sphinx. It offered some protection against air-raid damage, though the city had no serious bombing even when the German tanks were only a hundred miles away."

After dinner, when the plates had been cleared and we were almost alone in the large dining room with our cups of coffee, George Mitchner announced, "And now to business. I live on the family estate up in Duchess County, with my wife and son. The Mitchners have owned land there since Revolutionary times, and we have a family cemetery on the property."

Simon Ark interrupted with a question. "How many are buried there?"

"Counting babies who died at birth, I suppose there are about fifty. My parents are both there. "Lately, there's been a rash of grave robbing, coffins dug up and opened, the main crypt invaded. The local police put it down to vandalism by teenagers, but I think it's something more. Certain Satanic symbols have been found nearby."

"This interests me," Simon admitted, "though even Satanic symbols can be painted by teenagers."

George Mitchner shook his head. "No, this is a clear case of grave robbery, or at least desecration."

"There are two motives for grave robbery," Simon told him, taking a sip of coffee. "One is to steal valuable objects that were buried with the deceased, as in ancient Egyptian tombs. The other is to steal the body itself, as Burke and Hare did in nineteenth-century Scotland, for sale to medical schools."

"The bodies were not taken. Nothing was taken. It's as if the vandal simply wanted to view the remains."

My mind went back to Emerson again, opening the coffin of his dead wife after thirteen months. "What sort of a sick person would do that?" I asked.

A flicker of pain crossed George Mitchner's face. "That is why I appeal to you, Mr. Ark, to come see for yourself. I have every reason to believe that the graves are being opened by my son Andrew."

When we finally met him, in the big old house at the end of a tree-shaded lane in Duchess County, Andrew Mitchner hardly seemed like the classic representation of a grave-robbing ghoul. He was a personable, mild-mannered young man with a ready smile and a firm handshake. Some of his father's features were apparent, especially in the shape of his brow and the curve of his shoulders.

"I'm pleased to meet you both," he said. "Father tells me you're here to suggest some security measures for the family graveyard. We've been troubled by vandals lately."

"Have you seen anyone in the area?" Simon Ark asked.

"Not at night. The graveyard and crypt are over the hill. They can't be seen from the house."

If we had wondered at the source of the Mitchner family income, it became obvious the moment we walked into what must have been the drawing room. The walls were lined with black-and-white photographs of giant cargo ships, and a scale model of one occupied a place of honor on a side table. "We're a maritime family," George Mitchner explained. "Always have been. Andrew's learning the business."

I guessed the son's age in the late twenties, a bit old for youthful pranks. I was still studying him when his father announced, "And this is my wife Abby."

If Simon and I expected to be greeted by a woman of Mitchner's age, we were startled by our first glimpse of her. She was a second wife, o course, a woman closer to Andrew's age than his father's. Her red hair may not have been natural, but her smile was warm and sincere as she greeted them. "It's a pleasure to have visitors here," she said, striding up to shake our hands. "We're too far from Manhattan for most people."

"It's wonderful country up here," I said. "Those Italian cypresses are like something on a picture postcard."

"All credit for the landscaping belongs to my father," George Mitchner said. "He remodeled the house and greatly improved the grounds. But we should get moving if you wish to see the cemetery while it's still daylight."

I thought for a moment that all of us would be going, but Andrew and Abby Mitchner stayed behind. Simon Ark had been unusually quiet during our time in the house, but once outside and striding through the crisp April air, he seemed to return to his usual self. He often claimed to be two thousand years old, and at that age suppose anyone can grow a bit quiet at times. Still, I suspected there was more to it than that. The Mitchner family hadn't been what either of us expected.

"There's one of the Satanic symbols I told you about," Mitchner said.

We'd approached the old family cemetery, bounded by an iron fence. There were stone posts where a gate might once have been, and it was on one of these that a crude pentagram had been spray-painted in red. Simon made a sound of derision. "Anyone can draw a pentagram. The dictionary tells you it's an occult symbol. True Satanists would be much more imaginative."

"Are there any teenagers in the area?" I asked Mitchner.

"Sure, there are a few on neighboring estates."

"How about the one next door?"

"A boy named Ronnie, around sixteen. He likes to ride horses. Ronnie King. Sometimes I have to chase him off my property."

"Maybe he's—"

But now we could see the first of the open graves, only partly filled in. Digging down to reach the coffin would have been hard work, a lot harder than spray-painting pentagrams. "This is the grave of my great-grandfather. It was the first one to be opened, two weeks ago. A few nights later, the crypt was broken into." He indicated what was really a stone mausoleum, built into the side of a hill. I could see from this distance that the padlock on the door had been recently replaced, shining like new.

"Exactly what does this graveyard ghoul do?" Simon Ark questioned. "I can see that the coffin has been opened—"

"He does nothing! Perhaps he looks at the bodies, but nothing more. In all cases the remains seemed intact. Nothing obvious was removed."

"Why do you suspect your son?"

"Four nights ago I was standing by the bedroom window just before retiring. There was a full moon, and suddenly I saw Andrew coming out of the garage, heading in this direction. He was carrying a shovel. The following morning I came down here to look and discovered that my wife's grave had been desecrated. His own mother's grave!"

"Have you reported this vandalism to the police?"

"Of course! I've called them all three times. All they told me was that they'd increase the road patrols in this area. That was when I decided I needed private help. If it is Andrew, I don't want him arrested."

Simon and I stood at the edge of the newest grave, staring down at the coffin. "Was there evidence that it had been opened?"

"Oh, yes! The lid was still ajar. When I think of Margaret suffering an indignity like this, after all she went through— And from her own son!"

"When did she die?" I asked.

"Four, almost five, years ago. She had a great many things wrong with her. She'd been in and out of hospital and finally it got to be too much for her poor body. She was only fifty-five."

Simon Ark pushed a bit of the dirt into the grave with his foot. "What was Andrew's reaction to all this? I gather you haven't confronted him with your accusation."

"Not yet. I wanted your opinion first, Mr. Ark. He seemed as shocked as I was at this outrage, so I made no reference to seeing him with the shovel."

Simon nodded. "It may be good for us to depart and then return after dark. If four nights have passed since the last outrage, it may be time for this ghoul to return."

Mitchner's face revealed a depth of pain we hadn't previously observed. "Why is he doing it, Mr. Ark? Has some devil taken control of him?"

"That's what I intend to find out."

We returned to the house, but now young Andrew Mitchner was nowhere to be seen. Abby was in the garden, tending to the season's first tulips. "The magnolias are ready to blossom," she told her husband. "One more warm day should bring them out."

"She's a wonder with flowers," Mitchner said as we went inside.

"Does she know of your suspicions? Simon asked.

He shook his head. "I've told no one but you two."

"Still, I should speak with her. She may have observed something that would be helpful."

Abby got up from her knees as we approached, shielding her eyes from the afternoon sun. She still held a trowel in one hand. "What do you think? Can we install a security system down there?"

"A really effective one would be quite expensive," I told her. "Of course, a simple alarm siren would scare them off. That might be all you need."

She rubbed a dirt-stained hand against the side of her jeans, then turned toward Simon as he asked. "Do you have any ideas about this vandalism, Mrs. Mitchner? It always helps to know if we're dealing with wild teenagers on a lark or adults with some darker purpose in mind."

She thought for a moment before responding, then said, "The spray-painted symbols seem more the work of young people, but I can't imagine anyone opening a coffin years after burial. That would have to be an awfully sick individual."

"Perhaps. If the symbols are to be believed, this could be the work of Satanists."

"Why would they open the graves? George tells me nothing was removed. It's not as if they wanted a skull or something for their obscene rites."

At that moment Mitchner called her from the house.

"Abby, could you come in now? Dinner is almost ready."

"We have to be going anyway," I told him. "I'll phone you in the morning with a quote on the job."

"Do that."

We drove down the highway a couple of miles as darkness began to settle over the land. "We have some hours yet," Simon Ark said. "Remember, Mitchner spotted his son with the shovel at bedtime."

"You think it'll be tonight?"

"That depends."

We had a light supper at a restaurant overlooking the Hudson River and drove back to the Mitchner estate shortly after eight o'clock. "We'll take up a position near the graveyard and watch until midnight." Simon suggested. "If nothing happens by then, we'll try again tomorrow."

Happily, the night was not too chilly. I found a good spot on the hill above the crypt, giving us a good view of the cemetery's entrance. "No one would climb the fence when there's an open gateway," Simon reasoned.

We were silent for a time, but after a while I became convinced no one would come. I started making conversation in a low voice. "I suppose Abby Mitchner is right. It would take a really sick individual to go about opening coffins."

"But what about Emerson? Was he sick or unbalanced? He opened his wife's coffin, remember."

"I don't know, but there is a possible explanation for that."

"Which is?"

"In those days people were occasionally buried alive, by accident. You have only to read Poe on the subject."

"And you think Emerson opened the coffin to be certain she was dead? After thirteen months?"

"Well—"

"He must have been certain of her death or he would never have allowed her burial. And he must have known that after all those months nothing would be left to stir memories of their days together."

"Then why? Was it something so obscene that we could never imagine it?"

"Hardly, my friend. Remember when we talked of the public life, the private life, and the secret life? Emerson was a minister at the time, a man of God. I doubt if he had a secret life, and if he did he would hardly have written about it in his journal."

"Then what explanation has been offered for his behaviour?"

"Students of Emerson say it never happened—that it was a dream or a metaphor. Are we really to believe this, when the remainder of the journals are quite rational and true? Whatever else may have happened, Emerson really did open that coffin."

I was about to continue the conversation when I spotted a light moving among the trees on the other side of the cemetery. "Simon!" I whispered. "Look there!"

"Get down," he cautioned.

"Is it—?"

The light was one of those battery-powered camping lanterns. The figure, dressed in dark clothing, set it on the ground and produced a can of spray paint. This time he began spraying the ground itself, running a long red line over earth and grass and stones, all along one side of the graveyard fence.

"We much catch him and get to the bottom of this," Simon decided. "Go around behind him, and I'll head him in your direction."

I was getting a bit old for playing games in the middle of the night, especially with an opponent who might be both dangerous and deranged, but I followed Simon's instructions and made a wide sweep of the paint sprayer in his circle of light. When I had him between me and the little hill where Simon was hiding, I gave a short, owlish hoot. The figure paused in his spraying to glance in my direction, and that was Simon's signal to rise up and bellow in his deepest voice, "Stop this blasphemy in the name of the Lord!"

The figure dropped his spray can and turned to run, knocking over the lantern as he sprinted directly toward me. I had only to move a few paces to grab him with ease. Hanging onto him was something else again.

"Slow down, mister! We want to talk to you."

"Get your hands off me!"

He lunged for freedom, and we both went down together, hitting the ground with a bone-jarring thud. He rolled over on top of me with ease, and I quickly realized that my fighting days were long past—if they'd ever existed in the first place. Luckily for me, Simon was behind him by this time and took the fight out of him with a blow to the back of his neck.

"Get the lantern," he told me.

If I'd expected it to be young Andrew Mitchner with the spray paint, I was disappointed. It was a spike-haired teenager in black leather who looked as if he'd escaped from some third-rate biker movie. Beneath his pants I could see brown leather riding boots.

"Who are you?" I asked.

"None of your business!" Despite the defiant attitude, somehow he didn't look like a street punk. Maybe it was the setting. Up there we were a long way from Manhattan.

We helped him to his feet, and Simon asked, "Why would you want to desecrate these graves?"

"I didn't desecrate anything," he muttered, rubbing his neck where Simon's blow had fallen. "I was just having some fun with my spray paint."

"You dug up those coffins."

"Like hell I did! The old guy probably did it himself. He's a nut about cemeteries. Did you ever read his book?"

That was my first clue, though Simon had tumbled to it much sooner. Leather-clad biker punks with spray cans don't read obscure books by obscure authors. They probably don't read any books at all. This kid was a neighbour.

"Do you want us to take you home to your family?" Simon asked. "Your father might not approve of what you've been doing."

"You don't know my family."

"I imagine you're Ronnie King from the neighboring estate. Mitchner's been chasing you off his property when you come riding, hasn't he?"

"Yeah. So what?"

"So you decided on this form of revenge," Simon told him. "Does it give you special pleasure to dress like this when you go out vandalizing property? The ultimate revolt against your parents' values?"

Simon Ark's words had somehow subdued him, as if he'd been a circus lion facing the trainer's whip. "You don't need to take me home," he mumbled. "I know the way."

"Who's been digging up the graves?"

"I don't know! Honest, I don't!"

"You must have seen someone around."

"Nobody, I swear! I saw the gardener partly filling their first grave the morning after it was opened, that's all."

"Yet he left this last grave open."

"The police were here looking at it. I watched them from our place. Old man Mitchner was with them."

"Didn't you know you'd be blamed if you kept returning here with your spray can?"

The kid looked away. "I don't care."

Simon nodded. "You wanted to be caught, didn't you?"

Ronnie King didn't answer.

"Go on, go home," Simon said finally. "Don't come back here again."

He picked up his lantern and trudged off, head down. After a moment we could see only the glow of it, receding into the woods.

"How'd you know it was Ronnie King?" I asked Simon.

"He was wearing brown riding boots under his black leather pants. I remembered Mitchner saying he'd chased Ronnie and his horse off the property. That camping lantern seemed a bit fancy for a town kid, too. I guessed it might be the neighbour."

"You know, Simon, until he mentioned it I'd forgotten George Mitchner's little book on cemeteries. I should find a copy at the office and read through it."

"You can do that tomorrow, my friend. I think we can head home now. The graveyard ghoul won't be appearing tonight."

"How do you know it wasn't Ronnie King?"

"He didn't bring a shovel."

We kept a complete file of all Neptune Books titles in the executive editor's spacious office. It took me only a moment to locate the slim volume with its lavender jacket. At first glance it looked like a book of poetry, which might have been one reason why its sales were disappointing at the time it was published. Actually, it was a 135-page essay on cemeteries, beginning with the burial customs of the ancient. Egyptians and their habit of burying treasures and even favorite pets along with the deceased. Everything he would need for the afterlife was provided.

There was even some discussion of the nineteenth-century fear of being buried alive, and of the short-lived fad for coffins with a small bell attached, so help could be summoned if a person found himself in that predicament. The book closed with a mention of modern pet cemeteries, with speculation that someday soon city land might be too valuable to devote to burial grounds. I decided the thing would have made a better magazine piece than a book, but then again I hadn't handled it.

I sought out the editor I wanted—genial, pipe-smoking Chris Billican, who had an office down the hall from me. "Remember George Mitchner?"

"Cemeteries. How could I forget? We sold nineteen hundred copies and remaindered the rest."

I sat down in his visitors' chair. "Wrong jacket. It looked like a book of poems. You should have appealed to the ghoulish crowd. Anyway, what do you remember about the author?"

"Country squire type. A real gentleman. Owned a lot of ships, as I remember it."

"What made him write a book about cemeteries?"

"There's one on the family property up in Duchess County. He told me they fascinated him since he was a kid."

"Nothing else?"

"Not that I can remember. It's a book I try to forget."

"Thanks, Chris."

I wondered if George Mitchner's fascination with cemeteries might extend to digging up coffins in the dead of night. When I suggested this to Simon Ark later that day, he tended to downplay it. "Unless he has a split personality, Mitchner would hardly call me in to investigate if he were the villain."

I had to agree with that. "What do we do next?"

"Mitchner and his son are in the city today. I have telephoned Abby Mitchner to ask if we could visit her."

"Now?"

"As soon as we can drive up there."

It meant another call to my wife Shelly to explain why I wouldn't be home for dinner. She'd put up with Simon Ark's antics for most of our married life, but I knew she grew tired of them at times. I phoned her, and it went about as I'd expected. Then Simon and I were off to the Mitchner estate once more.

Abby Mitchner was waiting at the door for us when we pulled up to the house. "I don't know what I can tell you that George hasn't already gone over," she told Simon.

"He's often away, while you are on the scene. I want to know about servants, neighbors, anyone else who could be desecrating those graves."

"There's no one. We have only two regular servants—a woman who cooks and cleans, and a gardener. Neither of them live in, so they wouldn't have been here overnight." She spoke the words like an actress still uncomfortable in her role as lady of the manor. "As for the neighbors, the only nearby ones are the Kings. Their boy, Ronnie, likes to ride his horse on our property, but otherwise he seems to be a good kid."

"Could I see your stepson's room?" Simon asked suddenly, as if the thought had just occurred to him.

"Whatever for?"

"I want to get some idea of his interests."

She weighed the idea and then decided. "I'll allow you to glance into his room. Naturally, I couldn't allow a search of his drawers or closet."

"Just a glance would be helpful."

She led the way to the second floor and stopped before a closed door. "He's been known to lock it," she informed us, but it was unlocked this day. The bed had been made, and the room was quite neat. Simon's attention was immediately drawn to a shelf of books near the bed and I focused on them myself. There were a few classics—Shakespeare, Cervantes, Dante—and some textbooks that might have been left over from his college days—*A Brief History of the United States*, *A Handbook of Toxicology*, *Advanced Calculus*. At the end of the shelf was a thick volume entitled *A History of Witchcraft*, by Montague Summers.

"He has a wide variety of interests" Simon murmured.

"I never see him reading. He dislikes modern novels."

There was a television set in the room, with its own VCR and a few tapes of recent popular films. Nothing else of interest seemed visible. Simon strode to the window and gazed out on a view that took in the driveway up to the house. "Your room is around back?"

She nodded. "George and I have the master bedroom. Would you like to see that, too?"

"It won't be necessary."

We went back downstairs, and Simon asked her a few other questions. "Do you visit the graveyard much yourself, Mrs. Mitchner?"

"No. I went over with George to inspect the damage, but before that I hadn't been there in a year. They're not my family."

"How long have you known young Andrew?"

She smiled at the questions. "He's not much younger than me. I met him, I believe, on the day of Margaret Mitchner's funeral."

"You knew your husband's first wife?"

"No, but I had a business relationship with George at the time. I was doing some freelance public relations work for his shipping company, and felt I should attend the funeral."

"How would you describe your relationship with Andrew?"

She shrugged. "He hasn't moved out yet. I assume if he didn't like me, he'd find a place of his own."

We finished up then, and Abby Mitchner walked us to the door. "I'll have to tell them you were here," she said.

"Oh, it's no secret," Simon assured her. "Tell them, by all means."

I knew before Simon told me that we'd be spending another night in the graveyard. "He'll be coming tonight," Simon assured me.

"The ghoul?"

"If that's what you wish to call him."

"Andrew Mitchner. But why tonight?"

"Because she'll tell him we looked in his room. He'll know his time is running out."

"The witchcraft book!"

"We shall see, my friend."

We didn't have long to wait that night. We'd taken up the same vantage point on the hill above the mausoleum, and shortly after dark we heard someone approaching through the woods. The figure carried no lantern, and seemed to rely upon instinct or familiarity to find its way among the grave markers. Simon spotted the figure first, when the moon came out from behind a cloud, and touched my arm lightly.

"He's coming right toward us!" I whispered.

"Toward the mausoleum," he corrected.

By moonlight I saw the shovel raised and heard the clang of metal as it hit the padlock. He gave it two more blows and then paused, reaching into his pocket. He'd wanted to avoid using the key, but now he had to. This padlock must have been stronger than the first one.

"He's inside," I whispered.

Simon drew a flashlight from his pocket. "Come on!"

We made our way silently down the hill and to the open mausoleum door. I heard the squeak as another coffin lid was raised. Simon pointed the flashlight and turned it on. The graveyard ghoul had been busy at his tasks and hadn't heard our approach. Now he turned, startled, and the full horror of it met my eyes. It was young Andrew Mitchner, as Simon had known it would be. By the light of a single candle stub, he had opened another coffin and was using a scissors to cut a few strands of long white hair from the decomposing corpse inside.

"There is no need for that, Andrew," Simon told him calmly. "You took what you needed the last time."

"How did you—?"

"Close down that lid and we will talk."

I didn't know quite what there was to talk about when we'd caught him in the act, and I was beginning to wish that one of us had brought a weapon. We waited outside while he screwed down the lid and then joined us. By the light from Simon's flash, I could see his face clearly, and if I'd expected the twisted, hairy features of some were wolf-like creature, I was disappointed. Even his eyes showed none of the madness one might have expected, only a look of concern.

"Will you tell my father?"

"He'll learn your true purpose quickly enough," Simon remarked.

"Then, you know—?"

"Yes, I know. Things are not always what they seem. You had no ghoul-ish motives in opening these coffins as you did. You were only trying to prove that your mother Margaret was murdered by your father five years ago."

Later, when we were alone, I told Simon, "I thought it was the book on witchcraft that gave you the clue."

"No, no, my friend. Montague Summers's volume is merely a popular history, with no mention of ghouls or graveyards. Your eye was drawn to that instead of to Shakespeare."

"What does Shakespeare have to do with it?"

"Just as Hamlet avenges the murder of his father, Andrew set out to avenge the murder of his mother, another victim of poison."

"The book on toxicology!"

"Of course. Such a book on the effects and detection of poisons would hardly have figured in the ordinary college course. He didn't become a doctor, after all."

"What could the toxicology text possibly tell him that would make him dig up his mother's body five years after her death?"

"That traces of arsenic can be found in the victim's hair even after hundreds of years. A recent examination of Napoleon's hair suggests that he was poisoned."

"My God! But why did he dig up the other grave, and open two coffins in the mausoleum?"

"As with a killer who murders four people to hide the identity of his true victim, Andrew wanted to keep his father from learning the pur-pose of his desecration, at least until he'd gotten a lab report on the hair. Tonight's final coffin opening, as he told us, was to further cloud the motive while also obtaining another sample of hair to be tested against his mother's hair. Virtually everyone's hair has a tiny amount of arsenic in it. The quantity is the important thing."

"What will you tell his father?"

"Nothing. He'll learn the truth quickly enough without our help."

I thought about the young second wife, about how she'd been working with George Mitchner already at the time of Margaret's death. Motive enough, I supposed especially if a messy divorce would have meant a huge settlement and endless alimony.

The story made the papers a few weeks later: *Police Question Shipping Tycoon About Wife's Death; Exhumed Body Shows Traces of Arsenic.*

"You saw the papers?" I asked Simon Ark when we met for lunch the following week.

"I saw them. Young Andrew tells me an indictment is expected."

"As you say, Simon, things are not always what they seem. Do you think you could clear Ralph Waldo Emerson's name as easily?"

"I already have."

"How could you?"

He leaned back and sipped his drink, smiling at my reaction. "I can never prove it, of course, not at this late date. But I can supply an explanation that has nothing to do with ghouls or madness or burial alive."

"What's that?"

"Emerson opened his wife's coffin after thirteen months simply to retrieve something he'd buried with her."

"Like what?" I asked dubiously.

"Remember that Emerson was a poet, my friend. What could be more natural than for him to have composed a poem on his beloved wife's death and have slipped it into the coffin with her. More than a year later, he wanted that poem back. His journal says only that he visited Ellen's tomb and opened the coffin, not that he looked upon her body. I think her retrieved that poem and published it. Possibly it was *To Ellen* or one of several others he wrote about her death."

Perhaps Simon was right, as he has been about so many things. I like to think so.

MASTER OF MIRACLES

"**H**ave you ever heard of Thaddeus Lusk?" my old friend Simon Ark asked me on the telephone one day in late summer. "Lusk? I don't believe so." I was semiretired from my editorial duties at Neptune Books, but still doing some manuscript reading at home. Simon's call had caught me half napping over a first novel about childhood innocence, and I was thankful for the wake-up call. "Who is he?"

"He used to be a stage magician and performance artist in his younger days, one of those people who painted their bodies blue and rolled around on stage. Now he's in California and has started a new religion. They call themselves the Luskites."

"I guess California is the place for new religions."

"My friend, I have had reports that this religion is more devilish than sacred, with false healings that sometimes cause deaths. I must go out there to see for myself. I would be grateful if you favored me with your company."

My wife Shelly was resigned to my eternal travels with Simon, and this time when I told her she merely shrugged and said, "I suppose California is better than Tibet, or some of the other places he's taken you."

"He's never taken me to Tibet."

"He probably will, any day now."

Thaddeus Lusk's new religion had its headquarters in the redwood country of northern California, along the narrow coastal fog belt where tall trees and giant conceits seemed to grow side by side. Simon and I flew to San Francisco and rented a car at the airport, driving north along the rocky Pacific coast for hours before reaching our destination.

No one seemed to know how the town of Pineapple Grove had gotten its name. There certainly had never been pineapples grown anywhere in the area. Some thought the original settlers had called it Pine Apple Grove, with the first two words being combined over time. There was no motel in the town, and we were lucky to get a twin-bedded room at a bed-and-breakfast. The proprietors, Sarah and Wayne Hammond, were a middle-aged couple who seemed to enjoy welcoming newcomers to their home. Sarah showed us our second-floor room, scurrying about to puff up the flowery pillows on the chairs.

"This your first visit to redwood country?" she asked.

"Indeed it is," Simon Ark told her. "This is a lovely area."

"We think so." If she found anything odd about his black suit and ancient, lined face she made no comment on it.

"My friend here is a New York editor," he said, no doubt hoping that the word editor would mean newspaper reporter to her.

"That so?" She fluffed another pillow.

"We've come to interview a man named Thaddeus Lusk. Do you know him?"

She crossed herself as if he'd spoken a taboo name. "We don't talk about him."

Later, after we'd unpacked and ventured downstairs to the sitting room, Simon brought up the subject again with Wayne Hammond. "I'm sorry if I upset Mrs. Hammond earlier by mentioning Thaddeus Lusk."

"It's not a popular name with her," Hammond admitted. "She thinks he's the Devil himself. I just think he's a sick man with delusions that he's God or the Devil. I don't know which."

"The Devil?" That perked Simon up at once. It was what he'd traveled across the country to hear. Ever since I'd first known him, Simon Ark had been claiming he was a two-thousand-year-old Coptic priest, wandering the world in search of Satan. I viewed him more as a highly intelligent sleuth of the occult, a still-vigorous man in his seventies who'd written a couple of books for my company on Satanism and witchcraft. As far as I knew, the dwindling royalties on those books had been his sole source of income over the years. (But hadn't he seemed a vigorous man in his seventies when we first met, decades ago?)

"Lusk lives in a redwood temple and calls himself the Master of Miracles," Wayne Hammond continued. "When his followers gather there they chant and wear aqua-colored robes. Then he gets up on a stage, does a few magic tricks, and cures people."

"You sound as if you've seen all this."

"No, sir, not me! But there's a lad here in town who got himself an aqua robe and sneaked in there a few months back. He told us about it."

Simon Ark smiled slightly. "I would be grateful for the name of this person, and where I might find him."

Sarah Hammond had entered the room, and she responded before her husband could speak. "His name is Gerry Webster. He owns the Quik-Fill gas station down the street, and he's no lad. He's twenty-eight years old."

"Still a lad to me," her husband argued.

It was dinnertime, but since the Hammonds supplied only breakfast to their guests, we went in search of nourishment in town. They'd directed us to the Redwood Cafe and I wondered how many of those there might be in this neck of the woods. On the way we passed the Quik-Fill, which had a drive-thru car wash next to it, but a sign in the window announced the station was closed from six to seven, apparently a one-man operation.

The Redwood Cafe was a plain, uncluttered room with a dozen tables and a bar at one end. About half the tables were occupied, and three men stood at the bar. I had a thought. "Simon, if Gerry Webster just took a break for dinner he might be here eating it, unless he lives close enough to drive home."

It was an idea. When the tired blond waitress got around to taking our order, Simon asked her, "Is Gerry Webster here tonight?"

She glanced around. "Sure, that's him in the black T-shirt and jeans at the bar."

He was chatting with two men, and when they left I went over to speak to him. "Mr. Webster? Gerry Webster?"

He glanced around. His face was nicely tanned; his hair seemed bleached by the summer sun. "That's me. What can I do for you?"

I led him over to the table and introduced Simon Ark. He sat down to join us and ordered a beer from the waitress. Simon came right to the point. "I understand you have had some contact with Thaddeus Lusk."

"You mean that nut case up in the woods? The Master of Miracles? Yeah, I went out there once."

"Could you take us there?"

"What for?" he asked with a trace of suspicion.

"My friend here is a New York editor," Simon explained vaguely, as if that answered the question.

"What, one of those tabloid things? Sure, I guess I could show you the way. Lusk doesn't go in for sex orgies, though, if that's what you're expecting. He's more into magic tricks and miracle cures."

"You've attended his services?"

"Just once. My girlfriend Kelly used to go up there with her mother before the old lady died. She had one of those aqua robes so I wore it one night and crashed the party. Only it wasn't much of a party. Lusk came out and talked for a half-hour about cleansing ourselves, and he did his healing. Then he threw a few fireballs at the stage like a magician and ended up commanding a shower of rain to fall out of the darkened sky and douse those little fires. He said the fires were Satan's work and the rain, like our aqua robes, signified the goodness and power of the Lord. It was a pretty spectacular conclusion, if you buy that stuff."

"What about the healing?" Simon asked.

"A few people came up on crutches. One woman was in a wheelchair. He told them it might be a few days before they felt the full effects of his healing hands. Then, of course, Lusk took up a collection. They always do that, don't they?"

"When is the next service scheduled?"

"Tomorrow night. They're every Tuesday, with special ones now and then."

"Could you take us there?" Simon asked. "Before the service, so I could speak with Lusk if possible."

"I couldn't. Maybe Kelly could. He doesn't even know me."

"Could you ask her for us?"

"Well—I suppose so. I'll be seeing her tonight after I close. Come by the station in the morning and I'll let you know."

After dinner, Simon and I strolled around the three or four blocks of the town, looking in store windows. There seemed little else to do. At one point a car went by and I thought I saw Sarah Hammond behind the wheel, heading back home to her bed-and breakfast. By the time we arrived there a short while later, she and her husband were in the parlor watching television together.

"This town is not exactly the liveliest place on earth," I told Simon the following morning as I watched a trailer truck loaded with logs driving along the highway in front of the house.

"You've been spoiled by New York, my friend. I have a feeling the pace will pick up once we meet with Thaddeus Lusk."

"What kind of a name is Thaddeus, anyway?"

"He was one of the twelve Apostles," Simon reminded me.

"Oh, that Thaddeus."

Our breakfast of ham and eggs with sourdough bread was quite filling, and over coffee Wayne Hammond asked us, "Did you talk to that lad at the gas station last night, about Mr. Lusk?"

I nodded. "We're going back this morning. He may be able to help us." Mrs. Hammond said nothing and I wondered if she'd seen us when she drove through town.

Webster's girl, Kelly Block, worked at the tourist center in town, and she'd arranged to stop by the gas station on her lunch hour to meet us. Promptly at noon, she drove up in a ten-year-old Ford with a dull blue paint job. The license plate read TREE-1 in dark letters against a white background. She was about Webster's age, with long brown hair and a ready smile, and wore a badge on her khaki shirt promising *Redwood Tourist Information*. A button on the other side read *Hug a Tree*.

Gerry Webster introduced us and Kelly said, "Hi, you the folks want to meet Thaddeus Lusk?"

"We are," Simon replied.

"It's not easy. He has bodyguards around him at all times. But we can give it a try tonight if you'd like, before the service at eight. Why don't you meet me back here at seven? It's only a fifteen-minute drive to the temple." She turned to Gerry. "You want to come, too?"

He shook his head. "I have to keep the station open till nine. Have fun without me."

Simon and I spent the afternoon driving around the countryside, enjoying the grandeur of the Pacific and the back roads that snaked through the towering majesty of redwood country. We saw no sign of Lusk's temple in the woods, nor any people wearing aqua robes. Returning for another dinner at the Redwood Cafe, I noticed that our rental car was covered with dust from traveling on those dirt roads during our afternoon excursion. It was not quite six o'clock and the drive-thru car wash seemed to be still open, though no workers were in sight.

"Is that your place, too?" I asked Gerry Webster.

"No, no. Fellow name of Murphy runs it. Sort of a loner, a Vietnam vet who drifted up here after the war. There are others in the hills, they say, but I stay away from them. Murphy's harmless, though. There he is now."

He was a man of indeterminate age, scowling at us over a growth of red beard. Dressed in an old army fatigue jacket and pants, he sauntered forward and asked, "You want a car wash?"

"I think we need one," I answered.

"That's seven dollars for a plain wash, just the outside. We also offer a five-dollar noonday special. There's a vacuum cleaner and cloths at the other end if you want to do more. Stay in the car and close your windows." I paid him the seven bucks and he hit a button on the wall behind him. The noisy mechanism sprang to life. I put the car in neutral and took my foot off the gas. We started moving forward on the track. First there was a watery spray from all directions, followed by globs of liquid soap and agitation by a battery of long felt strips that seemed to dance over the car. We could see nothing through the windows as the curtain of cloth pennants struck at us again and again. Then the car forced its way between pairs of whirling brushes that cleared our vision. Dryers bathed the car in warm air and we burst through a final curtain of cloth into daylight.

"Better than a fun house," remarked Simon, confessing he'd never been through a car wash before.

"Never?" I was astounded.

He shrugged. "I don't drive a car. Why would I need a car wash?"

We drove away without bothering to vacuum the interior or towel off a few remaining streaks of water. I circled the block and came up to park in front of the Redwood Cafe. By the time we'd eaten a light dinner and returned to the Quik-Fill, Kelly Block was already there. She was dressed as she had been earlier and I asked, "No robe for the services?"

She grinned. "It's in the car. But I don't have anything for you two. I'll get you through the gate as my guests." She told us she'd have to drive, so I climbed into the backseat, leaving the front one for Simon. As she pulled away she waved to Webster and called out that she'd see him later.

"How long have you been a Luskite?" Simon asked her when we were under way.

"I've never really been one," she answered easily. "It was my mother who thought his curing powers might help her."

"Was it cancer?"

She nodded. "He told her to cease medication and rely on him, but his cures didn't work. She was dead in three weeks, and I watched her die. That was last winter. I should have quit then, but I've still been coming around."

"Mrs. Hammond believes Lusk to be the Devil," Simon remarked.

"Well, I wouldn't go that far."

She'd turned off the main highway onto a road that wound through the woods, virtually shutting off what sunlight remained. "It's not far now."

Presently we came to a fence with an open gate. A burly man in an aqua-colored robe stood blocking our path. She gave him her name and told him we were guests from New York who wanted to interview Thaddeus Lusk. The guard produced a cellular phone from beneath his robe and tapped in a number. He spoke a few words, listened, and then waved us through.

The temple came into view at the next turn, lighted in the near-darkness by a line of luminarias that stretched down the road and around the main building, a low, churchlike structure of redwood logs topped by six wooden spires of equal height. A small stage seemed to occupy the area in front of the place. Kelly followed the road around the temple to a log house that seemed to match it on a smaller scale. There was some parking here, though it was obvious the main parking area was in front.

Another muscular guard like the one at the gate ushered us inside and almost at once we were in the presence of Thaddeus Lusk. Somehow he was not at all what I'd expected, no embodiment of evil, no horns growing from his forehead. In his aqua robe he reminded me just a bit of the traditional depiction of a medieval monk, short and stocky, with a halo of white hair fringing his otherwise bald head. "You have brought me visitors, Kelly?" he asked.

She introduced us and I thought I saw Lusk flinch just a bit at the mention of Simon Ark's name. "Have you come for tonight's service?" he asked us. "Certainly we will be interested in seeing it," Simon replied. Lusk smiled slightly. "Are you a religious man, Mr. Ark?"

"I am a seeker after the truth. I thought I might find it with the Master of Miracles."

"You have come to the right place for your interview. Anything I can tell you about the Luskite faith—"

Simon hesitated a moment and then asked, "Why are there six identical wooden spires atop your temple?"

'The Luskite doctrine holds that each human being is endowed with five senses plus another, the so-called sixth sense."

"But the number six has other connotations," Simon went on. "Repeated three times, as in six-six-six, it becomes the number of the Devil."

"Is that so?" Thaddeus Lusk said, wide-eyed as an innocent child. "Imagine that!"

"People tell me there have been messages on the Internet accusing you of being Satan himself."

"No, no, no!" The little man threw up his hands in disbelief. "I'm only a poor magus attempting to spread the word of the spirit and the senses. Those who say otherwise are heretics!"

"You are a former magician and performance artist," Simon said with a touch of accusation in his deep voice. "I imagine your magical trappings are no more than stage trickery designed to fool the gullible."

Lusk merely smiled benevolently. "Come and see for yourself. I must prepare for the evening service now. We can continue with the interview later."

We followed him outside where cars were beginning to fill the parking area. Kelly whispered, "He's going to be very upset when he learns you're not really doing an interview. This might be the end of my days as a Luskite."

"Would that bother you?" I asked.

"Not particularly."

Since there was no place to be seated, it was obvious that the congregation stood during the service, which Kelly assured us was fairly brief. "There's a great deal of milling around and talking afterward," she said. "Here comes Mr. Hines. He always does the opening."

"Who's he?"

"Drew Hines, Lusk's deputy. He's in charge of the church's business operations."

Simon watched the slender blond man come onto the stage, moving toward the microphone. Like everyone else except Simon and me, he wore the trademark aqua robe of the Luskites. Drew Hines adjusted his glasses and began reading a few short announcements, mainly work assignments for the coming week. Then he introduced Thaddeus Lusk as the congregation took up a low chant of welcome. At that point I guessed there were about two hundred people in the congregation. It wasn't a huge crowd by any means, but given the location, in the middle of the woods, it was pretty impressive. "Some of them drive fifty miles or more to be here on Tuesday nights," Kelly Block told us when I commented on it.

As the chanting died down, Lusk held up his hands for silence and began to speak. His sermon was more an appeal for money than anything else, pointing out that a famous (unnamed) film star had recently joined the church and would attend their Tuesday evening service some week in the future. The celebrity had given a generous donation to the Luskites, and it was hoped that others would do likewise. Then Lusk held up his hands and instructed those in need of healing to come forward. One man with a cane and a bad limp seemed to walk better after Lusk laid on his hands, but others were warned that the cure was not an immediate thing and was tied to continued prayer and fasting. I wondered to whom they were supposed to direct their prayers, since God hadn't been mentioned. As the curing ended, the cadre of guards moved quickly among the congregation with their collection baskets.

Lusk said a few more words, announcing to murmurs of surprise that a special service would be held on Thursday evening to make an important announcement. Then he went into his concluding fireball routine, hurling what appeared to be flaming darts. As they struck the stage, six little fires rose at or near the spots, obviously fueled by a propane gas line under the flooring. Then Lusk stepped forward and raised his hands to the starlit heavens above. "Let the aqua of our robes and the purity of our deeds bring forth the waters of salvation to quench these fires of the damned before they consume us all!" he commanded.

Almost at once, rain began falling from the cloudless sky, drenching both Lusk and the stage as the half-dozen fires died to nothing. The congregation chanted its approval. "That was spectacular," I admitted. "Does he end every service like that?"

Kelly nodded. "Unless the weather is bad and we have to go into the temple."

People were greeting each other and congregating in small groups as Lusk returned to his house with Drew Hines and one of the bodyguards. We followed along and, once inside, we waited while the Master of Miracles changed into some dry clothes.

"Miss Block," Simon asked, "have you ever been out here in the daytime?"

"Of course. Many times."

"I could see there are no trees above that stage. Is there anything else up there?"

"Nothing but the sky," she replied. "And one of those bird screens."

"Bird screen?" he questioned.

"You must have seen them along the coast or in Florida. Resort hotels often have them over their swimming pools. They're a dome-shaped construction of thin plastic wires, almost invisible to the eye but they keep birds out. Lusk doesn't like birds interrupting his services."

The Master of Miracles joined them after a few moments. He'd shed his wet aqua robe and was wearing a white terrycloth one instead. "Did you like my closing?" he asked with an impish grin.

"Very effective," Simon admitted. "You should have remained on the professional stage."

"Now on with the interview," Lusk said, settling into one of the chairs.

Kelly Block cleared her throat. "I have to tell you something, Mr. Lusk. I brought Simon Ark and his friend here under somewhat false pretenses. They're connected with Neptune Books in New York, but not with any news magazine. This is not an interview as such."

His face seemed to harden at her words, and I feared she'd gotten herself in big trouble. "You know our rule against strangers, Kelly, and you know the penalty."

"Yes. I'm sorry."

"Please leave."

She got to her feet, telling us, "I'll wait in the car." Her face had the frightened look of a trapped rabbit.

"We should be going, too," I said, but Simon remained seated, his eyes on the little man.

"I hope you don't intend to punish her for bringing us," he said.

Thaddeus Lusk closed his eyes for a moment, as if communing with a voice only he could hear. "It's out of my hands now. Kelly Block will be gone by noon tomorrow."

"Gone? What does that mean?"

"Exactly what I said. Good night, gentlemen." He turned and left the room.

Kelly was waiting for us in the car, but Simon Ark would not tell her exactly what Lusk had said. "It may have been a threat of some sort. I'm not certain. In any event, I think you should be very careful for the next day or so."

"I'm always careful," she replied, joining the line of cars that was beginning to leave the parking area. "He won't do anything."

But she fell silent during the brief drive back to Pineapple Grove. When she dropped us at our rental car she said simply, "Maybe I'll see you around tomorrow." Then she was gone.

When we got back to our room Simon suggested I phone Gerry Webster at his home and tell him about the possible threat against Kelly. I tried not to alarm Webster, but he said he'd drive over and check up on her.

The following morning we breakfasted again with the Hammonds, and Wayne wondered how long we thought we'd be there. "Do you need the room for someone else?" I asked.

"No, it's not that. We just heard you were out to the Luskite service last night. My wife and I don't get involved with cults and things like that. We're churchgoing Methodists."

"Who was it that saw us there?" Simon asked.

Wayne Hammond didn't want to answer. It was his wife who said, "Mr. Murphy from that car-wash place. Sometimes he drives out to the services. He phoned this morning to say he saw both of you there with that tourist lady, Miss Block."

"We had a brief conversation with Thaddeus Lusk," I admitted. "Simon here is a student of miracle cures and we were interested in seeing him."

Hammond stared hard at Simon's lined face. "If you'll pardon me for saying it, you seem a bit old for a student."

"Oh, one is never too old to learn, Mr. Hammond. As for our stay here, I would guess another day or two. We should be gone by the weekend."

"Murphy says there's to be another service tomorrow night," Sarah Hammond said. "Will you be going to that one, too?"

"We may, if we're still in town."

I was anxious to get away from the Hammonds after breakfast, and we drove down the street to the few shops clustered around the restaurant. In a souvenir and gift shop I found just about everything that could possibly be made from a redwood tree, and finally chose a small square mirror set off by a wide polished wood frame. It looked like something Shelly would like. As we were leaving the shop, Simon noticed Gerry Webster just opening his Quik-Fill station down the road. We drove down there and Simon asked him, "Is Kelly all right?"

"She's fine. She was a little nervous last night so I stayed with her and followed her in to work this morning. That's why I'm a bit late opening."

"Is she coming here this noon?"

"I think so. She often does. Why do you ask?"

Simon grew serious. "I didn't tell you last night, but Lusk said she'd be gone by this noon. It wasn't clear what he meant."

"She's certainly safe at her tourist office."

I suggested that Simon and I take a ride down there to be sure. "Which way is it?"

Gerry Webster pointed. "Five minutes north, a log cabin on the left with a big sign. You can't miss it."

Her blue Ford was parked in front and we could see her through the window, explaining something on a map to a couple of women. "I guess it's a false alarm," I said.

"Wait, my friend. It's more than an hour until noon. Let us park here and watch."

We parked and watched and nothing happened. I was beginning to think this whole journey had been a waste of time. At five minutes to twelve, Kelly came out and got into the Ford with the TREE-1 license plate. "What now, Simon?"

"Follow her, not too close."

I thought she was heading directly to the Quik-Fill, but as we approached she suddenly turned into the car wash behind another vehicle. I remembered Murphy's noontime special and saw her reach out the window to hand him five dollars. "What now?" I asked. Another car was already in line behind her.

"Follow her through the car wash but let me out here. I want to be watching the other end when she comes through. It's just twelve o'clock."

I did as he said, gave Murphy my five bucks, and started through. "Weren't you just here yesterday?" he asked.

"This car attracts dirt."

As soon as the initial spray and soap hit my windshield I could see nothing. Then the hanging strips of cloth battered the car from above and the whirling brushes went to work on the sides. Finally, there were the drying blowers and then the cloth strips parted and I was back in the day-light. Simon Ark was standing there, his face drained of color. I drove up to him and lowered the window. "What is it, Simon? What happened?"

"She never came out."

We persuaded Murphy to halt the line of vehicles and shut down the mechanism once the cars inside were clear of it. Then the three of us walked through the car wash together. There were lights near the floor, though I hadn't realized it while going through. "See, mister," the red-bearded man told us, "these walls are prefabricated sheet steel. There's this one side door that's kept locked. If she drove in the entrance, she had to drive out the exit."

"You saw her drive in," I said. "You took her five dollars."

"Kelly Block? Sure, I know her. She must have come out the other end and you missed her, that's all."

"I didn't miss her," Simon insisted, turning to me for support. "When I came around to this exit a green Buick with an older couple was just coming out. Then there was a white Ford with a male driver wearing a moustache and a baseball cap, and a red Toyota with a young girl at the wheel. You were the next car out," he said to me. "None of the cars was Kelly's, and none of them had her TREE-1 license plates."

We walked back through the car wash again, searching for clues, but there was nothing. Both car and driver had vanished without a trace. "Take a ride down to her office," Murphy suggested. "I'm sure she'll be back there by the end of her lunch hour. You guys just missed her somehow."

We walked back to our car. I tried to calm Simon's frustration by suggesting that Murphy might be somehow involved, but he brushed that aside. "There were other cars coming in. He had to take their money and send them through."

"I couldn't see a thing with all that soap and suds on my windshield. Someone in the car ahead of me could have gotten out and grabbed Kelly from her vehicle. She might have left the car wash on the floor or in the trunk of another car."

"Then what happened to her car?"

There was no immediate answer to that question. We went next door to the gas station and I broke the news to Gerry Webster. "We think something's happened to Kelly," I told him. Simon quickly outlined the details of her disappearance.

"That's impossible," Webster insisted. "People don't vanish while going through a car wash!"

"Her car is gone, too. There's no explanation for it."

"Did you check back at her office?"

"We're going there now," I told him.

He closed the station and came with us, but when we reached the tourist bureau it wasn't yet one o'clock and the girl behind the desk said simply that Kelly was out to lunch.

We waited past one.

We waited until two. The girl inside had no idea where she was.

Webster insisted we check on her apartment so he guided us over there. It was a garden complex just outside of town. There was no sign of her car and she didn't answer the door. "Are you sure it was Kelly's car you followed this morning?" he asked.

"It was hers," I assured him. "We were in it with her just last night."

"Then I think we'd better phone the sheriff."

But the sheriff's office didn't want to hear about people missing only two or three hours, even if they had disappeared while going through a car wash. We were told to call them back if she didn't reappear in twenty-four hours.

"It's Murphy," I decided. "Whatever was done, Murphy must have had a hand in it." Although Simon Ark remained silent, Gerry Webster quickly agreed. After all, Murphy had admitted attending the Luskite services.

Back at the car wash, business had slacked off following the noonday rush. Murphy was reading a San Francisco newspaper in his tiny cubicle while waiting for customers. "We want to ask you some more questions about Kelly's disappearance," I said as he stood up to greet us.

"I told you everything I know."

"We'd like to examine that side door into the car wash."

"I told you, it's locked. Sometimes I come in that way in the mornings, but usually I use this front door." He took us around and showed us the locked door, but Webster wasn't convinced. "Thaddeus Lusk had you do something to her, didn't he?"

"Calm down, sonny. I didn't touch your girl, and nobody else did either. You folks are imagining this whole thing."

Another ten minutes of talking and speculating got us nowhere. When Kelly failed to reappear at her office or apartment the rest of the afternoon, we dropped Webster back at his station and drove out to Thaddeus Lusk's temple in the woods.

Somehow the place looked different by daylight. Though it was after six when we arrived, there was no service scheduled and only a half-dozen cars were in the parking area. The announcement of our arrival by the guard had brought Lusk's top deputy, Drew Hines, out to greet us.

"You're a night early," he said. "The special service isn't until tomorrow."

"We've come to see Mr. Lusk," Simon told him.

"You saw him last evening. He's doing his meditations now."

"Tell him it's about Kelly Block. I'm sure he'll see us."

"I can't—"

"If he doesn't see us tonight he'll be seeing the sheriff in the morning." Simon was not to be turned away.

Finally Hines took off his glasses and polished them, considering the possibilities. If he feared Lusk's reaction for disturbing his meditations, he must have feared Simon Ark even more. Simon inspired that reaction in people who didn't know him well. "Stay right here," Hines told us. "I'll be back."

Presently we were ushered into the log temple itself, where rows of pews and a sort of altar gave it the appearance of an ordinary house of worship. Thaddeus Lusk was waiting there in the aisle, wearing his aqua robe. "Gentlemen, it is a pleasure to see you again."

"We've come about Kelly Block," Simon told him. "I'm sure you know she's disappeared."

"That's unfortunate, if true."

"It's true all right," I chimed in. "She vanished this noon from the car wash, along with her car."

"How extraordinary!"

Simon's eyes were blazing as he locked gazes with the man. "If this is another of your magic tricks, I suggest you produce her at once."

"I know nothing about it. My powers are such that they sometimes manifest themselves without any conscious direction from me." He frowned. "I thought someone said Kelly had been out here today, but she's certainly not here now. If you doubt me, you have permission to search the entire compound. Mr. Hines will accompany you."

"I think we'll do just that," Simon told him. He turned toward the door and I followed him out.

"How are we going to search for her?" I asked.

"If she's here, her car is probably here. That's harder for them to hide."

But the blue Ford was not among the six cars in the parking area. There was a Rolls Royce, obviously Lusk's, an MG, a Dodge Neon, a Chevy, a Saab, and a Ford van. One of the outbuildings was a garage and we had

Hines unlock the door for us. There was no car inside, only some soiled dropcloths, cans of insect spray, a couple of empty paint cans, and a shotgun with a box of shells.

"What is the shotgun for?" Simon asked.

"This is the woods," Hines pointed out. "We have all sorts of creatures at night, including bears. Mr. Lusk won't have a weapon in the house, so we keep it out here."

"Aren't the guards armed?"

"Only with Mace and they've never had to use that. The people who come here are believers, Mr. Ark."

We left the garage and walked back to the stage, which was elevated about five feet above the ground. A latticework covering ran around it like a skirt. "Can we see under here?" Simon asked.

"What for?"

"It's high enough to hide a car."

He sighed and opened one section so that we could walk beneath the stage in a crouching position. There was no hidden car, nothing except a ladder and a coil of thin plastic hose and the propane gas lines that produced the jets of fire for Lusk's act.

"I'm satisfied," I said, retreating quickly from the odor of a rotting animal.

Simon Ark followed after a moment, and once back in the fresh air stood staring up at the sky. In the daylight we could see the sun reflecting off the thin plastic wires of the bird screen, high above the stage. After dark it would be completely invisible.

"Notice how some of them are thicker," Simon told me. "Perforated plastic tubing for the rain trick."

"That doesn't tell us what happened to Kelly Block," I said.

"No," he agreed. "It doesn't."

Drew Hines saw us to our car and we drove off through the gate. It wasn't until we got back to the Hammonds' place that I noticed a little blue smudge on one of my hands. I showed it to Simon but it washed right off and I thought no more about it.

The following morning, the sheriff finally agreed to enter the investigation. He was a local lumberman named Jed Sweeney, a gray-haired man in his fifties.

He listened to our account of the disappearance and talked to Gerry Webster, but beyond that he wasn't too helpful. "Probably just decided to take off for a few days," he decided. "Folks do that sometimes, especially when they've got no family ties."

He went around to Kelly's apartment and had the landlord unlock the door, but nothing appeared out of place. Her clothes and toilet articles seemed to be where they belonged. Of course, if anything had been missing we'd have had no way of knowing. Simon watched the sheriff going through the motions and suggested he put out an alarm for the missing car. "I was just going to do that," he told us, going back out to the radio in his car.

"He doesn't seem to believe our story about the car wash," I said.

"That's understandable."

"Do you think she'll reappear, Simon?"

"If she does, it'll be at Thaddeus Lusk's special service this evening."

When we arrived, around seven-thirty, the parking area was already half full. One of the guards waved us into an empty space and we joined the others as darkness began to fall in among the redwoods. Promptly at eight o'clock, Thaddeus Lusk was introduced and walked onto the stage. He launched into a combination sermon and fund-raiser not too different from what we'd already heard. But there was one surprise.

"I've summoned you here tonight to hear the joyous word directly from me. The Luskite Church is now a recognized institution! Starting in January, we have a contract to place our weekly service on cable television for all of America to see!"

The congregation burst out with applause and cheers. Simon and I moved closer through the crowd for a better look. "Now!" Lusk shouted. "Journey with me to this new tomorrow of our dreams! Journey with me as I douse the fires of Satan one more time!"

The fiery darts left his hands, the flames leapt from the stage as they had before. He stepped into their midst, raising his hands to the heavens and calling upon rain the color of their aqua robes. As it started to fall, I heard his scream, a split second before the entire stage and Thaddeus Lusk were enveloped in a tower of flame.

We surmised later that he must have smelled it, smelled the gasoline that flowed through those tubes and rained down upon his head. He screamed when he realized what was happening, but by then nothing could have saved him. When the fire trucks and ambulance arrived, quickly followed by Sheriff Sweeney, all they could do was pull the charred body from the ruins of the smoldering stage.

We quickly established it was Drew Hines who started the pump for the water that was to extinguish the fires on stage. The sight of Thaddeus Lusk's horrible death had left him shaken, still trembling a half-hour later. Sheriff Sweeney unscrewed the top of a water tank behind the garage and took a sniff. "Gasoline. It's a wonder the flames didn't shoot back along those tubes and cause an explosion."

"I shut it off at once," Hines said, "but not fast enough."

"What do you make of this?" the sheriff asked no one in particular.

"He was murdered," Simon Ark said, "in a particularly horrible manner. Someone who'd seen his act and knew how it worked slipped back here, emptied out the water, and filled this tank with gasoline."

Sheriff Sweeney kicked at the side of the tank. "What does it hold—twenty gallons?"

"About that. It worked perfectly on Tuesday night."

"The killer came after Tuesday, then. How would he get that much gasoline without attracting attention?"

"Perhaps he owned a gas station," Simon speculated.

"Webster at the Quik-Fill? What motive would he have?"

"If he thought Lusk had done something to Kelly Block—"

But Gerry Webster had heard of Lusk's death in the fire, and before we could decide to question him he pulled up in his truck. "It's all over town," he told us. "What happened?"

The sheriff quickly ran through the facts as we knew them. Webster frowned and asked, "Have they found Kelly?"

"Not yet."

"Search for her! He must have her hidden here somewhere."

"We searched yesterday," I tried to tell him.

But the temple and garage and grounds were searched again. This time even Lusk's own house was searched. There was still no sign of Kelly Block. "Maybe Lusk had nothing to do with her disappearance," I suggested. "Maybe his killer has her, and killed Lusk because he knew about it."

"Perhaps." But Simon's eyes were on the line of cars now beginning to leave the parking area and head for the gate. Most had waited till now perhaps thinking it was some sort of ultimate magic trick. But now th truth had sunk in, and women sobbed as their husbands led them to wait-ing cars or vans. There would be no more magic this night.

Suddenly Simon Ark grabbed the sheriff's arm. "Stop those cars from leaving! Close the gate!"

"What?"

"You heard me. The killer may still be in here."

"That gasoline could have been left hours ago, even yesterday," the sheriff argued. But he signaled his deputy to hold up the line.

Simon hurried along the rows of cars, searching for something. We tailed along and I was surprised to see him stop at a white Ford that was showing its age. "Get out," he told the driver, a young man with a mous-tache who was wearing a baseball cap.

"What's all this?" Sheriff Sweeney asked.

With a sudden motion Simon yanked off the baseball cap, revealing a coil of long brown hair underneath. "This is Lusk's killer," Simon told us. He peeled off the moustache, too, and we were staring into the angry face of the missing Kelly Block.

"With Lusk's background and preference for magic tricks," Simon told us later as we sat in Sheriff Sweeney's tiny office, "it seemed likely from the beginning that Kelly's disappearance was some sort of trickery dreamed up by him. She might even have suggested it herself. She would vanish at Murphy's car wash, and reappear tonight at this special service where Lusk would announce his television contract."

"How'd she do it?" the sheriff wanted to know.

"If you think about it, there's only one possible way. She couldn't pass through the cars in front of or behind her. She had to change the appear-ance of her car and herself. A dull blue paint job had to become white in an instant, and she had to change from a woman to a man. How was that possible? The car was simply coated with a water-soluble paint that would come off quickly under the whirling brushes of a car wash."

"Wait a minute," I objected. "The license plate number—"

"The real plate number was painted over in white, and the TREE-1 number painted on top of that. It all washed off, like the car's blue color-ing, and we had a whole new car. It was still a Ford, but its color and the driver's sex—changed by a cap and moustache—were different. I let it go right by me."

"But we walked through that car wash twice. Why didn't we see the remains of the blue paint?"

"Because two or three cars, including ours, went through after she did. All that water, and what remained of the blue paint was flushed down the drain."

I simply shook my head in amazement. "How did you know?"

"Remember those empty paint cans in the garage at Lusk's compound? You got some of the blue paint on your hand but it washed right off later. That told me how it was done, and it told me Lusk had to have been part of it. He only pretended to be angry with her. I suppose the painting was done several days ago so people would get used to seeing her in that car. As long as she stayed out of the rain she was safe. But all this told us one thing with a certainty: Kelly Block had to have been in on the trick. Her driving the blue car, going through the car wash at noon, and disguising herself as a man were things only she could control. It was a safe enough trick. We've seen for ourselves how impossible it is to see the car ahead of or behind you as you go through. No one noticed the car's change in color. She couldn't have known I'd be at the other end watching for her, but she knew whatever we did the blue car would have vanished from sight. I assumed she would reappear at this evening's service. When she didn't, I realized she must have turned on him."

"But if she was willing to do this at Lusk's bidding, why did she want to kill him?" the sheriff asked.

"Because he persuaded her dying mother to cease all medication. Kelly watched her die, and it couldn't have been pleasant. I think she wanted Lusk to suffer, too, though his suffering lasted less than a minute. She went out to the temple yesterday with cans of gasoline, probably stolen from Gerry's station, and substituted it for the water in the tank. She knew the gas flames on stage would ignite the gasoline as soon as it started falling from those perforated plastic tubes. Lusk even let slip that he thought he saw her there yesterday."

"Why were you so sure she was in the crowd tonight? She'd already arranged the death trap."

"She'd watched her mother die," Simon Ark said. "She'd want to watch her mother's killer die, too."

When we flew back to New York two days later, Kelly was being held for psychiatric evaluation. We never did learn what happened to her. But then, as Simon remarked, we never learned what happened to Thaddeus Lusk either.

THE GRAVESEND TRUMPET

"**H**ave you ever heard tell of the Gravesend trumpet?" the old vicar asked Simon Ark. We were seated around a glass-topped table in the garden of St. John's rectory on a sunny September afternoon, discussing the local legends that had brought Simon and me to this corner of England.

"Trumpets have something of a mystical allure," my friend replied, in that deep, dark voice of his that always hinted at unfathomable mysteries. "I imagine they have sounded in this very church on Easter morn, and the Feast of Trumpets was a Jewish festival marking the beginning of their ecclesiastical year. During séances, mediums have often used trumpets to establish communication between the living and the dead."

"But the Gravesend trumpet is something else, perhaps unique to this area around the mouth of the Thames. Our town is not called Gravesend for nothing. Do you know much about its history?"

I contributed the one fact I knew. "Pocahontas is buried here."

"Ah yes, your American Indian who saved John Smith's life and then married another. She came to England with her husband and died here in sixteen seventeen. You may visit her grave in the cemetery at St. George's Church." The vicar, whose name was Ronald Neims, was said to be nearing eighty and looked every year of it. Simon Ark had sought him out when he decided to research a book on English country legends. Before I retired from Neptune, I'd published a book he wrote on witchcraft, and I felt sure the firm would be interested in this one as well. A publishing friend in London had suggested we contact Vicar Neims, himself long retired but a font of information regarding local legends. "Actually," he continued, "your mention of Pocahontas is not so far afield as you might think."

"How is that?" Simon asked.

"You may know that mediums sometimes use American Indians to help establish contact with the dead. Mediums will speak with an Indian guide on the other side, who then attempts to bring forth the spirits they seek. I know at least one woman here in Gravesend who claims to have used Pocahontas herself in this manner."

"Does the Church of England approve of such things?" I asked, think-ing that the old vicar might be one who made his own rules.

He held his gnarled hands wide, as if encompassing all the world's knowledge. "Nothing is beyond the scope of man's curiosity, sir."

Simon Ark allowed himself a rare smile. "We seem to have gotten off the subject of the Gravesend trumpet."

"Ah yes! The trumpet! Like the Holy Grail, its history is rooted in leg-end. But surely it is a very old thing, perhaps dating back to Biblical times. Some say it is the trumpet of the Last Judgment, which will summon the dead from their graves."

"And it is here, in Gravesend?"

"It is. In 1921 an archeologist named Hamstitch uncovered it in Egypt, near the town of Luxor on the Nile. Like treasures of King Tut and others, the trumpet was thought to be cursed. Legend has it that Hamstitch blew on the trumpet and died almost at once—died of old age, though he was a relatively young man of forty-six."

"Do you believe such a thing?" Simon asked.

"I only know the facts. After the man's death, the Cairo museum refused to accept the trumpet. Some thought it could be infected with a deadly virus."

"Very possible. And how did it come to be in Gravesend?"

"Hamstitch had a daughter living here. She inherited the trumpet and turned his house into a small museum. Her descendants carry on the tradition."

Simon Ark nodded. "I would want to see that. Could you make arrangements?""

"Certainly," the vicar said. "I believe Naomi opens the museum rooms only by appointment, but I can phone her for you."

I merely shook my head. "You're telling us this man Hamstitch dug a trumpet out of the desert sand after two thousand years, put it in his mouth, and blew on it? Why would he have done such a thing?"

Ronald Neims shrugged. "Perhaps because his first name was Joshua."

I have known Simon Ark for most of my life, and he still remains a mys-tery to me. At times he claims to have been a Coptic priest in Egypt almost two thousand years ago, wandering the world in search of Satan and his minions. There are even occasions when I half believe him, much to the consternation of my wife Shelly. Here I was off in England with him again, and I could already imagine her reaction when I phoned her that evening with the story of the trumpet.

But in truth, the Victorian mansion with the faded Hamstitch Museum signboard outside was almost enough to make a believer out of me. It seemed a perfect habitat for ghosts and ghouls, a place where Simon Ark might well have to face Satan for a final reckoning. Perhaps that was why I was so startled by the appearance of the perky young woman barely five feet tall who opened the door and greeted us with, "You would be the Americans, here to see the museum room." Then, getting a better look at Simon, she asked, "Why are you dressed all in black? Are you a priest or something?" Her brown eyes were alive with amusement.

"Not at the present time," Simon assured her. "But Vicar Neims sent us. I believe he phoned you in advance."

"The vicar is always sending someone. I think I'm his pet charity." She glanced past us toward the car. "Didn't he come with you?"

"He seemed hardly able to move out of his chair," I told her.

"Don't let that old fox fool you. He's chased me around the dining table more than once." She sighed and held out her hand. "Anyway, I'm Naomi Swift. Welcome to the Hamstitch Museum. That will be two pounds each, please."

Somehow I hadn't been prepared to pay a fee to the vicar's pet charity, but I was relieved to unload four of the heavy one-pound coins from my pocket. She held out her left hand and I noticed the wedding ring on it. "Do you and your husband live here?" I asked.

"No, no. George is a funeral director. We live above the funeral parlor. I only come over here when there's someone to escort through the museum." The coins had disappeared into a side pocket of her frock. "Step this way, please."

We walked to a pair of sliding doors, done in dark oak like the rest of the gloomy interior. Gold lettering announced the Hamstitch Museum, and Naomi Swift inserted a key in the lock. This place would make a great haunted house," I remarked.

"The exterior has been used in films," she announced with some pride. "George is always after me to sell it, but I feel it can only appreciate in value. Besides, it brings in quite a few pounds each week. In July and August, the height of the vacation season, the tour buses stop here. And we get some in the autumn, too."

Simon and I followed her into the museum, a single large room occu-
pying the east wing of the house. It consisted entirely of shelves and glass
cabinets filled with curios gathered in Hamstitch's brief lifetime of travels.
The room had only one entrance, and the windows were barred to prevent a break-in. "Most interesting," Simon observed after several minutes'
study. "These signs and descriptive captions indicate much of the mate-
rial is from Egypt, a country with which I am quite familiar. How is it the
government there allowed him to violate its strict laws against removing
such archaeological finds from the country?"

"Many of those laws were not in force during my great-grandfather's
time. And as I understand it, customs officials could always be bribed."
She led us to the far end of the room. "The vicar said he told you the story
of this trumpet."

And there it was, resting on an old steamer trunk and covered by a
protective plastic dome. It appeared to be made of bronze, with a long
straight tube some three feet long and a flared bell at one end. I associ-
ated such trumpets with the Middle Ages, not ancient Egypt, but the
descriptive card next to it clearly stated *Bronze Trumpet–2nd millennium
B.C. Discovered near Luxor on Hamstitch's final visit, 1921.*

"So this is the famous trumpet that killed him," I remarked, reaching
out as if to touch it.

Naomi graciously lifted the protective lid. "This is it, and it was shipped
back to England in that very trunk after his death."

Simon Ark lifted it gently and asked, "Then the vicar's story is true? He
aged and died after blowing this trumpet?"

She smiled a bit. "The family has never believed that the trumpet was
cursed. It's more likely that the mouthpiece was coated with some sort
of poison, though none was found later. His death came quickly, but the
business about his sudden ageing seems to have been exaggerated. My
husband thinks it more likely that he was killed by one or more of the
native workmen he'd hired. The English members of his crew were all in
town buying supplies when it happened. But it was all so long ago. Who
can tell now where the truth lies?"

"The vicar believes he might have been inspired to blow the trumpet
because his name was Joshua."

"Well, of course the Biblical Joshua and his men blew their trumpets
to tumble the walls of Jericho. Perhaps that impelled my great-grandfather
to this rash act. But I certainly don't believe there's any Pharaoh's curse

on the trumpet. I've often been tempted to blow it myself, just to prove how harmless it is."

"I would not advise that," Simon Ark cautioned. "If there was a poisonous substance—"

Naomi Swift shook her head. "It's been examined by scientists. There's nothing on it now, if there ever was." She took the trumpet from Simon's hands. "Look, I'll show you."

But before she could blow on it we were interrupted by the arrival of a dark-haired young woman, taller and more shapely than Naomi. "I saw the cars outside," she said. "Are you giving a tour?"

"Hello, Ruth." Naomi put down the trumpet and replaced the protective lid. These gentlemen are researching local legends and Ronald wanted them to see our trumpet." She introduced Simon and me to her neighbor, Ruth Russell. "Sometimes when we have bus tours Ruth helps me out."

The woman gave us a friendly smile. "Naomi should show you the rest of the house. It's pretty much as it was when the Hamstitch family lived here."

When Simon and I hesitated, Naomi had a suggestion. "If you're staying over in Gravesend tonight, why don't you come back in the morning? I'm a bit pressed for time now, but I could show you the whole place then, and you could meet my husband. He knows more about my great-grandfather than I do."

"I was thinking we might seek out Pocahontas's grave," I told her. "What do you think, Simon? Should we come back tomorrow?"

"Of course you should!" Naomi insisted. "Phone me in the morning and we'll set up a time. I won't even charge you extra."

"And I'll show you that grave," Ruth Russell said. "It's a lovely spot."

We followed her in our car across town to the cemetery at St. George's Church, and then on foot to the grave of Pocahontas. "You know, she was only twelve when she saved John Smith's life," Ruth Russell told us, "and only twenty-two when she died here of smallpox. She converted to Christianity at age eighteen and married John Rolfe, an Englishman ten years older. They established a tobacco plantation and she gave birth to a son. The family traveled to England in 1616, when she was twenty-one, and she became something of a celebrity. She visited Sir Walter Raleigh and was presented at court. She contracted smallpox the following March, when the family came here to board a ship back to America."

"You make a fine guide," Simon told her.

She shrugged. "The story is well known here. Earl Mountbatten's wife was a direct descendant of Pocahontas."

"Mediums often use the spirits of Native Americans to contact the dead in the next world. Has anyone ever attempted to use Pocahontas in this manner?"

Naomi's neighbor smiled. "Mrs. Neary claims she has. She's Gravesend's resident psychic."

"With séances and everything?" I asked, remembering that the vicar had mentioned a local medium.

Ruth Russell smiled. "Even with trumpets, I believe, though I have never personally attended one of them. She's a fraud like all of them."

As we strolled back to our cars, Simon asked, "What is your opinion of the trumpet at the Hamstitch Museum?"

She snorted. "It's a good story to scare little children. Naomi swears that one of these days she's going to blow it herself and shatter the myth forever."

As we parted at the cars, I thanked her for showing us the grave. "It was nothing," she assured us. "What time will you be at the house tomorrow? I'll come over and help Naomi with the tour."

"Perhaps around noon," I suggested. "We want to be back in London by evening, if possible."

Our small hotel was pleasant enough, and we learned that ships' pilots often stayed in its rooms while awaiting the arrival of a cargo vessel to be guided up the Thames. Everywhere there was evidence of the town's seafaring history, and one wall of the hotel lobby commemorated the distinguished visitors who had been received there in the past and conveyed to London.

We slept well and woke to a dreary mist off the sea. The previous day's sun had disappeared, at least for the present. I phoned Naomi Swift and arranged to meet her at the museum at noon. Simon and I breakfasted at a nearby restaurant and looked in a few shops until it was time to drive there. "It took me awhile, but I've finally gotten used to driving in the left lane," I told Simon, slipping behind the wheel of our rented car. Then "Look! There's the vicar coming out of that hardware store."

He was carrying a small stepladder when I pulled alongside of him "Can I help you with that?"

"Oh! It's Mr. ..." My name escaped him and he shifted his gaze to Simon. "Mr. Ark! So you're staying in our town for a bit."

"We were here overnight. Mrs. Swift graciously offered to show us the rest of the Hamstitch house today."

"A fine young woman. She's a stalwart of St. John's."

"Let me carry that for you," I offered again, opening the car door.

"No no! I wouldn't hear of it! My vehicle is just around the corner and this weighs next to nothing. It's the only exercise I get."

Except for chasing women around the dinner table, I thought, remembering what Naomi had told us. I didn't argue with him, but Simon had something else to ask. "Vicar, is Mrs. Neary a member of your little flock, too?"

I saw his face harden. "Lydia Neary? I have nothing to do with the woman. She is a charlatan of the worst sort. You'd be wise to keep your distance from her." He turned and disappeared around the comer with his short ladder.

"I guess asking a vicar about the local psychic wasn't the wisest thing to do," I remarked.

Simon did not answer directly. "He's remarkably agile for a man his age."

"Naomi Swift told us that. Remember?"

She was waiting on the porch of the house, sheltered from the increasing rain, wearing a baggy blue dress with a silver belt. A slim handsome man at her side quickly introduced himself. "I'm George Swift, Naomi's husband. I understand you people have a special interest in the Hamstitch Museum."

I shook his hand and explained. "My friend Simon Ark is working on a book of legends and superstitions. The vicar told us about the Gravesend trumpet."

"That's certainly a misnomer. It could more accurately be called the Luxor trumpet, because that's where Naomi's great-grandfather found it."

"And this was in 1921, a year before the opening of King Tut's tomb?"

George Swift nodded. "Some of the same people worked on both excavations. The area around Luxor was rich in treasures."

"Here comes Ruth," Naomi said as the dark-haired woman came up the walk. "She wants to come along on the house tour."

The five of us entered the place with Swift leading the way. The weather had made it gloomier than on our previous visit, and he quickly snapped on the lights as we climbed the wide staircase to the second floor. "This is my floor," Ruth Russell explained. "I give a little talk for every room. This is the master bedroom at the top of the stairs. Interestingly enough, Joshua Hamstitch's widow never slept here after his death. She used one of the smaller rooms."

"As if she feared his ghost might come?" Simon asked.

"Who knows?"

I felt some historical perspective was called for. "It's not such a bizarre practice. After George Washington's death, his widow Martha moved to a smaller bedroom. I believe there were other presidential widows who did likewise."

We moved on to the next room, an upstairs parlor filled with Victorian memorabilia. Naomi drew a sharp breath as we entered the room, and went at once to a broken window that looked out on the rear of the house. The rain was coming down harder now, soaking the curtains and the carpet below them. I could see a rock about the size of a golf ball on the carpet. "The neighborhood children know the house is empty. This isn't the first time they've used our upstairs windows for target practice."

George Swift quickly found a piece of cardboard to keep out the rain until the pane could be replaced. "That's why we barred all the downstairs windows, to keep them out. We have an alarm system for the downstairs, too, of course. Some of the items in the museum are quite valuable."

Naomi carefully picked up the rock and the pieces of broken glass. Simon and I helped her carry them to a wastebasket in the adjoining bath-room. Then she soaped and washed her bare hands in the sink and dried them on a towel. "Ugh! Sometimes I think George is right about selling this place. The upkeep can be a nuisance."

Ruth showed us the rest of the upstairs rooms, including the bedroom used by Mrs. Hamstitch following her husband's death. "Musty," Simon commented to me as we left it. "This whole house has the odor of death and decay about it."

"I suppose that's not surprising, since Hamstitch filled it with relics from Egyptian tombs."

We ended at the museum room again. It was unchanged from the pre-vious day except that the lack of sun cast a dimness over it that even the overhead fights could not fully dispel. Naomi grinned at her husband. "Is this the day you're going to blow the trumpet, George?" She'd lifted the protective plastic lid.

"And drop dead of old age? After you, my dear." This was obviously a familiar topic between the two of them.

"Well, let's close it up," Ruth Russell urged after we'd looked over everything for the second time.

We strolled back into the foyer and Naomi was pulling the doors shut when she suddenly remembered, "I didn't put the lid back over the trumpet." She hurried inside, leaving the doors ajar.

George Swift glanced after her with something like concern. It was a moment later, when we heard the first high notes of the trumpet sound through the house, that his expression turned to panic. "Naomi!" he shouted. "Don't—"

By the time the four of us were through the door, the trumpet was silent. It lay on the floor next to her fallen body. It was Simon who reached her first and turned her over. But even before I had a glimpse of her face I realized that her hair had turned gray. "She's dead," Simon Ark said.

Ruth Russell screamed. "That's not Naomi! It can't be Naomi!"

For the body on the floor before us, wearing Naomi Swift's blue dress and silver belt and wedding ring, was that of an elderly woman.

Ruth was hysterical by this time, and we took her to a nearby room to calm her while Swift phoned for the police and an ambulance But it was much too late to do anything for Naomi, except determine the cause of her death. The police, in the person of PC Higgins, had serious doubts about the story we told. He was a young man, no more than thirty, and he ceased writing in his notebook almost at once. "Sir, you are the husband of the deceased?"

"I am," George Swift said, his voice grim.

"And you claim that Mrs. Swift entered this room alone, blew on this trumpet, and died?"

"That's what happened. The four of us were standing in the foyer, just outside the door. There is no other way into or out of the room, and not even a closet in there. All the exhibits from Hamstitch's archaeological digs are displayed on open shelves."

"Well, the lady's fingerprints should determine her identity."

"I'm not certain my wife's fingerprints are on record anywhere. We may be able to tell something from her teeth, though. Naomi had all her teeth out while still in her twenties."

The constable knelt by the body on the floor, feeling gently between her lips. "I believe these are false, too, but I'll leave that for the pathologist. There are no obvious wounds on the body. Unless the autopsy turns up something, I'll report it as a suspicious death due to the circumstances, but apparently natural."

"Natural!" Ruth Russell had joined us from the other room where she'd been resting. "Nothing could be less natural! It was supernatural if it was anything! She wasn't out of our sight for more than thirty seconds. The door was open all the time. She'd been kidding with George about blowing on the trumpet to dispel the myth of Joshua Hemstitch's death."

"Yes," PC Higgins said. "I'm familiar with the local legend. Nobody believes that, do they?"

"We didn't until now," Swift replied. "But if there's not a curse on that trumpet, please tell me what happened to my wife."

The constable stared down at the body. All he could say was, "She died."

It was obvious that Simon Ark had no intention of leaving Gravesend until the mystery was solved. We saw no more of Swift that day as he returned home to make funeral arrangements. His parting words to us were, "I wish I had never seen that damned trumpet. When this is over, "I'm going to destroy it."

Ruth Russell, still buried in her grief, left the house when we did. Since there was no evidence of an actual crime, the police did not seal the place. The rain had let up a bit, but it was still a foul day. As she was getting into her car, Simon called out to ask her, "How would I get in touch with the psychic, Lydia Neary?"

"Stay away from that woman," Ruth warned. "I told you she's a fraud. Naomi hated her and so do I. There's no communicating with the dead." She closed the door and drove off.

"The vicar must know how to reach her," I suggested.

"I suspect his reaction might be the same as hers. The phone book might be a more likely source."

Naomi's tragedy, whatever it was, preyed on us throughout the day. When word reached Vicar Neims, he came at once to our hotel seeking details. "PC Higgins told me you two were on the scene. What sort of monstrous thing is this?"

We'd come downstairs to meet him in the hotel's small pub. I was aware that the bartender and a few customers kept their eyes on us while we talked. Simon told him what little we knew. "Perhaps the autopsy will clear everything up," I suggested.

"How can it be cleared up?" the vicar wondered. "If the body is not that of Naomi Swift, where could she be? If the body is hers, what devil's work could have done this to her?"

"We understand the trumpet is being examined," Simon told him.

"It was examined many times over the years."

"Something new might have been added." He told the vicar about the broken upstairs window.

"You believe someone gained entrance to the house through that window? Don't they have an alarm system?"

"Only for the downstairs, apparently," I told him.

Vicar Neims shook his head, still unable to comprehend it all. "And you both actually saw her die?"

"She went back into the room, picked up the trumpet, and blew it. She was out of our sight for less than thirty seconds," I told him.

"What did it sound like?" he asked. "I've always imagined it would have a special sound, something to summon the demons of Hades."

"It may have done that," Simon agreed, "but it sounded like an ordinary herald's trumpet, announcing the arrival of a king. She only blew it for a few seconds, then there was silence. We ran right in, but we were too late for her."

The vicar slowly let out his breath. "What do you think it was, Mr. Ark? What did this to her?"

"A powerful evil, certainly. I believe it's important that we try to contact her."

"Contact?"

"Through Mrs. Neary, if necessary."

Surprisingly the vicar's reaction was not nearly as negative as Ruth's had been. "The woman is a charlatan, of course, but if you wish to consult her I'll consider coming along."

Simon spent the remainder of the afternoon and evening at various odd tasks. I accompanied him to the hardware store, where we'd encountered the vicar with his stepladder. He wondered if another purchase had been made, perhaps a taller ladder that had to be delivered, but the clerk was of no help. By this time, the rain had all but stopped, and we went next to the local newspaper office where he requested papers for the past two months. He pored over the columns with interest, but if he found anything relevant, he did not communicate it to me.

In the morning, PC Higgins called and joined us for breakfast. He wanted an official statement of our version of events at the Hamstitch Museum. During the conversation we learned that the autopsy had been completed. "Rigor mortis had not set in and preliminary tests showed no trace of poison. There was none on the trumpet, either. Death seemed to be due to heart failure, but our pathologist wants to run more tests before he releases the body. He did say that her height, weight, eye color, and false teeth are all consistent with Naomi Swift, but he insists the body is that of a woman in her seventies."

Simon Ark nodded. "I believe I may be able to help with this investigation. Let me contact you later today."

After that, Simon and I sought out the psychic, Lydia Neary. She was a stout Irish lady with graying hair and a brogue. Her little house on the outskirts of town had lace curtains and a scent of lavender. "I do séances," she told us. "A lot of people don't approve, but I do them anyway."

"Do you ever use Pocahontas as an intermediary when contacting the other side?" Simon asked.

"Frequently. She has a special affinity for Gravesend, since she died here."

"I would like you to hold a séance this evening to contact the recently deceased spirit of Naomi Swift. There would be six people, counting yourself."

"A good number, a proper number. If there are too many brain waves in the room, sometimes contact cannot be made."

I asked, "Who would these people be, Simon?"

"The three of us, plus George Swift, Ruth Russell, and Vicar Neims."

That brought a snort from the Irish lady. "Vicar Neims wouldn't be caught dead here."

"I may be able to persuade him. What time is good for you?"

"Not before eight. We need darkness."

"Fine. Eight it will be."

"My fee—"

Simon waved it aside. "We will talk of that later."

We returned to our hotel to make the necessary phone calls. "What are you trying to do, Simon?" I asked at one point. "Have you become a believer in the supernatural?"

"I always have been, if you include the labors of Satan in your definition."

"Then you believe it really happened?"

"We shall see, my friend."

On the phone, Swift was reluctant, Ruth downright hostile, and the vicar hesitant. "I still don't know what good that woman can do," he told Simon.

"She can tell us if Naomi Swift is dead or alive."

"Highly unlikely."

"Take my word for it, Vicar. You promised to help out."

"And I shall. Are Swift and that Russell woman coming?"

"They are, reluctantly."

"Very well. I will see you there at eight."

Lydia Neary's husband met us at the door and ushered us into the parlor. Simon had spoken to PC Higgins on the phone while I was downstairs, and I'd half expected him to be present, too, but at eight o'clock there were only George Swift and the vicar in attendance. While we waited for Ruth, Vicar Neims spoke to Lydia Neary. "One can find more contact with the hereafter in my church than around this table listening to your bells and trumpets."

"I offer a choice, Vicar, for those unsatisfied with organized religion."

Swift was growing nervous. "Let's get on with this before I'm sorry I came."

Ruth arrived just then, escorted into the room by Mr. Neary. She took the only empty chair, opposite Lydia, and the medium ordered us to hold hands. "This is sheer bunk!" Ruth grumbled, but she grasped my hand with one of hers. To my left was the vicar, then Lydia and Simon and Swift, on Ruth's right.

"No speaking," Lydia Neary instructed us, "and do not break the circle. The lights will now be dimmed." Obviously her husband was working the switch, and darkness descended on us.

All was silence for a moment and then Lydia's dreamlike voice reached us. "We are gathered here to contact the recently deceased spirit of Naomi Swift. I call once more upon the spirit guide Pocahontas for aid."

After another moment, she repeated the message. This time there was a glow of undulating phosphorescent cheesecloth above our heads, bring-ing a distasteful grunt from the vicar. "Silence, please," Lydia said at once. After a moment, her message was answered by a distant female voice, undoubtedly a recording, speaking in a strange tongue. "Can you talk to us in English?" Lydia asked.

"Yes," the voice responded.

"What is your name?"

"I am Pocahontas, daughter of Powhatan, ruler of the Algonquin tribes."

"Pocahontas, I seek the recently deceased Naomi Swift."

"Naomi Swift..."

"Can you guide her to us? Her husband and friends are awaiting word from her."

"Naomi ..."

I felt Ruth's hand squeezing mine.

Then a familiar voice was heard. "I am here. I am with you!" It was the voice of Naomi Swift, and suddenly the door opened and she stood there bathed in light.

"No!" her husband yelled out. "It can't be! You're dead!"

He broke the circle and leaped to his feet, but before he could reach her PC Higgins intercepted him. "Sir, I am arresting you on a charge of attempted murder. You are not obligated to say anything unless you wish to do so, but what you say may be put into writing and given in evidence."

It was Simon Ark who sorted the whole thing out, later that night. The vicar was still there, and PC Higgins had returned to Lydia Neary's house after taking George Swift into custody and recording Naomi's statement at police headquarters. "It was a remarkably clever plan," Simon told us.

"Clever and diabolical," the constable agreed.

"They only made one slip-up, but that was the one I noticed. Naomi was wearing a wedding ring the first time we met her, and the body in the museum was wearing it, too. But when she cleared up the broken glass and then washed her hands, she wasn't wearing the ring. Her hands were bare. What had happened to it? There was only one possible explanation. The entire scene was set up in advance, and Naomi had to substitute the dead body for herself as quickly as possible, in less than thirty seconds. A duplicate dress and belt and shoes were no problem, and they put her ring on the dead woman in advance, to save precious seconds."

"They just happened to have a dead woman of the right height, with brown eyes and false teeth," I remarked sardonically.

"You're forgetting that George Swift is a funeral director. I assumed that some time in recent weeks he handled the funeral of this nameless woman, no doubt with a closed coffin and few if any relatives. He noticed the general resemblance to his wife and decided on his scheme. The coffin was buried full of sand or stones and the body was kept in his freezer. I spent some time at the local newspaper office yesterday looking over recent death notices. The woman had to be someone not well known in Gravesend whose funeral had been handled by Swift. I found two possibilities, both women in their seventies from nearby villages."

PC Higgins took up the story. "Mr. Ark gave me their names and addresses over the phone and asked me to show their neighbors a picture of the dead woman. It was the first woman I checked on, one Rosemary Watkins who died a month ago at a nursing home in Cooling. She had no family, and the home made funeral arrangements with George Swift."

Vicar Neims was still doubtful. "What in God's name did they hope to accomplish by such bizarre trickery? And how was Naomi able to make the substitution? You were right outside the open door."

"Swift's supposed motive was publicity that would increase the value of that ancient trumpet and the house and museum themselves. Strange as it might seem, a notorious history does not scare off modern buyers, and he admitted to wanting to sell the place. But he had another motive as well—to kill his wife in a safe and foolproof manner that would defy detection. The reason for that can only be surmised, but one might question his relationship with Ruth Russell for a beginning. With Naomi dead, the valuable house would be his and he'd be free to marry again."

Lydia Neary and her husband had listened to all this with something approaching awe. "Why did you come here to my place?"

"I needed to get Swift away from his house. When Constable Higgins established the true identity of the dead woman, he was able to obtain a search warrant for the funeral parlor. Naomi hadn't turned up and there were only two possibilities. Either she was hiding in their house or she was dead. Happily the constable discovered a third possibility."

Higgins nodded. "I found her bound and gagged in a basement storage room. She'd been injected with some sort of muscle relaxant that probably would have stopped her heart in another couple of hours."

"But how did she make the switch in the museum room?" the vicar asked again. "The windows were barred, and there was no closet or hiding place."

"Ah, but there was," Simon told us with a bit of a smile. The trumpet, three feet long, rested on an old steamer trunk which had been used to transport it from Egypt. Naomi is barely five feet tall and the dead woman was about the same height. With no rigor mortis present, her body was easily folded into the trunk the previous night, with the duplicate dress and the wedding ring already in place. Naomi opened the trunk, lifted the small body out, climbed inside, and blew on the trumpet just before she closed the lid. Simple, all in less than thirty seconds."

"What if we'd thought to open the trunk?" I asked.

"I'm sure she and her husband would have treated it as a bizarre and tasteless joke. As for the rest, they gambled on the pathologist not detecting that the body had been previously frozen. Perhaps they were going to try this stunt during one of the autumn bus tours, but our arrival gave them a smaller and even better audience. Of course, Naomi slipped out of the steamer trunk and returned home after we left the house, never suspecting the true fate her husband had in store for her. Once she was dead, I suspect he would have added her to the coffin of someone due for cremation."

"What will become of them?" Mrs. Neary wondered.

"Prison for him, certainly," the constable predicted. "Naomi Swift may convince the prosecutor that she was the intended victim and not a criminal."

Simon nodded. "It is good sometimes when we can solve a mystery before the murder rather than after it."

"But what about Joshua Hamstitch?" I wondered. "How did he really die?"

"My friend, that is something we will never know."

SOURCES

Day of the Wizard. *Chase*, September 1964
Funeral in the Fog. *Weird Tales*, Summer 1973
The Avenger from Outer Space. *Ellery Queen's Mystery Magazine*, October 1979
The Weapon Out of the Past. *Ellery Queen's Mystery Magazine*, April 7, 1980
The Sorceress of the Sea. *Ellery Queen's Mystery Magazine*, August 18, 1980
The House of a Hundred Birds. *Ellery Queen's Mystery Magazine*, February 24, 1982
Prisoner of Zerfall. *Espionage*, November 1985
The S.S.S. *Mystery Scene*, November 1986
The Way Up to Hades. *Alfred Hitchcock's Mystery Magazine*, January 1988
The Virgins of Valentine. *14 Vicious Valentines*, Avon Books, 1988
The Stalker of Souls. *Stalkers*, Dark Harvest, 1989
The Society of the Scar. *Predators*, ROC, 1993
No Blood for a Vampire. *Vampire Detectives*, DAW, 1995
The Graveyard Ghoul. *Night Screams*, ROC,1996
Master of Miracles. *Ellery Queen's Mystery Magazine*, May 1999
The Gravesend Trumpet. *Ellery Queen's Mystery Magazine*, September 2005

CRIPPEN & LANDRU, PUBLISHERS
P. O. Box 9315 Norfolk, VA 23505
Web: www.crippenlandru.com
E-mail: info@crippenlandru.com

Since 1994, Crippen & Landru has published more than 100 first editions of short-story collections by important detective and mystery writers.

☞ This is the best edited, most attractively packaged line of mystery books introduced in this decade. The books are equally valuable to collectors and readers. [Mystery Scene Magazine]

☞ The specialty publisher with the most star-studded list is Crippen & Landru, which has produced short story collections by some of the biggest names in contemporary crime fiction. [Ellery Queen's Mystery Magazine]

☞ God Bless Crippen & Landru. [The Strand Magazine]

☞ A monument in the making is appearing year by year from Crippen & Landru, a small press devoted exclusively to publishing the criminous short story. [Alfred Hitchcock's Mystery Magazine]